GRAYSON DAY AND THE BLACK DIAMOND

BY

JACOB BRADY

Library of Congress Control Number:
2022917266

Acknowledgments

Developmental Editor: Clara Abigail
Line Editor: Kandi Neal
Copy Editor: Rikki Brady
Proofreader: Ana Joldes
Cover Designer: Rebecacovers

For God, in hopes of turning people into angels and merging our physical world with His spiritual Kingdom.

Contents

Chapter 1: Creative Energy 1

Chapter 2: A Lacing Welcome 21

Chapter 3: Oscar's Friend..41

Chapter 4: The Days Before Icefall 56

Chapter 5: The Reville's Gift..73

Chapter 6: The City in the Clouds 90

Chapter 7: New Tongue at Cassiel's Lake 107

Chapter 8: The Lacer Initiation Process 124

Chapter 9: Ambrielle Stone...142

Chapter 10: Puzzles at Adriel's Pond 157

Chapter 11: The Missing Necklace...173

Chapter 12: A Way to Win 186

Chapter 13: The Black Diamond...201

Chapter 14: Hell on a Holy Day..220

Chapter 15: Chain Link 239

Chapter 16: The Stream of Serenity...256

Chapter 17: Invasion of Amethyst House 271

Chapter 18: Deceptive Tradition 291

Chapter 19: Shaders..314

Chapter 20: Return of Wind and Evil...328

CHAPTER 1

Creative Energy

B lack on the Right. White on the Left. Gray in the middle. These were the three Earths that Grayson and his disobedient asteroid shower propelled toward at top speed. The trillions of jagged boulders refused their master's commands, threatening to end life in the middle world.

"HALT! HALT!" Grayson bellowed.

He tactfully front-flipped off the lead stone and glided through the black abyss. His emerald crown floated into nothingness like the future souls of those on Gray Earth. Unless he could prove himself a dependable savior once more, this time for his own people, the constant clash of Black and White would prove to be Gray's everlasting demise.

Grayson launched himself in front of his world, back into the agonizing blast zone of good and evil's pull. His body stretched Right. His body stretched Left. More Left. More Right. Farther Left. Grayson's paper-thin flesh wrapped around the middle world like a sequin cloth over the table of a Thanksgiving feast.

His stomach growled as all the rocks in the universe collided against him. The asteroid's sharp edges drove Grayson through Earth's atmosphere, over the oceans and seas, across the plants and trees. The only audible sound was a familiar scream, far too potent for him to continue his dream.

"Grayson!" screamed Cristina. "You better be out of bed. I woke you up an hour ago. You can't be late again!"

Grayson opened his eyes and ruffled his long brown hair. He stretched his arms and legs across the bed in frustration. Why did his mom have to interrupt everything? He told himself he would imagine a more satisfying conclusion to the dream later in the day.

Grayson stumbled to the bedroom closet, slipped on an outfit of his mother's choosing, and stared into the reflection of his dark brown eyes in the bathroom mirror. Hopefully, he could get through his daily quote without further disruption.

"Creativity is the key to an extraordinary life. All people are creative to some degree; only a select few have the mental discipline to make their fantasies a reality. Belief and visualization are essential," said Grayson, finishing with a yawn that caused drool to fall from his bottom lip onto his freshly ironed collared shirt.

"Wake up!" Cristina yelled.

"I'm already dressed!" Grayson fired back.

"Then come downstairs, sweetie pie. Ethan's already here. I have to leave for work. And breakfast is getting cold."

"Your breakfast is also slowly disappearing," called out Ethan through a mouth full of food. "You better hurry up, sweetie pie!"

"Ethan Clark! Are you making fun of what I call my little boy?"

"Of course not, Mrs. Day. I think that's a very fitting nickname for your little boy," said Ethan.

Grayson clenched his jaw and crossed his arms as much as his uncomfortable dress shirt would allow. He had told his mother just last week to stop using those childish names in front of his friends.

The usual siren of despair erupted from Grayson's phone, giving him ten minutes before it was time to leave for school. Ten minutes seemed like an eternity; he would actually have time to eat breakfast. Grayson fixed his hair, checked to see if his abs were visible, and hurried downstairs, passing the *WELCOME TO HIGH SCHOOL* sign hanging in his living room. Grayson and Ethan's co-middle-school graduation party would be taking place in Grayson's house later that very same evening, hence why Cristina had dressed him up.

"Another year down," said Ethan in a high-pitched voice that didn't match his manly build, "and what do you know? I'm still twice your size."

"Twice my size? I'm three inches taller than you, buddy," said Grayson, using the last piece of toast to calculate his vertical advantage. "That button-down shirt makes you look like a tree trunk that just got inflated with a bicycle pump."

"Yours makes you look like a tree branch on its way to Sunday service."

Grayson brought his toast into the living room and plopped himself down on the couch, where he was free to express his frustration with the graduation poster hanging above his head.

"Did my mom already leave for work?" Grayson asked.

"Yeah, your dad did too," said Ethan, handing Grayson a half-ripped piece of paper. "She told me to make sure you read her note before we leave."

Grayson Vincent Day, I cannot believe the day is already here, when my baby boy is all grown up and finished with school. Congratulations! You know how proud I am of you. Have fun, and make sure you bring Ethan home with you today to help set up for tonight's party. Love, Mom.

"If either of my parents says the phrase *finished with school* one more time today, I may run away and never come back, just to make them eat their words," muttered Grayson, handing the note to Ethan. His heart dropped; he shouldn't have referred to running away as a joke.

Ethan took the note and patted Grayson on the shoulder. "It's okay," he assured, "you don't need to feel bad just because Mitchell decided to be a jerk and ditch my family for his girlfriend. It's been three years—you replaced him as my brother a long time ago."

"I don't have any siblings—you know you've always been my brother," said Grayson.

"I like being a big brother more than a little brother, anyway," said Ethan with a deep, prideful exhale as he kicked his feet onto the couch ottoman. "You're right, though—our parents need to save that phrase for when we graduate college."

College graduation, the *real* last day of school—*that* would be the day Grayson could finally enjoy himself. Whether it was the first day of a school year or the last day never made any difference to Grayson. As someone who was not a firm believer in the modern-day education system, he saw tonight's "graduation party" as nothing more than a tragic send-off to more pointless schooling. Other than the dirty-blond-haired boy sitting across from him, Grayson didn't know anyone else who was bothered by school as much as he was.

"Quinton texted me and said he's running late. His mom's driving us today," Ethan told him.

Grayson spent the last five minutes at his house kicking himself for his careless runaway comment. Ethan never discussed his feelings when it came to Mitchell deserting his family; he let his pain out in other ways. Getting Ethan worked up on the last day of school was the last thing Grayson wanted to do. Ethan's anger and irritation tendencies often became more apparent after the mention of his brother.

The two boys sat in silence. Grayson pulled out his brand new GemPhone. His parents had let him upgrade last month after his outdated smartphone had shattered. Grayson twirled the weightless square tablet in his hand, marveling at the beautiful sapphire gem on the backside, still surprised his parents had spent the amount of money they did on an eighth-grade graduation present. He swiped his hand through the air above the screen and began to scroll through the same tweets he had already seen earlier that morning.

An arrival message from Quinton gave Grayson a reason to click away from the endless supply of political news. Grayson and Ethan grabbed their school bags and marched through the front door into the freefalling snow.

"May 17 is a day you boys will never forget," said Mrs. Williams once the boys had loaded their belongings into the trunk. "Are you two as excited as Quinton for high school?" she asked, playfully rubbing her son's bushy hair.

"Oh yeah, definitely," lied Ethan.

"More school—how could we not be excited?" exclaimed Grayson.

Mrs. Williams checked everyone's seatbelt status. "I'm glad Quinton has a group of friends that take education seriously. I requested off work so I could drive you boys to school today. I told my husband maybe he should go into the office early for a change."

"Mom, they're messing with you," said Quinton. "Ask Dad— they hate school. He hears them talk about it all the time."

"Is that true?" asked Mrs. Williams, taking a swift peek in the rearview mirror. "You boys hate school?"

"It's not our favorite," admitted Grayson.

"We hate it," said Ethan, not bothering to downplay his feelings. "If we're late again today, we get a month of detention to start off high school."

Mrs. Williams clapped her hand on the steering wheel. "How could you possibly be late so much? My husband drops you three off fifteen minutes early every day."

"Grayson and I always take a slight detour before going to class," said Ethan.

Grayson elbowed Ethan to shut him up. Quinton cautiously looked to the backseat.

"What kind of detour?" Mrs. Williams asked as the car came to a stop at the final red light before the school.

"You don't wanna know," said Grayson quickly, but Ethan spoke anyway.

"We go to the forest behind the school. We found an inspirational book buried in the snow a couple of years ago. We keep it out there and read a passage each day before class. A Lacer wrote it."

The light turned green. The car gear shifted to park.

"Get out," said Mrs. Williams, pressing a button to open the trunk. "Both of you, get out now."

"Mom! Don't make them get out! It's not a big deal!"

"Get out!" she screamed. "Don't bring up that crazy Lacer stuff around my family. Oh no, not in my car. Get out!"

Despite Quinton's pleas for them to stay, Grayson and Ethan hopped out the back door, grabbed their bags from the trunk, and headed for the nearby forest. By stopping early, Mrs. Williams had unknowingly saved them a great deal of time.

"Looks like we won't be sleeping over at Quinton's house this summer," said Ethan, skipping down the sidewalk. "Quinton should've told her that we like Lacers."

"Or maybe her husband could've told her," said Grayson. "We got *Mr.* Williams interested in Lacers months ago."

Every day on the way to school, Mr. Williams had asked Grayson and Ethan to recite some of their favorite quotes from the enlightened book they loved so dearly. He was one of the few people Grayson knew who did not flat out despise Lacers. After listening to his dad and friends talk about them all year, Quinton was beginning to come around as well—apparently, their open-mindedness hadn't rubbed off on Mrs. Williams.

"At least our parents don't hate Lacers," said Ethan.

"How do we know that?" asked Grayson. "They never answer any of our questions about them."

"My dad told me to check the internet last time I asked."

Grayson laughed. Everybody knew there wasn't any reliable information on the web when it came to Lacers.

The snow decided to give the air a chance to dry when the boys reached the forest. The steady rising sun effortlessly broke through the clouds, showering the trees in front of them in rays of illumination. Grayson loved sunny days; he enjoyed reading the Lacer book more in natural light rather than from the flashlight on his phone.

"Are we really gonna do what we said?" asked Ethan as he high-stepped through the powdered ground and around the pine trees. "If we leave it for another kid to find, then today's our last day reading it."

"I think it's the right thing to do. We already understand the main idea—let's pass the torch."

The boys sat down underneath a frail tree. Ethan reached into the hollow trunk and pulled the thick leather book out of its hiding spot, commencing their daily ritual. He opened *The Laws of Nature*, and together, they chorused a line from the inside of the front cover.

"Nature made you; therefore, it is for you, not against you. Take the time to understand your creator, and you will be rewarded with the power to craft any life you desire."

"And now," echoed Grayson, "the time has come for our final message."

"Would you like to do the honors?" asked Ethan, handing Grayson the book.

Grayson closed the book and then opened it again, this time on a random page. He shut his eyes tight and aimlessly pointed to a spot on the paper.

"Got it!" said Ethan, taking the book back and tracing his finger along the scripture Grayson had pointed to. "You ready?"

"Shoot!"

"If you believe you are different, then you are different; those who possess a mind state of normality are on a path to live a life that many others have already lived."

A jolt of energy ran through Grayson's body — this had happened before. A brief flash in his mind told him his life had a purpose. A purpose other kids didn't. He saw himself at birth, carrying a unique power, then he saw himself strengthening that same power before he died.

"Wow, that was a good one to end on!" said Ethan. "Let's go. I'm not starting high school in detention."

Grayson remained on the ground with his eyes closed and his arms crossed. "I think I'm gonna stay for a while."

"Oh god — not this again. You have fun out here. I'll see you in class. Make sure you leave the book out in the open so someone else can find it." Ethan kissed the dusty leather goodbye and ran to class.

If Grayson was going to risk being late to school, he needed to make this visualization time count. He tried to resurrect the split second of energy the quote had given him and turn it into a plan for his life. He saw the same pictures he always did: He was doing something he loved — something different, something fun — but he didn't know what that something was.

Creating fascinating scenarios in his head was the only thing Grayson genuinely enjoyed, and unfortunately, there wasn't a job in the real world for that. The concept of time lost all meaning whenever he imagined himself as a hero in a world full of ordinary people. Grayson liked his life. He had a great group of friends, caring parents, basically everything he could ask for, yet there was always the little voice in the back of his head telling him he would end up with the same basic life all adults had. That was his one fear.

Grayson had just replaced himself in the asteroid shower, ready to save the world, when his phone buzzed. Ethan's text message telling him to hurry up arrived at 7:26 a.m. Grayson had four minutes before school started. He left the creative bible out in the open and sprinted to class, yelling behind him, "Thanks for changing my life! I hope another kid like me finds you!"

Grayson darted through the trees, past the parking lot, and crossed the front gate into Pine Ridge Middle School for the last time. This mediocre public school in northern Colorado had been his "home" for the past two years, and the thought of never coming back made a second strike of energy blast through his body.

All aspects of Pine Ridge were appalling. The chipped cement blocks that made up the campus accurately represented the far-from-exceptional staff members. He grabbed the rusted door handle leading into the F Building, swung it open with a screech, and ran up the cracked staircase, taking them two at a time. The thought of being able to daydream all summer long forced a smile out of him as he entered Mr. Cole's classroom for the final time.

The clock in the back of the room read 7:29 a.m. Grayson patted Ethan on the back and gave him a wink. Ethan shook his head in disbelief. Grayson proceeded to the front of the class, where his desk stood directly in the middle of the room, no more than a foot away from Mr. Cole's projector. Mr. Cole had realized early on that the Grayson-next-to-Ethan seating arrangement was not going to pan out, and consequently, they were separated for the remainder of the year.

Grayson tossed his backpack onto the dusty carpet and raised his head until his dark brown eyes met Mr. Cole's cold, loathing stare. Feeling a little cocky that he had made it on time, Grayson let an enormous grin stretch across his face. Mr. Cole returned it with a look of pure disgust before raising his hand in the air to silence the class.

Once the last of the murmurs had stopped, he began, "Just because it's the last day of school doesn't mean everyone gets to roam the class freely. Pick a seat and stay in it. This class is lucky I didn't give out a test today, given the way some students here have behaved."

Mr. Cole deliberately grimaced at Grayson and Ethan. "After today, you will no longer be eighth-graders; you will be in high school. That means you will be taking a final exam or even writing an essay at this time next year. My point is—more is going to be expected of you. I am, of course, only speaking to those of you who will actually be attending high school," said Mr. Cole, as he once again hit Grayson and Ethan with a not-so-friendly look before his closing anthem. "I encourage all of you to enjoy today but also prepare and better yourselves for the days to come. I wish most of you the best next year."

With those cheerful remarks, Mr. Cole walked to his desk in the back right corner of the classroom, where he plopped himself down in his black leather chair and engaged in a magazine.

Ethan stood up from his desk; the kids around him nervously glanced up from their phones to make sure he wasn't starting any trouble. He managed to reseat himself in the empty desk to Grayson's right without doing anything worse than kicking a kid's backpack out of the walking aisle. The kid didn't look happy, but Ethan's impressive fistfight record kept him from expressing his thoughts on the matter. Grayson and Ethan made eye contact, attempted to keep straight faces, and then burst out laughing.

"Did you hear Mr. Cole say, 'I wish *most* of you the best next year?'" asked Grayson as tears came rushing down his face.

"Yeah, that was almost as funny as him trying to make it sound like we aren't smart enough to go to high school," said Ethan. "Neither of us have ever gotten anything lower than a 'B' on our report cards."

Mr. Cole had made several outrageous comments throughout the year, and while he might have made his dislike of Grayson more public than other teachers, he was certainly not alone. All his life, as far back as he could remember, Grayson had had trouble with his teachers. Impressing his instructors didn't rank high on his list of life goals, yet he did at times wonder why they all had it out for him. Yes, he was always late to class, and yes, he did talk during lectures more than he should; however, for some strange reason, Grayson got the feeling that his behavior was not the issue.

Ethan said, "I think I just realized why some of our friends are actually excited for high school."

"What's your conclusion?" asked Grayson, spinning his GemPhone on the desk like a coin.

"The teachers actually like them."

"That's good for them, but think about all the experiences we would've missed out on if we were content living a normal life."

"Let's be honest," said Ethan, "we haven't experienced anything new in a long time."

"Okay, here's an idea," proposed Grayson, taking a deep breath. "This summer, let's go to Denver, explore downtown, and search for some new inspiration."

"No way am I going downtown again! We already did that. Maybe you forgot!"

"I didn't forget. I just don't think that sneaking off from our parents for thirty minutes to a theater and auditioning for a play counts as exploring the city."

During their experimental sixth-grade years, Grayson and Ethan had tried out their acting skills. They quickly learned that being a movie star was not a realistic goal for their future, as it required a great deal of being serious, a task neither of them excelled at. A lack of other ideas throughout the past three years led Ethan to start a conversation that came up a lot between the two of them.

"Why do people hate Lacers if they don't know anything about them?"

"Would you shut up?" whispered Grayson. "The last thing we need is Mr. Cole hearing us say that word; he'll put us in detention faster than Quinton's mom threw us out of the car."

Mr. Cole overhearing their conversation would undoubtedly have a nasty result, yet that had little to do with why Grayson had avoided Ethan's question. Truthfully, he didn't have an answer as to why Lacers were treated differently. From the bits and pieces of information Grayson had clawed out of people over the years, he hadn't heard a single scratch of evidence to make him think Lacers were here to harm others.

"Do you think they really have magic staffs?" Ethan asked.

"I don't know about staffs. But I know they like fancy jewelry."

To Grayson's knowledge, he had only come across one Lacer in his life. He had been outside playing tag with his good friend Tommy Hudson when a boy about five years older than them walked by wearing all black and had a magnificent amethyst necklace around his neck. Tommy, who didn't like Lacers, stared at the boy as he passed.

The young Lacer had simply turned, faced them, and said to Grayson, "You really shouldn't hang out with this closed-minded child."

Tommy got defensive and yelled at the Lacer to leave. Grayson never said a word to the boy but secretly agreed with him, although he would never have told Tommy this in a million years. Anytime Grayson went out in public, he was always on the lookout for neck attire similar to what the Lacer boy had been wearing that day. Years had passed since that interaction, and he hadn't sighted a necklace like that since.

"I'm sure there are plenty of Lacers out there," Ethan assured. "They probably just stay far away from regular people like us."

"Good point. Who would wanna deal with someone like Mr. Cole if they didn't have to?"

Mr. Cole had spent the year teaching the class about people who had been treated horribly because of their skin color and their religious beliefs. In Grayson's opinion, Lacers were just the newest victims of the cruel world he lived in. He could only hope that one day they would be treated fairly—maybe then he could be allowed to learn a little more about them.

The bell marking the end of the first hour sounded. The boys grabbed their bags and headed for the door, happy never to see Mr. Cole again. They walked out into the dimly lit hallway and went their separate ways toward their next classes.

Grayson's last day as a middle schooler breezed by. The saying *time flies when you're having fun* would not have accurately described what happened to Grayson. His day went by fast because he slept through his remaining classes.

Once the final bell of the school year sounded, Grayson strolled out of the school's back exit and waited for Ethan under an oak tree adjacent to the bus lane. Grayson didn't like riding the bus. It was loud, and it somehow made kids his age act like toddlers on a playground. Today, thanks to Ethan infuriating Mrs. Williams, the bus was unavoidable.

I'll just sit in the back like I always do, thought Grayson.

Grayson spotted Ethan walking alongside two obnoxious, short, and stocky boys who would be riding the same bus as them. One of them was Mr. Cole's son, John. As they got closer, Grayson noticed that the three of them weren't necessarily walking together; instead, the kid farthest from Ethan was holding John back from hitting Ethan in the face.

Only about ten feet away now from the tree Grayson stood under was Ethan backpedaling and waving his finger at the two kids, yelling something that sounded a lot like, "Shut your mouth, Johnny bear, or Daddy's gonna have to put you in detention on the last day of school."

John and his friend continued toward the bus, embraced in a backward hug. Ethan stopped next to Grayson.

"And you were mad at me for almost being late to school," said Grayson with a big smile on his face.

"Oh, come on, we can't get in trouble now. School's over! Maybe with some luck, he'll try to fight me once we get on the bus."

It was not as if Grayson didn't want to see Ethan fight Mr. Cole's son; John deserved a good punch or two for all the trash-talking and rumors he had started. It was just that every time Grayson spoke to a police officer, he got the same feeling he did every time he talked to a teacher.

Once the boys exited the bronze fence, leaving the school grounds for good, they made a right toward their bus, where everyone was piled around the doors, waiting for them to open. Grayson made his way through the cluster of people. Their aging bus driver, Donny Bruce, stood by the steering wheel, wearing his typical black baseball cap and always colorful button-down shirt. Today, he was not alone.

An elderly man with straight silver hair down to his shoulders and an oversized trench coat wrapped around his body stood beside

Mr. Bruce with a stern expression on his face. It looked like they were having a serious conversation. Neither one had broken eye contact, and they seemed oblivious to the fifty students waiting outside.

Grayson turned around and nudged Ethan. "You know who that is?"

Ethan gave a nonchalant shrug and pulled out his phone.

Some of the kids waiting were getting restless. It had started snowing again, as it did year-round in this particular part of Colorado, and with it being the last day of school, Grayson was growing anxious to board himself.

The bus doors opened. The silver-haired stranger stepped out of the vehicle and steered clear of the students, limping his way to the bronze gate. The old man turned in Grayson's direction—only for a moment. He said nothing. He did nothing. The man's face looked normal, yet it made Grayson's inner soul tremble. Inside the stranger's skin, inside his eyes, Grayson saw himself.

The mystery man made a swift turn around a corner and vanished. Grayson stumbled onto the bus in a trance. He faltered down the aisle and sank into his usual bench in the back right corner. His backpack knocked a leather book off the seat. Grayson didn't notice.

He looked around, trying to locate Ethan, but found John's circular face glaring down at him in anger. Still in a daze, Grayson barely had time to duck as John swung his right hook. Grayson turned his duck into a spear tackle, sending John to the floor. He had just scrambled to his feet when a blow to the back of the head brought Grayson to his knees.

"How dare you go after him when he wasn't looking, you coward!" shouted Ethan as he landed a nose-breaking jab on John's friend.

The punch to the head snapped Grayson out of whatever trance he had been in. Ethan's abrupt entrance to the fight gave Grayson an opportunity to put John away for good. He chose to finish him with an elbow to the temple.

Mr. Bruce jumped into the middle of the action. He grabbed Grayson with one hand, Ethan with the other, and shoved them both against the back wall of the bus with surprising force. John, who did not need any telling from Mr. Bruce, struggled to his feet and headed back to his seat, pulling his friend with him.

Just when Grayson thought he was about to get yelled at, Mr. Bruce said, "Not bad. It looks like you two will be fine in *high school* next year." He released the boys' shirts and went back to the driver's seat, chuckling.

There was something in the way Mr. Bruce had said *high school* that made Grayson flinch. It was almost as if he were one of the teachers telling him he wouldn't make it that far, yet Grayson felt like Mr. Bruce was encouraging him.

"I can't believe I'm about to say this, but our last day of middle school did turn out fun," said Ethan, filling in the row across from Grayson. "One of your books fell out of your backpack, by the way."

Grayson bent down to pick up the leather book Ethan had pointed to. Engraved in the front cover itself were the words *Grayson V. Day*. It was *not* one of his schoolbooks. Although it was much smaller, only about ten pages in length, this book reminded him of the Lacer book from the forest.

All ten pages were completely blank. Grayson turned the book around and ran his fingers through a spiral-shaped crevice on the inside of the back cover. The crease was half an inch deep, coated with a rigid texture. It had his name on it—it had to be his. Maybe his mom had custom-made a diary for him and slipped it into his backpack before school.

Then Grayson felt it.

As he continued to hold the book in his hands, the energy from earlier that morning returned. It radiated through his hands, to his arms, until it overwhelmed his entire body. The energy was not a figment of Grayson's imagination—it discharged from the book itself, and the longer Grayson held it, the stronger it became. A vision of the silver-haired old man told Grayson they possessed a similar power, the same power Grayson needed to strengthen before he died. The power was somehow a purpose for his life. He threw down the book before it unhinged his mind.

Ethan proceeded to lie back across the bench, using his backpack as a headrest. Grayson, on the other hand, was unable to process what had just happened. He stuffed the empty book inside his backpack, not daring to speak a word of its powers. He squished his cheek up against the window and watched as the bus pulled out onto the main street, away from Pine Ridge.

For most of the trip back to Snowside, he stared out of the fingerprint-covered bus window, watching people shovel snow, make snow angels, and attempt to sled down their icy driveways. Grayson's mind started to wander. He saw pictures in the clouds, messages written in the trees of the passing forest, and even people's full life stories simply based on the facial expressions of their snowmen.

As the bus entered Snowside, it made its first left before climbing the incredibly steep road that led to Grayson's house at the top of the hill. Grayson, Ethan, and about five other students gathered their belongings and headed for the front of the bus. Ethan slammed his backpack into John's shoulder on the way out. Grayson avoided Mr. Bruce's eyes, but Mr. Bruce caught his arm and pulled him back.

"The minute you get home, hide the book," he said.

Everything around Grayson and Mr. Bruce went pitch-white and froze. Time itself slowed to a dream-like pace. The weight of the book pulled down Grayson's backpack and rooted him in place.

"Why do I need to hide it?" he asked, completely unaware of the words leaving his mouth.

"There's a power inside it," Mr. Bruce told him. "There will be people at your house when you get home. They must not know about it."

"What power?"

"The book is filled with creative energy."

"But creativity isn't a real power," argued Grayson. "It just lets people imagine themselves with power."

"That can be even more dangerous," said Mr. Bruce. He released Grayson's arm.

CHAPTER 2

A Lacing Welcome

The school bus raced down the neighborhood streets, the wake of its black tire tracks imprinting the snowy pavement like referee stripes.

"Where do you think you're going?" asked Grayson, grabbing Ethan's arm and yanking him back onto the sidewalk. "We have to set up for the party."

"I'm throwing this in my house," said Ethan, taking the backpack off his shoulder and tossing it inside the already unlocked front door.

As the boys walked next door to the house at the top of the hill, Grayson suddenly became very aware of his own backpack. He hadn't forgotten about the book with his name, but he now felt the need to hide it for a reason he couldn't quite put his finger on.

Grayson and Ethan stepped off the snow-covered porch and onto the hardwood floor. With both their parents preparing food right around the corner, Grayson listened to his gut feeling and immediately tossed his backpack into the coat closet.

"Look who it is," announced Jeff Day, giving Grayson and Ethan a round of applause as they made their way to the leather couch in the living room. "You did it, boys!"

"Did what, Dad?" asked Grayson, sinking into the cushions. "We're like halfway done with school. I think you guys forgot about high school and college."

"The easy part's over. Now it gets difficult," said Rob Clark, skipping over to join Jeff on the couch ottoman, his messy blond hair bouncing as he went.

"Ha! You can say that again!" said Jeff, lifting his glasses from his nose to his bushy brown hair.

Grayson and Ethan remained expressionless on the couch. Grayson hoped the dads were getting all their dad jokes out of the way before the party. He wasn't sure how his dad could think Rob's comment about high school being harder than middle school was funny; obviously, high school was going to be harder.

"Hey, middle-school graduates and funny dads, how about you come help Cristina and me with the food?" asked Susan Clark, who was doing her makeup in the reflection of the microwave door rather than helping.

Cristina was locked in. The only thing that distracted her from the dozens of serving dishes that still needed to be filled with appetizers was Grayson's appearance in the kitchen. She momentarily forgot about the tasks at hand and embraced Grayson with a bear hug—well, as much of a bear hug as she could; she was a tiny woman. Like her husband and son, Cristina also had brown hair, but hers was longer, at least twelve inches past her shoulders.

During this hug with his mom, Grayson noticed the gentle material of her sweatshirt. It was much softer than the itchy collared shirt she had picked out for him earlier that morning. Grayson pulled away and saw his dad keeled over laughing at another one of

Rob's jokes. Jeff was wearing sweatpants and a wrinkled t-shirt that said, *Dads will be Dads.*

Grayson pulled away from his mom and crossed his arms. "Let me get this straight. You and Dad get to change into your dress clothes right before the party, but I had to suffer all day at school? I could barely even sleep in science today; the sleeves kept bunching up under my arms."

"Oh, shoot! That reminds me!" said Jeff, swiftly taking off up the stairs. His glasses tumbled to the floor.

"I hope they broke," said Cristina as she filled the final chip bowl. "We all know he wears them for looks."

"Rob, I wonder how you'd look with glasses?" asked Susan. She had finished her makeup and was now painting her nails. "Ethan, sweetie, I know you would look great with glasses."

While many things did happen to annoy Ethan, Grayson really felt bad for him when it came to dealing with constant and absurd compliments from his parents. Rob and Susan never missed an opportunity to point out Ethan's accomplishments or potential triumphs. Ethan usually put in his headphones whenever Susan started rambling. This time, he plugged his ears but lifelessly let his hands fall to his lap and his mouth drop to the floor moments later.

Jeff had merrily trotted downstairs wearing a shimmering, sapphire-colored cloak. "Rob. Susan," said Jeff, handing each of Ethan's parents an amethyst cloak. "Cristina, dear, when was the last time we wore these bad boys?"

Grayson never did hear the answer to his dad's question; he was too busy imagining his parents wearing these ridiculous costumes at the graduation party. They *sparkled.* "Man, these babies are tight. Both literally and figuratively," said Rob, sucking in his gut.

"I'm gonna have to go easy on the pizza tonight," said Jeff, patting his stomach.

Grayson couldn't take another dad joke, especially not while they were dressed like complete morons.

"We're canceling this party," announced Grayson. "I'm already embarrassed, and nobody's even here yet."

"I know what will cheer you boys up," said Cristina, pinching Grayson's cheeks with her hands and making him smile. "How about another graduation present? Susan, is it ready?"

Susan peeked into the backyard and nodded in confirmation.

"I don't care how good this surprise is," said Ethan, opening the back door for him and Grayson. "We aren't having a party unless you change into something normal."

Ethan turned out to be very wrong, indeed. The boys stepped through the doorway and stumbled backward to the ground out of fright.

"WELCOME, LACERS!" shouted a vast crowd of people simultaneously. They jumped out from behind the marble pillars, behind the patio furniture; some of the more daring visitors even jumped down from the roof.

Jeff helped Grayson to his feet. Ethan scrambled upright and clenched his fists, ready for a fight. There would be no fight. Grayson knew what these people were—he knew why they were here. This was the moment he'd dreamed of his entire life.

Just like the parents, all the guests were wearing colorful cloaks. Many fancied an emerald or ruby shade, giving the backyard a Christmas feel. Ethan's parents and about ten other Lacers wore amethyst, while only three others joined Jeff and Cristina in the sapphire category. Grayson caught a glimpse of one shiny white cloak in the back of the group, but his parents sat him down in a rocking chair next to Ethan before its owner's face came into view.

"I bet one of them passes out," teased Rob.

"It's not funny," said Cristina, grabbing Grayson's hand.

"What? I almost passed out at my Lacing welcome party," said Rob, who'd received a slap on the arm from Susan.

Grayson couldn't decide if this was a dream. Maybe he had fallen asleep during one of Mr. Cole's lectures and made up the whole scenario—that had to be it.

Jeff shook Grayson's shoulders, bringing him back to reality. "Congrats, son," said Jeff. "You did it!"

Grayson took a prolonged inhale to compose himself. He cracked his neck and shook his head side to side. "Congratulations on what?" he asked, pointing to the crowd of Lacers who were now walking into the house. "Being a Lacer? The whole world hates us."

While it had never gone precisely like this in his head, Grayson had run through the thrill of being told he was a Lacer an infinite number of times, and not once had he ever been upset by the news. Now he was forced to face the consequences of his lifelong dream. Grayson could keep his identity a secret and live his life as a lie, or he could tell the truth and lose his friends. "Are you absolutely sure we're Lacers?" asked Ethan, violently shaking Grayson's arm. "Grayson, it's actually happening, oh my god!"

"I'm sure a million questions are running through your heads right now, and all I have to say is sorry. We're all sorry," said Jeff, motioning to the other three parents as he took a seat across from the boys.

"What could you possibly be sorry about?" asked Ethan, who was bouncing in his chair like a little kid on a sugar high.

"For not telling you boys you were Lacers years ago," interjected Rob.

Rob's statement left Grayson dumbfounded. How could his parents possibly have hidden the fact that they were Lacers from him for fourteen years?

"Why didn't you tell us?" asked Grayson with a bit of an edge to his tone. "We've been wasting our time in school all these years—"

"You haven't been wasting your time in school," interrupted Jeff, giving Grayson a stern look telling him to calm down. "We would've told you sooner, but it's against the law to tell children they're Lacers before they finish eighth grade."

Grayson wanted to know who made Lacers hide their identities from their own kids. Was it the government's law or one the Lacers themselves had created? He was unable to ask this pivotal question—Ethan wouldn't give him a chance.

"What exactly is a Lacer? Like, what can we do?" asked Ethan, rubbing his hands together like he was starting a fire.

"A Lacer is an individual whose mind is ten times more creative in every aspect of thinking than a regular human's. In other words, there is no limit to what a Lacer's mind can accomplish," explained Rob. "Even regular people have the ability to make anything they dream come true, but unfortunately, they block their creativity with negative thoughts and energy. We let ours flow, enabling us to find solutions they can't."

Ethan stopped bouncing and looked at Grayson. Rob's speech was by far the most interesting and informative thing that either boy had ever heard leave his mouth. It sounded like a quote straight out of *The Laws of Nature*. Rob looked pleased with himself.

Jeff brushed some lint off his sapphire cloak and tried to outdo him. "Being a Lacer means you can accomplish whatever you set your mind to. Our entire existence revolves around creativity and, well... karma, too, but that's a topic for another time. Anyway, as Lacers, we can make whatever we imagine in our heads happen in real life. Trust me, that's not as easy as it sounds. It'll take both of you years to master all of your unique visualization techniques."

It didn't matter what the world thought of him or even what his friends thought of him; Jeff and Rob had done enough to make Grayson remember that being different was okay, better actually. Grayson thought of sitting in school for eight more years; he already knew what that would be like. Being a Lacer... now *that* was a mystery, a whole new journey he had in front of him. Grayson was ready to seize it.

"There is only one way to master all these skills," said Rob. "Which is why... this August... both of you... *will be enrolled in a Lacer training program!*"

Rob's announcement forced Cristina to spring off the coffee table. "Only if you want to, of course! There's always an option to

stay home for the first year. Maybe you guys would rather do that—
"

"No way!" yelled the boys.

"You mean we get to learn how to use superpowers? We do have superpowers, right?" asked Grayson.

"Do we get a magic staff? I know Lacers have necklaces. Grayson saw one once. But I heard they have staffs too," said Ethan.

"I guess you'll just have to wait and see," replied Susan, beaming at the sight of Ethan's happiness.

Grayson was speechless. The anger at his parents for not telling him he was a Lacer sooner had converted into pure excitement for his undetermined future.

"Now, I'm not sure if you two forgot, but there's a house full of guests waiting to congratulate you on making it through the first step of becoming a Lacer," said Jeff.

"First step?" Grayson asked. "I thought you said we were Lacers."

"Not officially. We'll explain more after the party, sweetheart," said Cristina. "You don't need to worry about what lies ahead right now. Talk with these Lacers. Pick their brains. I promise at least a couple of them will have some interesting stories to share."

"At least my friends will. Your mom's friends can be a little boring sometimes," said Jeff playfully after the moms had walked away.

Jeff and Rob followed their wives inside, beckoning for the boys to do the same. The two young Lacers sat together, taking a moment to process their current situation. Grayson figured this was about the time they usually would have shared a brotherly hug had there not been a group of complete strangers watching them through the window.

The Lacers made themselves right at home inside the Day residence; some had their feet propped up on the couch with the remote in hand. Others had broken into the alcohol cabinet and were now pouring their third drink of the night.

Susan waved Ethan over to talk to her friends, leaving Grayson alone in the middle of the kitchen. Not knowing how to start a conversation with a Lacer gave Grayson an excellent excuse to make his way toward the food. Everything looked delicious. There were chips, salsa, cheese dip, chicken wings, and pizza—all his favorites.

In Grayson's absence from the house, the Lacers had re-dressed the living room and kitchen with more lively decorations. They had turned what was once a modern home with lots of silver and white decor into a jungle. Green vines dangled from the ceiling, as did bright yellow lightning bolts to ignite the room. Swirling balls of fire danced around from guest to guest, keeping them warm on an otherwise chilly evening. The glittery golden sign that had previously read *WELCOME TO HIGH SCHOOL* had been flipped over, now reading *WELCOME, LACERS.*

"Watch out, Grayson! You don't wanna touch that. It'll shock you," said a Lacer wearing a sapphire cloak with an orange tie underneath.

Grayson promptly transformed his curious grasp at the hanging lightning bolt into a handshake, where the Lacer's limp hand met his steady one with uneven force.

"Simon Lowery," said the Lacer with a cheerful smile. "It's nice to finally meet you."

Grayson and Mr. Lowery had a typical introductory conversation. Grayson admitted he was still adjusting to the thought of himself being a Lacer. Mr. Lowery relived the thrills of his Lacing welcome party and said he currently lived in Texas with his family.

"My dad told me that I've only completed the first step of becoming a Lacer," said Grayson. "What else do I have to do?"

"Woah! Watch your shoes!" said Mr. Lowery, pointing to a puddle on the floor where he'd carelessly spilled some of his drink. "What were you asking? Oh, right—the Lacer Initiation Process... You've got a long way to go before you become an Official Lacer."

"Like a year of training?"

"It's probably your father's place to tell you that."

"Well, what's the training like?"

"Definitely can't discuss that with you... Oh my! This cheese dip is fantastic! Your mom is an excellent cook. Here, have some," said Mr. Lowery, gesturing toward the bar top.

Grayson watched in awe as the first Lacer he'd ever met unsuccessfully attempted to balance his food in one hand and his drink in the other. After creating a mess too big to ignore, Mr. Lowery turned around to grab a napkin. Grayson saw his chance to escape and hurried off. He had to find out if all Lacers behaved like Lowery. What was he getting himself into?

After thirty minutes of small talk, bouncing around from Lacer to Lacer, Grayson began to wonder why there was a party at all. Nobody he met was quite as obnoxious as Lowery, but they were all overly energetic and refused to answer any of Grayson's questions about becoming a Lacer.

Grayson was about ready to give up and hide upstairs when he noticed a tall, distinguished-looking Lacer standing alone on his phone in the corner of the kitchen. He was wearing a white cloak. Grayson eagerly darted between the crowd in hopes that this accomplished gentleman could tell him something useful. Sure enough, as Grayson approached him, the man lifted his gaze from his phone and smiled.

"Ah, able to free yourself at last?" asked the Lacer, extending his hand.

Grayson returned the smile and took the man's firm grip.

"Hello, Master Emerson! I'm glad you could fit our party into your schedule today," interjected Jeff, barging his way through the kitchen.

Grayson watched as his father and this Lacer, whom he had just addressed as a Master, hugged each other as though they were long-lost friends. Emerson towered over Jeff. His spiky black hair made his white cloak shine as bright as the lightning bolts hanging from the ceiling. No other Lacer at the party wore white. Emerson wasn't drinking, and he wasn't playing with vines; he was relaxed, composed, and meant business. Grayson could tell Emerson had control over not only himself but the rest of the party as well.

"Please, Jeffery, Grayson here was the first one on my list," said the Master in a gentle tone. "I don't think there's any question that you would fit in perfectly with us, Grayson. After all, my city's initiation program has instructed bright, creative minds like yours far before any other program."

"So, you'll be my teacher?" asked Grayson cluelessly.

The two men laughed.

"If you were to choose us, then I would most certainly watch over your teachings," replied Emerson. "But to answer your question more precisely, no, I wouldn't be one of your instructors."

"*If* I choose you? I thought I had to attend a Lacing program after eighth grade. What other options would I have?"

"Oh, you have to attend *a* Lacing program," said Jeff, massaging Grayson's shoulders. "You just don't necessarily have to choose Master Emerson's program."

"It would be your best choice, of course, right here in the Colorado Mountains, nice and close to home. Unless Master Lowery has already convinced you to move to Texas."

"Now, Emerson, let's try not to influence Grayson too much before he gets to meet the other mayors," said Jeff.

"Mr. Lowery is a Lacer Master just like you?" asked Grayson, cutting off his father.

"He's the mayor of the Lacing city in Texas called Firenight Valley. So yes, he holds the rank of Master as all mayors do," said Emerson, sounding thrilled that Grayson hadn't heard this from Lowery himself.

"Master Lowery didn't mention any of that... What's the name of *your* city?"

"I'm glad you asked. You see, Grayson, for the past several decades now, most Lacers refer to our city as Mount Icefall. However, I have always preferred to call it 'The City in the Clouds.'"

Grayson started to daydream again. There was something so magical about that name. He imagined an enormous city so high in the air he could touch the clouds. It was not until Ethan ran up to him and started yelling about a Lacer Master that Grayson refocused on the present.

"He runs the program we're going to attend!" bellowed Ethan, pointing in the direction of Mr. Lowery.

"Might attend," corrected Grayson, nodding at Master Emerson.

"Oh, hello, sir," said Ethan, clearly embarrassed.

"And you must be Ethan Clark. It isn't an every-year occurrence I get to meet two intelligent Potential Lacers at the same party," said Master Emerson.

Emerson put his arm around Ethan and began to give him the same spiel he had given Grayson. Jeff then grabbed Grayson's arm and led him back into the living room, where they stood with their eyes locked.

"I know what you're gonna say," said Grayson.

"What am I going to say?"

"That I need to talk to more Masters before I pick a program."

"Yes, exactly. Elliott Emerson can be rather persuasive when he wants to be, and I don't believe he should've pressed you as hard as he did. The entire purpose of this party is for you to decide which city has a program that best suits you. It's wise to give every mayor time to show up before you make your decision."

"But I don't wanna talk to forty-eighty more mayors."

"My dear son, do you really think that each state has a Lacing city? If that were the case, our system would allow you much more time to choose. We only have five true Lacer cities here in America," said Jeff, placing his glasses back on his head. "Each of the five mayors picks which Lacing welcome parties they want to visit to recruit the best pupils for their program. New York and California usually have enough Lacers in their own states to fill up their open spots, but I wouldn't be surprised if Florida stopped by, so we'll need to keep the party going for at least another hour."

Grayson returned to the backyard for some fresh air. The sun had set in Colorado, and the only light outside came from the balls of fire that dribbled their way around the icy pavement and snowy bushes like basketballs. He sat down in the nearest patio chair and closed his eyes, doing his best to enjoy the silence. He was still shaking with excitement. "No more school," he said to himself.

Through the window, Grayson looked at the party, and a rather obvious thought crossed his mind. If these people were Lacers, shouldn't they have their fancy necklaces and magic staffs with them? Grayson had heard from one of his school friends that Lacers kept their staffs around their waists. But surely, over fourteen years, he would have noticed if his parents carried a big piece of metal with them. And there was no possible way his parents could have hidden their necklaces, even if shirtless activities like swimming were not that popular in Colorado. Grayson did not like the secrecy of these Lacers.

He spent another ten minutes outside before the cold became too much to bear, and he went back into the noisy house. As he entered, an older couple wearing earmuffs and scarves bid him farewell, but not before slipping him a twenty. After five minutes,

Grayson had said goodbye to practically the whole party and easily made over three hundred dollars. Even Master Lowery slid him a fifty, muttering something about nice sunsets in Texas.

Aside from Ethan, who was still standing starstruck, talking to Emerson with the rest of his family, the kitchen was now empty.

The doorbell rang.

Cristina rushed over and swung the door open, revealing three late arrivals. Grayson did not need to see his dad's shocked expression or Emerson's angry one to know that these were the mayors of the other Lacing cities. Why they all arrived together, he did not know, but he had never been more nervous.

They took turns shaking hands with Cristina before introducing themselves to the rest of the house. Ethan broke away from Emerson upon the arrival of the other three Masters; he now stood side by side with Grayson. They met Mistress Swaney from California, Master Richmond from New York, and Master Pickman from Florida.

The charming Mistress Swaney gently grabbed Grayson's arm and led him over to the couch, where she took a seat and gestured for him to join her. Ethan sat at the kitchen counter with the mayor from Florida while Master Richmond from New York entertained their parents. Emerson remained in the corner on his cell phone; he had a snarl on his face.

Grayson's conversation with Mistress Swaney went fairly well, although he didn't hear too much about her program since he could not take his eyes off her wavy black hair, which she continuously twirled. Grayson did throw in the occasional "oh wow" or "yeah definitely." He constantly had to remind himself that he was speaking with a powerful Lacer, not a supermodel. She spoke of the beautiful scenery in the Bay Area yet mentioned nothing of her program's training.

Grayson met with Master Pickman next. Pickman was a bald, middle-aged man, also dressed in a sapphire cloak. Grayson's informal conversation with Pickman consisted mainly of his city's favorable location, where the annual Miami Bikini Competition was held. The two of them agreed this would not be a bad spot to train; however, just like Master Lowery and Mistress Swaney, he did not want to share key information.

Lastly, he spoke with Master Richmond from New York. Grayson had never visited New York and thought it looked like an opportunistic place to live. Richmond did not disappoint. He described his school's spectacular view of the city and listed several important contacts inside the Lacer government—a thing Grayson did not know existed—for future job references. Grayson asked many questions about the Lacer government, all of which Master Richmond hinted he would eventually unveil if Grayson chose to come to New York.

Just like Emerson, Master Richmond was a serious Lacer. However, Emerson's calm and powerful aura seemed to put him in control of the entire room, even above Richmond—perhaps his white cloak played a part in this. Grayson and Master Richmond joined the others in the kitchen. Ethan had just completed his third interview with Mistress Swaney; he was sweating an awful lot.

"Well, you did it, boys! All done talking for the day!" said Rob Clark.

"Are you two Potential Lacers ready to pick where you want to go?" asked Emerson.

Everyone froze.

"Emerson, you know it's the protocol to wait until the next morning for them to decide," said Master Richmond sternly.

"Oh yes, I'm well aware," replied Emerson. "I just thought I would give both families the option to inform us now. Making a single phone call to Master Lowery would be much easier for them than calling all of us tomorrow."

"We just need a minute to discuss it," said Grayson.

After countless reassurances from their parents that it was perfectly normal to wait until the next morning, Grayson and Ethan insisted that they only needed a second alone before making a decision. As the boys sat down on the couch, there was such tension in the air that Grayson could feel the Lacer Masters' cold stares piercing straight through him.

"Colorado," said Ethan. "It has to be Colorado."

Grayson agreed; he had liked Emerson the most, but he couldn't help but feel like something was off. It was clear how everyone else in the room felt about Emerson. Still, there was no denying he had done the best job recruiting them.

Several minutes passed with Ethan rambling on about how he thought Emerson could read minds and how New York still didn't compare to Mount Icefall. Grayson came up with as many counterarguments as he could, but eventually, even he had to admit that the positives of going to a training program in their home state outweighed the negatives.

They made their way back to the eight silent Lacers. Ethan announced their decision. When he did, the room remained quiet.

Master Pickman and the beautiful Mistress Swaney wished the boys the best of luck and thanked them for their time. Much to everyone's surprise, the once sophisticated Master Richmond did nothing of the sort. He stormed out of the house without a word, shoulder-checking Emerson on the way out. Emerson's cloak was brushed to the side, revealing a short silver clip strapped to his waist with a red marble inside it. He kept his hand on the clip until Richmond was far from the house's premises.

With the other Masters gone, Emerson took a deep breath and gave himself a confident nod for winning over Grayson and Ethan. He didn't stay long to celebrate. Emerson thanked the boys and their families for trusting him and his program; he assured them they had made the right choice. Emerson's soft voice from the beginning of the party had transformed into a deep, commanding tone. He hadn't lost his manners, but he no longer needed to persuade his hosts. Emerson disappeared out the front door and trekked through the freefalling snow.

The Clark family was thrilled with the party's outcome. In their opinion, there wasn't a finer Lacer anywhere than Elliott Emerson.

Jeff had a much different view on the night's events; however, he waited until the Clarks went home to share his concerns. Ethan gave Grayson a brotherly hug before he, Rob, and Susan danced down the hill to their house one driveway over.

"It was completely against protocol for him to rush you like that," bellowed Jeff.

Cristina seemed to think Emerson had only tried so hard because he saw Grayson's potential and chalked it up to Emerson realizing what the others didn't see.

"You're just happy he's going to the city you wanted," said Jeff, still infuriated.

At those words, Cristina turned and marched up the stairs. Before Grayson even had time to ask his dad why his mom wanted him to stay in Colorado, Jeff said, "We'll discuss everything in the morning." He snatched a blanket off the top of the couch, making himself comfortable for the night.

Grayson grabbed his backpack out of the storage closet. His water bottle fell out of the front pocket as he climbed the hardwood stairs. He continued until his feet reached the gentle light-brown carpet that led to his bedroom at the end of the hall. He always loved his room; it was far enough away from his parents so that they couldn't hear him and Ethan up late playing video games or wrestling.

He shut the door and changed into his pajamas for the night. The old-fashioned clock hanging over his bed frame read 12:30 a.m. Had this been a normal last day of school, Grayson wouldn't have even considered going to bed this early, but it was not a typical day by any sense of the word, and he was exhausted.

He pulled out his GemPhone for the first time in what seemed like years. There were at least twenty messages from his friends, most likely wondering where he was — friends he was sure would not want a thing to do with him after today. Grayson put the little sapphire gem into its charger and placed the phone he wouldn't need as much in the years to come down on his nightstand.

He recounted all the money the Lacers had given him. Three hundred and fifty dollars was the most money he'd ever held in his life, yet it meant nothing to him. What could he buy when he already had everything he wanted?

Just as he was walking toward his dresser to stash it away, Grayson abruptly threw the money into the air and dove for his school bag. Memories of the old man from the bus came rushing back. He desperately reached his hand into the darkness of the already unzipped backpack, praying that the energy-filled book was still inside.

CHAPTER 3

Oscar's Friend

As night turned into day, the snow in Snowside transformed into rain. Miles below the storm clouds, kids of all ages emerged from their houses to play. Rushing down the right lane of the road came a group of eighth-grade graduates, who, until they reached the red brick house at the top of the hill, could not be tamed.

Grayson began to stir in his sleep for the first time all night, thanks in no small part to an excessive amount of doorbell ringing from his worried friends. The ringing stopped just as his eyes and mind were on the brink of waking, and Grayson fell back into a deep sleep.

***

The dusty living room shutters behind Jeff's head were open, but not an ounce of sunlight could be found in the house. Jeff reluctantly rolled off the couch and stumbled across the dark kitchen to open the door. A cool gust of wind blasted through the house like a rocket, yet it was the screams of four anxious teenage boys that nearly blew Jeff's ruffled hair clean off his head.

"Grayson's perfectly fine—"

"Yes, I'm sure, Tommy—"

"He's just a little tired, Quinton, that's all—"

Jeff proved to be no match for the persistent group of kids, who insisted on seeing their buddy. Cristina hurried downstairs at the sound of the doorbell, stuffed the remaining party decorations in the closet, and rushed to the door. After many reassurances that Grayson was in perfect condition, she was able to fend off Quinton and the others with a "family emergency" tale. The boys sprinted down the hill to get the scoop on Ethan.

Despite Jeff and Cristina's decision to loudly resume their previous night's argument, Grayson managed to sleep until eleven. The gloomy weather around the house hadn't made its way into his bedroom. Grayson's consciousness returned as he gently traced his finger over the creases of his name on the front cover of the energy-filled book from the bus. He clutched it tight in his arms, just as he had before going to bed, and tried to recall his crazy night of dreams. When he looked back on his last day of school, his night of hallucinations didn't seem all that wild.

Grayson didn't want to let go of the book. If he did, perhaps his usual morning drowsiness would come over him. He was also terrified to let it out of sight after last night's scare.

Knowing he couldn't carry it around the house without revealing it to his parents, Grayson rose from the comfort of his blankets and securely buried the book under the contents of his dresser. His energy did not dissipate as he snatched his phone off the nightstand and began his day.

Grayson wasn't in the mood to expose his true identity to his friends, so he ignored their messages, repeated his daily quote, and proceeded to rummage through his closet, thinking to himself, *What would a Lacer wear?* All the Lacers at his welcome party had been wearing an array of custom cloaks, which did not happen to be in his current wardrobe—he wondered when he would get his own. Grayson decided he would pick the shiny white cloak like Master Emerson.

Grayson did not understand why his dad was so angry with Emerson. Jeff had acted like Emerson did something horrible when he had simply done a better job recruiting than the other mayors. Grayson refocused on his outfit selection for the day and went with black sweatpants, a red sweatshirt, and his usual pair of beaten-up shoes.

It was pure silence downstairs when Grayson trotted into the living room. Cristina was in the kitchen cooking eggs while Jeff was sipping a cup of freshly brewed coffee and watching the Lacer News on television. There, in the middle of the screen, stood a ruby-cloaked reporter holding a microphone.

"That's funny. I've never seen this station on our channel guide," said Grayson.

"Just upgraded to the deluxe plan this morning," said Jeff, proudly smacking the remote in his hand. "It's about time we get some reliable information in this household."

"You two still mad at each other?" asked Grayson, making his way to the kitchen counter.

"Heavens, no." Cristina smirked as she shoved a plate of eggs, bacon, hash browns, and toast across the counter. "Your dad just needed some time to let it sink in that you picked my city over his."

"You trained at Icefall?" asked Grayson, jumping out of his seat. "What does it look like? What's the training like?"

"It was one big jungle last time I was there. It's been remodeled since then," said Cristina with one eye on the TV.

"Emerson shouldn't have rushed you to make a decision," repeated Jeff. "You could have woken up today and decided New York was the place for you."

Cristina rolled her eyes.

"Oh, come on, you know my city is cooler. We float over New York!"

Grayson nibbled at his hash browns, wondering if he had made a mistake. Although his mom said it had been remodeled, Grayson didn't see how any jungle could be better than a floating city. Emerson had made Icefall sound irresistible… Had he lied?

It was too late to switch programs now. Cristina had already called Master Lowery to let him know Grayson would not be moving to Texas. Now that all five mayors had been informed of Grayson's decision, the deal was finalized.

Cristina joined Jeff in the living room to watch the news, leaving Grayson alone at the bar top to eat his breakfast. With the living room directly behind him, he usually didn't have trouble hearing the television; however, Jeff continuously lowered the volume throughout the course of Grayson's meal. Cristina ferociously snatched the remote from Jeff to ensure she'd heard one segment clearly.

"Oscar has evaded death once again and is on the run. E.R.O.L has released a statement claiming they are actively trying to contact Oscar and are willing to provide him with top security until his hunters have been apprehended."

Grayson went to sit by his parents, determined to find out if this type of action was an everyday occurrence in the Lacing world or if Oscar's manhunt happened to be the story of the year.

"What's E.R.O.L?" asked Grayson as he wrapped himself in a blanket.

"Stands for the Enlightened Republic of Lacers," said Jeff, turning off the TV. "It's our government."

"Hey! I wanted to watch that!"

"You can watch the news some other time. Right now, we need to talk," said Jeff, tossing the remote to the side.

"Fine. About what?"

"Well, don't you want to know where your dad and I work?" asked Cristina.

Grayson looked at her like she was crazy. He already knew both of his parents worked for a car insurance agency in Denver. Then he remembered: As Lacers, they were forced to lie to him about everything. The way his mom had so casually addressed her lie made Grayson's internal body temperature rise. He threw off the blanket and impatiently gestured for her to continue.

"I'll go first," said Jeff, handing Grayson his iced coffee. "I'm the Head of Security at the Black House."

"The Black House is the Lacer version of the White House," said Cristina, answering the question Grayson was about to ask. "It's also in Washington D.C., just more secluded."

"I'm not gonna lie," said Grayson, his eyes wide in shock, "that sounds like the most awesome job in the world… So, you're kind of like Secret Service?"

"For lack of a better term," said Jeff. "The title Head of Security doesn't exactly live up to its hype. There was talk of laying off my security team, and understandably so. A Lacer hasn't committed a crime for several years. There's nothing to protect the house from."

"Not one Lacer has committed any type of crime?" asked Grayson.

"No, not for a long time. We tend to be a happy group. You'll see what I mean when you get to Icefall. The Lacers there are even more cheerful than the ones who came to your welcome party," said Jeff, cleaning his glasses before placing them back on his head.

"What do you do, Mom?" asked Grayson, taking a sip of his dad's coffee. "Are you the Lacer Queen or something?"

"No, I'm a secret investigator for E.R.O.L."

Grayson choked on an ice cube and spilled coffee all over his lap. The thought of a little woman like his mother investigating anything other than the neatness of the house was hilarious.

"If I could tell you the types of stuff I investigate, I bet I'd knock that doubtful smirk off your face," said Cristina, crossing her legs.

"No, I'd probably just laugh more."

"Don't underestimate your mother. She's a tough little cookie," Jeff said. He gave Cristina an approving nod. "But enough about us, you have another surprise tonight."

"Another party?"

"No. Elliott Emerson's going to stop by and give you something. Don't ask what," said Jeff, cutting off Grayson. "It's a post-Lacing welcome surprise. He should be here around four. Your mom and I took off work today, so we'll be here."

Grayson cleaned the coffee off his sweatpants and went upstairs to contemplate what Emerson could be bringing him. A staff, a necklace, or a cloak were his most hopeful picks. He texted Ethan to share the good news, locked his door, and opened the energy-filled book from the bus.

Grayson didn't know what his next step should be. He could ask his parents about the book, but the way he had come across it made Grayson feel like it was for him and him alone. He flipped through the pages, and to his astonishment, there was a tiny message written in the bottom right corner of the last page that he'd overlooked the first time. The message was two words long: *Bottom Right.*

Grayson frantically turned all the pages again, checking the bottom right corners carefully in hopes of finding the meaning of the phrase. This time he saw nothing new but continued to examine the spiral-shaped crevice on the inside of the back cover. Grayson needed someone else's input. It was time to bring Ethan into the mix. The two boys worked better when they combined their creative abilities.

***

On this foggy afternoon, the Clark house didn't have the typically warm, welcoming feel it usually presented its guests with. The front gate was shut, and the blinds were closed. Grayson hopped over the picket fence, landed in a puddle of water, and went to ring the doorbell. He stopped when he heard yelling coming from inside. He recognized Ethan's high-pitched cries, Susan's screeches, and Rob's howls, but there was another unfamiliar voice. The Clarks had been so exhilarated with the outcome of the welcome party. Grayson didn't know what could've changed, nor did he know to whom the fourth voice belonged.

He returned to his house for safety, only to find himself in a more intense situation. Jeff and Cristina stood a foot away from the television. The news was on. The volume was loud.

"This is the first attack on the Black House since its creation. Extensive damage has been done to the building's defenses. Luckily, there are no reported deaths at this time… When we come back, an update on Oscar's last known sighting and Lisa Johnson's theory on how he could be connected to today's attack."

"I take one day off, and this happens?" yelled Jeff as he swung open the coat closet and darted for the front door. "I'll try to stop by for a few minutes at four o'clock, but no promises," he said, slamming the door behind him.

"What the heck is going on?" asked Grayson. "Did the Lacers' main government building just get attacked? And how is Dad going to get from here to Washington D.C. and back again by four o'clock?"

Cristina's hands were covering her mouth. She took a long time to respond, and when she did, all she said was, "Yes, the Black House has just been attacked."

"Is this Oscar dude the Lacer who did it?"

"Gosh, no," said Cristina, offended. "If anything, he's probably trying to hunt down the Lacers who did."

"How's Dad going to get there in time?"

"His necklace."

"But how?"

"Not now, Grayson!" Cristina burst out. "You don't need to be watching this! Go to your room!"

Rarely did Cristina ever raise her voice, and on the few occasions she had, never had her words reached the decibel point they just did. Grayson went to his room, thinking maybe his mother was tough enough to be a secret investigator after all.

Grayson paced around his room for hours. *Maybe that's what Ethan and his family were arguing about,* thought Grayson. *They could've been worked up over the attack.*

Had there not been a fourth person at the Clarks', Grayson would have settled on this conclusion. It didn't matter—there were currently much more troubling issues at hand. Grayson was worried about his dad. As Head of Security, Jeff would be right in the middle of the action. Grayson didn't know what Lacers were capable of, but anyone who had the nerve to attack the Black House had to be powerful. Even though his mom had said Oscar had nothing to do with the ambush, Grayson pictured his dad in a fierce battle with the mystery man from the news.

He continued pacing. Master Emerson would be arriving soon; hopefully, he would fill Grayson in on the situation. Grayson took a shower and willingly dressed himself up. He wanted to look professional when receiving his surprise. If he got his own necklace, Grayson decided he would help his dad at the Black House with whatever new powers it gave him.

Ten minutes before Emerson's scheduled appearance, Jeff barged into Grayson's room wearing his sapphire cloak. He was panting and dripping rain and sweat.

"I can't stay for long. I've got to get back," said Jeff. "Come downstairs so we can make this quick."

"What's going on at the Black House?" pried Grayson as he followed his dad to the living room.

"We haven't found the attackers yet, but everything's under control. Oh, and be gentle with your mom tonight—today's been hard on her," whispered Jeff, nodding to his wife, who stood only a couple of feet away in her sparkling cloak.

Two uneven knocks on the door shook the atmosphere of the house. Jeff swung open the wooden barrier. The night sky's darkness was broken not by Master Emerson's gleaming cloak but rather by the messy white hair and tangled gray beard of a scruffy-looking man wearing a ripped brown jacket.

As Jeff jumped back from the doorway, Cristina ran forward to embrace the elderly man, tears pouring down her cheeks. "I thought you were him," she cried into the stranger's shoulder.

In some strange way, Grayson knew what she meant. At first glance, this dirty hitchhiker reminded Grayson of the old mystery man from his bus stop on the last day of school. The four of them awkwardly made their way to the living room. Only Cristina's sobs broke the silence.

"Walter Frost," said the man in a stern, low voice. He extended his hand to Grayson. "I haven't seen you since the day you were born."

Grayson tried to respond; however, he found himself unable to think or move from the second the two of them shook hands. The energy Walter Frost brought into the house was more potent than the energy from the book on the bus.

"Why were you there the day I was born?" asked Grayson, recomposing himself.

"Oscar invited me to come," he replied, releasing Grayson's hand.

Grayson curiously stared at Frost. Why would the Lacer from the news, that was on the run, invite Walter Frost to watch his birth? Surely it was a different Oscar. Frost returned Grayson's gaze. Grayson felt the old man inside his head.

"You didn't tell the boy?" he asked.

"We haven't heard anything yet," said Jeff.

"What is it, Walter?" pressed Cristina, begging him for information.

"I would've thought you'd already known," said Frost, taking a deep breath. "He was found dead at a ski resort about an hour ago. I did all I could to track him down. I'm sorry."

Cristina broke down in tears. Jeff rushed to her side. Grayson didn't even know who had been killed. Who could have died to make his mom this upset?

"Walter, what was the name of the ski resort where they found Oscar?" asked Jeff, holding his wife tight in his arms.

"This is impressive, even for President Starr," said Frost. "He was there at the ski resort. And you're his Head of Security at the Black House, are you not? I figured he would've told you."

Jeff's expression was impossible to read. It was clear Frost's comment had bothered him. "When it comes to power, President Starr keeps his circle tight."

"He is your father-in-law... I guess it wouldn't hurt to inform you," said Frost, taking a seat on the couch. "I hopped on Oscar's trail the day after he went missing, so I was far behind. I tracked him to Snowy Summit Ski Resort here in Colorado. I arrived just as President Starr and a group of his buddies were leaving. Starr didn't seem happy. I'm going to guess Oscar's killers got it first."

"Is this the same Oscar from the news?" asked Grayson.

They all looked at him like they had forgotten he was there. Cristina's eyes were swollen shut. Frost nodded toward Jeff.

Jeff revealed that Oscar was Grayson's grandfather, Cristina's dad. Grayson had been under the impression that all his grandparents had died before he was born. He didn't know what to do with this information—he hadn't even known the man. He decided his only proper response was to comfort his mom, who had just lost her father.

Cristina, Jeff, and Grayson joined Walter Frost on the couch. Cristina wiped her eyes and nose, trying to pull herself together. Grayson was sure that his mom would not have let a man as filthy as Walter Frost sit on their furniture under any other circumstance. His deranged hair, torn clothes, and repellent smell were all in plain sight, yet his expressions and mannerisms gave the old man a look of sadness and defeat.

Grayson inferred from Frost's story that Oscar must have been carrying something valuable on him; that was the only reason a group of murderers, as well as the Lacer President, would've been hunting him down. He restrained himself from asking more questions, knowing this was not the right time.

"Let's just get this over with, and I'll get out of your hair," grunted Frost as he pulled out a piece of paper. "Sign this."

Potential Lacer, please select the city you intend to live in throughout your initiation process. Then sign on the dotted line.

Colorado Mount Icefall
Florida Sunlight Peak
California Moonlight Canyon
Texas Firenight Valley
New York Floating Fortress

Grayson circled *Icefall* and quickly scribbled his name with his non-dominant hand. He didn't want to take his right arm away from his mother.

"Okay then," said Frost, placing the signed paper in his jacket. "I'll be giving that to Elliott."

"Is that all you had to give me?" asked Grayson, who had been waiting for a surprise.

Frost pulled a small cardboard box out of his jacket, set it on the couch, and got up to leave. Grayson left the box alone, keeping his focus on his mother.

"Wh… why did Elliott send you here?" stammered Cristina.

"He didn't. I asked to come. I wanted to pay my respects to Oscar's family."

"Thank you, Walter… P… please make sure G… Grayson doesn't get himself into t… trouble this year," whimpered Cristina as Frost closed the door behind him.

"Does he teach at Icefall?" Grayson asked.

"Lives there," corrected Jeff.

Jeff and Grayson tried to console Cristina, but she immediately ran upstairs to be alone.

"Take care of your mother tonight," instructed Jeff. "I've got to get back to work and find the Lacers who did this."

Jeff slammed the door behind him. Grayson ran over to the couch and tore open the box—maybe whatever this surprise was could somehow help his family. Neither a staff nor a necklace rested inside the wrapping paper, but rather a shiny emerald cloak. The glistening material made the air around it glow. Grayson held it up to himself and then threw it down in disappointment.

He ran upstairs to check on his mom, all the while wishing he had a necklace instead of a cloak to help his dad bring these murderers to justice. Grayson couldn't help but feel like he knew a lot more about his grandpa's death than he should have. He found Cristina lying on the bed, looking through old photographs.

"We hadn't spoken since the day you were born. He left for good after that. That's the real reason your dad decided to take my last name, kind of a way to remember him. It would've been nice to say goodbye." Cristina pointed to a picture of her younger self standing next to a tall man with gray hair.

It was the stranger from the bus stop, the one who had left Grayson the book.

CHAPTER 4

The Days Before Icefall

"You're an idiot," said Ethan.

"It was against the law for me to contact you. How can you not accept that?"

"You should've at least texted me. They wouldn't have known. What kind of brother are you, not willing to break the rules for your own family?"

"What kind of brother am I? Do you think I wanted to keep everything a secret from you? How about 'Welcome home, Mitchell. It's good to see you again. I really missed you?'"

"Oh, Mitchell, I missed you so, so much! I hope you had fun at Icefall with your girlfriend while I was stuck living at home and going to school."

Mitchell slammed his bedroom door closed.

Grayson didn't blame him.

✳✳✳

Throughout his last three months at home, Grayson spent most of his time listening to Ethan complain about Mitchell's cowardly act of following the law. Unlike Grayson, Ethan never dove into the depths of a problem; he saw the issue he was face to face with and got too angry to see what had caused the problem in the first place. Grayson thought the Lacer government was the real issue.

During a family breakfast one chilly July morning, Grayson mentioned Ethan and Mitchell's quarrel to his parents.

"That's why most Lacer couples only have one child," said Cristina, "to avoid what's happening with Mitchell and Ethan right now."

"It's a terrible law," agreed Jeff, "but that's just the way it has to be for the time being."

"Why does it have to be like that?" Grayson argued. "Why can't kids know they're Lacers from the time they're born? Then nothing has to be a secret."

"How do you think you would've been treated in school if everyone knew you were a Lacer?" asked Jeff through a mouthful of bacon.

Grayson thought long and hard about his dad's question before answering truthfully, "Everyone would've probably treated me the way Mr. Cole did."

"Correct!" said Jeff. "You know how I know you're right?"

"How?"

"Because Mr. Cole *did* know you and Ethan were Lacers—all of your teachers did. They had to be *warned in advance*," said Jeff spookily. "Until Lacers are seen as equals in the eyes of society, the law will stay as is, for the safety and well-being of our own kind."

Cristina stood up from the table without excusing herself. Grayson thought his dad had said something to make her angry, but then he saw a tear fall to the ground. His mom was crying again. She wouldn't emerge from the bathroom until long after Grayson and Jeff had finished eating.

"That's the first time I've seen her cry this week," said Jeff as he did the dishes.

"She cried two days ago when you were at work."

Despite her occasional meltdowns, Cristina was slowly bouncing back from her father's passing. She had returned to her job a couple of days ago, which kept her busy. The less time she had to think about it, the better off she seemed. Grayson always made sure he was at his mother's side during her breakdowns. Part of him felt like he should have been more upset about his grandfather's passing, but it was hard—he had never spoken to the man.

Other than each day at breakfast, the only time Grayson saw his dad was on Sunday evenings when the Clarks had everyone over for their weekly cookout. The Black House had Jeff working overtime to construct an entirely new defense plan for their building. The security breach had apparently sent E.R.O.L into a full-on panic. Not wanting to stress his wife out further, Jeff waited until Cristina went inside to refill her drink with Susan before updating the rest of the table.

"The guys who attacked us were pretty darn good," said Jeff. "They blew right through our first line of defense, but then they stopped without even trying to break into the house itself. I think they were trying to send a message."

"Do you think they're the same Lacers who killed Oscar?" wondered Ethan.

"Probably. The two crimes were committed on the same day... I hope it was them. One crazy bunch of Lacers is enough."

"How do you know it was multiple Lacers? You haven't caught anyone yet," Grayson pointed out.

"There's not a Lacer on Earth powerful enough to damage our defenses like that alone. And trust me"—Jeff paused to take a sip of his drink—"Oscar may have been old, but it would've taken more than one Lacer to put him down. Your grandpa wasn't someone to mess with."

"That's an understatement," said Rob, wolfing down Susan's cooking. "Once Jeff finds these killers, they're getting sent straight to me. It's about time I get to slam some criminals into our empty cells."

"I miss my days in the Atlantic," said Jeff, nodding his head in remembrance.

"It's not the same without you," Rob replied. "Hopefully, we'll be reunited in D.C. by this time next year. Just tell President Starr to give me that promotion."

"You know Starr and I aren't close. But God knows I'll find a way to get you to the Black House somehow. This attack might be the break you've been waiting for."

Grayson had learned a lot about the Clarks during these cookouts. Rob directed the Lacer prison somewhere off the East Coast. He claimed having a total of five elderly prisoners made it seem like a retirement home more than anything else. Susan referred to herself as a *stay-at-home Lacer*, not because she did anything different than a regular stay-at-home mom—she just liked the title more. Unfortunately, the Clark family member Grayson was most interested in did not attend these get-togethers. Mitchell spent his summer locked away in his room to avoid any additional disputes with his brother.

"You hear that purring? I think Mitchell has a cat up there or something," Ethan would say each time Grayson came to his house.

"Yeah, that's annoying. Let's go to my place." This was Grayson's strategy to get Ethan's mind off Mitchell.

***

The end of summer was rapidly approaching, and both Grayson and Ethan had failed to solve the mystery of Oscar's book. After Walter Frost's visit, Grayson had shared every bit of information with his best friend. Jeff and Cristina remained unaware of Oscar's gift; however, the boys had had many enlightened discussions revolving around the topic. They'd spent several hours contemplating the meaning of the phrase *Bottom Right* and had come up with no logical conclusions as to what it could mean.

"This book makes me feel smarter every time I hold it," said Ethan, relaxing in Grayson's room.

"I've been calling it creative energy," said Grayson. "I think it only feels like that because my grandpa touched it. I felt the same thing when I shook hands with Frost, and they're both powerful Lacers, according to my dad."

"Or maybe this is a dangerous weapon. It could be what his killers were after."

"I don't think an empty book is a weapon. Oscar probably just wanted to let me know he cared about me before he died."

With no further clues to help maintain their curiosity, the boys accepted that the book was nothing more than a personalized diary for Grayson with a slight hint of Oscar's creative energy left behind. They did, however, use this energy to help them decide what to tell their friends about the upcoming school year. Early in the summer, they had announced that they would be switching school systems, but now, with only a week left at home, Grayson had changed his mind and wanted to tell the truth.

With Mrs. Williams out of town, Quinton and his dad had jumped on the convenient timing and decided to throw a going-away party for Grayson and Ethan. If they were going to tell their friends the truth, that was the right time and place to do it.

"The only one who really hates Lacers is Tommy. The rest of them are starting to come around," said Grayson as he freshened up for the party.

"I'm fine with telling the truth," said Ethan, flexing in Grayson's mirror. "I'm not worried about Tommy. I'll take him down if he tries to pull a fast one on us."

"No fighting," said Cristina as she dropped an empty suitcase off in Grayson's room. "If you're going to tell them you're Lacers, that's your decision. But remember, we have a Lacer Initiation Process Code of Secrecy... That means you can't tell them about your welcome party, your cloaks, and especially don't tell them about Mount Icefall. You can say that you're going to train but be vague."

Grayson and Ethan were running a little late because of Cristina's lecture. They hurried through Snowside's streets, reminiscing on all the years they spent ding-dong ditching the neighbors. Quinton lived on the opposite side of the neighborhood; no matter, the boys knew every shortcut and were there in no time.

The night turned out to be a lot more fun than Grayson had expected. Quinton's dad ordered eight extra-large pizzas, which the boys nearly finished, despite there only being six of them. They played video games, shot hoops in the backyard, and engaged in a tag-team wrestling tournament, an event that used to be an after-school tradition until Grayson's mom had suddenly decided it had become a safety hazard. With midnight approaching, Grayson and Ethan nervously sat their friends down in Quinton's loft to tell them the truth.

"Okay—remember—we're still your friends after we tell you this," said Grayson.

"You're not moving out of Colorado, are you?" asked their friend Evan. "You guys said you were only going to high school twenty minutes away from here."

"We're not moving out of Colorado," answered Grayson softly.

"Did you get expelled for having too many absences?" asked Quinton. "I swear, if my mom made you guys late by making you get out of the car, I'm gonna rip her a new one when she gets home."

"It's not that either. Listen—"

"Did you get in trouble for the fight on the bus?" asked Tommy.

"We're Lacers," said Ethan, who was sick of playing twenty-one questions.

The loft became silent after Ethan broke the news. Tommy and the others shifted anxiously on the couch.

"I knew it!" yelled Mr. Williams from the first floor of the house. "Thanks for sharing all those quotes with me this year! The guys at my office love them!"

Grayson and Ethan laughed at Mr. Williams's enthusiasm, and slowly some of their friends did, too.

"See? We aren't that scary," said Grayson, harmlessly raising both hands in the air.

"Well, like, what can you guys do?" asked Brian Stedway, wiping off his glasses to get a better look at Grayson.

Brian's curiosity opened the floodgates. Quinton, Evan, and Brian took turns asking one question after the next. Grayson had a feeling his friends had always had these questions about Lacers buried deep inside of them. He answered as many as possible without breaking the Lacer Initiation Process Code of Secrecy. Only Tommy remained silent.

"I have no clue what we're going to learn," said Ethan, "but we'll show you guys next summer!"

Tommy was not interested in Grayson and Ethan's unique abilities. He was the first to have his parents pick him up. Apparently, his stomach was hurting from eating too much pizza, which Grayson found fascinating, considering he hadn't complained at all during basketball or wrestling. But with midnight approaching, Grayson and Ethan weren't far behind him. They answered a few more of their friends' questions and headed downstairs to leave.

"If you boys hear some good quotes while you're off training, text them to Quinton so he can tell me," said Mr. Williams, who had been listening to the entire conversation. "The weather is terrible. Do you boys need a ride home?"

"Will do, Mr. Williams. And our parents are right around the corner. We wouldn't dare walk home through this snowstorm," assured Ethan, with his fingers crossed behind his back. "Thank you again for having us."

The boys hugged their friends goodbye and promised to stay in touch throughout their year apart. They left the warmth of the house, returning to the familiar powdery roads.

"Snowball fight!" screamed Grayson as he nailed Ethan in the back of the head.

The two of them spent nearly an hour playing on the way home. Grayson wanted to take in every moment; something in the back of his mind told him this innocent period of his life would be over once he left for Icefall.

"One last time?" asked Grayson.

"One last time," repeated Ethan, as the two of them rang the doorbell of their neighbor across the street before sprinting into their separate houses for the night.

Four years of endless doorbell ringing, and never once had the owners suspected the two teenage boys from one house over—or maybe they just didn't have a problem with kids being kids.

***

Two days before departure, Grayson ran into Ethan's brother for the first time all summer. Mitchell was outside doing yard work when the two of them got to talking. He was of average height, and like the rest of his family, he had blond hair. The only physical difference between Mitchell now and the day he had "run off" three years ago were his muscles. Mitchell was twice Ethan's size, and that was saying something. Grayson was sure he could've entered any bodybuilding contest and won.

"I wish Ethan could understand I didn't have a choice," said Mitchell.

"I'll try to talk to him about it," promised Grayson, "but you know he's a hothead just like you."

"I'm not anymore," insisted Mitchell, tossing his shovel into the dirt. "Training really makes you keep your emotions in check."

"How many years is training?"

"Only three until you're an Official Lacer. I'm in Icefall's E.E. program, so I'm going back for my fourth year—not sure if I'll last five."

"E.E. program?" asked Grayson.

"Oh, that stands for Extensive Education. You get to decide if you want to do extra training or not. Some Potential Lacers can handle the training, others not so much. Trust me. It's worth it in the end—you just have to stick it out for a while."

Mitchell went on to explain how he had been in his room practicing "very advanced techniques" all summer. "My parents asked me to stay in there so you and Ethan wouldn't see any of it. Once we get to Icefall, I'll show you guys whatever. Come find me if you have questions about anything or just want to hang out on one of your off days! Hopefully, Ethan and I will be cool by then."

Normally, Grayson would have been eager to hear about the things Mitchell was practicing; however, Mitchell's comment about sticking out training was troubling him. This would not be the last time Grayson heard about unpleasant training.

In fact, the very next day, he eavesdropped on his parents talking about it in their room. Eavesdropping wasn't something Grayson approved of, yet he decided to make an exception since they were talking about him.

"He can handle it, Cristina. You're overexaggerating how bad it is," said Jeff. "We don't need to tell him any more than he already knows."

"Fine. I guess you just want him to be behind the other kids. You know darn well most parents don't keep their mouths shut anymore," fumed Cristina as she swung the bedroom door open right into Grayson's face.

"Ouch! I… uhhh… I came up here to tell you that I'm going to the store to buy more milk, and this is how I'm rewarded?" said Grayson, lying sprawled out on the floor, trying his best to act like he wasn't listening to them talk.

Cristina dashed to his aid. "I'm so sorry, Grayson bear, let me run to the store for you. Do you want whole milk or one percent?"

"Whole, I guess," replied Grayson, praying that they were, in fact, out of milk.

"Okay, honey, you go to your room and keep packing while I'm at the store."

Packing. This was not an area Grayson excelled in, although he was almost done as far as Cristina knew. The empty racks of clothes

Grayson had shown his mother were really shoved under his bed. With less than twenty-four hours until he left for his new home, he did not have any other choice but to start rounding up his belongings.

He began by gently folding the outfit he would wear to move in the next day. After refolding the shirt five times so it wouldn't wrinkle, Grayson viciously threw everything he owned into suitcases. He finished in half an hour. Sure, none of his bags would close; nevertheless, he was done for the night.

"Grayson! Come downstairs!" bellowed Jeff. He didn't sound happy.

Grayson walked to the living room as slowly as possible, attempting to brainstorm everything he could possibly be in trouble for. When he arrived downstairs, Grayson could tell he wasn't the person Jeff was angry with.

"Your mother believes we need to prepare you for the process you're about to go through," said Jeff, rolling his eyes.

"Well, she's right, isn't she?" mumbled Grayson.

Jeff gave a long sigh. "Buddy, you have to understand that not knowing what's going to happen is all part of the journey. That's how it was for your mom and me."

"Why can't you just tell me about some of it?"

"You aren't supposed to know about the initiation process beforehand because it's a tradition. How you handle and react to the training is up to you," said Jeff.

"You've seen how the outside world treats our kind. Well, the training you'll go through is to prepare you for that," explained Cristina.

"Your mother and I have been in dozens of awkward situations over the years, whether it was your friends' parents talking bad about Lacers or your schoolteachers. The only reason we were able to keep our cool was because of our training," said Jeff, reinforcing what Mitchell had said about learning to keep his emotions in check.

"I don't want to spoil the process for you, but be ready, sweetheart," said Cristina. "We just got your move-in information in the mail. Here you go! Open it now so we can all see the plan."

Grayson took the letter from his mother's outstretched hand and read it out loud.

Dear Mr. Grayson Day,

Welcome to Mount Icefall! Please read the following information carefully.

Page 1

Required items:

→ *Emerald (first-year) cloak*
→ *Staff*
→ *Globe carrier*
→ *Plain black t-shirt*
→ *Plain black shorts*
→ *Minimum of one suit*

Page 2

Recommended items:

→ *Clothes*

→ *Swimsuit*

→ *Toiletries*

→ *Bedsheets*

→ *Television*

→ *Snacks*

→ *Phone / phone charger*

→ *First-aid kit*

Page 3

Move-in Information:

Take the frontage road labeled, "Road Closed. Icy Streets Ahead. Danger!" located just east of Snowy Summit Ski Resort.

Please arrive at the front office to check in no later than 5 p.m. on August 30ᵗʰ.

Room number: ER-44 (Emerald Residence Hall)

Roommate: Ethan Clark

Kind Regards,

Master E. Emerson

Mayor of the Lacing City in Colorado, Mount Icefall

"Am I supposed to learn how to magically make a staff by tomorrow?" asked Grayson.

"You could try to," said Jeff, slapping Grayson on the back, "but there's no need. We're going to stop somewhere on the way to Icefall for you to get one. That's the next step in the Lacer Initiation Process. First, your party, followed by your cloak, and then your staff right before you start training."

Grayson was so happy he forgot how to breathe. He had waited all summer for tomorrow, and now it was going to be even better than he'd imagined. He didn't know if he could wait.

"Can I please see your staffs?" begged Grayson for the hundredth time of the summer. "Or at least your necklaces?"

Jeff always answered his son's requests with the word *no*. Today he told Grayson that despite his necklace currently being around his neck, it was physically impossible for him to show it. "The moment a Lacer becomes a parent, their necklace turns invisible until their child receives their own necklace."

"Does that mean you can show me your staff tomorrow after I get mine?" asked Grayson.

"You're not seeing it," said Jeff firmly. "Maybe after you complete your first year of training."

Cristina hadn't heard any of this. She began reciting all the items she had already bought for Grayson over the past couple of weeks, then ran to the kitchen to grab a pencil and paper to write down everything she had missed.

"Did you know they were allowed to have snacks in the dorm this year?" Cristina asked Jeff as she scribbled down the names of Grayson's favorite after-school goodies.

"What's the first-aid kit for?" asked Grayson nervously.

"Most likely just a precaution," reassured Jeff.

"Most likely?"

The Days arrived at the local grocery store around 10 p.m., only nineteen hours before Grayson's check-in time at Icefall.

"Why did they give me my checklist the night before I move in?" asked Grayson as he stopped the cart in the middle of the dessert aisle.

"Get used to doing things last minute," said Cristina. "Now hurry up. We don't have all night. Will you eat frosting bites? Yes, you will. I'll get them just in case. Oh, and remind me to grab that milk you wanted earlier."

By the time Grayson reeled the cart into the checkout, it was overflowing with cakes, cookies, candies, and pretty much every sweet ever produced. Cristina swiftly took Grayson's wallet out of his pocket when he wasn't looking and used the cash from his Lacing welcome party to pay. Grayson and his mom got into a tug-of-war match at the checkout counter.

"You're not going to need this cash for anything else. The only reason our friends gave you money at the party was to buy the items on your checklist," said Cristina, yanking the final twenty out of Grayson's hand.

When they got home from the store, Cristina went into full-on psycho mode.

"Jeff, grab the big plastic bin from the pantry. Yeah, okay, this should fit most of the snacks," said Cristina, talking to herself. "I guess we can put the rest in your suitcase upstairs."

This comment forced Grayson to jump off the couch where he had been relaxing since they got home. "Yeah, I'll go make some space!" he yelled as he took off up the stairs.

As quickly as possible, he emptied the suitcase that was least full and started piling up the other ones even higher with wadded-up clothes. It was no use.

"Grayson!" gasped Cristina. "You call this packing?"

Cristina's original plan to go to bed at eleven and wake up at ten was no more. Together, Grayson and Cristina repacked everything. Jeff insisted this looked more like a mother-son project and hurried off to bed, but not before Cristina gave him the evil eye. Grayson was unsure why his mom said she needed his help when she continually refolded everything he'd "folded wrong."

Once the end was in sight, Grayson noticed Cristina was moving slower, as if she did not want to finish packing. He could see tears welled up in the corner of her dark brown eyes as she gently placed the last of his clothes in the suitcase.

"I'm gonna miss you too, Mom," whispered Grayson as he gave her a tight hug.

Grayson did not know how long he sat on his bedroom floor comforting his mother. Time seemed to slow as he reflected on the first fourteen years of his life. So many years of wondering what direction his life would go, yet he knew when his alarm sounded the following day, he would be closer to answering that question than ever before.

CHAPTER 5

The Reville's Gift

"Creativity is the key to an extraordinary life. All people are creative to some degree; only a select few have the mental discipline to make their fantasies a reality. Belief and visualization are essential," said Grayson, staring at himself an inch away from his bathroom mirror. "Wow... It worked..."

It was move-in day. For the first, and most likely the only time in Grayson's life, he was awake before the rest of the house. He heard his dad loudly slurping coffee before leaving for work. He heard Cristina snoring from the master bedroom. And a couple of hours later, he heard Jeff re-enter the house, announcing his return from a short morning shift.

"Cristina! Wake up! Do you know what time it is?"

"Oh my!" gasped Cristina. "We have to leave in half an hour. Go wake up Grayson!"

"Wake up, son!" bellowed Jeff, swinging open Grayson's door. "It's time to go... Oooh, you're awake. Cristina, he's awake."

"Well, why didn't he wake me up then?"

"I just woke up," lied Grayson, who didn't care to admit that he'd spent the last five hours fantasizing about the magic staff he was about to get.

Had Grayson not lost track of time and noticed that Cristina's alarm hadn't gone off, perhaps move-in day morning would've been less chaotic. Cristina ran around the house frantically, marking off all the items on her checklist. She shoved a bagel with cream cheese at Grayson, who had been hauling his neatly packed suitcase down the stairs.

"Eat quick, honey. We're gonna have to open up all these suitcases again to make sure we packed everything."

"We're gonna what?" asked Grayson, hoping his mom was kidding.

"Just do what the woman says," muttered Jeff. "There's no point in arguing with her this morning."

"We've got to be at Fancy Folks in an hour," said Cristina as Grayson sat down at the kitchen counter to eat his bagel.

"Fancy Folks? I thought I was getting a magic staff. What the heck is that?"

"*That* is the place you'll be getting your staff. What the heck did you think it was called, *The Staff Shop?*" Cristina smirked.

Grayson's one and only job consisted of a final room sweep to make sure he had not forgotten anything. Jeff had already loaded the television and nightstand into the truck. Aside from two wooden dressers and the sheetless bed, the room was empty. The black backpack with his grandfather's book was the only item Grayson still needed to take. He tiptoed behind his mother, who was now repacking everything she had unpacked.

"I know we haven't told you a whole lot about the process, but hopefully, you've realized you won't be having too many books to put in that backpack of yours," said Jeff as he rearranged the luggage in the trunk.

"Oh, yeah, I know that. I... I just really like this backpack," stammered Grayson.

Jeff gave him a confused look before going back inside.

I just really like this backpack? Why the heck did I say that? thought Grayson.

He reached into the car to make sure the bag was zipped up all the way; sometimes, he could feel the energy through the material. When Grayson pulled his head out of the backseat, he turned right into the Clark family. Caught off guard, Grayson was forced to grab onto the car door to stop himself from slipping down the driveway.

"You don't seem very happy. What's up?" asked Grayson as he regathered his footing.

"Picture time," replied Ethan, stone-faced.

Sure enough, it was picture time.

"Okay, get over by the garage door, you handsome boys." Susan Clark beamed. "Go on, Mitchell, get in there."

Ethan reluctantly put his arm around his brother. Refusing to do so would've only dragged picture time on longer. The moms took close to four hundred pictures before Cristina announced she had captured the perfect one.

"All right, time to head out," declared Rob, checking his watch. "We'll lead the way if you want to follow us, Jeff. Fancy Folks is just below Icefall. I know the route pretty well by now. After all, it's Mitchell's fourth year," he said proudly, indicating to Ethan's sharply dressed brother.

Grayson and Ethan tried to convince their parents to let them drive together; however, Cristina and Susan insisted every moment left with their boys was precious. The Clarks' minivan reversed out of the driveway. Jeff stepped on the gas to keep up with Rob's lead foot. Grayson had never traveled south of Denver. He tried to absorb as much of his surroundings as possible, which was not easy because they were driving directly into a snowstorm going ninety miles an hour.

Things got interesting when Jeff exited the highway onto Rock Road. They followed the twisty dirt path to a little town located beneath a mountain range. Jeff was forced to hit the brakes for the first time to avoid hitting pedestrians, who were flowing from the streets into various bars and restaurants. Numerous eyes followed the Days' luxurious vehicle through what was evidently a poor area.

"It's go time!" said Jeff, blasting his 90s greatest hits playlist at full volume.

He took a sharp left turn into a parking lot outside of a crowded blue building, with the illuminated words *Fancy Folks* stamped over the doorway. Had Grayson not known what he was there to purchase, he wouldn't have thought there was anything unusual about the store.

Jeff whipped into a tight space across from Rob. Grayson started sweating, the nerves of pure unknowing finally setting in. What if he had to show his powers in front of his family to be allowed a staff? He didn't know anything yet. Grayson imagined Oscar's book sitting in his lap; he recalled the feeling of its creative energy flowing through his body. *This is what you always wanted, a chance to do something different*, thought Grayson, taking a deep breath.

Grayson rushed after Ethan, who had been too eager to wait. He let out a gasp of astonishment as he entered Fancy Folks. He now knew why the store was jam-packed. Grayson felt as if he were back outside, not in the parking lot, but rather in some type of rainforest. The walls around them were decorated with emerald trees, dangling branches, and countless animals.

"You two go check the place out. We'll check you in," bellowed Rob over the jazz music played throughout the shop.

"Are these people Lacers?" asked Grayson.

"The employees are. The customers aren't," said Jeff. "We're trying to slowly merge our culture into the regular world. Starting in a low-profile town like this is the best way to do it."

The store was massive. Grayson and Ethan wandered aimlessly through each section, all of which seemed to have a different theme. The jungle entrance led directly to an ocean scene where Fancy Folks sold their beach clothes. Thrashing waves displayed on the surrounding walls eventually turned into swirls of fire. Grayson stopped to examine the design of the apparel. The colorful cloaks were similar to his emerald one, although they were not made of the same shiny material.

Grayson looked around for Ethan and eventually found him admiring a maroon dragon necktie. He moved on to the next area of the store, where the blaring fire disappeared and was engulfed by a black thunderstorm. Lightning strikes ran down the walls until they were cut off by a glass display shelf filled with the most elegant jewelry Grayson had ever seen.

This was clearly the most popular part of the store. Dozens of employees frantically removed diamond necklaces, sapphire rings, and ruby earrings from their cases. The lines were backed up with customers raising their hands, trying to flag down the passing workers.

"Do you have any necklaces in this color?" shouted a short, hairy man, pointing to his yellow blazer.

"We only carry emeralds, rubies, amethysts, sapphires, and diamonds. Sorry, sir!" replied one of the employees.

Grayson squeezed through the crazed shoppers until he made his way to one of the necklace displays. The top shelves were decorated with different color chains, while the bottom shelves had an array of gem shapes.

Grayson had always liked jewelry but never asked for any because the stuff he wanted was always too expensive; this seemed to hold true for most Fancy Folks customers. Grayson saw the price of a diamond necklace listed at ten dollars and laughed. Obviously, all this jewelry had to be fake. The Lacers were tricking people. Nobody would sell real diamonds for that low of a price.

"Excuse me," said a woman, waving to an employee behind the display counter. "Did you really find all these gemstones on a newly discovered island?"

"Yes, ma'am," said the worker, proudly tapping the sign behind his head.

Our recent expeditions to the Atlantic
are driving our competition into a panic.

The necklaces were so cheap that Grayson didn't care if they were real or not. He could buy one of these today and wear it until he got his official necklace. Just as he was about to ask if he could try on a ruby necklace with a silver chain, his dad appeared.

"Oh, there's my son. Don't be getting ahead of yourself and start trying on necklaces at this age. We'll see if you get that far."

"Get that far in *what?*" demanded Grayson, begging his dad for information.

"The Lacer Initiation Process. Not everyone makes it far enough to get their necklace. They're ready for you upfront. This is your first trial. I guess we'll just have to wait and see if you're up for it," he finished, trying to sound as scary as his sarcastic tone would allow.

Your dad is joking. Your dad is joking. Of course, he's joking. He's always joking. These were the hopeful thoughts Grayson clung to as he made his way back to the front desk. A tall girl only a few years older than him waited behind the counter. The emerald necklace she wore matched her bright green cloak. Her cloak sparkled.

"This way." She smiled, directing him toward a closed curtain labeled *Staff Members Only.*

Grayson hesitated. He looked back at his family and then pulled the curtain to the side, revealing a steep, dimly lit staircase. The Lacer with the emerald necklace followed his lead and closed the curtain behind them, completely silencing the noise from the store. Grayson could hear his own heartbeat. The two of them continued down the endless steps in silence. After three straight minutes of walking, they reached a metal doorway.

"Uh, should I go in?" Grayson asked the Lacer.

She ignored his question, let out a little giggle, and pointed at a piece of paper posted next to the door.

Dear Potential Lacer,

Once through this door, you will undergo a series of tests. Now, not to worry, these examinations require no prior studying because there are no correct answers. However, it is essential that you answer each question with absolute honesty. Your staff creation depends on it. With that said, we hope you now understand no outside influence can alter your actions during this process. We want your staff to suit you perfectly. Please indicate to the Fancy Folks employee (without talking) that you're ready to begin.

After reading the instructions twice, Grayson confidently nodded to the Lacer. He prayed the sign had indeed been telling the truth about "no correct answers." She pressed a button on the opposite side of the door, which triggered a camera to pop out of the wall. The camera scanned the girl's necklace with green and red lights. The heavy metal door creaked open…

The entrance sealed itself immediately behind Grayson, leaving him in a crowded hallway. On his right, thousands of sparkling crystal balls hung from the wall. Numerous colored walking sticks occupied his left. Grayson stood on a narrow bridge, with what looked like TV screens on both sides of the floor. Being sure to stay on the bridge, he took a step forward. The floor vanished from under him, and he fell deeper underground.

The fall was not steep. Grayson landed on his backside and sprang up to evaluate his surroundings, his heart pounding. He was in a small, quiet room with a wooden desk. Grayson sat down, half-expecting the chair to disappear beneath him. He flipped open the paper test lying on the desk in front of him.

Question 1: What is your current height and weight?

Grayson jotted down *5'10, 150* and took a sigh of relief. If all the questions were about him, he really didn't have anything to worry about. He moved on to the next one and laughed out loud—someone had to be playing a joke on him.

Question 2: What is your favorite color?

Grayson wrote down *Black* and then began to flip through the test to see if the following questions were also kindergarten-level. The next few did happen to be just as easy as the first two.

Question 3: Would you rather live underwater or in a cloud?

Question 4: Do you prefer iron or gold?

Unfortunately, as Grayson reached the middle stages of the exam, the questions required a bit more thinking.

Question 17: If a giant panther attacks you, would you rather use the air to playfully make it float or turn a nearby tree into a ladder so you can climb to safety?

Panthers seemed like pretty vicious creatures; he circled the option that didn't involve playing with a wild jungle cat. By the time Grayson got to the final question, his head was ready to explode.

Question 30: If you were on fire, would you prefer to extinguish it by casting water droplets from the sky, jumping face-first into a pile of mud, or making a huge gust of wind sweep you off your feet so that the flight would put out most of the flames, keeping you alive long enough until the swamp you land in puts out the rest of the fire?

Grayson picked the last option for that one; the extra few seconds on fire would be worth the thrill of flying. He rose from the desk to find his next set of instructions.

A stone cauldron slowly shifted out of the wall. Ancient scriptures covered the rock like tattoos, and inside its vast basin, a black substance twisted and twirled, reminding Grayson of outer space. He tried to touch it, but the air around it would not allow him to. He shook his head clear, refocused, and found his next task written above the cauldron.

Throw your test into the darkness, return to the hallway above you, and make it to the other side of the bridge.

Grayson tossed his test into the black space and watched it swirl around like a whirlpool before disappearing. He strolled over to the area where the floor had vanished. Sure enough, the roof opened, and this time the floor raised him to the same white carpet bridge as before. Without warning, the hallway went pitch black. Grayson could barely see the crystals on the wall. A robotic voice spoke. The force of its every word shook the bridge.

"Prepare yourself! Three, two, one, go!" it thundered.

The screens on the floor surrounding the bridge lit up, and an enormous brown panther with two massive fangs charged Grayson. He hit the deck as the wild creature sprang through the air attempting to claw him. Grayson spun himself around to maintain a visual of the panther, but it was already gone.

This was his chance. He jumped to his feet and darted across the bridge. He was nearly there when this time, three panthers appeared. Grayson did not need a creepy overhead robot voice to tell him to turn around. His plan was to get to the trapdoor and hide underground. At the rate the beasts were gaining on him, he was forced to improvise.

Grayson felt the first one right on his tail. He leaped off the bridge, across the screens, and onto the wall full of sticks. He grabbed the first stick he could find. It fell off the rack, sending him tumbling once again.

Grayson stuck the stick out to break his fall, but it plunged through the TV screen, causing his head to smack against the metal rack. The screen lost its color, and two of the hungry panthers evaporated.

It all made sense. The screens on the floor were floor projectors. Now that Grayson knew these were not real jungle cats, he was able to think straight. He grabbed two more sticks from the shelf behind him and pushed himself off the projector onto the bridge. When the remaining panther pounced, Grayson stuck the stick in its mouth, prying it open, rolled across the bridge to the other projector, and punctured it with the second stick. The final panther vanished.

Although he was gasping for air, Grayson did not let his guard down. He cautiously jogged across the bridge with two sticks held at the ready. This time, nothing attacked. When Grayson arrived at the small square space on the other side, the lights flicked back on, and another stone cauldron emerged from the wall in front of him.

"Step up to the Reville and place your arm over the darkness," said the overhead voice.

Grayson took an educated guess that the stone object was the *Reville* he needed to place his arm over. He stretched his hand over the black pit and waited for something to happen.

The Reville started making sounds that reminded Grayson of ocean waves crashing. The blackness in the center began to spin, and a five-foot golden rod shot into his hand. He held it firmly and let the fresh gold flow through his body.

A mystical green sphere shot out of the darkness and landed on top of the golden rod. Grayson watched in amazement as a vague white mist traveled through the emerald ball. *BAM!* He flinched as a pure gold carving placed itself on the upper quarter of the rod, intertwining the sphere and the handle with golden vines.

The room went silent again. Grayson ran his fingers on every part of the emerald and gold, admiring it. "This is proof I belong in the Lacing world," he muttered to himself. At last, he had his very own magic staff—another step completed in the Lacer Initiation Process.

Grayson remained in front of the Reville, holding his staff until the wall beside him shook. He looked down at the weapon he didn't know how to use yet and decided he would have to pretend it was a sword to scare off whatever was about to attack him. He cocked his staff back in a striking position, ready to swing at any giant panthers. The wall finished retracting. The only thing that jumped on him was his hysterical mother.

"Oh, Grayson, thank goodness," she sobbed. "I was so worried. I just kept thinking about how scared I was when I did this. Are you sure you're all right? I see a scratch on your arm."

"Not bad, not bad at all," said his father. "The guys upstairs were pretty impressed with how quickly you destroyed the projectors. And that jump you made off the bridge, man, that took guts."

Grayson assured his mom he was in perfect condition and relived the thrills of the battle with his dad for quite some time. Then they caught a glimpse of his staff.

"Oh my. Jeff! Jeff, the globe! Look at the green globe!"

"I see it! This is great! He'll be the first one in the family, won't he? I mean, not even Oscar had an earth staff, did he?" asked Jeff.

"An earth staff?" asked Grayson.

Jeff explained how the green sphere at the top of Grayson's staff represented the earth element.

"They're quite rare," interjected Cristina. "Not unheard of, but rare."

"Supposed to be a little more difficult to control than the other elements. Nothing we can't sort out."

Grayson nodded along reassuringly, although he didn't know exactly what an element was.

Cristina ushered him forward. "Ethan's waiting upstairs, honey. We should probably head back up."

The three of them walked to the hidden elevator Jeff and Cristina had used.

"Almost forgot," said Jeff. "Grayson still needs to pick his globe carrier."

A variety of colored waist clips hung on the back wall of the elevator. Each of them had a small space in the center, just like the one Master Emerson had underneath his cloak at Grayson's welcome party.

"Most Lacers pick a color that matches their rod. Yep, here's a gold one." Cristina beamed. "What'd you think?"

Grayson took the tiny clip. "Looks fantastic. What the heck does it do?"

"Give your staff a bang on the ground," ordered Jeff.

Grayson lifted his staff off the floor and slammed it down. The staff disappeared from his hand and was nowhere to be seen. Instead, a little bright green ball floated in front of his face. Grayson grabbed the globe out of the air and held it in his palm.

"Throw it to the ground when you want your staff to reappear," said Cristina. "But for now, just place it in the clip."

Avoiding the second part of his mom's instruction, Grayson chucked the sphere at his feet, and in a puff of green smoke, his staff reappeared in his hand. Grayson repeated the process a couple more times until Cristina snatched the globe in midair, just as Grayson was going for one final throw. She placed it in the golden clip for him.

"Don't worry about your mom taking it away from you," whispered Jeff as the elevator opened back at the main level. "It'll always come back to you."

The elevator doors opened in a dressing room at the main level; the sign on the door read *Out of Order*. Grayson wasn't sure how a dressing room could even be out of order, but the passing customers didn't seem to question it. Grayson and his parents returned to the front desk. Ethan and his family sat in a group of chairs by the exit.

"It's about time," said Ethan, discreetly flashing a white clip with a red globe inside of it. "Let's get to Icefall so we can try these babies out."

"Do we need to pay first?"

"No," said Jeff. "You don't need to worry about doing that anymore."

"Uh… paying for stuff?" asked Grayson.

"You two will see soon enough," said Rob as he led the way outside.

"No way did you actually jump onto the rack carrying the rods. That's insane!" said Ethan.

"I panicked! How did you avoid the panthers?"

"Panthers? I was attacked by a flock of birds," said Ethan as he slid into the back seat next to Mitchell. "I'll see you at Icefall!"

"Here we go, baby!" said Jeff, once more pushing the car's speakers to the limit. He followed the Clarks' minivan off the town's main road toward a sign that read: *Snowy Summit Ski Resort.*

"Jeffery! Do you have to blow out our eardrums every time we step foot in the car?"

"Sorry, sweetums, maybe you should play some of your exciting country music. That'll really get Grayson hyped up to move in."

Listening to his parents argue over two types of music he couldn't care less about was not exactly how he thought their final moments in the car together would be spent. Fortunately, a distraction on the road ahead forced them to shut it off. Rob pulled over and waved for Jeff to do the same.

"The entrance to the tunnel is right up the road. We just have to wait for the professional photography crew to get out of our way!" yelled Rob, indicating to a mom and dad who were kneeling, taking pictures of their daughter in front of a bright orange *Road Closed* sign.

Cristina smiled. "See, Grayson? Susan and I aren't the only parents who take pictures."

Grayson barely heard her. He was busy trying to recall the directions to Icefall from his letter. "Take the frontage road labeled Road Closed," he muttered to himself.

"This doesn't really look like a frontage road," said Grayson louder. "We'd fall off the side of this hill if we drove past that sign."

"Another road pops up once we get through the rough patch of snow. Be sure to give it some gas, so you don't get stuck, but not too much; you don't wanna spin out of control going down the hill," said Rob confidently. "Okay, they're gone. Let's get a move on."

Grayson strapped himself in tight, clinging onto the seat in front of him for dear life. Jeff zoomed past the sign and began to plow through the snow. Grayson couldn't see a thing through the powdery air. He didn't have the slightest idea how his dad was navigating through the treacherous terrain. Just as the car seemed to get stuck and Grayson was able to relax, the car dropped. Grayson would have flown through the roof had it not been for his seatbelt.

"Hold on!" bellowed Jeff as the car continued to free fall.

Grayson closed his eyes, bracing himself for an impact that never came. Instead, peeking with one eye open, he watched the car land flawlessly onto a steep downward sloping road. Jeff accelerated even more as the car picked up enough momentum to skyrocket them up the oncoming hill and into a dimly lit tunnel.

CHAPTER 6

The City in the Clouds

Cristina's deep breathing was the only disturbance in an otherwise silent tunnel. Grayson gazed out the window. Torches placed along the rocky walls lit their path as they traveled upward through the mountain. A steady flow of water ran on either side of the road. It was so peaceful that Grayson could hear skis and snowboards gently gliding along the ice above him.

"Wow, it's changed so much," said Cristina. "The entrance, the tunnel—it's a completely different feeling from when I trained here."

"I gotta give it to Emerson; he's fixed up this entrance pretty darn well. Still wasn't quite as much fun as entering the Floating Fortress in New York, but let's face it, nobody is topping my city," said Jeff proudly. "Still, this was way better than that boring ski lift your mom used to take to get here!"

"It was safe, Jeff. Not boring!" snapped Cristina.

There was natural light up ahead. Jeff settled on a parking space toward the edge of a vast clearing, giving Grayson a perfect view of the countless ski trails that intertwined on the lower half of the mountain. Right below him, Grayson saw a group of skiers at what they surely thought was the mountain's summit. Farther in the distance, glimmering jewelry ignited the streets of the town. Grayson extended his staff to full length and raised his hands to the sky. He was on top of the world.

"No time to check out the view today," said Jeff, pulling Grayson away from the cliff's edge. "Check-in time is in two minutes. You don't want to get into the habit of being late, trust me."

Grayson rushed across the parking lot to a single-story building with glass walls. Forty-foot-high piles of snow encapsulated both sides of the structure, creating a barricade around the city. Murky clouds loomed over the entryway like demons hiding the treasures of heaven. Rumbling thunder shook the mountain top, conveniently rattling open the minuscule glass door for Grayson and his family.

Dozens of silver cubicles, all of which were stocked with state-of-the-art computers and office phones, rested below an immaculate ceiling mural, bursting with splatters of paint, as if all colors of the rainbow had forgotten their natural order and mixed themselves together, creating a new symbol of joy. Yellow and purple swirled their way down the wall like a lily in a lightning storm, enlightening the spectacle two rows down, where the Clarks stood in front of a desk labeled *New Personnel Check*. Behind her desk, a frazzled woman frantically flipped through folders of paperwork.

"My apologies, sir. All the files are saying the same thing. Oh, perfect, are you the Days? Would you please hand over your room information?" asked the woman.

"What's the problem, Rob?" asked Jeff, pulling Grayson's letter from Icefall out of his pocket.

The woman scrunched her eyes together. "This is most bizarre. Both of your forms have you in room ER-44; however, the computer database has you in ER-11. I already checked a pair of girls into

Room 44 about an hour ago. As of right now, Room 11 is the only option."

"Does it really matter?" asked Ethan impatiently.

"As a matter of fact, it does, Ethan," said Susan. "In Emerald Residence Hall, floors two and four are for the men, and floors one and three are for the women."

"You're telling me our boys will be living on a floor with only girls?" demanded Cristina. "Susan, we can't let this happen. There must be another option!"

The woman frowned. "Unfortunately, ma'am, that's the only room we have available."

And that was that. The two families, assisted by one of Icefall's employees, went back to their cars to grab the luggage. Mitchell hugged his parents goodbye and wished Grayson and Ethan good luck in the program. He promised they would be seeing each other a few times throughout the year. Ethan gave his brother a half-hearted farewell before Mitchell made his way alone through the building, his suitcase rolling behind him in one hand and a metal crate in the other.

"Right through here, ladies and gentlemen," directed a buff worker by the name of Paul, propping open a side door. He carried Grayson's television and led the families up a narrow hallway that came out on the other end of the building. When Paul unlatched the backdoor, Grayson was forced to duck his head to avoid hitting the cloud above him. He could only see the snow at his feet.

"It's a little overcast today!" yelled Paul through the roaring wind once everyone had made it outside. "Emerald Residence Hall is on the far west side of the city. This trail will lead us straight there. Come on now, keep up. It's not getting any warmer."

The freezing weather did not seem to be slowing down the two mothers, both of whom were practically racing Paul to the room so they could scout out any "potentially dangerous" floormates that their boys might have. Grayson and Ethan both agreed their moms' lists would most likely include every girl on the first floor.

"Don't worry, Cristina. I'll give that front office a piece of my mind on the way back. Putting our two beautiful boys around all these girls is just asking for trouble," said Susan.

The chatter Grayson heard coming from the dads in the back of the group deeply contrasted with the mothers' point of view.

"Oh man, did our boys luck out! I mean, for gosh sakes, I was stuck with two former wrestlers across from me during my first year, couldn't even get a good night's sleep with them banging into the walls every second," said Rob.

"Maybe our boys will finally get girlfriends," said Jeff. "Grayson always tells me he's too busy for one."

Grayson's ears turned bright pink under the hood of his jacket. Had anyone else heard what his dad said besides Ethan, he would have been appalled. It was true, though; Grayson had never dated a girl, much less kissed one. He had a couple of crushes back in middle school, but the problem was that he and Ethan always ended up liking the same girls. This meant the two of them usually spent more time arguing about whom she would like more than actually talking *to* her. Grayson decided he would make being less shy a point of emphasis during his first year away from home.

"Right up here on the left!" shouted Paul.

The bright silver, rectangular building had four floors and quite a few windows. Paul scanned his ID, causing a sliding glass door to retract into the wall, and Grayson rolled his suitcase off the snowy path onto the white marble tile. Room 11 of Emerald Residence Hall was in the back corner of the first floor. As the group proceeded deeper into the building, the sound of screaming girls grew louder.

"At least one side of our room won't have neighbors. I call that side," muttered Ethan.

"It's gonna be a fun year for you, kids," chortled Paul, opening the door to Room 11.

Grayson walked in first. The spacious, two-window room was exceptionally neat aside from a couple of scratches on the left side of the wall by Ethan's bed and a busted tile on the ground under Grayson's, which Paul shoved back into place before he left. There was a couch in the center of the room and a dresser against each wall. Two wooden desks surrounded the black table where the television was stationed. The miniature closets were located directly across from the bathroom by the door. It was perfect.

The dads helped Grayson and Ethan unpack while the moms were busy cleaning the "filthy" room.

"Grayson, dear, these were on your desk; you'll be needing them," said Cristina, thrusting two folded-up papers in Grayson's outstretched arm. "It's your to-do list and a map of the city... Oh, Susan, let me see the wet towel. This desk is disgusting."

It took over an hour to set up the room. Grayson and Ethan had finished their one and only task relatively fast—putting their clothes in the dressers. The dads hooked up the television within minutes, yet they were slowed down by Susan when it came time to hang pictures on the wall.

"Seriously, Robert? If you hang the picture directly across from the window, there is going to be a glare, and if it has a glare, how is anyone going to see our boy's handsome face?" asked Susan. "Yep. No. Yep! Okay, another inch to the right. Much better!"

"I told her to leave that picture at home," complained Ethan, who was sitting on Grayson's bed. "I mean, honestly, why would I want a picture of myself in my own room? I can just look in the mirror anytime I want."

Other than the controversial wall hangings, the room was shaping up nicely. Grayson briefly visited the bathroom. When he re-entered the main room, both the moms were crying for the hundredth time of the day.

"I just can't believe this day is already here," bawled Cristina into Ethan's shoulder. "I just... I just can't... I mean, I'm just glad Grayson has you here with him."

"I'm glad I'm with him too," said Ethan, giving Grayson's mom a comforting pat on the back.

"I... I feel so bad we have to leave them here without even telling them about... about the program or... or the city," stammered Susan, who was now rushing over to give Grayson a hug.

Grayson did not know why the moms had decided to swap kids, but he figured they were too distraught to care. As long as they had a shoulder to cry on, it didn't matter.

"They're better off not knowing what's going to happen. I'm sure the boys don't want us to ruin the surprise," said Jeff cheerfully.

The rest of the goodbyes took nearly as long as it had taken to set up the room. Grayson promised to call his mom every chance he got—which, according to Cristina, wasn't going to be very often once their training started. Eventually, the families made it back to the doorway, mainly because Jeff and Rob were practically pulling their wives into the hall.

"Yes, I love you too," said Ethan.

"Of course, we'll be careful," assured Grayson.

"All right, to hell with it," whispered Jeff as the rest of the parents walked down the hall, and Grayson was about to close the door. "If I were to give one piece of advice to the two of you, it would be this: Don't draw attention to yourselves on the first day. Stay quiet unless you are spoken to, and do not, *do not* ever talk back to your instructors. I promise it'll only make your life more difficult."

"Jeff, honey, what are you doing?" called Cristina from down the hall.

"Sorry, I left my wallet. I'll be right there, sweetie," bellowed Jeff before lowering his voice again. "Now, I might see you for Christmas. But for gosh sakes, try to have some fun this year," he said, indicating to the neighboring doors. With that, Jeff turned his back on ER-11 and walked out of Emerald Residence Hall, his gray trench coat brushing the white marble as he went.

***

They were alone. Grayson turned to Ethan; this was the moment they had both been waiting for all summer. The boys charged each other and met in midair with what they liked to call "a real man's hug."

"I can't believe the day is finally here!" yelled Ethan as they jumped up and down.

"I know. We're practically in college now!" exclaimed Grayson. "But without the school part!"

"Okay, first things first," said Ethan as he sprang toward the wall where his seventh-grade school picture was proudly positioned above the dresser. "This is going in the closet for the rest of the year."

"And second things second," roared Grayson, removing his green globe from its carrier.

He threw it on the ground and turned his full-length golden staff at Ethan. Ethan tossed his red globe on the floor and immediately swung his chalk-white staff at Grayson's head. Grayson ducked just in the nick of time and placed a perfect counterstrike right in Ethan's gut with the rear end of his staff. Ethan stumbled back against his bed. The two roommates swung their staffs relentlessly at each other until Grayson ended the match by stabbing Ethan's shoe.

"Time out," panted Ethan, limping onto the couch.

"There's no time-outs! Do you quit or not?"

"I thought we said nothing below the waist."

"Oh, sure, I can't hit you in the foot, but you can try to take my head off. I'm up one-zero in our series," said Grayson, determined to make sure this first duel counted as a win for him.

"All right, whatever. Let's go find some food. I'm starving," said Ethan, changing the subject.

Feeling awfully good about his performance, Grayson strolled over to his desk and unfolded the map of Icefall.

"Ethan, check it out! Look at all those skyscrapers! I guess the clouds were covering them when we walked in."

The entire diagram was colored, labeled, and three-dimensional. Half of Grayson's desk was covered with pop-up buildings by the time it was completely unfolded. According to the map, the tall structures, such as the hotels, offices, and apartments, were in the middle of the city, centered around Icefall Lane. The street itself seemed to be the hotspot for restaurants and shops.

The boys cleaned up before heading into the city. Ethan took a shower, which left time for Grayson to explore his new home. Their dormitory view could've been spectacular; it could've been horrendous. Grayson could not see a thing with the storm clouds threatening to swallow the residence hall. As he was heading to the closet for a jacket, he stepped on the second sheet of paper.

To-do List (Must complete by August 31st):

- Visit "The Guardians of Icefall" and choose your very own guardian.
- Have a fantastic time in the city! Enjoy yourself!
- Arrive at Emerald House at 5 a.m. sharp on September 1st. Be dressed in a black t-shirt and black shorts. Bring your phone, your staff, and as always, a positive attitude!

"These letters just keep getting better and better," said Grayson, handing the paper to a wet-haired Ethan, who had a towel around his waist.

"So what? We just go get ourselves a personal protector from a store and run around the city for one more day until… wait! Five in the morning? On the first day? These people can't be serious! Let's be honest, who the heck is going to bring a positive attitude at five in the morning?"

"That's not the part I'm worried about," said Grayson. "We have to wear a t-shirt and shorts. If the weather's anything like it is today on September 1st, we're gonna freeze."

"I'm sure this Emerald House is inside. Come on, let's go eat. We can stop by the guards' place on the way back. Although, I don't know how comfortable I feel with some Lacer guarding me."

Grayson threw on a jacket and clipped his globe carrier on the side of his jeans. He followed Ethan down the hall and out the sliding glass door.

"We need to go right," said Grayson, repeating the route he had memorized.

Despite the jacket, Grayson was still freezing. He couldn't tell if it was nighttime or if the clouds were masking the sunlight. Either way, it was difficult to navigate through the fog. The snow covered most of the dirt, and the only light came from the occasional torch stuck in the ground.

Tree branches dangled over the path, hinting at the surrounding nature. As bad as Grayson wanted to investigate the nearby wildlife, he was afraid he would lose his sense of direction in the clouds; he didn't want to get lost in the jungle his mother had told him about. A set of yellow eyes peered at them through the branches, giving the boys another reason to stay on course.

Their journey continued until a miraculous garden lined with thousands of flowers and plants materialized from the mist. Lanes of water flowed around the stems, and the moonlight parted the clouds, reflecting down onto the flower bed like a projector on a movie screen. A wooden sign with the title *Bezaliel's Garden* hung next to a batch of purple lilies. Grayson had never felt so at peace with the earth.

"I think we're lost!" yelled Ethan, who had passed the garden without noticing it was there. "Come on, let's try another path."

"Lead the way," said Grayson, taking one last look at the glorious scenery.

After a couple more wrong turns, they heard cheering and music up ahead. Lights came into view, blinding Grayson and causing him to walk right into Ethan's backside. The two of them tumbled into a set of heavy oak doors. The boys jumped to their feet to find themselves at the doorstep of a church.

"Look!" exclaimed Ethan, pointing to a sign labeled *Icefall Lane*.

Grayson turned his back on the church and gazed down the road. His jaw dropped. An array of shops and restaurants were situated on his right and left. In front of him, prancing up and down the street, were hundreds of Lacers in their colorful cloaks. They each danced to the deafening music at their own rhythm and pace, making the road look like a concert of three different music genres. Lacers were not the only creatures roaming Icefall Lane; each Lacer had a wild cat by their side. These animals had exceedingly long bodies, short legs, and their oversized tails slithered across the pavement like cobras.

"In here!" said Ethan, ducking into a restaurant called *Marty's Brews*.

Grayson scampered through the crowd of Lacers and closed the door behind him, drowning out the music from the street. He stood in a small bar with only ten tables and a single stage, where a long-haired Lacer passionately struck the keys of a piano.

A hostess fancying a ruby cloak popped up from behind the check-in booth. "What... Oh, what do we have here?" she asked. "Some new faces! I love this time of year! Will it just be the two of you tonight?"

Grayson nodded, caught off guard by her enthusiasm and sudden appearance.

"I'm sorry, but you two aren't old enough to sit at the bar yet. I hope that's not a problem."

Grayson assured her it wasn't and plopped himself down in a booth next to the stage.

"What the heck were those things on the street?" asked Grayson.

"I don't know," said Ethan, "but they reminded me of the purring I heard coming from Mitchell's room all summer."

"And that crate he had with him today! You don't think?"

"If it was one of those giant cats, that means we'll probably get our own too... Woah! They have everything!" exclaimed Ethan, who had just flipped open the menu. "They even have steak. We *have* to get steak for our first night out! I'll pay for it. I have a hundred dollars."

The two boys ordered steaks and sodas. Grayson told Ethan he would pay him back. The food was delicious, and the service spectacular. Jeff had not exaggerated the cheerfulness the citizens of Icefall possessed. Everyone was in such a good mood that Grayson was starting to think it was some sort of Lacer holiday.

Regardless of the night's enjoyments, Grayson was dreading the moment the waitress would bring the check. He would have to borrow money from his parents to pay back Ethan. Why hadn't *his* parents given him money, or at least let him keep his own? Maybe his mom thought he would live off the frosting bites and cookies she had packed…

The check never came. The waitress bid them good night and cleared off the table without the slightest mention of payment.

"Maybe we pay at the front?" said Grayson, sliding out of his seat.

"Uh… ma'am? " Ethan said, waving down the hostess. "We didn't get a bill. But I have money. Are we supposed to pay up here?"

The hostess snickered. "Oh, silly me, I always forget how clueless you newbies are. Your money's no good here."

"It's free?" asked Grayson.

"It is for now. Once you finish your program and become Official Lacers, you will be expected to pay in other ways." She smiled.

"What other ways?" asked Ethan with a skeptical expression written across his face.

"We Lacers believe kindness, hard work, and good deeds are the best form of payment." And with that, the cheerful woman ushered them out the door and onto the noisy street.

Maybe Grayson's old buddy, Tommy Hudson, was right about these Lacers—they were totally insane. He was all for free steak dinners, yet he couldn't see how anyone made a living if everything was free. Surely Lacers didn't work for fun because, let's face it, working was not fun.

The grandfather clock hanging from the church informed the city of midnight's arrival. With the clouds still covering the nearby skyscrapers, groups of Lacers made their way out of the busy bars and disappeared down dirt paths, stumbling as they went.

Grayson and Ethan wove their way in and out of the city's residents toward the Guardians of Icefall. According to the map, it was located a block away from Marty's Brews on the opposite side of the road.

In the middle of the street, a gorgeous stone waterfall fenced in by a ring of fire parted the clouds. Fish and sea creatures alike filled the base of the waterfall; they hid in the depths of the pool as a towering figure approached their home. A giant black bear happily made his way over to say hello to his aquatic friends.

One of the passing Lacers stopped in her tracks to address the bear. "Laura, is that you? It's been almost a year! Now, you play nice, Karman," she said to the wild cat at her feet.

Grayson and Ethan didn't wait to see if the bear answered or not. They sprinted inside the Guardians of Icefall for safety.

"Hello. Hello. Welcome! I'm Marjorie. How can I help you?" asked an aging woman sitting behind her desk as she brushed her long silver hair away from her reading glasses. "Coming to get your tasks done early? I love it!"

If it was possible, this woman had even more enthusiasm than the hostess from Marty's Brews. Grayson decided he wouldn't mind if all the Lacers at Icefall were extremely friendly, but it would take some getting used to. Where he grew up in Colorado, it was considered uncommon if the greeters even looked up from their phones when customers came in.

"You're the first P.L.s of the year," she continued. "That means you'll be able to pick which guardian you want before the rest of your class!"

"Sorry, but what exactly is a P.L.?" asked Grayson.

"And what do you mean by 'pick our guardian?'" Ethan added. "Do we just choose someone who works here to watch over us?"

"P.L. stands for Potential Lacer. You're going to have to get used to all the acronyms, sweetheart. We use them a lot. As for your question," she said, pointing to Ethan, "guardians aren't Lacers. They're creatures. You will have to forgive me for not explaining sooner. Most parents happen to tell their children about guardians long before they ever step foot in this store. It seems many Lacers have forgotten our code of secrecy also applies to their children."

The jungle cats on Icefall Lane were guardians. Grayson and Ethan were about to get their own protectors. Grayson wasn't sure he wanted one—they didn't look like the nicest pets in the world.

"There's no need to be scared, honey," said the woman gently, as if reading Grayson's mind. "The little guardians you'll get tonight won't be anything like the ones out there on the street."

That was the second time Grayson felt like a Lacer was inside his head. Walter Frost had given him the same vibe during their encounter, and Ethan claimed Elliott Emerson had the ability as well. Grayson trudged to the back of the store where Ethan and Marjorie were peering through a tinted glass window.

"Grayson! These things aren't scary," said Ethan.

Grayson looked through the dark glass into a room full of long-tailed kittens. Most of the creatures appeared to have gold or brown fur, a few were white or silver, and a lonely black one slept in the corner.

"What's wrong with it?" asked Grayson.

"That poor thing has been here since last summer. Nobody wants the bad omen."

Marjorie explained that the color black was a symbol of bad karma in the Lacing world. Black had always been Grayson's favorite color growing up, probably because it made him harder to see while ding-dong ditching the neighbors.

"I want it anyway," said Grayson, deciding he would take his chances with a little bit of bad luck. "If I don't take it, it may never get picked."

Just when Grayson was convinced this situation could not get any weirder, Marjorie pulled a ski mask over her face.

"Guardians get attached to the first human face they see," she explained. "I'm going to bring the black one out first. Mr. Clark, you turn around, so it only sees Mr. Day's face."

Marjorie walked around the tinted glass, marched through the howling horde of cats, and picked up the timid creature hiding in the back. She carried the animal in her frail arms and placed it on a table that had suddenly appeared in front of Grayson.

Grayson's brown eyes met the guardian's blue eyes. He could feel a connection between them. He took the animal into his arms and the next few minutes became a daze. He seemed to fall in love with the little creature. The guardian contently purred as it gently rested its head against Grayson's chest. Grayson could tell how much it already cared for him.

"I'll take the white one closest to the door," said Ethan, who had eventually made up his mind.

The next thing Grayson knew, the two guardians were sprinting out the store's entrance, directly toward Emerald Residence Hall. They seemed to know the way better than he did.

CHAPTER 7

New Tongue at Cassiel's Lake

The day before training began was the best day of Grayson's life. It was hard to tell if this was because he had his own magic staff, because he did not have to pay for any of his delicious meals, or possibly because he had an entire city to explore without parental supervision.

Grayson and Ethan wanted to get into a good routine before their first 5 a.m. training session the following day. When their alarms went off early that morning, they rushed to the window and saw that the previous night's clouds had dissolved. Not bothering to change out of their pajamas, the boys hurried up to the roof for a better view of the city. They dashed to the railing, where they were presented with their first genuine look of Icefall. As Grayson gazed out upon the city, he realized he no longer needed to repeat his daily quote—in his mind, it had already come true.

Streams of water flowed in every direction. Lakes and ponds hid beneath the thick layer of trees, and dozens of dirt trails crisscrossed over the landscape, making it possible to navigate from Emerald Residence Hall to Icefall Lane.

Icefall Lane itself was blocked from view by a hundred glass skyscrapers. Blue electric currents circulated through the windows to power the buildings. The energy from the skyscrapers illuminated the city and jungle in a bright sapphire light. Vines dangled from the tower's rooftops down to the street, creating an alternative exit for Lacers who didn't want to wait for the elevator. Grayson could see Lacers sliding down the vines like fire poles. He and Ethan made themselves comfortable. They watched the unique beauty of Icefall, knowing they had chosen the right city to train at.

The sun slowly crept over the east side of Icefall, making its way above even the tallest skyscraper. Grayson closed his eyes and faced the star, letting its beams soak into his skin. After a dreadful night's sleep, Grayson was going to need all the sunlight in the world to stay awake. His lack of proper sleep was not caused by an uncomfortable bed but rather by a five-foot-long tail constantly whipping him in the face. His new pet had not been in the mood to sleep.

"Do these things go to the bathroom or not?" asked Ethan as he and Grayson walked their guardians around the residence hall. "I guess not. You would think that lady last night coulda told us something useful about taking care of them. I'm going back inside."

Grayson found his guardian just as interesting as the city itself. While he was still unsure if it ate, drank, or slept, he knew it could understand him—maybe not the exact words he spoke, more the tone in which he said them.

"Make sure you put some water down for them," said Grayson as the boys left the residence hall, eager to explore in broad daylight.

This time it only took ten minutes to get to Icefall Lane. The correct trail from the residence hall led directly through the forest to the city. Even on a cloudless day, the forest remained relatively dark. Aside from the few spots where the trees were thin and sun rays were able to sneak through, the only light came from the occasional torch or campfire. Blue currents radiating from the skyscrapers sheltered the landscape as well.

Halfway through their journey, the boys came to a circular pond where a metal bridge replaced the trail. The blue electricity sent vibrations through Grayson's body as he skeptically crossed over the glowing passage. The boys heard the growl of a nearby animal in the trees and raced into the city.

The same bunch of well-dressed Lacers from the night before danced up and down the street with a drink in hand, listening to the melodic music being echoed from the rooftops. As he sat down at a breakfast café called *Eggs for Days*, Grayson couldn't help but admire how these Lacers lived. He and Ethan each requested two meals, and their waitress gladly crammed the table with the food of their choosing only moments after the order was placed.

After a delicious breakfast, the boys landed back on Icefall Lane. They moved along the street, pointing out inspirational clothing and jewelry stores. They even peeked their heads through the side window of the church, where they saw hundreds of Lacers sitting in rows, listening to a white-cloaked man speak from a podium.

"I wonder what religion they believe in," said Ethan, hopping down from the bench they had been using to look through the window. "My parents never really mentioned that stuff. Did yours?"

"Oh, crud!"

"Watch out!"

"Ughhhh, ouch!"

Grayson had lost his footing on the icy bench, fell right into Ethan, and as a result, they had both plummeted into a pair of girls walking on the path behind them. The four of them got to their feet, each as confused as the next as to how they had all ended up on the ground.

"I'm so sorry! Are you two okay?" Grayson asked the girls in his most apologetic voice.

"What the heck was that?"

"I'm really sorry, I just sorta slipped off the… I mean, I fell off the…" Grayson was at a loss for words. The girl who had just yelled at him had to be some sort of angel. She was wearing skater shoes, ripped jeans, and a thin V-neck shirt that was far too summerish for the top of a mountain, all of which were black. Her hair was just as dark as her outfit, aside from the occasional blonde highlight running through it. Clearly, she wasn't the type of girl to wear makeup; however, her tan skin mixed with her bright blue eyes and rosy lips were more than enough to make up for that. It did not matter how angry her face might have been at the current moment; Grayson saw nothing but beauty. He had almost forgotten she was still waiting for an answer. Luckily, Ethan jumped in.

"We were just looking through the window."

"Well, are you kindergarteners? Can you not keep your balance on the little two-foot bench?" she fumed, brushing snow off her shirt.

Grayson could see Ethan's temper starting to rise, as it so often did. Beautiful girl or annoying teacher's kid on the school bus, Ethan did not enjoy people yelling at him. Right when Ethan opened his mouth to start shouting back, the second girl spoke.

"Ambrielle, I don't think they meant to… Do you have to yell at them?" she whispered in a frightened voice as if Ambrielle might slap her across the face for defending them.

Grayson had been so focused on Ambrielle that he hadn't even noticed her cute blond-haired companion. This girl was at least half a foot shorter than Ambrielle—which meant she was probably average height because Ambrielle was very tall for a girl—and her green eyes matched the emerald cloak she was wearing.

Ambrielle glared at her along with Grayson and Ethan as if she couldn't decide with whom she was angrier, then she said, "Come on, Harlie, we're leaving."

"Do you guys live in Emerald Residence Hall, too?" blurted out Grayson desperately. He couldn't let Ambrielle leave while she was still mad at him.

"Yes, on the fourth floor," replied Harlie quietly, although her eyes were on Ethan rather than Grayson, who had asked the question.

Grayson thought back to the original room he and Ethan were supposed to stay in, and he was almost positive it was on the fourth floor, which meant…

"Are there any other girls on your floor?" asked Grayson, determined to keep the conversation going even if Ambrielle was staring off into space.

"Not that I know of," muttered Harlie. "There was some sort of confusion with our room number."

"Ha! *Some sort of confusion.* That's all this place is. A bunch of confusion. A group of partiers who can do all sorts of magic, yet they can't get a freaking room number right," mocked Ambrielle with her arms folded.

"This place is amazing!" snapped Ethan. "Sorry if *you're* too mad all the time to enjoy it."

Ambrielle looked him right in the eyes. "We'll see if you still think that after our first lesson."

And with that, she walked away. Harlie took one more look at Ethan and hurried off after her.

Grayson and Ethan followed the trail until they reached a campfire behind the church. This was the farthest they had traveled away from their dorm. The wind picked up speed, and gentle snow showered from the sky. They were against one of the city's walls, or at least what Grayson assumed was a wall. The massive snow pile stood at least forty feet high, much like the one around Icefall's entrance building.

"What was that girl's problem?" grumbled Ethan once they were settled into the campsite.

"I don't know. Did you see her eyes?"

"What? Um, yeah, how could I not? She was giving me a death stare the whole time we talked. Well, anyway, it seems like we found out who got our original room."

"Yeah, maybe we should ask them if they wanna switch back. You know, to be nice and all," said Grayson, who didn't like the idea of Ambrielle being on a floor with all guys. *What if she started to like one of them?*

"*To be nice?*" asked Ethan. "They weren't very nice to us, were they? Well, I guess the blond girl, what's her name? Harlie... I guess she was kinda nice… That doesn't even matter. We can't give up our room! We live next to all the girls!"

Grayson didn't answer, but he was quite sure he would rather make Ambrielle happy by switching back. What girl would he meet on his floor that was better than her? *Maybe someone who doesn't scream at you*, said a little voice in the back of his mind.

Grayson had been gazing off into the distance, daydreaming, when any and all thoughts of Ambrielle were driven out of his head. Seeing a woman in bright purple robes soar through the sky, nearly hit her head on the roof of a nearby skyscraper, and plunge back down to the ground, surely to her death, was an incident terrible enough to shock even the bravest of Lacers. Grayson and Ethan jumped to their feet. Together, they navigated through the trails in mad pursuit of the horrible Lacer who would catapult someone across a city.

"It looked like she was launched from over here!" yelled Ethan. "Yeah! Just up ahead, I hear voices!"

Grayson followed closely, thinking to himself, *Ambrielle was right. These people aren't as nice as we thought.* A Lacer had committed a crime, and Grayson was a witness. Grayson wanted to call his dad; maybe these were the same Lacers who had attacked the Black House and killed Oscar.

"There they are!" said Ethan. "All right, I'm going after them."

Grayson grabbed Ethan's arm and pulled him around the backside of a tree, out of view from the group of Lacers.

"Are you out of your darn mind?" Grayson demanded. "These guys just sent a woman halfway across Icefall, and your plan is what, exactly? To run up there and start throwing punches?"

"You're right," said Ethan, reaching for his globe carrier. "I'll hit 'em with this." He extended his staff to full length.

"We don't even know how to use our staffs!"

"Mine controls fire, and there's a torch right by us. I'll figure it out!"

"Look at them! They're wearing blue cloaks! That means they know way more magic than us. They'd probably turn us into dust before we even got close enough to hit them."

"Come on. They're even laughing at what they did. We have to do something."

Ethan was right. The three grown Lacers were all doubled over laughing, clinging onto some piece of circular machinery. Grayson figured this object must've had some role in killing the poor girl.

"Yeah. Yeah. I agree," said one of the Lacers, chuckling. "We're gonna be late if we don't hurry."

"I'll see you on the other side," said another, walking up a short set of stairs onto a circular platform surrounded by a metal railing.

"*Lacer confirmed,*" echoed a robotic voice. "*Preparing landing zone four. Launching in three, two, one.*"

Grayson watched in amazement as another Lacer went soaring through the sky, closely followed by his two friends. No crime had been committed. Grayson and Ethan left the scene even more astonished by Icefall and the Lacers within it.

***

"You said your staff controls fire?" asked Grayson on the way back to the residence hall. "My dad told me mine controls earth, but I don't know what he meant by that—everything is on Earth."

"I *think* mine controls fire," said Ethan, aiming his staff like a loaded shotgun at one of the torch sticks on the side of the trail. "It doesn't seem to be controlling it right now... Yours probably controls trees and stuff like that."

After many failed attempts to uproot the surrounding trees and extinguish the nearby fires, the boys concluded that they wouldn't be getting the best of their elements without further instruction.

"These are the worst staffs ever," said Ethan, kicking over a torch.

"Would you calm down? We'll probably learn how to use them at training tomorrow."

***

By late afternoon it was confirmed guardians did not eat or drink. They did, however, have a knack for smacking the boys with their puffy tails that were far too large for the rest of their bodies.

The four of them went for a walk, this time in the direction of the garden. Ethan hadn't noticed it the night before, and Grayson wanted to see it during the day. On the way, they came across another launch pad, landing pad, whatever it was called. Grayson tried to get this one to launch him, but it said *Identification Required* every time he pressed the launch button.

The boys never quite made it to the garden. Their legs were tired from walking, and the baby guardians were also slowing. Ethan led the way through an opening in the trees, where a vast body of water rested. In what was an otherwise calm lake, the only ripples came from a shirtless Lacer kicking his feet back and forth in the water like he was riding a bike. Next to him was a fully-grown silver guardian.

The Lacer twirled his curly blond hair and hummed a pleasant little tune, bobbing his head from side to side. The golden chain wrapped around his neck clung to a sapphire gem in the shape of a star.

"Hey there! New P.L.s? Right on!" said the Lacer. Everything from his personality to his hair reminded Grayson of a surfer dude. "Come on over and dip your feet in the water. The temperature is perfect. And I have a feeling the sunset is going to be spectacular tonight!"

"Hi, I'm Grayson," said Grayson as he took off his shoes, put his feet in the lake, and sat down by the Lacer.

"Ethan."

"Grayson and Ethan. I'll try to remember that. I've always been terrible with names. Oh, I'm Jasper, by the way, and this is Rad," he said, pointing to the guardian. "There it is! This could be up for sunset of the year!"

Grayson and Ethan let their legs soak in the water while Jasper built make-believe houses in the sand and wrestled with Rad, who looked to be going easy on the surfer.

"Come on, Rad! Let's see if we can get Sonia to come out again," said Jasper, rolling over to the lake and splashing the water.

Grayson and Ethan turned away to hide their laughter. Jasper was an entertaining fellow, to say the least. The boys suddenly yanked their feet out of the water as a stingray surfaced from the lake. Rad went face to face with the sea creature.

"Ask her how many fish she's caught today," said Jasper, placing his hand on the top of Rad's head.

Rad wrapped his long tail around his own body and set it on the stingray. Jasper tilted his head in curiosity and said, "Only five fish? You can do better than that, Sonia!"

Sonia snarled at Jasper and Rad and resubmerged.

"You can talk to stingrays?" asked Grayson, perplexed.

"I can talk to any animal with Rad's help. Unless the animal isn't in the mood, of course."

"Can you call Sonia back up here so we can try?" asked Ethan.

"I think Sonia is busy catching more fish. You wouldn't be able to communicate with her anyway; your guardians are too small to be respected by an animal as dangerous as a stingray. Not to mention you need one of these," Jasper told them, spinning his necklace.

"When do we get our necklaces?" asked Grayson.

"Oh, not for a couple of years. If you make it that far through the Lacer Initiation Process. It's okay, though. Your guardians need that time to grow."

"So, our guardians protect us from other animals?" asked Ethan.

"They protect and communicate," corrected Jasper. "Most animals would never attack a Lacer, but you never know; one day, your guardian may talk you out of a sticky situation. It's good to let guardians build their own network. The more friends they have, the more you have. The sea creatures around here love Rad to death — the birds, not so much. Your guardians are too young to go exploring alone. Make sure you travel with them for now."

Grayson no longer felt all that safe at Icefall. Jasper made it sound like animals could pounce from the forest at any given moment. If Grayson's guardian couldn't protect him yet, what would happen?

"Not to worry," said Jasper when Grayson asked him about this. "No decent Lacer would ever kill an animal, so animals don't randomly hunt and kill Lacers."

It was getting dark, and the boys were getting hungry. "Good luck at training tomorrow," said Jasper, flipping his hair as Grayson and Ethan dried their feet and laced up their shoes. "Maybe I'll see you two back here for another sunset. Cassiel's Lake is my favorite place in the city. Don't even bother going to Yahoel's Lake; there's too much noise there to enjoy Mother Nature."

The boys assured Jasper they would be back. They headed into the forest, their little guardians prancing along behind them.

***

Ethan was in an unbelievably lousy mood by the time dinner came around. "Oh, yeah. She was right. Now that I think about it, *not everyone* here is nice. *She* isn't! And stop defending her," he said as they walked into a restaurant on Icefall Lane.

Grayson had made the mistake of defending Ambrielle, and Ethan, who was determined to hate her, would hear none of it.

"I'm just saying… it *was* my fault we knocked them over," said Grayson, placing his napkin across his lap.

"What about when those girls bumped into us with their couch in the hallway just now? Did we flip out on them? No, we handled it like adults and helped them move it."

Grayson did not see what these two scenarios had in common, and at any rate, he did not think Ethan had the right to talk about *handling things like an adult* considering he had been ready to fight three Lacers earlier in the day for using a launchpad. Yet, to Grayson's displeasure, Ethan had so far been right. Ambrielle was the only person at Icefall who had been rude to them.

In appreciation of lifting their couch, the girls from down the hall had invited him and Ethan in for tea. This was an offer the boys had been too polite to refuse. In Colorado, fancy tea dates were not common; however, being from Maine, Faith and Brooke found this type of socializing to be perfectly normal. Personally, Grayson found tea a little upscale for a group of teenagers.

At dinner, the boys wolfed down their identical orders of chicken fingers in no time and headed back to the residence hall to meet Dylan and Jeremiah, a pair of fellow first-year residents they had met while walking, for game night.

With their first training lesson only hours away, Grayson and Ethan had planned on locating Emerald House before the end of the night. They didn't want to worry about finding it at 5 a.m. the following morning. However, the map told them it wasn't far from

Emerald Residence Hall, and game night sounded much more enjoyable.

Dylan greeted them at the door. He was a short, heavier set boy with curly brown hair, the opposite of his roommate Jeremiah, a tall, lengthy, African American kid with clean-cut hair. Although differing in appearance, their personalities were quite similar.

"Just met Jerry here yesterday," said Dylan through a mouthful of food. "He's from California, and I'm from Arizona, but we both have family in Chicago."

"You want some food? We got plenty!" said Jeremiah, force-feeding Grayson some pizza. "We decided to stop by every single restaurant today. Gotta stock up on as much food as possible," he said, indicating to their refrigerator, which was so full it couldn't even close properly.

"What was the point of that? Those restaurants aren't going anywhere," said Ethan.

"Yeah, they might not be going anywhere, but *we* might not be going to *them* much longer. We have our first initiation lesson tomorrow morning," said Dylan.

Dylan explained how his dad had accidentally let it slip that first-year residents were forced to eat in designated spots, reminding Grayson of what his mom had asked his dad on his last night at home: *Did you know they were allowed to have snacks in the dorm this year?*

"Down, girl! Bad Cakes!" said Dylan. "What did I tell you about jumping on our guests? Why can't you just relax on the bed like Fluffy?"

"You named your guardian Cakes?" asked Ethan.

"Yeah, because she looks like a zebra with her stripes. Get it? Zebra Cakes! I just didn't want to include the word zebra in her name in case she got offended." Dylan beamed.

"How do you know it's a girl?"

"I can just tell."

Jeremiah, Dylan, and Ethan spent the next hour exchanging childhood stories. None of them seemed remotely stressed about their first lesson; Grayson, however, hardly spoke. *Just because we have to eat in designated areas doesn't mean the food will be bad,* he thought. *Maybe we just eat in groups, or at a certain time.* Then there was the lesson itself. There was something about Ambrielle that made Grayson think she knew many things about Icefall that he didn't. She had made it clear their first initiation lesson would not be fun; obviously, she hadn't been referring to the food tasting bad.

Things started to get boring, so Dylan pulled out a deck of cards and some poker chips. None of them knew how to play poker properly. Their version of the game went like this: Everyone drew six random cards from the deck, they all added up their cards, and the person with the highest "score" won. It turned out to be competitive, even though the game took no skill whatsoever.

"*No!* Not again. I'm already way too full," said Dylan. It had been decided that the person with the lowest overall score in each game had to eat a slice of pizza. This was the best way the boys could ensure a good night's meal before tomorrow's unknown food circumstances.

Dylan announced his retirement from pizza poker by throwing his cards across the table and eating what had to have been his fifteenth slice. Everyone laughed as they watched him struggle to keep it down.

Ten o'clock rolled around, which meant it was time to head back to the room. Grayson stood up from his chair and cleaned up all the cards Dylan had thrown when he lost. *Ace of spades, five of spades, king of spades.*

"Is 'spades' a name?" Grayson asked Ethan as they walked down the staircase to the first floor.

"Spades? Like the card suit? I suppose… if you want it to be. Let's be honest. Anything is better than Zebra Cakes."

"It's just Cakes," corrected Grayson with a grin.

After a busy day of traveling, Grayson curled up next to Spades on his bed, the two of them completely exhausted. Ethan turned off the lights while Spades licked Grayson's face and repetitively smacked his tail against the wall. Grayson decided that Spades was definitely a boy.

He pulled out his phone for the first time all day and set his alarm for 4:45 a.m. He figured fifteen minutes should be plenty of time to throw on his black t-shirt and shorts, brush his teeth, and walk to Emerald House, which, according to the map, was only five minutes from the residence hall. If there was a list of life skills that Grayson was yet to learn, being on time would top the list.

Grayson forced himself to close his eyes, refusing to think about the following morning; he knew doing so would only stress him out more. Before he drifted off into what would turn out to be his last good night of rest for many months, Grayson remembered his father's last words to him: *If I had to give one piece of advice to the two of you, it would be this: Don't draw attention to yourselves on the first day.*

CHAPTER 8

The Lacer Initiation Process

"**D**onny Bruce, it's good to see you. Start the engine; we have a lot to talk about," said Oscar.

"This bus may very well be the first vehicle on Icefall Lane," said Mr. Bruce.

"I guess you could say that makes this school bus different from other buses," replied Oscar. "But is it really? It's still yellow—there are thousands of yellow buses in the world."

Mr. Bruce smiled. "But this bus is at Icefall. That has to mean it's different."

"Indeed," replied Oscar. "This particular school bus is in elite company, willing its way on a dangerous journey that only a few like it have foreseen, better yet, that only a few like it dare to follow until the end. However different may it be, does this make it as different as it could, perhaps, be?"

"How about a nice new paint job, Oscar? Surely, that would separate it from the others."

The bus turned white.

Oscar tilted his head to the side. "Now, it is certainly distinguishable among its peers. But what are we to make of their identical windows? Their identical wheels and gears?"

Mr. Bruce snapped his fingers. "Away with the windows. Given we are on a Colorado mountain, ice skates make for a better ride than wheels," he said with another snap and shake of the bus. "Best not to be predictable. Multiple gears, without a doubt."

"Here we have it, Donny, a unique bus. Though, undoubtedly, more could be changed. New walls? Different seats? Perhaps a peephole for a windshield, where the driver must gaze upon traffic like a pirate peering through his spyglass for treasure? There are, positively, an infinite number of modifications to be made if this bus is to reach its peak of difference."

"I see, Oscar, you haven't lost your imagination even after death," said Mr. Bruce with a wild laugh. "I present to you a new batch of questions: At what point, after how many adjustments, does this school bus convert itself into something else entirely? Can we still call it a school bus at all? Or do you believe it to be true that if it began as a bus, it will always be and could be nothing other than a bus? Is it possible to be too different, to stand out too much?"

"Oh, that would all be up to the bus," said Oscar kindly. "If, while transforming, this bus doesn't approve of each new group it finds itself in, it may continue to transform until it is in a league of its own."

Grayson lay peacefully in his usual back right corner, his legs crossed, his hands gently folded. "I'm guessing I'm the bus?" he asked.

"My grandson, it was nice of you to finally join us... I believe, at training today, you may answer that question yourself," said Oscar. "Begin the drive, Donny. Unfortunately, Grayson, your stop will be our first."

"What do I have to do?"

"Simply exit the bus. Our timing should take care of today's work."

"I'll be back," said Grayson, nodding to his grandpa and Mr. Bruce.

Mr. Bruce opened the door. "We know," he said.

Grayson floated off the school bus into the peaceful snow sprinkling on Icefall Lane. The bus skated down the vacant street, toward the distant church, at the speed of an injured turtle. Grayson's shapeless body glided across the road in a cloud of gray mist. It crept past the skyscrapers, through the forest, and into Emerald Residence Hall with one question on its mind: Am I different from the other Lacers?

Grayson's subconscious mind levitated through the closed door of the dorm. It plunged like an Olympic diver into its owner's head, which had been resting peacefully on a pillow, until two blaring sirens erupted, waking him with a jolt.

"We gotta—we gotta leave soon," mumbled Ethan.

"Nooooo," yawned Grayson, blindly reaching for his phone to hit snooze.

The boys drifted in and out of sleep until their alarms sounded for the second time. Grayson rolled out of bed and stumbled over the trash can on his way to the light switch. He changed into his required black clothing and slicked his hair back to look good on the first day of… whatever this was.

"This better be a one-time thing," groused Ethan. "Way too early."

"Hurry up. And don't forget to grab your staff and phone."

The adventure from Emerald Residence Hall to Emerald House was not as smooth as Grayson had imagined. As the sliding glass door retracted, the warmth of the residence hall dissipated into a gray cloud, which floated inside the dormitory, creating an indoor rainstorm. The boys covered their eyes and stumbled through the heavy air without the slightest sense of direction. Grayson grabbed onto the back of Ethan's shirt, and the two of them fell face-first into the mud.

Grayson wiped himself clean on his t-shirt and hobbled through the hazardous weather in his gym clothes. Behind him, Emerald Residence Hall had disappeared into the clouds. With the cold disrupting Grayson's thinking, he couldn't recall the path to Emerald House. Ethan took the lead, and after a couple of wrong turns, they found themselves at a two-story cement block just outside the forest.

"You sure this is it?" asked Ethan.

"The map said it was around here."

Grayson was really hoping he was wrong. He didn't think a building without paint, windows, or a roof qualified as a house. And considering the theatrics of the structures in Icefall City, Grayson had expected to train somewhere a bit more exciting. The trees, lakes, and skyscrapers were all in the distance as Grayson and Ethan sprinted through the pebbled mud and up the short set of stairs to the wooden front door of the house.

Ethan yanked on the heavy lever, and the door descended into the floor, opening to a training facility half the size of a football field. The turf floor was split into four sections with a square pool in the center. An ancient stone statue stood proud on a pedestal in the middle of the water, donning a glimmering emerald necklace.

Each of the four sections around the pool had a different theme. Directly in front of the entrance, a circular lava pit crackled its spews of heated rock onto the surrounding torch sticks. Green, blue, yellow, orange, and red fireballs danced around from torch to torch, reflecting colors onto the lava pit like a disco ball. Across from the firestorm, a collection of fans hung from a glass wall, enclosing a small section of the house like a racquetball court. Inside the glass, the fans exhaled different color air, creating a never-ending tie-dye tornado.

Past the pool, another two training areas lay hidden in the back of the house. Grayson could see streams of electricity jolting through a crowd of power units, threatening to send sparks to the nearby garden, where two trees elevated past the inner balcony on the second story of the house and above the non-existent roof. Vines from the garden draped down the balcony in the shape of slithery serpents.

He was in such awe of his surroundings that it wasn't until Ethan desperately cleared his throat that Grayson noticed a group of eighteen identically dressed Potential Lacers standing single file in front of the pool, across from six irritated instructors. He ran over to the line and stood up straight with his hands behind his back, doing his best to mimic the others.

Grayson stopped his eyes from wandering and locked them onto his six instructors, all of whom looked disappointed. Five of the instructors were dressed in green workout clothes; the sixth instructor wore a suit and tie, making his authority clear. He had patchy black hair, black eyes, and was much thinner than his colleagues. He nodded with a stern expression, signaling for a short, middle-aged man to take action. It was Jasper. Jasper flipped his blond hair and strutted over to Grayson and the others, holding out a plastic container as he went.

"Place your phones in it," growled the lead instructor.

Grayson's teachers in school had constantly yelled at him and given him detention, but not once had a chill ever run through his body like the one that just did when this Lacer spoke. Perhaps the absence of a roof and constant mix of rain and snowfall played a role in Grayson's body temperature dropping, but only possibly. Everyone pulled their phones out of their pockets and set them in the container as Jasper passed. Once they were all without their mobile devices, the lesson began.

"Welcome to the Lacer Initiation Process. My name is Ridley Crimson. You will address me as either *Master Ridley* or *Sir*," informed the head instructor, straightening his tie. "I will be overseeing your first-year training to ensure this Initiation Group, or I.G. for short, stays on pace for its completion ceremony, which as of now is set for April 9, just over seven months from today.

"You will be close friends with everyone in this I.G. by the time that day arrives. You will eat your meals together. You will train together eight hours a day, six days a week. You are a team. You will treat your instructors, as well as yourselves, with the utmost respect. Anyone who fails to do this will be banished from the program. If you can't treat your own kind with respect, you most certainly won't be able to control yourselves in the world of savage humans we live amongst.

"Right now, all of you are considered P.L.s or Potential Lacers. If you ever want to be an Official Lacer like those partying, enjoying life on Icefall Lane, you will need to complete three years of training. An entire I.G. never makes it through the year; a few always drop out and become Gavens. You don't want to be a Gaven. There's no fun in that, so stay in the program. Ah, well, that's enough for now, I suppose. I believe we have some late arrivals."

Grayson held his breath, hoping the instructors wouldn't remember exactly who had been late. After all, they all had the same clothes on.

"What time did they arrive, Ms. Myles?"

"Five past five," replied a plump, curly-haired woman.

"Hmmm," pondered Master Ridley. "We'll do introductions later… What should we say? Five push-ups? One for each minute."

Push-ups? Grayson had not expected Lacers to use physical exercise as a punishment. No matter though, five push-ups were a piece of cake; however, he didn't know when to do them. Master Ridley was staring elsewhere with his arms crossed.

"Uh… do you want us to do them now?" Grayson casually asked, not realizing he probably should have raised his hand before speaking.

Luckily, Master Ridley didn't seem to mind. "Oh, yes. Please do," he replied with an insincere smile.

Grayson and Ethan awkwardly spaced themselves out from the rest of the line and dropped to the floor. They finished with ease and hopped back into the line.

"Huh. Does anyone happen to recall my opening speech?" asked Ridley. "Specifically, the part about being a *team*. Or is the rest of this I.G. too selfish to do five push-ups?"

The entire line looked around in confusion. Ridley hadn't instructed anyone else to do push-ups… One by one, each of them dropped to the turf floor, and during the set, Grayson twisted his head to the side to watch the rest of the I.G. He was troubled to see some of the group struggling with the task, although they all managed to finish.

Grayson felt terrible. He had just made a bunch of girls do push-ups because he had been too lazy to get out of bed on time. And… *Oh no, Ambrielle.* Grayson had been so distracted he'd forgotten she was here. He doubted that she would ever talk to him again after this with her temper.

"You! Yes, you!" yelled Ridley, pointing at Ambrielle's shy roommate Harlie. "Harlie Laurence, correct? Why did you only do four? Did you think I wouldn't notice?"

"I thought… I thought I did all of them," she stammered.

"Perhaps I am mistaken," said Ridley. "Why doesn't everyone do another set, just to be safe. And count *out loud* this time!"

"One two one three two three four three five four five."

Everyone in the I.G. was doing their push-ups at a different pace, and many of the P.L.s were now too tired to do all five. Grayson didn't bother getting to his feet this time.

"Again!"

It was hopeless. Grayson's arms were wearing down, Ethan was breathing heavily, and some kids were unable to do them at all.

Ridley forced them to attempt another ten sets before ordering them back into single file. "Maybe you just need a break," he suggested. "How about a dip in the pool? Ms. Myles, please adjust the temperature."

Grayson watched stubby Ms. Myles waddle over to the water, extend her blue globed staff, and place its tip in the water, causing a slight ripple.

"It's ready," she said.

Grayson and the rest of the I.G. skeptically trudged toward the pool. He couldn't tell if Ms. Myles had made it warmer or cooler—hopefully, warmer. It was already freezing without a roof, and warm water would relax the muscles, helping them complete the push-ups.

"Jump!" said Ridley.

Grayson watched the first P.L.s plunge into the water. He himself hesitated for a moment, then jumped. He couldn't tell whether he was hot or cold; his body was too numb. After the initial shock passed, Grayson began to shake. He must have been swimming in an ice bucket. The pool was full of twenty trembling Potential Lacers.

"Out!" barked Ridley.

Grayson climbed out. The water dripped from his body onto the turf. He got hit with a nice cool breeze, making him colder than he'd been in the pool.

"Toes over the edge," instructed Ridley.

Grayson placed the front of his soaking shoes over the pool. He felt as though he might fall in from shaking.

"Jump!"

Grayson didn't hesitate this time—he submerged again. When his head resurfaced, he saw half of the I.G. still standing on the edge. They all jumped in at different times, sending water splashing every which way. It was at this moment that Grayson realized there was a problem. It was supposed to be done like the push-ups, in sync.

The I.G. pulled themselves out of the pool. Grayson knew Ridley was about to yell, so when he did, Grayson tried to mirror his jump to that of his I.G. Half of the group jumped right away, and the rest waited, leaving Grayson as the last man standing.

When they resurfaced for the third time, Grayson's lips were blue. He gazed around the pool, where he saw Harlie and a couple of other P.L.s crying. That was the final straw. He had to stop this.

"Jump!" yelled Master Ridley.

"Stop! Wait!" yelled Grayson, and to his surprise, nobody jumped.

Everyone's eyes were on him, including Ridley's. Grayson figured he was about to be punished, so he spoke quickly, "Everyone jumps together! On my count! One! Two! Three! Jump!"

Once the I.G. was back in position with their toes over the edge, Grayson had time to think about his actions. He'd drawn lots of attention to himself—he'd spoken without being spoken to, and worst of all, he'd instructed his peers to *wait* before following Master Ridley's orders, going against just about every piece of advice his dad had given him. Grayson looked down at the pool as Master Ridley approached him. He could feel Ridley's eyes going through his spine. Then Ridley clapped.

"Well done, Mr. Day," he said as the other instructors joined in the celebration. "Finally, someone took charge. This I.G. needed a leader, and it seems Grayson here has risen to the occasion. Give me one good set of push-ups and meet over by the lava pit to warm up."

A leader? Grayson didn't see how being cold made him a leader. Regardless, all eyes were on him as he dropped into a push-up position and began the count.

"Down! Up! One! Down! Up! Two!"

He continued this cadence as loud as his trembling voice would allow until they reached five. Master Ridley was satisfied.

"Not perfect, but good enough for now. Over to the fire station."

Determined not to draw any more attention to himself, Grayson kept his head down on the way to the lava pit. The I.G. eagerly collapsed to the turf for warmth. Grayson found Ethan sitting across from Ambrielle. Ethan was soaking wet and did not look happy. Grayson was unsure if this was because Ridley had bossed him around for the past hour or simply because of Ambrielle's presence.

Ambrielle, on the other hand, still looked beautiful, messy hair and all. The black gym outfit looked better on her than the others. It didn't stray too far from her typical dark style.

"Thank you, man," said Dylan, taking a seat next to Grayson. "You really saved us."

Ridley gave the I.G. ten minutes to warm up, talking to them as they rested.

"I assume by now everyone knows a Lacer's staff allows them to control one individual element on this planet. I also assume each of you knows which element it is that you can control. Nevertheless, I'll reiterate them just so we're clear. Element number one is water, the blue globe. Water is a common element to control, perhaps the most common aside from element number two: fire."

Grayson looked across the lava pit toward Ethan. He had a feeling this would be the area Ethan would train in.

"Lacers who control fire have a red globe," continued Ridley. "Element number three—wind—a white globe. Followed by element four—electricity. My yellow-globe friends control this one. Lastly, the rare fifth and final element that only about five percent of all Lacers control—earth itself. These Lacers have green globes."

"Hey, sir! I got a couple of questions about this stuff," said a spiky-haired boy with large glasses. Master Ridley did not look happy about being interrupted, yet the boy pressed on, speaking rather fast as he did. "Why would an element be called wind instead of air? Isn't wind just made up of air? Also, I was taught in school that electricity isn't a natural element of the earth, so why would it be included with the others?"

Ridley just stared at the boy as if perplexed by the fact that someone could speak in such an irritating manner. "Your name?"

"Kevin Workman, sir! I have a few other questions—"

"Ahem, ahem," said Ridley, stopping Kevin mid-sentence with the clearing of his throat. "I think you've asked quite enough already, thank you. First off, your brilliant point of *wind being made up of air*. While obviously, that *is* true, moving air is wind, and the only thing our *wind* controllers do is move the air… And as far as electricity not being a natural element of the world, I suggest you look up in the sky during a storm once in a while."

"Well, actually, sir, lightning happens to be caused by air expansion, as well as—"

"Stop talking!" boomed Ridley. "Get to your designated stations. I trust you can figure out where you belong."

Grayson hopped to his feet and headed for the garden. He caught a glimpse of Ambrielle on the way. She was standing by the pool with her arms crossed, waiting with her usual annoyed expression, until the round woman, Ms. Myles, approached her with instructions. Ambrielle was by the pool; that meant she could control water. *Water has to be the best element,* Grayson thought. *Isn't the world like seventy percent water?*

Grayson passed through the dozens of bushes and hundreds of flowers that encompassed the garden's perimeter like a fence and came to a stop underneath two trees that acted as a roof for the work area. Jeremiah and Jasper approached the garden, but then Jeremiah broke away and headed for the electricity station.

"What's poppin', fellas? Oh, hey there, Grayson! You're in my group? Awesome!" said Jasper, addressing Grayson and another boy sitting under the trees. "I'm Jasper Crimson. Y'all can just call me Jasper, and uh, yeah, I'm gonna be teaching y'all about this earth controlling stuff."

"You're Master Ridley's brother?" asked the boy under the tree. "I'm Liam, by the way. Liam Dixon." He outstretched his hand to Jasper and Grayson.

"Oh yeah, the ole scary Ridley's my brother," kidded Jasper, shaking Liam's hand. "Y'all don't have to worry about that, though. I'm a lot more fun than he is. Last year I almost made it the full year without the I.G. even knowing we were related."

"Well, you don't look anything alike," said Grayson.

"Yeah, man, you're totally right! I'm short. He's tall. I'm blond. He's dark. Crazy how that stuff works, isn't it?"

Grayson knew he could relax. Jasper wasn't going to make them do push-ups or take an ice bath.

"Wow. It's really just the two of y'all I gotta teach this year? I guess we're just a rare breed," boasted Jasper, patting his side where his green globe was. "The first thing y'all gotta know about controlling the earth element is that it's hard, hard but sick! Earth is everywhere, right? That means y'all are gonna be able to control your surroundings no matter where you are, giving you the tactical advantage over all these other dudes in your I.G."

Grayson liked the sound of having an advantage over the other elements; that meant he'd probably be able to beat Ethan in their next duel.

"We gotta start with the easy stuff first, just like everyone else. Both you boys go stand in front of that flower bed. All right, look," said Jasper, pulling a red rose out of the ground and shoving it toward Grayson and Liam's faces. "Get a real good look at the stem. The roots are the key to getting anything out of the ground. You need to have a clear image in your head of what exactly it is you're uprooting. You guys got it memorized? Okay, good. Now, both of you get in front of a flower, picture the roots, and then imagine them being pulled up from the ground. You're gonna need your staffs."

Grayson and Liam removed their green globes from the carriers on their waist, threw them on the dirt, and grasped their full-length staffs, which had emerged from clouds of green smoke. Grayson lined up over a bed of lilies about six feet away from Liam. He aimed his staff at a flower with one arm, doing his best to imagine it being ripped from the ground. He had only been at it for a couple of seconds when Jasper interrupted his thoughts.

"Both of you, stop," he said, snatching Liam's bronze staff and gripping it in a proper striking position. "If you only use one hand to hold it, you have no control. Use two hands. Your movements will be more precise."

Grayson clasped both of his palms around the golden rod and tried to recall what the stem of the rose had looked like. He figured the stem of a lily wouldn't be any different. The lily shifted side to side in the dirt but refused to part ways with the ground. Liam was cursing under his breath and looking over at Grayson repeatedly as if uprooting the flowers was a competition. With so many distractions, it took Grayson nearly an hour before he mustered enough focus to uproot the flower completely.

Liam threw his hands up in anger. "Is this thing glued to the darn ground?"

Grayson took a break while he waited for Liam to finish. He plopped down under a tree to hide from the snow and watched the other element groups in his I.G. Grayson suddenly felt incredibly lucky. Some of the other instructors seemed a bit more intense than Jasper. He saw Ambrielle and four others doing laps in the freezing pool. Ethan and his large group of fellow fire controllers were back on the turf doing push-ups, and Harlie and Jeremiah were doing jumping jacks.

Liam eventually got the flower out of the ground, letting out an egotistical yell of excitement. He pranced over to the tree where Grayson sat. "I don't know what the problem was... This stuff is usually a walk in the park for me," he said proudly, although out of breath.

"If getting a flower out of the ground was this hard, I can't even imagine a tree," said Grayson.

"Trees aren't bad," said Liam, shrugging his shoulders. "I uprooted one yesterday."

"It's almost time for breakfast," said Jasper, giving the boys high fives. "Try to get one more flower out of the ground before we eat."

Grayson uprooted his second lily just as Ridley called the I.G. over to the center of the house.

"You've completed your first four-hour training session of the day. The dining hall is up on the second floor. Each group will return to their stations, take their designated ladders to the balcony, and wait outside the double doors."

Grayson walked over to the garden and climbed the hidden ladder on the backside of the tree; he wondered why the architect of Emerald House hadn't included a staircase. The I.G. gathered around the set of doors just as Ridley had instructed. Grayson worked his way through the group, patting Jeremiah on the shoulder as he passed, and found Ethan standing alone near the edge of the balcony, looking down at the training floor.

"This sucks," muttered Ethan.

"Yeah, it does," said Grayson, not wanting to tell Ethan he had actually had fun with his instructor.

"Oh yeah. It looked like Jasper was really working you to death," grumbled Ethan. "What'd he make you do? Talk to a tree?"

The dining hall turned out to be one big table with twenty seats. The instructors ate separately. The breakfast was okay; it was healthy, it was small, but not bad. Grayson thought he might have enjoyed it a little more if Ethan hadn't been complaining about the people in his group.

"Like, how stupid do you have to be?" Ethan asked. "Kevin almost knocked me into the lava and then had the nerve to complain when Mrs. Foster made us do push-ups."

The end of breakfast hour was announced by Master Ridley, who came storming in carrying a bag of watches. There was something about his presence that made Grayson want to punch him. Why couldn't Jasper be in charge? He was so much cooler.

"Pipe down. Pipe down," said Ridley, standing on a ledge so he could get a clear view of the table. "You can kiss your phones goodbye for the year."

Ridley was interrupted by disapproving groans.

"Quiet! I think you all can make it a few months without checking social media. There's nothing on there anyway unless you enjoy people calling Lacers a bunch of freaks. However, luckily for you guys, I have another way for us to communicate." He smiled, waving the bag of watches. "Instructors, pass these out."

The other five instructors each took a handful out of the bag and passed a watch to each P.L. at the table. Mrs. Foster, Ethan's fire element instructor, walked swiftly through the dining room, her red hair bouncing along with her. The two younger male instructors Grayson hadn't met yet were at her side. Jeremiah informed him the tall bald one was his electricity instructor, Mr. Boxer, which confirmed the heavier set man was the wind instructor, Mr. Hill.

"These should not come off your wrist for the remainder of the year," continued Ridley. "This is how we will communicate with you when you aren't present in this house. For example, when we send you back to your dorms, you should receive a message in three hours to remind you to return here for lunch. These digital watches can also be used for individual messages. Let's say that Ms. Myles needs a task completed—she may ask one of her trainees to complete it for her. Lastly, you *will not* go wandering around Icefall Lane unless told to do so by an instructor. There is no reason for you to be there. This is the time to train, not to party. Mark my words, anyone who does not comply with these rules will be sorry."

CHAPTER 9

Ambrielle Stone

"Come on. We could just stop by Marty's Brews really quick. It's right on the edge of town. None of the instructors would have a clue," said Ethan, walking back from a tiny, proportioned lunch at Emerald House.

"Too risky. They could be spying on us. Besides, we need to get some rest before our second training session," said Grayson, greeting Spades as he entered the dorm.

"Whooo's a gooood boyyy? Come here, Ace, jump up," said Ethan, patting his bed.

"You named him Ace?"

"Yeah, I thought of it while we were jumping in the pool. I liked your idea of naming them after a deck of cards. Ace is the perfect name for my guardian. Aces can be high or low, and this dude is definitely bipolar."

"Ace and Spades—very clever."

Thankfully, lunch at Emerald House had just been lunch; Grayson had expected another workout. Jasper had been the only instructor there, and he had sat quietly while everyone ate; although, he did remind the I.G. to keep their wristwatches on and return at 5 p.m. for their next lesson, giving Grayson three hours before he needed to be back.

"Oh great, our first message," said Ethan, tapping his watch. *"One of my fire trainees needs to deliver a large pizza to Emerald House; it doesn't matter who, but get on it. –Mrs. Foster."*

"You better get going," said Grayson, curling up under his covers.

"I ain't doing it! That kid Kevin who almost knocked me in the lava should do it."

Another message appeared on the watch screen.

"Someone in my group needs to bring me one too. Make sure it has sausage. –Jasper," read Ethan.

Grayson didn't feel like doing anything other than sleeping, but how could he avoid the message from Jasper? He and Liam were the only two P.L.s in Jasper's group.

"Come on, Grayson, *you better get going,*" mocked Ethan, pulling him out of bed.

Just as Grayson was about to slap Ethan, he heard yelling from the hallway. They opened the door and followed the voices to a lounge by the front entrance, where they found their I.G. arguing.

"I'm not going!"

"I'll go next time. I need to get some sleep!"

"There's Ethan. Make him go get it!"

Ethan got bombarded by the fire group the moment he walked over. He refused to go, and the yelling only increased. Luckily for Grayson, Liam was resting in one of the armchairs, apparently calm.

"Rock, paper, scissors, to see who goes?" asked Liam.

It sounded fair. Grayson held out his hands and made the first shape that came to mind. He lost.

"I had a feeling you were going to do paper," said Liam. "Almost everyone does. That's why I always start with scissors."

"Good thinking," said Grayson, rolling his eyes.

Grayson left the residence hall without waiting to see which P.L. from Ethan's group had been elected. He wanted to make this a quick trip so he could get some sleep. He followed the glowing torches until he eventually made it through the forest, past the towering buildings, and onto the crowded street. Grayson maneuvered his way through Icefall Lane, looking for a pizza shop. He found one at the end of the street by the church.

Grayson ordered a large sausage pizza and waited at a high top for them to finish cooking it. He was picking it up from the counter when a girl Grayson recognized from his I.G. walked through the door.

"Grayson," he said, with his hand outstretched.

"I know who you are. I'm Brenda Lewis," said the girl, shaking his hand before placing her order. "Thanks for getting our I.G. together this morning. You really saved us. Oh, by the way, your roommate is a real piece of work."

"Try living with him. I'll see you later—gotta bring this to Jasper."

By the time he paced through the training floor of Emerald House and climbed up his designated ladder in the back, Grayson's legs were exhausted. He found it rather difficult to climb while holding an enormous pizza box.

"Thanks, buddy!" said Jasper, taking the pizza from Grayson. "Now go get some rest."

"What's taking my group so long?" asked Mrs. Foster impatiently, who had suddenly appeared from the doorway and grabbed Grayson's shoulder, her bright red hair flaming.

"Oh... um... hi. I think they were just arguing over who was going to bring it to you, but they should be here soon," stammered Grayson.

"Arguing?" said Mrs. Foster furiously. "Someone must always step up immediately and get the job done. I'm going to have to make them think long and hard about this tonight."

"Oh no, no, no..." said Grayson apologetically, doing his best to cover up the mess he had made. "They were arguing over who was going to bring it because they all *wanted* to! You know, to make a good first impression!"

"Oh, I guess there's nothing wrong with that," said Mrs. Foster, in a surprised yet pleased voice.

"So, um... are you two roommates?" asked Grayson, changing the subject.

"All of us instructors live in this house," answered Jasper. "We got the whole place to ourselves when you goons aren't here."

"Is Mrs. Foster here? Hi, Mrs. Foster," panted Brenda, running around the balcony with a pizza box in hand.

Mrs. Foster took the pizza without a word and disappeared back into the house.

"Well, anywho," said Jasper, breaking the silence, "you two better be off. Lots to do tonight. Better get some rest. And I promise this won't be an everyday thing. I know it's just you and the other boy in my group, so I'll try to keep your errands to a minimum."

With that, Brenda and Grayson swept from the house, taking separate ladders on their way down; neither of them knew if they could get in trouble for using the wrong one.

Although he was still exhausted from the morning, Grayson couldn't afford to be late for the five o'clock lesson. His pre-training nap was canceled. He and Ethan were the first to arrive at Emerald House that evening. The two of them started their own single-file line. Once all twenty P.L.s were present, the instructors emerged from their living quarters on the second floor, Master Ridley wearing his typical suit and unhappy expression.

"These evening sessions will focus more on teamwork, just as the beginning of our last lesson did."

Everyone in line hung their heads.

"That doesn't mean four hours of push-ups and pool jumps," said Ridley, raising the I.G.'s spirits. "Even though conditioning is important, our evening sessions will have an emphasis on building, planning, and landscaping. All three of which must be done to perfection if this I.G. is to have any hope of winning the annual Necklace Raid. Emerald House hasn't won this event in sixty years."

Grayson and the rest of the I.G. were now listening intently. Ridley was talking about a game, a competition. Grayson immediately felt the urge to start training, and he didn't even know how to play yet.

Ridley continued, "I'm going to allow Mr. Jasper to give a brief explanation of the tournament rules, given that it's his favorite part of the year."

"Good evening, boys and girls!" beamed Jasper, strutting over to take Ridley's place in front of the I.G. "The Necklace Raid is simple. There will be two other houses participating: the second-year Ruby House and our third-year friends over in Amethyst House. Y'all see the big emerald wrapped around our buddy's neck?" he asked, pointing to the ten-foot-high statue in the middle of the pool. "We need to protect that necklace and steal the other houses' necklaces."

Grayson hadn't thought about the older Lacers very much. Ethan's brother was going into his fourth year, so hopefully, they wouldn't be playing him in this tournament. Competing against Lacers that were Mitchell's size didn't sound like a game Grayson was interested in.

"Excuse me, I have a question!" snapped Ambrielle without raising her hand.

The room went silent.

Ms. Myles violently slapped her hands. "Miss Stone! It is extremely rude to interrupt an instructor, especially while he is giving important instructions. I will not tolerate P.L.s in my group who—"

"Isn't it stupid to have a group of inexperienced Lacers, such as us, participate in a game with Lacers who have been training for over two years now?" Ambrielle asked anyway, staring Jasper in the eyes.

"Miss Stone!" scolded Ms. Myles. "There were a number of things wrong with what you said, but most importantly, how dare you address yourself as a Lacer, as if you are equal to all of us who've earned that title. You are a P.L. until told otherwise."

"A Potential Lacer," mocked Ambrielle, making air quotes with her hands. "You mean as long as I keep my mouth shut and play two more years of capture the stupid necklace, you'll call me a Lacer? All of us in this I.G. are already equal to you. I don't believe in the tough act you put on to scare us."

Neither Jasper nor Ms. Myles said a word back to Ambrielle; perhaps they thought it best for Ridley to handle such a situation.

"Ambrielle Stone," said Ridley, flipping through the pages on his clipboard as he approached her. "It seems as if Daddy Stone has spoiled a thing or two about our initiation process, as I'm sure many other parents have. However, never again will you voice these opinions during a lesson, so why don't you do as you said and *keep your mouth shut and play two more years of capture the stupid necklace*, or maybe you'd rather drop out of the program already? Hmmm, that's what I thought. Everyone around the pool!"

The lesson began the exact same way the morning had. They jumped in and out of the freezing pool, which was even colder at night. They did an endless number of push-ups, and Ridley added in a new workout as well: running laps around the balcony while the instructors monitored from their lawn chairs. Grayson found himself in charge again, leading the push-up count, calling out when to jump into the pool, and yelling the lap number—not because he wanted to, but because nobody else had stepped up.

148

The thought of becoming an Official Lacer partying on Icefall Lane was the only thing driving Grayson through the workout. The first year of the initiation process was set to last seven months; Grayson's body was on the verge of failure, and it was only day one. As they worked out, Grayson wondered why Ambrielle had lost her temper over some tournament. She must've known something about it that he didn't.

The workout didn't conclude until Dylan ran over to the trash can and vomited. Grayson figured he'd eaten too much leftover pizza.

***

Ridley didn't mention Ambrielle's outburst for the remainder of the night. Before he ordered the I.G. into their element groups, he gave everyone motivation to stay in the initiation process.

"Don't be the P.L. who drops out on the first day. This is about time you start asking yourselves if the life of a Lacer is worth all this training," said Ridley, pointing at the group. "Keep in mind, Gavens don't get necklaces. Each of you will be gifted a necklace during the third year of the Lacer Initiation Process. That starts with you making it through tonight. Three years of hard work when you're young can and will make the rest of your life enjoyable."

Grayson remembered Jasper communicating with the stingray; he would never be able to speak with animals if he didn't tough out the process. And who knew what other powers Lacers' necklaces had hidden inside?

"This is the most excited I've been for the Necklace Raid in years," said Jasper, once he, Grayson, and Liam were all in the garden. "This year is better than the others for *me* because I already know both of you boys are gonna want to win this. Usually, I have a couple of trainees in my group who don't want to get their hands dirty. Not this year! Together, the three of us will come up with some creative ways to keep those older P.L.s out of our darn house!"

Grayson and Liam couldn't help but smile as Jasper continued to hype them up for the tournament.

"I think it would be best if one of you stayed back to defend our house while the other led the charge into an opposing house," said Jasper.

"Do we only get to attack one of the other houses? Or do we have to get both necklaces to win?" asked Grayson.

"Well, the tournament takes place over two separate nights, so it's better to focus on breaking into a single house each time we play. I would suggest going after Ruby House first since they aren't that much more skilled than you guys."

Grayson figured a whole year of training would put the Ruby I.G. far ahead of his. All he could do at the moment was uproot a flower.

"Don't worry, the first night of the tournament isn't for another three months," said Jasper, reading Grayson's agitation.

"How do the points work?" asked Liam.

"One point for each P.L. who gets into an opposing house, three points to take an opposing house's necklace off their statue, and five points to get their necklace all the way back to our statue."

Jasper then went on to explain the rules of combat. "Basically, everything is allowed, except for face shots with the staffs. It's a very rough game, and the other houses aren't going to take it easy on you. If you feel like you've had enough and wish to withdraw from the match, there will be a designated safety box for each house. Keep in mind, once you step foot in a safety box, there's no returning to the game."

Grayson had been all ears a moment ago but now had his eyes locked on Ambrielle, who was repeatedly being shoved from behind into the ice pool by Ms. Myles. This was the first time Grayson had witnessed an instructor lay hands on a P.L. Did she really deserve this? She'd disrespected the instructors, but what had she said that was so bad? She didn't seem to have spoiled anything. Grayson just wanted to talk to her. She didn't have an excuse to be mad at *him* anymore; *she* had just gotten the entire I.G. punished.

Conveniently, the perfect opportunity presented itself later in the night when Ridley called the I.G. away from their stations, back into single file.

"The Ruby House is located two blocks north from our house, the Amethyst about the same distance south. For those of you who know your directions, you know we're smack-dab in the middle of them, making us an easy target. We'll discuss that further tomorrow. For the last hour of training, everyone's going to walk outside, grab a tool, and start shoveling snow away from the battleground so we can begin to place defenses around our house."

Grayson followed the I.G. out into the darkness, where the only light came from the torches by the front door. He grabbed one of the shovels lined up against the wall of the house and waited to see which direction Ambrielle went. She immediately distanced herself from everyone else, making it clear she wasn't in the mood to talk.

How could she be? She was soaking wet and wearing a t-shirt while shoveling snow. He knew talking to her wasn't smart. She would probably yell at him. Grayson didn't care; he threw caution to the wind and walked toward her.

"Uh... hey," said Grayson in the most awkward voice possible.

"What?" said Ambrielle through chattering teeth.

Grayson didn't know what. He had no clue why he was talking to her. He panicked and said the only thing he could think of, "Er... I'm sorry about the other day. You know, when I knocked you over." Grayson knew bringing up that incident while she was already mad couldn't have been a smart decision, but she didn't tell him to leave to his surprise.

"I suppose you aren't that big of a moron compared to our instructors," she muttered, avoiding his eyes.

Grayson considered this a compliment coming from Ambrielle. She turned her back to him and began to halfheartedly scoop snow away from the house. Grayson was sure she didn't want him to know how cold she really was. He then made perhaps the dumbest suggestion of his entire life. "Do you want my shirt? It's dry... and, well... it's pretty cold out here."

Ambrielle dropped her shovel and gave Grayson her signature death stare. "Do I want your shirt?" she repeated sharply. "What's Ridley going to say when you walk back in shirtless? Do you ever think at all?"

"I'll just wear yours. The rest of my body's dry, so I'll be fine," said Grayson immediately.

Ambrielle appeared to think about this for a moment. "You're serious?"

Grayson nodded. He could tell Ambrielle was going to cave. She was clenching her jaw tight to stop it from shaking, and her face was blue. "I won't tell anyone. I promise."

"Ughhh," she groaned, checking to see if anyone in the I.G. was watching them. "Okay, turn around."

Grayson handed Ambrielle his shirt and covered his eyes.

The rest of the night was not a fun one for Grayson. He and Ambrielle shoveled snow side by side in silence. Grayson was so cold he could barely breathe. *Better me than her. Better me than her,* he repeated in his head.

Ridley would walk by them occasionally, yelling some sort of ultimatum, "Do it right, or go home!"

Mr. Hill and Mr. Boxer sat on top of the house, throwing snowballs at the P.L.s. Grayson hated how cool the instructors thought they were. Mr. Hill stood up to threaten Ethan for not shoveling fast enough and almost fell off the house. Ethan laughed at him, which resulted in Mr. Boxer pelting him with a block of ice.

"Laugh at an instructor again, Clark, and the next one will be even bigger," taunted Mr. Boxer.

"He's not gonna find a bigger snowball than that unless he wants to throw his bald head," muttered Ambrielle.

After the hour was up, they were called back into the house for dinner. It wasn't until Grayson climbed the ladder to the balcony that he realized Ambrielle's shirt was a size too small for him. He used both hands to pull it down as he made his way into the dining hall, taking a seat next to Ethan. The clock on the wall might have read 9 p.m., but it felt like two in the morning.

"Where were you outside? I couldn't find you," said Ethan.

"Ridley told me he needed someone to shovel snow on the backside of the house," answered Grayson, not wanting Ethan to know he had been talking with Ambrielle.

Dinner was just as small and healthy as the previous two meals. Grayson wanted to get back to his dorm and break open a box of frosting bites; however, the point of all the workouts and healthy food was to get him into good shape for the upcoming tournament. Once everyone had finished dinner, Ridley marched into the dining room.

"There are a few things I forgot to mention earlier. First off, anyone who is sent to Icefall Lane will wear a suit and tie. You need to look respectable in front of that many Lacers. You also need to wash the black workout clothes you have on; we don't need this house smelling like a hot yoga studio. Hopefully, you have an idea of what this initiation process is going to be like. For those of you who don't want to be here, you can always drop out of the program and go work an office job for the rest of your lives," said Ridley, laughing, looking right at Ambrielle. "Five o'clock sharp tomorrow morning. Now get out of here."

The I.G. strolled back to the residence hall in one large group. Everyone was too tired and depressed about the next morning to talk much.

"Hey," said Ambrielle in a whisper, tapping Grayson on the shoulder. "If you want, I can just follow you to your room so we can switch shirts."

Grayson told her that was fine. He couldn't seem too interested with Ethan watching. Ambrielle drifted off behind him, next to Harlie.

"What're you talking to her for?" asked Ethan.

"She has to stop by our room really quick," said Grayson.

Ethan didn't say anything more on the matter. They made their way through the first-floor hallway, stopping at the room right before the staircase.

"We're right here," Grayson told Ambrielle, who had continued walking.

"No way," she said. "You're the boys who took our first-floor room."

Not wanting to take part in the conversation, Ethan opened the door and shut it quickly behind him.

"What's his problem?" asked Ambrielle in a disgusted voice.

"He's still a little mad at you for yelling at us the other day," responded Grayson, opening the door for Ambrielle.

Grayson took off the shirt, flexed his abs as hard as he could, and handed it back to Ambrielle. Ethan had shut himself in the bathroom. Spades emerged from under the bed, carrying Grayson's backpack in his mouth.

"You want these frosting bites?" Grayson offered, pulling them out of the pocket. "I thought you didn't eat food."

"*He* doesn't want them, genius. He wants *you* to eat them," said Ambrielle, as if Grayson should already know this. "When you're hungry, they're hungry. When you're angry, they're angry. They read your emotions, feelings, and thoughts."

"How do you know so much about this stuff already?"

Ambrielle shrugged. "Maybe another time," she said. "Thanks for switching shirts with me, by the way."

And with that, she left the room. Ethan, who had obviously not been using the bathroom, came out at the sound of the door closing. He changed and went straight to bed without a word.

Grayson bit into a frosting bite, telling himself he was only eating it because he didn't want to starve Spades. When he was finished, he went to put them into his backpack—that was when he saw it. The book from his grandpa had been lying right below the box of frosting bites. Grayson had forgotten it was there. He picked it up and instantly felt its energy run through his body.

It was stronger than before.

CHAPTER 10

Puzzles at Adriel's Pond

During the first week of training, Grayson didn't have any time to think about his grandpa's book. The instructors tortured the I.G. every lesson with multiple, hour-long workouts, even if nobody caused trouble. After the workouts, Grayson used any leftover energy to shovel snow or control his element.

Within a week, Grayson had mastered uprooting flowers and switched his focus to larger plants. Jasper hadn't been lying when he said Lacers needed to picture every little detail of what they were trying to accomplish. Grayson would close his eyes and try to imagine even the smallest molecules of the root slowly being ripped from the ground. He felt like the exhaustion from the workouts lessened his ability to control earth.

There was no denying it; the lessons were bad. However, the part that bothered Grayson the most was that, even when the I.G. wasn't in Emerald House, they were still being burdened with tasks. Every night, Grayson's wristwatch would beep around two in the morning with a message from one of the instructors. Thankfully, Jasper usually wasn't the one who needed something. Ethan wasn't so lucky; Mrs. Foster loved to torture her group each night with pointless assignments, some of which didn't even benefit her.

"What did she make you do last night?" asked Grayson, cuddling in his sheets.

"Thirtyminuterun," yawned Ethan. "I think I would've dropped out and gone home if we didn't have the day off."

The I.G.'s first day off came on a Sunday after six straight days of training. A week ago, Grayson would've punched Ethan for mentioning dropping out, but Grayson had considered it himself by this point. Every muscle in his body ached, he was constantly hungry, and he had a permanent headache from lack of sleep.

Sleep—that was Grayson's plan for his day off. Yet, this plan did not pan out as he thought it would. It all started with Spades. Both Ethan and Grayson remained in bed with their eyes closed, not wanting to get up until breakfast at nine, but they were disturbed a few minutes early by a faint scratching noise. Grayson's guardian was pawing at the backpack under the bed.

"No! If I can wait until breakfast, so can you!" said Grayson, fighting the urge to grab the final frosting bite from his backpack, but eventually, he gave in. "Fine. If it'll get you to be quiet." Grayson pulled his bag out from under the bed and began to snack. Spades didn't stop whining; he started clawing at the tile with the backpack out of the way.

"Would you shut him up? I need sleep," groused Ethan.

"Uh oh," said Grayson with his head craned off the side of the bed. "He's trying to dig a hole."

"What the heck do you mean, he's trying to dig a hole? It's tile."

"That doesn't seem to be stopping him."

Grayson pushed the misplaced tile back into its proper position, picked up Spades, and set him on the couch.

"He probably just wants a more comfortable place to sleep," suggested Ethan. "He was used to sleeping on your bed; now you make him sleep on the floor."

This was probably the case. The decision to kick Spades off the bed hadn't been an easy one, yet it was for the best. Grayson didn't get much sleep to begin with. He couldn't have a tail whipping him all night. He spent the rest of his pre-breakfast time making a more comfortable bed for Spades by rounding up his spare blankets and pillows and arranging them in a circle at the foot of his bed.

"Come on, get up. We gotta leave," said Grayson, as he took his grandpa's book out of the backpack and placed it under his sheets to look at later.

Grayson had not heard or seen the phrase *Bottom Right* anywhere despite living in a Lacer city for a week. Over the summer, he had expected to find the meaning behind Oscar's code once he got to Icefall if it was, in fact, a code at all. Grayson took the increase of creative energy radiating from the book as a sign that he needed to keep searching. His only remaining option was to ask someone what *Bottom Right* could mean—someone who knew about the Lacing world but didn't have the power to get him in trouble.

The first person that came to mind was Jasper. As an instructor, Jasper could technically punish Grayson if *Bottom Right* meant something offensive or was the location of something illegal, but Grayson hardly expected him to do this.

Grayson entered the dining room of Emerald House and had a sudden change of heart. He couldn't risk the slight chance of ruining his relationship with the only instructor he liked. Besides, Jasper was Ridley's brother.

Grayson was placing his napkin over his lap, brainstorming ways he could investigate the phrase himself when help arrived.

"Hey, group leader," said Ambrielle in a sarcastic yet dreamy voice as she took a seat next to him.

"Please don't call me that again," said Grayson, beaming with internal pride.

"Group leader" was the name Dylan and Jeremiah had made up for Grayson since he'd been the one to make them work as a team and always led the count during workouts. Much to Grayson's displeasure, this name was starting to catch on more and more.

Ethan no longer said anything negative about Ambrielle. He claimed this was because he had decided to give her a second chance; however, the real reason was her roommate, Harlie. Anytime Ambrielle talked to Grayson, which happened to be a lot since he was the only P.L. who didn't hate her for constantly getting the I.G. punished, Harlie would also come to talk to Ethan. Sure enough, moments later, Harlie walked through the entrance and took a seat next to him.

"Hi, everyone," she whispered.

"Oh, hey... morning," replied Ethan in a deep voice Grayson had never heard before.

Ethan and Harlie engaged in conversation, giving Grayson time to ask Ambrielle about the meaning of Oscar's code.

"Your parents didn't really hide anything from you, did they? You know... about all this," asked Grayson timidly.

"Parent," corrected Ambrielle. "And no, my dad didn't... Why?"

"Oh, I'm so sorry. What happened?"

"She died when I was a kid—don't really remember. Anyway, what were you asking?" said Ambrielle, clenching her jaw.

"Oh, right. Do you know lots of Lacer phrases? Like anything they usually say that might be hard to understand?"

"I mean, maybe—do you care to venture an example?" she suggested, clearly confused on why this would matter at all.

"My parents would always use the phrase *Bottom Right.* I never knew what it meant," said Grayson.

"Bottom Right? That's it? Nope, never heard of it. Doesn't sound like a saying to me, probably a location of something... When did they use it?"

Grayson didn't know if telling her the truth about where he had seen the phrase was a good idea, but he couldn't let her help figure out what it meant unless she knew. It was probably nothing anyway.

"Well, they didn't actually say it."

"What? You just said—"

"I lied."

Ambrielle threw her hands up in the air. "Do you wanna ask me something that, I don't know, actually makes sense? Because this conversation doesn't seem to be going anywhere."

"It does make sense if you know the whole story. If you come back to my dorm after breakfast, I'll show you what I mean."

Ambrielle agreed to come, but unfortunately, she also asked Harlie to join them. Grayson didn't want Harlie or anyone else to know about the book.

"Ethan and I just told Dylan we'd go to the pond," Harlie said.

"Grayson, Ambrielle, you guys gotta come too! We're all going," said Dylan, gesturing to the table.

After breakfast, the I.G. headed back to the residence hall to change into their swimsuits.

"I'll meet you there. I gotta use the bathroom," said Grayson, finding an excuse to hang back at the dorm.

"Sounds good. Remember, we're going to Adriel's Pond. That's the one we walk past on the way to Icefall Lane," said Ethan, closing the door behind him.

Ambrielle appeared moments after Ethan had left. "Okay, what do you have to show me? We have to hurry because Harlie's nervous she's not going to have anyone to talk to without me there. I don't know why—she barely talks to me anyway."

"I think you scare her."

"Not my fault," said Ambrielle. "She's probably scared of butterflies, too."

"This is what I wanted to talk to you about," said Grayson, handing Ambrielle the book. "Bottom right corner of the last page."

Ambrielle examined the book while Grayson told her all about how he'd found it on the bus and how he knew it was from his grandpa. When he said the name Oscar Day, Ambrielle jumped off the couch where she had been sitting.

"Ha!" yelled Ambrielle. "I can't believe I didn't realize you're related to Oscar Day. This energy really is from a black diamond, then. It feels amazing. I feel so aware."

"A black diamond?"

"A black diamond necklace," said Ambrielle, still clutching the book. "Your grandpa has one."

"How do you know what kind of necklace my grandpa had?"

"He's one of the five black diamond holders. All Lacers know who the black diamond holders are."

"Only five Lacers have that kind of necklace?"

"Yeah, it probably wouldn't be good if everyone had that much power. They're supposed to be dangerous. That's crazy to think about, though. You can still feel the energy from the necklace just because your grandpa touched this book. I wonder what it feels like to actually meet someone who's wearing one."

"I think I *have* met someone wearing one," said Grayson.

"Who? And when?"

"This guy Walter Frost, he was friends with my grandpa. He came to my house after Oscar was murdered, and I felt the same energy when I shook his hand."

Ambrielle's jaw dropped. "Oscar was murdered? I saw he was on the run for some reason, but then the news never said anything more about it, so I figured he was fine. Why would they not put that on the news? And I can't believe you met Walter Frost. He lives here. Nobody's seen or heard from him in years. How strong was his energy?"

Grayson didn't know which of Ambrielle's questions to answer first. He told her everything he could remember about how Frost had been trying to save Oscar and how the Lacer government had also been involved, but Oscar's killers had gotten something from him first.

"It's all pretty confusing. I didn't know what they were talking about," said Grayson. "Oh, and uh, Frost's energy wasn't that different from this book, maybe a little stronger."

"Grayson, what if Oscar's black diamond necklace is in here?" exclaimed Ambrielle, ferociously shaking the book. "It doesn't make any sense for this book's energy to be as strong as Frost's handshake. Oscar hasn't touched this in months!"

Grayson wasn't sure if he wanted Ambrielle to be right. Even if she were, what was he going to do with such a powerful object? He could barely move a plant. And the instructors definitely wouldn't allow him to wear it. Ridley said P.L.s didn't get their necklaces until their third year of training.

Ambrielle went on to explain all about what she called *necklace law.* "I know Lacers can't take off their necklaces, but I think the black diamond ones are different. There's a good chance he could've left it for you."

Ambrielle was convinced the black diamond necklace was inside the book. Grayson wasn't so sure. It was a book—not a treasure chest. Ambrielle continued to shake it; she said she just needed time to think.

"Let's go to the pond and think there. Ethan and Harlie are gonna kill us," said Grayson.

"Fine. Bring your guardians so they can meet Comet and Stella. Maybe some other animals will be there, too."

"I'm guessing you weren't the one who named your guardian Stella."

"Uh, no. That's Harlie's guardian. She named her after some princess she likes," said Ambrielle, rolling her eyes.

"Come on, Spades. Come on, Ace," said Grayson, pulling the guardians away from the barrier of pillows he had arranged to stop Spades from digging his hole.

Neither Spades nor Ace wanted to leave the dorm. Grayson and Ambrielle carried them from the residence hall to the forest. The trees blocked the shining sun, and the bridge used to get to Icefall Lane radiated its blue electricity, lighting up the surrounding area.

Five members of the I.G. stood on top of the overpass doing cannonballs into the pond, Dylan and Jeremiah were setting up a table with a fresh batch of pizza they'd somehow gotten their hands on, and the remaining P.L.s were swimming in the water, watching the one-hundred-inch flat-screen TV hanging underneath the bridge. Eighteen guardians sat at the edge of the pond, keeping an eye on their owners.

"You brought them! I was gonna text you to bring them, but we don't have our darn phones," said Ethan. "Go on, Ace. You and Spades need to make some friends. Go talk to the monkeys over by that campfire."

Spades and Ace remained on the edge of the pond, not wanting to test their luck with animals bigger than them. Grayson and Ambrielle hopped into the water next to Ethan and Harlie. Jeremiah walked around with pizza boxes, handing out slices to an I.G. that had been deprived of filling food for a week.

"I wish I could, Jeremiah, but I gotta stay in shape," said Liam, who was standing on top of the bridge, flexing his muscles. "Someone's gotta lead this I.G. to a Necklace Raid victory."

Grayson didn't know how Liam could possibly think drawing attention to himself was a good idea. He tried to sound so confident it was obvious he was not. However, the boy next to Liam, who had also denied a slice of pizza, looked a little surer of himself. Grayson had heard Master Ridley refer to this boy as Xander Reed. Xander might have been short, but his muscles were not. He was the biggest kid in the I.G., no smaller than Ethan's brother, Mitchell. His wide body made him resemble a hot air balloon.

"No, please don't splash me. I can't get my hair wet," said Harlie.

Ambrielle didn't seem to care about getting her hair wet. She dove under the water and pulled Harlie's legs out from under her.

Harlie resurfaced, looking like she was about to cry. "It's going to be curly. I hate my hair curly."

Now that Harlie's hair was already wet, the four of them were free to splash each other. A tsunami wave ended up drenching them all.

"My bad, Grayson. Did we getcha?" asked Liam. "Have you met my roommate, Xander?"

"We haven't officially met yet, but obviously, I know who you are... group leader," said Xander with a condescending smile.

Grayson didn't even like it when Ambrielle called him group leader; Xander referring to him like that made Grayson tremble in anger. The fact that Xander was also standing rather close to Ambrielle did not help matters.

"I'm glad you already know me," said Grayson. "What's your name, again?"

"Xander Reed," said Xander, extending his hand to Ambrielle while keeping his eyes on Grayson. "Ambrielle Stone, correct?"

"Yeah," muttered Ambrielle, shaking Xander's hand.

Xander gave a stern nod to Ambrielle and one last smirk to Grayson before he paddled away. Liam did the same.

"They seemed nice," said Harlie. "Everyone here is so nice."

"You really can't tell when people are being fake, can you, Harlie?" said Ambrielle. "They were just trying to make Grayson mad. Not everyone here is nice."

Ambrielle's recognition of the situation only made Grayson like her more. Ethan, who wanted to back up Harlie, claimed Liam and Xander hadn't been that bad; although, Grayson was sure Ethan would've started a fight had Xander shaken Harlie's hand.

✳ ✳ ✳

Lunch at Emerald House that afternoon was better than usual. With their stomachs already full of pizza, the I.G. didn't bother touching their fruits or vegetables. After mealtime, Grayson, Ethan, Ambrielle, and Harlie returned to the residence hall.

"Let's get round two of this party started!" yelled Dylan.

Ethan and Harlie returned to the pond with the rest of the I.G., bringing the guardians with them. Grayson and Ambrielle slipped out of the group.

"Why are all your pillows under your bed?" asked Ambrielle as Grayson pulled Oscar's book out from his desk drawer.

"One of the tiles is busted. Spades and Ace have been digging a hole. They probably smell dirt or something."

"Spades is weird just like you then," said Ambrielle.

"We aren't weird. Here's the book. Whatever you're going to try, try it fast. I wanna go relax at the pond."

Ambrielle had assured Grayson at lunch that her new search technique was bound to extract the black diamond necklace. The new technique was her smacking the book on the dresser.

"Careful!"

"Why else would he have left you the book?"

"I think it only has energy because he touched it with the necklace on," said Grayson, who still didn't think the book had any correlation to the black diamond's current location. "The people who killed him probably took it. Or who knows, maybe nobody took it."

"You would think he could've written something more informative than *Bottom Right*," said Ambrielle, stuffing the book back in Grayson's desk drawer.

The second trip to the pond didn't last long for Grayson and Ambrielle. The two of them relaxed in the water, discussing other things Oscar could've left for Grayson besides the necklace—they didn't come up with anything good. Spades and Ace were also a problem. They refused to play with the other guardians and kept running back toward the residence hall. Ethan had to bring them back several times.

"President Maxwell Starr will be giving an urgent speech at the Black House in fifteen minutes. My sources tell me it is regarding the Reville Cycle. Be sure to stay around for our next segment."

Grayson had momentarily tuned out the music and voices at the pond to focus on the TV hanging underneath the glowing bridge. The mention of President Starr had grabbed his attention. He wanted to know what his dad's boss looked like.

Grayson remembered the Reville cauldron that had produced his staff, yet he had never heard of a "Reville Cycle."

A sound in the nearby forest stopped him from watching President Starr speak on the matter. Elliott Emerson emerged from the trees, his white cloak shimmering in the blue light of the jungle.

"A party at the pond on your only off day? I like the energy of this I.G.," said Emerson.

Dylan and Jeremiah jumped in front of the pizza boxes.

"It's okay. I'm not here to get you P.L.s in trouble with your instructors," reassured Emerson, gesturing to the other dozen pizza boxes Dylan and Jeremiah hadn't been able to hide. "I just wanted to see how everyone's first week went."

"Better now," said Dylan with a mouthful of food.

"I can see that," said Emerson.

Something strange happened next. Emerson looked at the TV, where President Starr was now giving his speech. He looked directly at Grayson and then back at the TV again. All twenty guardians, including Spades and Ace, gradually crept toward Emerson like they were going to attack him.

"Hello there, little guardians!" said Emerson. "Is this what you want to see?" He pulled a sparkling diamond necklace out from his white cloak.

Grayson and Ambrielle looked at each other. Guardians were attracted to necklaces... Could that be what Spades and Ace were digging for in the dorm? Before anyone could ask where they were going, they bolted back to the residence hall. Grayson's heart pounded with adrenaline—they had solved it.

"This is why we switched dorms," said Grayson, destroying the pillow barrier around his bed. "Oscar needed me to live here!"

They pushed Grayson's bed into the middle of the room and jumped to the ground by the broken tile. They didn't find a black diamond necklace underneath it—they found a lever. Grayson yanked the metal rod backward, causing the room to shake. He and Ambrielle jumped onto the bed for safety. The ground beneath the broken tile vanished, leaving a hole in the *bottom right* corner of Grayson's dorm.

Without speaking, Grayson and Ambrielle got off the bed and moved toward the hole, where a dangling ladder waited for them.

"After you," nudged Ambrielle.

Grayson's mother had always preached *ladies first*; however, in this scenario, Grayson felt like he had to be the first one to descend. He couldn't see how far down the ladder went or what it led to. It turned out he had nothing to worry about. His feet touched the ground after only a few steps down, causing him to walk headfirst into a hanging light switch. He pulled the string, illuminating the small room in which he stood.

Everywhere Grayson looked, he saw himself. The floor, the ceiling, and all four walls were made of mirrors. A square section of clear, non-reflecting glass wrapped around the middle wall like a massive fish tank, restraining a stream of fresh water from flooding the chamber. A bright silver desk and a white metal chair were neatly stationed against the mirrors in the corner of the room. Grayson sat down in his grandpa's office and yelled, "Come on down!"

"Wow," said Ambrielle, "it's so peaceful in here. It's so clean."

"Let's go! Start looking for the necklace!"

They rummaged through the papers on the desk and ran their hands across the glass, feeling around for any sign of energy. Ambrielle knocked her fist on the bottom right panel. "Does that sound hollow to you? It could be another trap door."

Grayson had just sat down next to Ambrielle to examine the floor when he heard Ethan barge into the dorm from above.

"Grayson! Where are you?"

"Down here! Are you alone?"

Ethan slid across Grayson's bed in the middle of the room. "It's just Harlie and me. What the heck! Is that a trapdoor? You know what? There isn't time! Get up here!"

Harlie turned on President Starr's speech while Ethan helped Grayson and Ambrielle out of the bunker.

"Grayson! I think it's on Channel Five! You aren't going to believe it. The Lacers on Icefall Lane... Emerson... they're all flipping out! It's about you know who, who left you the book on the bus!"

"*Longtime black diamond necklace holder, Oscar Day, was found dead at a ski resort several months ago,*" *said President Starr.* "*With Oscar having passed away over ninety days ago, his necklace should have returned into the Reville Cycle by now. Since it has not, we're left with two possible scenarios. Either his killers have taken the necklace, which the case investigators deem unlikely, or Oscar left the necklace in someone else's possession before his death. Possibly his daughter, Cristina Day, or his young grandson, Grayson.*"

The black diamond was here—there wasn't a doubt in his mind. Grayson just had to find it before someone else did.

CHAPTER 11

The Missing Necklace

There, alongside his best friend and two girls he had met a week ago, stood Grayson, bearing the news that he might very well be in possession of one of the most powerful objects on Earth. The trapdoor leading to his grandpa's office remained ajar. Grayson walked over to his bed in the middle of the room, sat down, and closed his eyes. Ambrielle frantically whispered to Ethan, explaining the rarity and power of a black diamond necklace.

"I won't say anything to anyone, I promise," said Harlie.

"Thanks, Harlie, I appreciate that," Grayson replied calmly. "I guess you were right, Ambrielle. I do have his black diamond."

"You don't have it yet! We have to find it!"

"You can't go down there," said Harlie, blocking Ethan and Ambrielle's path to Oscar's office. "That room was for Grayson to find, not us."

"Oh, move over, Harlie," said Ambrielle, swiftly ducking under her arm. "I've already been down there. And Grayson wants our help finding the necklace. Don't you, Grayson?"

"*We* don't have to find anything," he said. "Come on, Spades."

Grayson told Ethan and Harlie how the guardians at the pond being attracted to Emerson's necklace had helped them find the hidden room. He picked up Spades and carried him down the ladder, hoping the necklace energy would lead the guardian to the black diamond's hiding spot. Ethan and Ambrielle followed Grayson and Spades into the underground office.

Harlie tentatively watched from above. "I'm not going down there and messing around with his things."

Spades immediately pounced on the bottom drawer of the desk. Everyone froze.

Grayson opened the cabinet, revealing a silver sphere no bigger than a tennis ball. Spades grabbed it with his mouth and dropped it at Grayson's feet, eagerly waiting for him to play.

"You've got to be joking!" said Ambrielle. "He finds a toy. A toy. Ughhh! Keep looking."

Grayson narrowed his gaze. "If you'd been cooped up in a dorm six days in a row, you'd probably wanna play ball, too."

"He gets plenty of exercise because *you* get plenty of exercise. Honestly, didn't I already explain this to you?"

They continued searching Oscar's office late into the night. Harlie positioned herself at the door, monitoring the peephole, just in case any of the instructors decided to stop by for their occasional room checks. But the hallway remained empty, and an eerie silence swept through the residence hall as they carefully checked the mirror panels square by square for secret compartments. Each mirror stayed locked in place, as did the glass plates containing the ring of water.

After hours of work with no necklace to show for it, Ambrielle called it a night and headed back to her room with Harlie, who had fallen asleep guarding the door. Not long after, Ethan climbed the ladder and collapsed on his bed, leaving Grayson alone to gaze through a collection of old letters they had found inside the desk—they weren't really letters, just one-sentence reminders Oscar had left for himself, and the ink was badly smudged. Surrounded by his own reflection, Grayson gently smoothed out the old pieces of paper and fell asleep reading his grandpa's writing.

***

The following day, Grayson spent very little of his training session actually training. He was exhausted from an uncomfortable night's sleep on the office floor, so he was thankful for Ridley giving the I.G. an easy workout; however, his typically enjoyable training time with Jasper turned into a full-on press conference, with his instructors and the other P.L.s questioning him about the black diamond.

"You don't really have the necklace, do you?" asked Dylan.

"All you clowns get back to your station," ordered Jasper.

"It's definitely illegal if he gave it to you," said Jeremiah as Mr. Boxer pulled him away. "You're underage. But you would still tell us if he did, right?"

Grayson gave Jeremiah an unconvincing nod and returned to uprooting his plants.

"Sorry about that, buddy," said Jasper. "This whole thing is crazy if you ask me! I personally find it comical—an entire city worried about a first-year P.L. having a black diamond. Can't blame them, though. This has gotta be the biggest story in years."

Being smack-dab in the middle of *the biggest story in years* might have sounded like fun to Jasper, but Grayson knew firsthand it wasn't. Dealing with Lacers questioning him was one thing, yet dealing with absurd questions, getting no sleep, working out eight hours a day, all while preparing for a rapidly approaching Necklace Raid tournament against older P.L.s, was another.

By the middle of October, individual element training had become just as unbearable as the workouts. Grayson couldn't get through a single drill without Liam or Xander making a sly comment about his grandpa.

"Not too bad, I guess, for a black diamond holder's grandson," Xander would say whenever his wind group came over to watch Grayson train. "I got through my training sets perfectly today, just like Liam!"

Xander's ego was so big that Grayson sometimes wondered if he thought of himself as the second coming of Jesus. Xander always tried to boost Liam's confidence, which happened to be exceptionally low when his buddy wasn't around.

With all unwelcome attention, Grayson jumped on any possible opportunity to leave Emerald House. Whenever an instructor asked a P.L. to make an errand run to Icefall Lane, his hand was always the first in the air. The level of exhaustion both Grayson's physical and mental state had reached by this point in the year would often cause him to get lost as he maneuvered through the skyscrapers. Not only did these incidental detours require more walking, but they also resulted in extra workouts. If the instructor that sent him wasn't satisfied with Grayson's return time, Grayson would spend the rest of the training session in the ice pool. Master Ridley claimed the ice pool was an extremely effective way to build "mental muscle."

The cheerful Lacers of the city would also slow Grayson down by bombarding him with questions on topics he wasn't even slightly educated on. It wasn't until the day of President Starr's speech that Grayson learned Lacers got their necklaces from a Reville, the same stone cauldron they got their staffs from.

As the I.G. gathered around the lobby of Emerald Residence Hall on a Sunday morning, Ambrielle explained that the Reville Cycle was a never-ending process, which a Lacer's necklace would enter once its owner passed away. No two living Lacers could ever have the exact same necklace.

"There's a lot of things that make necklaces unique: its gem type, its gem shape, its chain. Other things, too, I think," she said. "But ninety days after a Lacer dies, their necklace enters the Reville Cycle, so someone else has a chance of getting it. Otherwise, there wouldn't be enough combinations for everyone."

"All right, time to stop talking, Ambrielle," said Ethan, rising from his lounge chair to address the I.G. "We did introductions last week, so today, let's start off with our favorite childhood story."

Ambrielle quickly stood up, leaving the group circle. "Time to stop talking?" she mumbled. "More like time to leave."

"I saw that coming," said Grayson as Ambrielle continued down the hallway.

This was the third Sunday in a row that the I.G. had agreed to meet on their own, without the instructors forcing them. Since they were all going through this process together, getting to know each other was probably a good idea, and after Emerson's appearance at the pond, it was too risky to bring unhealthy food out in the open again. After everyone had repeated their introductions multiple times at the first meeting, Grayson had memorized everyone's name and where they were from.

With all the backlash he was receiving about the necklace, Ethan agreed to replace Grayson as the I.G.'s vocal leader during these gatherings. "How about you go first, Xander?"

Xander's story about his first time riding a bike somehow transformed into him being the star quarterback for his youth football team, where his unique skillset often left fans wondering if he had his own black diamond necklace.

Given that Harlie was too shy to attend these get-togethers in the first place, and Ambrielle claimed these meetings were nothing more than a circle of pointlessness, Grayson and Ethan did not feel the need to return after Xander's story.

When training resumed the next morning, Grayson didn't see a whole lot of Xander. With the Necklace Raid tournament only a month away, element training significantly picked up, and group workouts were cut from the sessions. Grayson was already in the best physical shape of his life. His cardiovascular endurance was untouchable, and his chest and arm muscles had grown from the daily push-ups.

Grayson enjoyed learning the more advanced aspects of the earth element, not only because it was more fun but mainly because he didn't know how uprooting plants would help his I.G. win the Necklace Raid. The first helpful skill Jasper showed them was how to throw these plants at an enemy. This turned out to be relatively easy, considering all Grayson had to do was imagine hitting Liam in the face with a bush.

"When you're thinking about the action you want to perform, your staff can't be motionless in your hands. There aren't specific motions, it's all preference, but you gotta do something with it," informed Jasper.

Grayson had an idea of what he meant. For instance, when he would throw a bush, he'd swing his staff like a baseball bat in the direction he wanted it to go. It wasn't until Jasper showed them more complicated areas of element control, such as deception, that Grayson got really confused.

"Deception is just a fancy word for confusion. Deceiving enemies is one of the most useful defenses out there. Here's an example."

Jasper threw his green globe on the ground, caught his staff with one hand, and aimed it at the biggest tree in the garden. In one sweeping motion, he made the tree grow in size, so much so that it momentarily covered the entire first floor, making everyone, instructors included, jump onto the ground in fright.

"Woah there! My bad, everyone," bellowed Jasper, as if he'd even surprised himself. "But anywho, you two get the point. If you were to make your opponent *think* a tree was about to hit them, you should have plenty of time to escape."

Grayson knew he wouldn't be doing anything that exciting anytime soon; however, he was beginning to grasp the *"picture what you want to happen, then make it happen"* motto that Jasper preached each day. In middle school, Grayson had spent hours in class daydreaming about things he never thought would be possible. Now they were possible, and Grayson just needed his imagination to be more vivid to manifest them.

"Every Lacer is born with creativity, some more than others, but that doesn't mean it's a skill that can't be developed. With dedication, consistent practice, and a stress-free mind, levels of creativity will increase," said Jasper, raising his hand from his waist to his head. "If you want to make people think this tree is as big as the entire house, then study the tree and repetitively run the scenario through your brain. If you believe you can do it, then you can do it, but the only way to believe something is to practice it."

After Jasper's creativity talks, Liam always felt the need to try and prove he was a more skilled Lacer than "Oscar Day's grandson." Just to get his mind off Liam's annoying comments, Harlie would come over to the garden and check on Grayson whenever her element group was on a break. It was hard for Grayson to stay angry with Harlie around. She had a way of putting a positive spin on just about any situation.

Even during Grayson's worst sessions, when his energy levels were depleted, he proved his mind was more creative than Liam's. Jasper was stuck teaching Liam the same tree trunk crushing technique for over a week. Grayson had finished this task on his very first try by imagining rubber bands constricting the bottom of the trunk. He didn't feel the need to share his secret.

***

As October came to a close and the necklace remained lost, Grayson had run out of handwritten notes to read, and he began to lose interest in the underground room. The office was in the *bottom right* corner of Grayson's dorm, so he had solved the mystery of the book, and now he was starting to think there was nothing else to find. The words *black diamond* appeared nowhere in his grandpa's writing.

Regardless of Grayson's doubts, the four friends had expanded their search to the fourth floor. A month of looking for the necklace had given Grayson lots of time to hang out with Ambrielle. Neither Grayson nor Ethan expected to find anything in the girls' dorm. The two boys used any excuse they could to hang out with their crushes.

"There's no way I'm asking her to date me," whispered Ethan as he and Grayson walked up to the girls' place. "If she's too shy to go to our Sunday meetings with me, she's not gonna want to go anywhere else with me. I've just got to be patient. There's nothing for us to do anyway besides walk around the forest together. Man, I wish we could party on Icefall Lane!"

Ambrielle's shyness wasn't the reason Grayson had been delaying his plan to ask her out. It was the exact opposite. Ambrielle scared Grayson. She constantly hit him or called him stupid; sometimes, Grayson wondered if they were even friends. One day they'd talk and have a great time, and the next day she'd be extremely guarded, keeping to herself completely. Grayson wasn't sure if she was the type of girl who wanted a boyfriend.

"For the last time, it's not here," said Ambrielle as she climbed off her bed so Grayson could move it away from the wall. "I already checked the corners of the room."

"I already looked under my bed, too," said Harlie gently. "That's where Stella and Comet sleep. They would have noticed if something were hidden under there."

Comet was bright gold, and like Ambrielle, he always seemed mad at someone; usually, that someone happened to be Harlie's guardian, Stella. Stella had silver fur, yellow eyes, and wore a pink bow around her neck.

"Isn't she the most adorable guardian you've ever seen? I named her after my favorite childhood princess," Harlie would say.

Ambrielle covered her ears anytime Harlie told this story, and Comet would try to pull the bow off Stella's neck at the mention of the word *princess.*

This time Grayson and Ethan gave up searching for the necklace after a couple of minutes. They were running out of places to look.

"It's somewhere in that underground room," said Ambrielle, jumping onto the couch. "We're just missing it."

"Or maybe President Starr was wrong," said Grayson. "On the night Oscar died, Walter Frost said Oscar's killers were the ones who took the necklace. If I don't have it and President Starr doesn't have it, Frost's theory is the only logical explanation."

"Why would President Starr tell everyone you have the black diamond instead of them?" asked Harlie. "I'm sure they have evidence that his killers didn't steal it. That's not something the President would lie about."

"He probably doesn't want to scare everyone," replied Grayson. "Admitting that evil Lacers have a powerful object could start a panic. And it's not like we know President Starr... He could be lying."

Ethan crossed his arms. "I doubt the Lacer government is worried about one small group of bad Lacers. Think about how many good Lacers are here at Icefall alone, not to mention the other four cities."

"What if it's not just one small group?" said Ambrielle. "Look at our instructors. I don't think those jerks qualify as good Lacers."

"Grayson's dad told us the Lacers who killed Oscar are the same ones who attacked the Black House over summer," said Ethan. "Those are the only crimes committed by Lacers in the last sixty years. That means there's only one bad group out there."

"And our instructors are only mean to prepare us for the outside world," said Harlie.

Ambrielle rolled her eyes. "Our instructors are the worst. They're supposed to be our teachers, and we can't even ask them a question without getting shoved in the pool for three hours straight. I think it's time we teach *them* a lesson."

"Yeah!" yelled Ethan. "I'm on board. Mrs. Foster is the worst."

"Let's go mess up their house and see how much they like cleaning for a change."

"Wait... You're being serious?" asked Ethan as Ambrielle grabbed her coat and headed for the door.

"Yes, I'm serious. It's nighttime. They won't see us. We'll be quick."

"You can't!" pleaded Harlie.

"Actually, I can, and you aren't going to stop me."

"Yeah, you aren't going to stop us!" said Ethan, high-fiving Ambrielle. "Grayson, I know Jasper's cool and all, but you gotta at least come watch."

"I'll come."

"Well, I'm staying," asserted Harlie.

"We could've guessed that," said Ambrielle. "Let's go."

With animals watching them from the jungle, Grayson, Ethan, and Ambrielle crept out of the residence hall and ran across the snow-covered trails to Emerald House.

"What exactly are you guys gonna do?" asked Grayson as they approached the back wall.

"I'm making a wave from the pool and splashing Ms. Myles's apartment door with it," said Ambrielle.

"I'm doing the same thing to Mrs. Foster's door but with fire," said Ethan.

"You're gonna burn the whole house down."

"Stop worrying. They'll put it out."

The trio came to a halt behind the house. Voices were coming from the doorway. The instructors weren't asleep yet.

Ethan kicked the dirt in frustration. "Come on. We'll do it another night," he said.

"Hold on, wait. Listen!" whispered Grayson.

"The P.L.s in my group are delusional this year," said Mr. Hill, crying with laughter. "They actually think they have a chance of winning the tournament. The Amethyst House is going to crush them."

"You'd think at least a couple of them would realize the tournament is set up for them to lose," said Mr. Boxer.

They turned around for the residence hall with their heads down. Grayson couldn't believe how hard he'd been training for a tournament he was supposed to lose. They were passing the last thick patch of the forest when Grayson stopped dead in his tracks.

"What are you doing? It's cold out here!" said Ethan, waving Grayson forward.

Grayson didn't move. He had gotten so used to the bright eyes of animals watching him from inside the jungle that he barely noticed them anymore. Grayson met the gaze of the sharpest set of eyes he could find and smiled. He had a plan, but he would need the black diamond to accomplish it.

"You think the Ruby and Amethyst teams are scared of animals?"

CHAPTER 12

A Way to Win

The morning after Ethan and Ambrielle's failed attempt to prank the instructors, Ridley gathered everyone around a bulletin board in Emerald House. He wore a baggy black suit, and his jaw was clenched so tight his head was shaking.

"The skills you have learned to this point in the program are the skills you will have going into the first round of the Necklace Raid. You are all in better shape than when you first arrived here. You've built muscle as well as mental strength. You're more conditioned, and most of you have been eating healthier." Ridley stared directly at Dylan and Jeremiah, who still had food leftover from the first week of training. "During this final preparation week, we will let you work alone. You need to develop a strategy that will successfully penetrate either the Ruby or Amethyst homes while also keeping our Emerald House safe. I speak for myself and the other instructors when I say we won't be happy if that necklace is taken from our statue… Tournament rules are on the board. You have exactly a week to prepare. Begin."

Oh great, thought Grayson, *they're going to punish us for losing a game we're supposed to lose.* He went up to the board and read the rule sheet.

The Necklace Raid

Objective: Each of the three Potential Lacer training houses has a statue located somewhere inside. Each statue is wearing a necklace. Your Initiation Group's goal is to take the opposing houses' necklaces off their statues and return them to yours.

Points System:

One point for each participant who makes it inside an opposing team's house.

Three points to take an opposing team's necklace off its statue.

Five points for successfully returning an opposing team's necklace to your own statue's neck.

Rules:

1. *Only three protectors are allowed inside each house.*
2. *Players cannot break a statue to reach a necklace. They must find another way to retrieve it.*
3. *If a participant wishes to withdraw from the battleground at any point, they may submit themselves to the cell blocks located in the middle of the playing field. Once in the cell block, there is no returning to the tournament.*
4. *Opposing teams may also force players into the cell blocks. (Still no returning.)*

Dress Code: Stealth Suits will be provided on the day of the tournament.

Authorized Gear:

1. *Staff (with globe carrier)*
2. *Sticker Gloves*
3. *Ropes*

Seniority Rules: If there is a tie, the older I.G. will be victorious.

Time: The tournament will take place over two separate nights.

Night One: November 27ᵗʰ, 10 p.m. – 10:30 p.m.

Night Two: April 2ⁿᵈ, 10 p.m. – 10:30 p.m.

Grayson reread the rule sheet several times. He hadn't the slightest clue what sticker gloves were, but on his way to Emerald House that morning, he'd seen three steel cages placed on the playing field. He guessed Mr. Hill and Mr. Boxer had been up late building the cell blocks.

The I.G. walked outside to shovel snow away from the house and began constructing their defenses. To the right and left of Emerald House, Grayson could see the Ruby and Amethyst training facilities in the distance. The area in between each house was perhaps the most uneventful part of Icefall. Besides the shiny cell blocks in the middle, the Necklace Raid playing field consisted of rocks, snow, and dirt. And the houses themselves were mere cement blocks. Grayson was eager to get inside them and see if their interior was as unique as Emerald House's.

"Let's brighten this place up," said Jasper, handing Grayson a plastic bag. "Here's some seeds if you guys decide to plant trees. I can speed up the growing process."

Once the front lawn was clear of snow, Ethan called the I.G. into a huddle. "Before we set up our defenses, we need to decide what house we're going to attack. Any ideas?"

Grayson was about to give his thoughts when he was cut off by the snottiest girl in the I.G. He didn't know much about Madison Silver, other than the unpleasant things Ambrielle had told him, but the moment Grayson heard her voice, he wished he had headphones to block the sound.

"Yes, I have some great ideas. Well, they aren't really my ideas — they're Liam's," she said, as though she thought the whole I.G. would love this news.

Grayson already knew the rest of her plan was about to be terrible. Liam had just told Jasper he wanted to plant trees on the roof to scare off the other teams. Grayson had no reason to expect his other ideas to be any better.

"Liam seems to think," she continued in her whiny voice, "that we should attack both the Ruby *and* Amethyst Houses! We'll catch them off guard."

Yep. Dumb idea. Grayson didn't know exactly what skills the Ruby and Amethyst teams possessed; however, it was obvious they were more advanced than everyone in their Emerald group. Certainly, the only way to break into another residence was to use all their available personnel on *one* specific house. Grayson wasn't going to let Liam, Xander, or Madison lose this game for them.

"Absolutely not," said Grayson sternly from the back of the huddle.

Everyone turned around to face him.

"Why not?" pressed Xander, who evidently wasn't happy with Grayson shooting down his buddy's plan. "It sounds like a pretty darn good strategy to me, unless, of course, your grandpa is gonna fly out of his grave and help us."

Grayson lunged at Xander, tackling him into a group of girls, all of whom screamed. Xander's friend, Spencer Erving, jumped on Grayson from behind and elbowed him twice in the head before Ethan made his way through the crowd and kicked him in the face.

"Get off of him!" yelled Liam, pushing Grayson off Xander.

Everyone sprang to their feet, ready for round two of the fight.

"Cut it out!"

"Break it up!"

Dylan and Jeremiah jumped in between the five boys and broke up the fight for good. Once everyone was separated and tempers were cooled down, Jeremiah spoke. "Okay, now Grayson, I believe you were about to tell us your plan," he said gently.

Grayson massaged the back of his head where Spencer's elbow had hit him and explained his theory that it would take almost all of them to break into one of the other houses.

"Okay, let's take a vote," suggested Dylan, still trying to keep everyone calm. "Who thinks we should attempt to invade both houses?"

Grayson sighed in relief when only five or six hands went into the air.

"Raising both hands doesn't count as two votes, Liam."

The remaining fifteen hands shot up when Dylan repeated Grayson's plan. He was happy to see most of the I.G. still trusted his judgment—although part of him was now worried. This was a big deal. If they lost the Necklace Raid using *his* strategy, Liam, Xander, and now Spencer Erving would never let him hear the end of it.

Grayson's attack plan focused all their personnel on one house; however, his defensive plan remained a secret. Grayson had read the rules sheet carefully for a reason. The instructors would most likely frown upon his strategy, but there didn't seem to be a clear-cut law against it.

Grayson had one week to find the black diamond, learn how to communicate with animals, and turn the outside of Emerald House into a jungle to hide them. Even though his friends said it was impossible, Grayson set his mind on achieving this goal by any means necessary. If the instructors wanted the Emerald I.G. to lose, Grayson was more than willing to bend the rules to prove them wrong. Since booby-trapping the house's perimeter was the only part of this plan Grayson had any control over, he began immediately.

Grayson dumped out the bag of seeds in a circular formation around the house, making sure they landed close together, so any animals he brought into the playing field could hide in the brush. There would also be plenty of vines and branches to tangle the opposition with. While Grayson was proud of his tree structure, he personally thought Ambrielle's moat was the best defense.

"Is it against the rules to electrocute the other teams?" Harlie asked Mr. Boxer.

"Of course not. Anything is allowed. Nobody will get seriously hurt in the stealth suits."

Harlie turned to Ambrielle. "Maybe I could put power lines into your moat. If any of the other players try to swim across, I'll turn on the power and electrocute them. It'll be one giant electric pool."

Ambrielle, of course, agreed with this violent and brilliant plan. "I think we can finally be friends, Harlie."

The only defense Xander and his two fellow wind controllers, Danielle Green and Brandi Stark, had contributed for the tournament was rehanging the fans from their training station onto the walls outside the house. Grayson and Ethan both agreed this was the least creative idea they'd ever heard of, not to mention stupid, since it gave the opponents a way to climb the walls without using a rope or sticker gloves. After hearing Xander's braggadocious stories at the I.G.'s off-day meetings, Ethan decided to knock the fans off the house's walls just to give him extra work.

Ethan was also in charge of shaping his fire group's defenses, which was probably a good idea when taking Ethan's ability to beat people in fights into account. He placed numerous campfires around the battleground—some underneath Grayson's trees—in case, as a last resort, they had to make a ring of fire around the house by burning them.

Three days later, the I.G. put the finishing touches on the house's *decorations* and used their remaining time to practice climbing, throwing, and swinging from vines. Ridley informed the I.G. that the vines dangling from Emerald House's walls weren't all that different from the ropes they would carry with them during the match.

"Each participating house has metal spikes placed at the top of their walls," said Ridley, pointing to the pinnacle of Emerald House. "These spikes give the opposing I.G.s an object to latch their ropes around when trying to climb."

Ethan put the Emerald I.G. through a vine-climbing contest. Grayson, Ambrielle, and the other seven fast climbers would be the ones to attack Ruby House, while Ethan, Harlie, and the remaining nine P.L.s stayed back to guard Emerald House. Preparations were going great; however, Grayson was no closer to finding the black diamond necklace. Without it, the rest of his plan couldn't happen.

One evening, Jasper sent for Grayson to pick up a pizza. Grayson walked through the forest and deviated off the trail to Cassiel's Lake. Under the clear blue water, there were whales, jellyfish, stingrays, and many more creatures Grayson was sure would scare the Ruby and Amethyst I.G.s. If he could only get the animals to do his bidding, he would take them from the lake and relocate them into the moat. Grayson waved at the creatures from the surface, hoping they would remember him as a friendly Lacer if he did, in fact, find a way to communicate with them before the match.

Grayson considered asking someone else to talk to the animals for him, but it would have to be someone he trusted. If the instructors found out Grayson was the one who brought the animals onto the playing field and ordered them to attack the other teams, who knew what type of tortuous workouts they would put him through?

Grayson maneuvered between the cheerful partiers on Icefall Lane and was tempted to ask one of them for help. The pizza place was jam-packed. He placed Jasper's order and was making his way toward an empty table when someone shoved him from behind. Grayson spun around to see Mitchell Clark's face.

"Grayson!" shouted Mitchell. He paused to squeeze Grayson's bicep. "Good to see ya! Picking up the instructors some food? I remember those days! Look at you in the black workout attire! Those muscles are really starting to show."

"Good to see you, too! Take it easy. I'm sore."

"I bet you are," said Mitchell. "Here, I want you to meet two of my friends. They're only a year ahead of you in the training process. This is Dontae. And this is Hardy."

Despite being two years younger than Mitchell, and only a year older than Grayson, Dontae and Hardy were built like grown men. They were roughly six-foot-six, and their shoulder muscles threatened to break through the ruby cloaks they wore. If this was what all the P.L.s in the older groups looked like, Grayson now understood why Mr. Hill had called the Emerald I.G. delusional for thinking they could win.

Mitchell explained how he had met Dontae and Hardy. Grayson didn't hear a word he said... He had noticed a sapphire gem hanging underneath Mitchell's white tuxedo, and all other things lost meaning.

Mitchell could communicate with animals. And more importantly, even if Mitchell refused to plot against his two friends in the Ruby I.G., Mitchell wouldn't rat him out for asking. It was worth a shot—but there was a problem. He couldn't ask Mitchell for help in front of Dontae and Hardy, and the Necklace Raid was only three days away.

"Well, we've actually gotta run," said Mitchell. "But let me know if you and Ethan want to meet for dinner after your tournament."

"How about before?" pleaded Grayson.

"Before? You guys aren't allowed to eat on Icefall Lane... Wait, you know what?" Mitchell paused, scratching his long blond hair. "If I'm remembering correctly, I'm pretty sure the instructors let you eat wherever you want the night before the tournament."

Dontae and Hardy nodded in confirmation.

"Marty's Brews at nine?" asked Grayson.

"I'll be there!"

* * *

Grayson delivered Jasper his pizza and returned to his dorm, where he and his friends did one last half-hearted search for the black diamond. With no sign of energy in Oscar's office, Grayson was positive his grandpa had not left him the necklace.

"I think I found a way to make the plan work, but I don't know if you guys are gonna like it," said Grayson.

Ethan, Ambrielle, and Harlie listened intently.

* * *

"These Ruby dudes were really bigger than Mitchell?" Ethan wondered.

"Much bigger."

"Okay, then I guess we have to try. He still owes me for not telling me he's a Lacer," said Ethan, standing up from the couch to grab water. "But if he's friends with these other P.L.s, I'm not sure if he's gonna help us cheat against them."

"It's bending the rules," corrected Grayson.

"You shouldn't be mad at your brother; he had to lie to you," said Harlie. "I hope my little sister isn't mad at me when I come home this summer."

Grayson's eyes widened. "You have a sister?"

"Yes, Kimberly. I'm glad I don't have to lie for very long. She's only a year younger."

"Do you have any siblings, Ambrielle?"

Ambrielle sat motionless on the couch and stared at the floor. "I had an older sister. She was actually kind of like you, Harlie, now that I think about it… She passed away at the same time as my mom. It's just me and my dad in New York."

Grayson covered his mouth with his hand. "I… uh… I'm so sorry."

"I'm sorry. I had no idea," whispered Ethan. He brought a box of tissues over to the couch.

"Why did you come all the way to Colorado?" asked Harlie, putting her arm around Ambrielle.

"My dad told me to stay on the East Coast, but I wanted to get as far away from New York as I could. I would've trained in California if their mayor had come to my welcome party."

***

On the final day of preparation before the tournament, Grayson had never been more nervous in his life. It was just occurring to him how little he knew about the older groups they'd be facing. The only older Lacer trainees Grayson had met were Dontae and Hardy. This was probably because the instructors didn't want the older P.L.s spoiling the initiation process for younger ones. That night at Emerald House, Grayson tried to hide his nerves as the I.G. put the finishing touches on what he thought was a solid plan.

"Harlie, one last time, when are you permitted to turn on the electric moat?" asked Ethan.

"Only if five or more opposing players get past our first two lines of defense," recited Harlie.

"Liam, Xander... what is the only exception for you leaving the perimeter of this house?"

"If an opposing player steals our statue's necklace and tries returning it to their house," mumbled Xander.

"But that's not gonna happen because we aren't going to let them into the house," chimed in Liam.

The only reason Xander and Liam had agreed to guard the outskirts of the house was because Ridley had stated earlier in the week that keeping the other teams from coming inside was the most important job. Liam was sure to remind everyone of this any chance he got. Ridley also said that three random names would be drawn on the day of the match to guard the inside of the house as a last resort.

Once the evening review session had concluded, that was it for preparation. Ridley informed the I.G. they wouldn't meet the following morning, and everyone better come rested at night for the tournament. And sure enough, as Mitchell had said, Ridley lifted his ban on Icefall Lane for the night.

"Finally! I thought they'd never let us eat here again," said Ethan as he and Grayson walked through the forest to Marty's Brews. "Remember how good the steak was last time?"

The same hostess in magenta robes skipped her way through the bar and sat the two of them at a booth by the piano. Mitchell wasn't there yet.

"Good luck tomorrow night," she said merrily. "Enjoy yourselves! I miss those days!"

The positivity of the Lacers at Icefall Lane still struck Grayson as weird. He couldn't figure out why his instructors were the only negative Lacers in the city. Yeah, they were supposed to prepare him for the outside world's treatment, but the difference between his instructors and the ordinary citizens of Icefall was night and day. Was it even possible for the instructors to purposely change their personalities that much?

Grayson ordered a soda. For the first time in two months, he took a deep breath and relaxed. He even closed his eyes for a moment, letting the smooth tunes of the piano soothe his exhausted body. There were things he should've been thinking, even worrying about: getting injured in the match, his I.G. losing because of his plan, the workouts they'd have to do if they lost, Mitchell refusing to help, and of course, the black diamond necklace that he never would've found if it hadn't been for some unexpected visitors at dinner.

"Yo, Dontae, look who it is! It's that kid we're gonna bury in the snow tomorrow night!" said Hardy, his muscles stretching the shimmering material of his ruby cloak.

"Ohhh, man! You're right, Hardy," said Dontae, towering over the booth where Grayson sat. "Oscar Day's grandson! Oh no, what if he wears grandpa's necklace?"

"Let's see if he's giving off any energy," said Hardy, shaking Grayson's shoulder. "Nope. I guess we're good."

The two boys continued trash-talking. Grayson was only half-listening to them because he was slowly reaching for his staff to hit them. Just as he was about to throw his globe on the table, the two older P.L.s accidentally provided Grayson with the most useful bit of information in the world.

"...but what if he just took off the necklace before coming into town?" mocked Dontae.

"We would still feel the energy on him, wouldn't we?" Grayson got the sense Hardy was genuinely asking his friend this question.

"No, we wouldn't," said Dontae, correcting his friend while still trying to sound sarcastic to Grayson. "The necklace's energy doesn't linger."

Grayson shot up from the booth so fast that he knocked over his drink right onto Hardy's cloak. Dontae lunged at him but slipped on the wet floor. Grayson passed Mitchell on the way out and didn't look back to see if he was being chased. He didn't look to see if Ethan was following him. He just ran.

Grayson wasn't sure if it was because of all the conditioning he did at the lessons or because of his adrenaline, but he wasn't even winded when he stepped foot in his dorm. He knew where the necklace was.

Grayson pulled the book out of his desk drawer and began shaking it and smacking it on his dresser; he even debated cutting it open. "Think, Grayson, think," he said, punching himself in frustration. "Not now, Spades. I know I didn't eat my dinner."

The moment he finished the sentence, he laughed. How could he have been so stupid? Grayson pulled his bed into the center of the room and yanked on the lever beneath it, revealing his grandfather's hidden room. Grayson descended.

For the first time, he brought the book with him.

He pulled the light switch, and sure enough, placed perfectly in the spiral-shaped crevice engraved in the back cover was a teardrop black diamond with a glistening gold rim to match its chain.

CHAPTER 13

The Black Diamond

Grayson woke up on the morning of the Necklace Raid with a lot to do and a lot of decisions to make. He had twelve hours to learn how to communicate with other animals, convince them to defend Emerald House, and get them to Emerald House without the instructors noticing. Whether or not Spades had grown enough to earn the respect of these animals was going to be a major factor in the day's success.

"I feel bad we stood up Mitchell," said Grayson, rolling out of bed.

"Who cares? You found the necklace!" Ethan enthused. "Let's go to the lake right after we eat."

The boys made their breakfast at Icefall Lane a quick one. They hurried back to the residence hall, Grayson grabbed the black diamond, and they ran to Cassiel's Lake, Spades at their side.

"It's such a weird feeling. Everything moves around a lot," said Grayson, gently running the chain through his fingers and carefully latching it around his neck. He closed his eyes and let its energy radiate through his body. When he opened his eyes again, it felt as if he had a second set.

"Are you dizzy?" Ethan asked.

"Everything is blurry, but I'm not dizzy. I think it's because I'm taking in more details of my surroundings… All right, let's give this a shot."

Ethan was stationed on lookout while Grayson placed his hand on top of his guardian's head, just like Jasper had.

Hey, Spades, I don't know if you can hear me, but can you get an animal's attention? Maybe one small enough to respect you but big enough to scare the other teams?

Spades jumped around in excitement. His oversized tail smacked the lake water, and he ran off into the woods. Grayson guessed he had gotten the message. Spades returned from the forest moments later, accompanied by every animal Grayson could think of. Wolves, birds, snakes, and monkeys emerged from the shadows. Bears, lions, and tigers, which were ten times Spades's size, showed no interest in harming him; they stood by his side as loyal protectors. Fish, stingrays, jellyfish, and alligators surfaced from the lake.

Spades danced his way back to Grayson and bent his head down for Grayson's hand. Grayson and Ethan didn't know what to say. Spades had just brought out every animal in the forest by simply walking in.

The king of the jungle stepped forward. Spades placed his tail on the lion as Grayson placed his hand on Spades.

Why did you come out of the forest? asked Grayson.

The energy. The energy. The energy, repeated the lion. *Steve likes the energy.*

This was the first real taste of power Grayson had ever felt. With the black diamond, Grayson had an entire army of jungle animals at his command. The other animals inched closer to the radiating energy. Grayson petted them one by one as he and Ethan discussed which creatures could help in the tournament.

"We can't take all of them. How about the monkeys? They can hide up in the trees. And the stingrays for the moat?"

"Yeah, good idea," said Ethan. "We gotta bring the snakes too. They'll scare the life out of Dontae and Hardy. Oh, and the alligators."

Will all of you be here tonight? Grayson asked the lion. *I need help defending Emerald House from the other Initiation Groups, but I can't bring you until it gets dark.*

We'll be waiting, said the lion. *If you pick me, I'll destroy them all.*

Grayson thanked the lion and the other animals for their time and announced he would return at 8 p.m. to pick which ones he needed.

"We can't take the lion," whispered Ethan as he, Grayson, and Spades departed from the lake. "As bad as I want to win, we don't need anyone in the other I.G.s getting killed."

Now it was time for what Grayson had been looking forward to most since finding the necklace: telling Ambrielle. When the boys knocked on the fourth-floor dorm, Ambrielle and Harlie were still fast asleep.

"How can it possibly be taking you two this long to get ready? We just wanna talk—you're not going to a modeling contest!" yelled Ethan through the door.

"Shut up!" screamed Ambrielle. Ethan went silent.

Ambrielle emerged from her room. Grayson was quite sure she looked good enough to be in any modeling contest. "Come on in. Wait, what's that? Is that—"

"Oh, this?" asked Grayson, untucking the gold chain and teardrop stone. "It's just a black diamond necklace."

Ambrielle pulled Ethan and Grayson inside the room and sat them down on the couch. Grayson began his tale back on the night he'd seen Mitchell, Dontae, and Hardy in the pizza shop and told the girls everything in between.

"How could we have been so stupid?" Harlie asked. "I thought the only purpose of the book was to get you into the underground room."

Ambrielle clapped her hands together. "So, we did it. We just have to bring the animals to the moat and the trees before the match—our house will be protected, and we'll win. I can't wait to see the look on Ridley's face."

"Our house should be protected," said Ethan, "but there's still no guarantee we break into Ruby House and get their necklace off its statue, unless... Grayson, what if you wore the black diamond *during* the match?"

"To do what with it? Sometimes my vision gets all weird when I wear it. I don't even know if I could function properly with it on."

"Do you have your staff?" asked Ethan, his lips forming into a daring smile. "Let's go have a friendly battle outside. At least this time, we should be able to do something a little more complicated than a swordfight."

Ethan suggested that they go to the campfire behind the church since it wasn't a common hangout spot. On their journey, Grayson's vision went sideways. His reflexes were the only thing keeping him from falling over. The forest trees shifted side to side. He saw black squiggly lines running from the branches down to the snow. Although he couldn't tell for certain, Grayson was sure these were the tree's internal roots. Every tree had the same lines, and they all seemed to connect underground.

"How's this gonna work?" asked Ambrielle once they were all standing around the fire. "Are we all just gonna attack Grayson and see what he can do?"

"I say we just start with one of you for now," said Grayson, who was still having trouble standing.

Ethan stepped forward. The two boys hadn't dueled in months. Grayson knew Ethan wanted to battle at the campfire so he'd have the advantage, and unfortunately, he was standing right by the fire, which meant Ethan's attack would be fast. Grayson could use the dirt from the ground, but with no trees close by, his resources were limited. Even the bushes were too far away for him to develop any type of plan.

Grayson had a brief moment of panic where everything was distorted, and he couldn't think clearly—then he saw more black wavy lines on the ground. The lines reminded him of the roots he had imagined on the way over. Grayson didn't know if there were really roots under him or not, but Ethan had raised his staff. Grayson was going to have to trust his instincts.

"No face shots," said Ethan, who was looking around curiously for anything Grayson could use as a weapon.

"Go!"

Ethan immediately flung his staff sideways toward the fire, sending a flame right at Grayson's midsection.

Grayson, who'd been too busy thinking about what to do, didn't even have his staff out yet. He pulled the globe out of the carrier on his waist and threw it on the ground in front of him. His full-sized, golden staff emerged from the puff of green smoke just in time to block Ethan's flame. Grayson definitely hadn't planned this, but it must have looked cool based on Ethan's shocked expression and the "ooohs" and "aaahs" from Harlie and Ambrielle.

Ethan sent more fire in Grayson's direction, forcing him to dive sideways. Grayson dodged another three attacks. One, he used dirt to stop the flame; the other two, he purposely jumped to his right so Ethan would be forced to follow. Grayson knew Ethan thought he was retreating, which worked out well because he was leading Ethan into a crowded area of underground roots.

Grayson didn't know how to visualize roots he couldn't see grabbing Ethan's legs, so he pretended the wavy lines were the roots, which they might have been—he didn't know. He pointed his staff at Ethan's ankles and pictured the lines bursting through the dirt and latching on to Ethan. They did immediately.

Ethan fell over and stabbed the roots with his staff. He was able to burn some off his legs, but Grayson kept sending more. It was no use. Grayson now had control over both of his arms. He closed his eyes and concentrated on constricting the wavy lines. He only let up once he heard Ethan's staff hit the ground.

Grayson helped Ethan to his feet, and although he was obviously mad about losing, all Ethan said was, "You're wearing it tonight."

Ambrielle bobbed her head in agreement. Even Harlie didn't protest.

"Did you make those roots out of nothing, or were they already there?" asked Ethan, eager to understand how he'd lost.

"Already there."

"But how'd you know?"

"Just saw wavy black lines and was pretty sure they were roots."

"Wavy black lines?"

"Yeah, I can still kinda see them now if I look closely," said Grayson, pointing at the floor of the residence hall.

***

Once back in his room, Grayson reluctantly took off the black diamond; everything seemed so normal without it now. He still had a couple of hours before preparation at Emerald House. He needed to rest, but with his first real test so close and the entire I.G. counting on his plan to work, it was hopeless. Ethan had gone up to Dylan's dorm, which gave Grayson some alone time with his thoughts.

So, if I wear it tonight, there's a good chance I get caught. There's also a good chance it doesn't help me at all, and then I still get caught. My duel with Ethan was pure luck. But if I don't wear it tonight and we lose, I'll always wonder if it would've made a difference.

And that final thought was all Grayson needed to make his decision. Of course, he was going to wear it for the tournament. Why should the fear of failing influence him at all? He'd never let it before; otherwise, he wouldn't be at Icefall. Grayson needed to distract himself from the possible negative outcomes of tonight's tournament. He grabbed a pen and a piece of paper to write down everything he knew about the black diamond necklace.

1. *It showed me something I couldn't see.*

Grayson still didn't understand how he'd seen the underground roots.

2. *It makes controlling earth easier.*

Even if Grayson had been able to see the roots without the necklace, he would've had to work a lot harder than he did to get them out of the ground.

3. *It gives me hints about the future.*

He figured that was the best way to put it. Right before his battle with Ethan, he'd seen the underground roots for the first time.

That was pretty much it. All these points could be valuable in his team's victory tonight; however, the energy was going to be a major problem. If he wore it tonight, he would not be able to touch anyone, including his own teammates. This was going to be impossible during the pre-tournament preparations—they were all in too close of quarters. He needed to hide it on the battleground beforehand.

***

The sun rotated over the city, hid behind the skyscrapers, and disappeared for the night. When Ethan, Ambrielle, Harlie, and Grayson got to the lake, the animals were already waiting.

Spades apologized to the lion on behalf of Grayson for not allowing him to help. Grayson gave the lion a back rub before he pounced back into the jungle. The lion roared a great roar at the touch of the black diamond's energy. The snakes, monkeys, stingrays, and alligators awaited instructions. The others bowed to Spades before their departure.

The tournament is in two hours, informed Spades. *Your job is to stay hidden until it starts. Otherwise, Grayson could get in trouble. He says to protect Emerald House without seriously injuring the other teams.*

How will I get to the moat? I can't breathe out of water, said Sonia, the stingray.

Burt, the alligator, will hold water in his mouth. You and the other stingrays will stay in there until we get to the house. Just don't sting him! You're on the same team!

Burt and Sonia cried out in protest, but Grayson gave them both a back rub, and the flow of black diamond energy was enough to convince the creatures to give into Spades's orders. Burt gulped up a group of stingrays and some lake water while the five monkeys, Kolby, Kyrie, Kevin, Kelsey, and Kate, each carried a snake on their back.

They traveled fast through the dark forest. A light sprinkle of rain fell from the clouds as Ethan and Harlie led the pack, checking around corners to make sure they didn't run into any other Lacers. There were voices at Adriel's Pond, so they took the long way, passing the residence hall. Once at Emerald House, Ethan guarded the door, and Ambrielle and Harlie watched the back trail while Grayson called out orders.

Burt, let Sonia and the others out in the moat. Okay good! Now you follow.

The aquatic animals disappeared into the water. The snakes slithered up the trees. And the monkeys hung from the branches, out of sight. The ambush was set.

"Let's go!" said Ethan.

Grayson started to follow and then rerouted; he had forgotten to hide the necklace on the playing field. Grayson jogged to a thick tree and buried the black diamond deep under its roots as Emerald House's door creaked open. He saw Ridley standing inside, talking to another instructor. Grayson's mind went into panic mode. Ridley hadn't seen him yet. He still had time to make a break for it. He hesitated. His time was up.

"Day?" shouted Ridley, squinting to see through the rain, which was now pouring rather hard. "Get the hell over here!"

Grayson wasn't sure how, but he'd managed to get out of situations just like this one all his life. Sure enough, as he was approaching Ridley, another story magically appeared in his head.

"You aren't due back until eight-thirty. Why are you here?"

"I was looking for you, sir," said Grayson, in the most innocent voice possible. "You know how Harlie Laurence can get a little paranoid sometimes, right? Okay, well anyway, we were together, planning for tonight, when she saw the storm coming. She started having a breakdown because it was raining, and she was worried her electric moat might shock *everyone* instead of just the people in the water. I told her I would come double-check with you just to make sure nobody would get seriously hurt tonight."

Grayson knew he'd succeeded the second he saw Ridley's face. Ridley's mouth was wide open, and he was staring at the floor, clearly unaware that Grayson had stopped talking.

"Sir?"

"What? Oh yeah... uh... right, Miss Laurence. Yeah, no, she'll be okay tonight. Don't worry about her."

***

Grayson's friends were waiting outside the residence hall for him.

"We thought you were done for," said Ethan. "What'd you say to get out of it?"

"Just made up some stuff. I'm going to take a nap."

***

"*The green cloaks are coming! The green cloaks are coming!*"

This wasn't exactly the soothing waterfall noise he had been expecting to wake up to, but when Grayson got up and looked through the peephole to see Dylan and Jeremiah running around banging on everyone's doors with their emerald cloaks on, he couldn't be too mad.

It was time to get ready. Grayson threw on his black workout outfit. He wasn't sure why Dylan and Jeremiah had been wearing their cloaks; come to think of it, he didn't even know what those were for.

When Grayson emerged from his room, the rest of the I.G. was already in the hallway. Everyone was jumping around hyping each other up. Everyone aside from Harlie, who was sitting in the corner quite obviously frightened; for a moment, Grayson thought the story he had made up to Ridley about her had been true. Ambrielle had her back to Grayson, occupied with the task of bringing Harlie to her feet.

"Get up, you baby," said Ambrielle, violently yanking Harlie's arm. "We need you to electrocute the other teams."

***

Grayson and the rest of the I.G. marched through the mud and pouring rain to Emerald House, singing as they went. Harlie was in the back, crying into Ethan's shoulder. Liam, Xander, and Spencer were pushing people around because they "needed to warm up for the match." Grayson was happy to see everyone—aside from Harlie—wasn't as nervous as him.

The house looked the same as it always did: four element training stations in the corners, a pool in the middle, and a stone statue in the center of the water with an emerald necklace that shone brighter than usual. Once everyone was inside, the instructors emerged from the shadows, all of them in their sharpest suits and dresses. Jasper had even slicked his hair back for the occasion.

The I.G. went silent as Ridley popped his staff out to full length and aimed it at the balcony, where twenty plastic bags came flying toward the crowd, one landing perfectly in each P.L.'s hand. Grayson opened his bag and pulled out a full-body, pitch-black compression outfit. He hadn't the slightest clue how anyone expected him to fit into this toddler Halloween costume. When he checked the tag, it read: *Stealth Suit, Large.*

212

"All right, ladies and gentlemen, let's get the ball rolling. Change in the bathrooms. Let's make it quick—we're on a bit of a time squeeze," said Jasper. "Oh, and be sure to put your work outfit in the plastic bag when you're done."

Grayson was last in the boys' line. When it was finally his turn, he spent ten minutes getting the compression suit on and fell over at least five times when it was stuck around his ankles. The suit's material was thin but sturdy. It was some type of magically enhanced fabric. After placing his shoes back on his feet, he looked at himself in the mirror and was shocked to see such a resemblance between his mother's childhood gymnastics pictures and his current self.

"Head down. Eyes closed. Toes over the pool," instructed Ridley, just as he had on the first morning of training. "Ms. Myles is going to draw three names out of this bucket. The three of you selected will be the ones who stay inside this house as a last line of defense for the duration of the match. Ms. Myles, if you would."

"Dylan Foster," said Ms. Myles, coldly with no greeting, "Madison Silver, and Harlie Laurence."

Harlie being inside the house was a good thing. She'd have a clear view of when to turn on the electric moat. Madison being inside with her was not good. She was still mad at Grayson for shooting down her plan the day before, which meant she probably wouldn't be too friendly with Harlie. At least Dylan would be there to moderate things.

Jasper walked around the pool, handing a pair of gloves and a rope to each P.L. "Okay, kiddos… Sticker gloves, a rope, and of course, your staff. Those are the only pieces of equipment you're allowed. Press the red button on the back of each glove to activate them. And I hope for gosh sakes that you already know how to use a rope and your staff. Otherwise, you might as well forfeit. Haha, only joking, kids."

Grayson peeked his eyes open and saw a few of his peers attaching the rope to a loop in the back of the stealth suit. He did the same.

"Heads down, eyes closed!" said Ridley. "Focus. When we conclude here, you'll have five minutes to talk things over, finish planning, reread the rules, whatever the heck you want to do. When the horn sounds, the match has begun. The other instructors and I will be watching from the second floor. I don't care if it's emerald, ruby, or amethyst, but there sure as hell better be a necklace on our statue when that final horn sounds. All three teams are going to be wearing these black stealth suits. Hopefully, you know your I.G. well enough to decipher a friend from a foe. Good luck."

Grayson opened his eyes, and the instructors made their way up to the balcony. Most of the I.G. frantically ran over to reread the rules. All Grayson could think about was getting the black diamond back around his neck.

"Where is it?" asked Ambrielle, whispering into Grayson's ear.

"The front lawn. I have to wait until the match starts. You need to stay by me and cover."

Grayson and Ambrielle went to find Ethan and Harlie.

"Remember, it's just a last resort, but don't hesitate if it needs to be done," said Ethan.

Harlie nodded and made her way up to the roof where she would have a clear view of the battlefield, Dylan right behind her.

214

The rest of the I.G. separated into three groups. Liam and Xander were to stay just outside the house and guard its walls. Ethan, Jeremiah, and five others were preparing to station themselves on the front lawn to activate the booby traps. Grayson and his team of nine were stretching out so they would be able to charge Ruby House at full speed.

Grayson positioned himself closest to the door to ensure he would get to the spot where the necklace was before anyone else. The I.G. counted down from three and threw their globes at the ground, covering themselves in multicolor smoke. The horn erupted across the playing field.

OWWOHHHHHH. OWWOHHHHH.

Staff in hand, Grayson shot out the front door like a sniper bullet, not checking to see what anyone else was doing. The other houses weren't far away; the other teams would be there soon. Grayson reached the tree and did a baseball slide into the dirt. He frantically dug through the mud and pulled out the necklace. He clipped it around his neck as the rest of his attack squad caught up with him.

"Jeez, couldn't you wait for us?" asked Brenda Lewis.

"He knows what he's doing, Brenda," said Ambrielle.

"I wanted to be the first one out here to see which house is coming for us," said Grayson, tucking the necklace into his compression outfit.

It was pitch black outside, making it difficult to see. The heavy rain didn't make hearing any easier. Grayson led his group down the far-left boundary of the playing field so they could sneak up on

215

Ruby House. He was sure the opposing teams hadn't spotted them yet. His necklace hadn't given him any warning.

The longer they crept along, the more Grayson got a feel for what was happening around him. He could hear yelling from behind, which meant either the Ruby or Amethyst team was now attacking their house. As he got closer to Ruby House, it became obvious they were not the ones attacking.

Grayson pulled his team into a ditch where he had a perfect view of all twenty members of the Ruby team standing guard. The house had fire pits and water pools everywhere but very few trees. Grayson contemplated turning around to help guard Emerald House with his team. Seriously, what was the point of trying to win a twenty-against-ten battle? Everyone remained silent while Grayson decided their fate.

He took a deep breath. Grayson didn't know what made him do it. Maybe it was confidence from the necklace; maybe it was Ethan's voice in his head telling him to never back down from a fight no matter what the odds of winning were. They had to get that ruby necklace. Otherwise, their plan would fail.

"Charge!" screamed Grayson, jumping out of the ditch and heading for the entrance to Ruby House.

The underground roots, said a voice in Grayson's head. It was too dark to see the wavy black lines, but with five Ruby players about to plummet him, he had to try and imagine them anyway. They erupted from the ground the second he closed his eyes and aimed his staff.

Grayson summoned every root he could, tying the limbs of the opposition, whipping them in the face. He could tell they were confused. Both teams had on the same black compression outfits, making it look like complete chaos when Grayson opened his eyes. He saw a clear path to the front door. His team was doing a good enough job keeping the others distracted.

He bolted forward, running; he was running, almost there, then *plow!* Grayson had been running so fast that he hadn't noticed a massive hole in the ground. Dontae and Hardy were glaring down at him.

"Gotcha, punk," said Dontae, grabbing Grayson by the shirt and pulling him out of the hole. "Let's have some fun with this one, huh, Hardy?"

Grayson was in trouble—what was he thinking charging this house? There was a reason the Emerald team always lost... He tried to escape. If they touched him any longer, they would feel the energy. Grayson still had his staff, but with no trees around and too many distractions to use the roots, all he could do was prepare himself for a serious beating.

"You wanna know what our house is like? Here, let me introduce your face to its wall," said Hardy, picking Grayson up and throwing him right into the concrete.

As he flew through the air for what seemed like an eternity, Grayson braced himself for contact that never came. When he opened his eyes, he wasn't outside anymore; he was inside Ruby House. He hadn't gone through the door.

He had flown through the cement wall.

The inside of the house was nothing like what he'd imagined. The building was the exact same as Emerald House, but instead of element training stations, the whole room was filled with desks like one big lecture hall. In the middle of it all was the statue Grayson needed to climb. Still mesmerized by how he'd gotten inside in the first place, he casually walked toward the statue. Three players screamed down at him from the second-floor balcony.

"Hey, you! What the heck? How did you—"

Grayson ran for the statue. The three guards inside had been relaxing in lawn chairs, clearly not expecting anyone to get through their defenses. Grayson threw his rope around the statue's arm and began to climb like he was back in gym class. He pulled the ruby necklace off the statue's neck and fell to the floor. He clipped the necklace to his stealth suit where the rope had previously been, grabbed his staff off the ground, and sprinted for the front door.

"Get his right! I got the left!"

The three guards were trying to trap him. Grayson ran around the classroom, trying to escape, but he was exhausted. One of the guards illegally swung his staff at Grayson's face and connected, knocking him out briefly.

When Grayson regained consciousness, he was lying back outside in the mud. Well, part of him was. Grayson's legs were still on the other side of the wall. The Ruby guards tried to pull him back inside, but Grayson twisted and kicked his way free until he could get his whole body out. He only had a few seconds before they would come after him, so he got to his feet and ran using every bit of strength he had left.

"I got it! I got it!" he yelled as he passed through the still ongoing battle. "I got it! Retreat! Retreat!"

Grayson saw Ambrielle and a few of his other teammates break off from their fights and follow him. He also witnessed a couple of them being dragged to the cell blocks by the Ruby players. He put his head down and kept running through the rain.

Emerald House was a complete and utter disaster. Multiple people from both the Amethyst and Emerald teams were unconscious on the front lawn. The trees were on fire. The Amethyst players had driven what was left of the Emerald team back to the front entryway. The monkeys and snakes sensed danger and scurried off from the battle.

"Do it, Harlie! Do it now!" screamed Liam as he jumped over the moat.

Burt picked up the stingrays in his mouth and waddled out of the water just in the nick of time. Grayson plunged into the moat and paddled with all his might. He was almost across when Harlie turned on the electricity. Grayson and the entire Amethyst team were electrocuted. The stealth suit absorbed some of the blow, but the shockwave's power was still enough to make Grayson fall into the mud on the other side, too weak to get up.

He could hear the pursuing Ruby team closing in. He tried to climb to his feet, but his body was numb. He felt the ruby necklace being ripped off his suit, by whom he didn't know. Everything went black and white. He saw a woman's face—a woman he didn't know. The curls of her hair gently brushed against her cheeks. She was frozen like a photograph. The last thing Grayson remembered was taking off his black diamond necklace with the intention to bury it deep in the mud, where he now lay unconscious.

CHAPTER 14

Hell on a Holy Day

"The best times in life are temporary and are always a result of the worst times," said Mr. Bruce.

Oscar nodded. "Good and bad feelings don't last forever because neither are real. They are imaginary concepts that end immediately when someone's mind chooses to end them."

"I wish I could remember these conversations," said Grayson, resting in his usual back right corner.

"What do you mean by I?" asked Oscar. "You remember our last drive, do you not?"

"I remember it while I'm here now, but I won't remember when I wake up."

"You are not sleeping," said Oscar. "The brain sleeps. The mind does not. You are not your physical brain. You are the formless spirit within it... You remember our conversations perfectly well."

Grayson gazed out the back window and through the walls of the skyscrapers as if they did not exist. He looked through the trees and across the ponds until he found his physical body in the arms of Ridley, being carried inside Emerald Residence Hall. "If this is me right here, then who is that boy?"

"He is a simpler version of you. One that can be understood. Without the real you, your body is meaningless."

Grayson took a moment to contemplate his grandpa's words. He knew them to be true, but he couldn't understand why he was on a bus, having a conversation his physical self wouldn't remember.

"You are here because you are entering a tricky time in your life," explained Oscar. "It's your first year away from home, you have a powerful object in your possession, you deal with physical training that exhausts your mind, and you are young enough to let your relationships with other people affect your mood... You will carry the voices of peace that Mr. Bruce and I provide in the back of your mind as you live your life."

"How does that help if I don't remember?"

"The subconscious mind is too complex for a rushed explanation. It will have to wait until your next visit—it's time for you to return to your body... I'll say this once more before you depart: Neither good nor bad feelings are real unless you make them real. You can't help the world or the people around you if your mind isn't at peace. Oh, and Grayson, remember the lesson from our last ride: If you believe you are different from the other Lacers, then you are. Don't hesitate to do what you believe is right."

Mr. Bruce put the bus in park and opened the doors. The church was still far in the distance as the gray mist of Grayson's mind glided across Icefall Lane.

***

"Wooohoooo!"

"LET'S GO! WE DID IT!"

"I didn't let one person up our wall!"

Grayson stirred in his bed at the sound of the celebratory screams.

"Quiet down," urged Ethan.

"Is he still out, Jasper?" asked Ridley cautiously.

Grayson kept his eyes closed tight, trying to absorb where he was and what was going on around him. Had his instructors found the black diamond? Grayson couldn't remember what he had done with it.

"Like a light." Jasper chuckled. "I can't believe the kid pulled it off. I knew he was talented, but to do this... Whew."

They'd won! Someone from the Emerald team must have taken the ruby necklace from him while he was on the ground and brought it to the statue.

"Yes, quite impressive. How exactly did he pull this off?" asked Ridley. Grayson could feel this question wasn't directed at Jasper.

"I don't know," said Ethan. "I wasn't attacking Ruby House with him. I was guarding our house."

"Yes," said Ridley, "but you live with him. Perhaps you've seen him with or doing something unusual?"

"Oh, for gosh sakes, Ridley. The kid doesn't have it," interjected Jasper.

"The question is valid. According to the Ruby instructors, Mr. Day was spotted in some unlikely predicaments, not to mention a couple of participants claim they felt a powerful energy coming from Grayson himself. None of them can even answer how he got inside the house in the first place. I watch the kid train every day;

he's shown no ability to get past twenty second-year P.L.s. And why did half the animals in the forest decide to conspire against the Ruby and Amethyst I.G.s?"

"They didn't hurt anyone, Ridley. I'm sure they were bored and just wanted to have some fun."

Grayson remained still on his bed, trying to come up with another fabricated story. They hadn't found the necklace, and they had no way to prove Grayson was the one who convinced the animals to help.

"We're the best! We're the best!" chanted Dylan.

"Shut that darn door!" barked Ridley.

The door slammed shut, causing Grayson to flinch.

"You awake, champ?" asked Jasper.

He didn't have much of a choice other than to get up now, so he opened his eyes, fake yawned, and said, "What... what happened?"

"We were hoping you could tell us."

"W... Well," stammered Grayson. "I took a couple of blows to the head, so the whole match is kinda cloudy... But I remember a couple of the Ruby guards threw me inside their house to mess with me, and I locked the door on them before they could get inside."

"Uh-huh. And how did you get out of the house?"

"Well... I didn't, really. One of them hit me in the face with their staff," said Grayson, indicating a bruise on his cheek. "They threw me down into a hole outside the front door. Then, I think, someone distracted them, which gave me an opportunity to run."

"Told ya, Ridley. The kid got the job done—"

"You weren't stuck in a wall at any point during this match?"

"Stuck in a wall?" repeated Grayson curiously. "No, but I think my head hit a couple of walls. They beat me up pretty good. I was lucky to get away."

"Let the kid celebrate! Hell, the whole city is right now! Emerald I.G. winning the first round of the Necklace Raid hasn't happened in years," said Jasper, holding the exit door open for Ridley to follow.

Having spent most of the match away from his team, Grayson had plenty of stories to listen to during the group celebration in the hallway outside his room. Dylan had accidentally fallen off the roof right into a trio of Amethyst invaders, Ethan had managed to drag two others into a cell block, and best of all, Ambrielle had been the one who'd grabbed the ruby necklace from Grayson and placed it around the statue before time expired. She'd also rushed back to him after the match was over to hide the black diamond, which had been lying under Grayson's chest in the mud. It was now in her dorm.

"Where did all those monkeys come from?"

"I don't know, but I'm glad they were on our side."

For the evening, Grayson and Ambrielle were treated like royalty among their I.G. Grayson must have been asked thirty times how he managed to break into Ruby House. He would merely shrug his shoulders in response each time. Nathan Bowen and Kevin Workman, two boys Grayson had barely talked to this year, even bowed to him.

Although it was unspoken, Liam and Grayson had somehow developed respect for one another after the night's events. From what Grayson had heard, Liam had guarded the walls of Emerald House with a tremendous amount of fight. Grayson could tell Liam was jealous of all the attention he was getting, so he decided to thank Liam for guarding the house while he was gone. The two boys shook hands in the end.

Xander, on the other hand, had been taken away from his post by two Amethyst players and forced into a cell block. Having heard this information, the party became even more enjoyable for Grayson. Jeremiah brought a speaker and a couple of pizza boxes to the hallway. Grayson had no idea how Jeremiah managed to get that much food into the residence hall—he didn't ask. Grayson filled his empty stomach and danced to the music. Everything was going great, better than great.

Ambrielle was smiling, dancing, and appeared to be having fun for once. Grayson loved it when she wasn't so guarded. For the first time, he felt relaxed talking to her. He really wanted to be alone with Ambrielle. Getting praise from his team was nice and all, but she was the only person in the world he cared to talk to.

Grayson's strategy had worked, the instructors hadn't found the black diamond, and Xander had performed horribly. What was stopping one more thing from playing out in his favor? He asked Ambrielle if they could talk alone.

"Is your eye okay?" Grayson asked softly as Ambrielle sat down across from him on the couch.

Ambrielle laughed and poked her own bruise. "It's fine."

Grayson smiled. "You know, you were really great tonight."

"Grayson, why did you want to talk to me?" Ambrielle asked, curiously tilting her head.

Grayson remained silent for a long time, not because he didn't know the answer to her question, but because he was too scared to tell her the truth. He had wanted to kiss Ambrielle from the moment he saw her, and he figured tonight was the perfect opportunity. Grayson was sure she already knew he wanted to, so instead of telling her, Grayson closed his eyes and leaned in to kiss her. He could feel her leaning in, just for a moment... then she hugged him.

"Not exactly what I was going for," said Grayson, smelling Ambrielle's hair as she pulled away from him.

"I know. I know," she said. "It's just... I can't. It's not like I haven't thought about it or don't want to. I just can't."

Grayson's spirits were slightly lifted. She'd basically just said she wanted to kiss him.

"Ummm, why can't you?" he asked.

"My dad," said Ambrielle.

"Because of your dad?"

"Because of my dad."

Of all the answers Grayson had expected, this was not one of them.

"He's not the nicest man, and let's just say he wouldn't approve of you."

"Why? What the heck is wrong with me?" asked Grayson, louder than he'd intended.

"Nothing," corrected Ambrielle, shushing him. "He wouldn't approve of any guy. You'll see what I mean at the Christmas party."

"What Christmas party?"

Ambrielle put her face in her hands. "I forgot the instructors haven't mentioned it to everyone yet. My dad told me about it. I wasn't supposed to say anything."

Apparently, the I.G. would be spending the next few weeks setting up for a Christmas party where everyone's families would show up to surprise and celebrate with them. Grayson wasn't mad at Ambrielle for spoiling this; he'd almost had a heart attack at his last surprise party. He promised not to tell the others.

"Let's make a deal. If I can win over your dad at the Christmas party, I get to kiss you on New Year's Eve."

"You aren't talking to my dad at the party."

"We'll see." Grayson grinned with newfound determination.

***

Ridley gave the I.G. the next day off training. Ethan seemed to think this was because he and the other instructors were busy celebrating with the rest of Icefall. Grayson could hear Icefall Lane bursting with excitement throughout the night. *"Emeralds rule! Emeralds rule!"*

He really didn't know why their victory was a big deal to the citizens of Icefall, who hadn't even watched the match. He guessed Lacers just used any excuse they could to party.

Things returned to normal the following day. Training was back on. The instructors were in somewhat better moods than usual. The chants from Icefall Lane could still be heard from inside Emerald House. Each time the echoes of praise came through the house's non-existent roof, Ridley would nod in approval, and Jasper would sing along, using his staff as a microphone.

"We can't give an inch as far as training goes. We still have another round to win before this tournament concludes," said Ridley, desperately trying to keep a sense of urgency among the I.G.

Ridley never asked Grayson about the black diamond again, nor did the other instructors. Mr. Hill and Ms. Myles would keep their hands on Grayson's back longer than usual before pushing him into the pool to check for energy, but Grayson saw no need to risk bringing the necklace to training.

"Even if they think you have it," Ethan told him once, "they don't want anyone else to think that. I bet they feel special for beating the older initiation groups. You cheating would take all that way."

***

Ridley didn't mention anything about a Christmas party for another two weeks. It was a cool December morning, and Grayson had just given the I.G. a set of twenty push-ups because he'd decided to make a joke while Ms. Myles was talking.

"As I'm sure you're all aware, Christmas is rapidly approaching," said Ridley, with little Christmas joy in his voice. "And since you all surpassed our expectations in the Necklace Raid, the other instructors and I see it fit to throw a Christmas party here at Emerald House. As you know, no true pleasure comes without prior hard work. Starting tonight, you will all be setting up for the party. The mayor of Icefall will be in attendance, so our house must be spotless unless you want Master Emerson to kick all of you out of the program."

"How did you already know about the party if we're only having one because we won the Necklace Raid?" whispered Grayson.

"We still would've had one even if we lost. They're all full of it," said Ambrielle, pointing her staff at the instructors.

The I.G. frantically disarmed the booby traps outside the house. Grayson and Liam crushed the few burned trees still standing. Ambrielle and the water controllers emptied the moat. The fans, power cables, and campfires were demilitarized as well.

The final days before Christmas were filled with a lot of errand-running. Jasper sent Liam and Grayson to Icefall Lane to get decorations. He had always told them they could get food while there as long as they got him some as well. Ethan got lots of wake-up texts from his wristwatch telling him to go fix posters in the house because the wind had knocked them over. Ambrielle and Harlie spent most of their time shoveling the constant falling snow or setting up chairs for the party.

The I.G. finished decorating and cleaning Emerald House in a matter of days. But the instructors continued giving them busy work since they couldn't punish them with workouts for winning the Necklace Raid.

"You're so lucky it's on an off day," said Ethan. "My birthday was torture. I mean, you already have it easy with Jasper, and now you get out of this!"

Birthdays weren't something the I.G. discussed; in fact, they avoided the topic at all costs. When he happened to look down at his clipboard on someone's special day, Ridley found it quite entertaining to make the birthday P.L. suffer more than the rest of the group. He would give them an extra leg or ab workout—that was their present; they got to choose. Fortunately, Grayson would not have to deal with this.

For all of Grayson's life, December 25th had been much more than a day to receive presents. It had been a day to receive double presents. Being the only child his parents had to buy gifts for meant he was always in for a pretty good haul. However, not having any siblings wasn't the only reason Jeff and Cristina went out of their way to make this day special. Christmas Day also happened to be Grayson's birthday. Being born on the biggest holiday of the year had its pros and cons. The holiday season was always spectacular, but once the new year rolled around, it was another twelve months before he had something to celebrate.

On Christmas Eve, Grayson, Ethan, Ambrielle, and Harlie all huddled around the campfire behind the church. They weren't technically breaking Ridley's rules because they were a few hundred feet away from Icefall Lane. Ethan got the fire blazing, and together the four of them listened to the cheers from the bars and the peaceful chimes from the clock tower above the church. They curled up in blankets and snacked on the vanilla cupcakes Dylan had smuggled to them.

Grayson took a moment to appreciate the new life he had at Icefall. Everything was so different here, but that was exactly what he'd wanted his whole life, to do something different, something fun. While training wasn't always fun, winning the Necklace Raid had been a blast, and like Ridley always said, *no true pleasure comes without prior hard work*. Grayson watched the Lacers in the street laughing, drinking, having a good time; they'd put in years of training, and this was their reward. He'd be there in just a few short years.

Grayson imagined his mom here at Icefall years ago, thinking about the same things he was now. He did miss his parents, and the thought of seeing their faces and listening to their voices the next day was all the comfort he needed to fall asleep by the fire, under the shimmering stars, completely at peace.

***

Grayson woke up by the recently exhausted fire one year older than he had been the night before. Fifteen didn't feel a whole lot different from fourteen, although the thought of being halfway to thirty was a little scary.

The sun was already high in the sky and had begun to melt away some of the previous night's snow. Grayson checked his wristwatch—the Christmas party started in one hour. Ridley had also sent out a message informing the I.G. that they'd be dressing in their emerald cloaks for the first time. Grayson woke up his drowsy friends, and the four of them exchanged Christmas hugs. Ethan chased Grayson around the fire, trying to give him fifteen lucky punches before they set off for the dorms to get ready.

Once at Emerald House, Grayson tried his hardest to look busy. He walked around straightening posters, fixing branches on Christmas trees, doing everything he could to avoid carrying in the hundreds of food trays with the catering team. He didn't want to take the chance of spilling something on his cloak. Grayson thought it was obvious their parents would be coming. There was no way the twenty kids in the I.G. could go through that much food.

All the element training stations on the first floor had been temporarily cleared out by the instructors and replaced with seating for the feast. Grayson looked up at the stone statue in the middle of the pool. The emerald and ruby necklaces around its neck made him wish he had his own necklace on. With the instructors still suspicious, Grayson had decided it best to let Ambrielle keep the black diamond hidden in her room until things cooled down.

"All right, P.L.s, listen up," announced Ridley once everything was in place. "We have some guests who will be attending the party with us today. Let them in, Jasper."

Jasper hauled open the front door; it was like he'd removed a wall on a dam. The house was flooded with a swarm of anxious parents. Harlie and Jessica Baker immediately started crying. Grayson, on the other hand, opened his mouth wide in fake shock and was embraced by his charging mom with a bear hug, his dad with their usual handshake.

"Happy birthday, sweetheart!"

Cristina examined every inch of Grayson's body. She pulled some cream out of her purse and started dabbing it on his bruises. She stacked questions on top of questions, not even giving Grayson time to answer.

"You don't have it, do you?" Cristina asked, finally pausing to ensure Grayson could respond.

Grayson knew the question would be asked, and he wanted to tell the truth. But when it came down to it, he just couldn't risk having it taken away from him, or even worse, having his I.G.'s victory revoked for cheating. Grayson assured both his parents he hadn't inherited the black diamond from Oscar. Cristina hugged him again and said she hadn't believed those rumors for a second.

Jeff didn't seem convinced. "It's a good thing you don't, son," he said firmly. "If you were ever to be caught with that, lord knows what kind of mess that would create. Nothing like that has ever happened before in the history of our kind."

Well, that didn't make Grayson worry at all. He knew he needed to take his dad's warning seriously and never risk being caught with it again. He couldn't get his family into trouble.

The three of them sat down at a table, enjoyed some lasagna, and caught up on their months apart. Jeff and Cristina both said they'd been working more since Grayson's absence. They also congratulated him on winning the first round of the Necklace Raid—apparently, it had made the Lacer News. Grayson found it nice to be recognized for something other than the missing necklace, even if the necklace was the only reason he had won the match.

Ethan and his parents joined them at the table. The six of them back together made Grayson feel like he was in the Clarks' backyard on a Sunday, grilling out, when his only worry in the world was what he'd scored on his science test. While being back with his loved ones was great, Grayson hadn't forgotten his main objective of the evening. He scanned the room until he found Ambrielle and her mammoth of a father sitting at a table in the corner. The two were sitting far apart from each other, not speaking.

Just as Grayson was about to step away from his table, Mitchell Clark arrived at the party. After greeting his parents, Mitchell pulled up a chair next to Grayson and Ethan.

"You two sure you don't wanna run away again?" asked Mitchell, slapping Ethan's shoulder.

"We were just imitating you," replied Ethan.

"I was so confused," said Mitchell, ignoring Ethan's joke. "Then I talked to Dontae and Hardy. I hope they didn't scare you too bad. They weren't being serious. I used to do the same thing to them."

Since Grayson couldn't tell Mitchell the real reason he'd run out of Marty's Brews that night, he and Ethan both acted terrified of Dontae and Hardy. Mitchell asked them repeatedly if they'd thought about dropping out of the initiation process; each time, Grayson assured him they weren't going to.

"This is probably going to be my last year of training," Mitchell told them. "Even if I were to qualify for the fifth year, I don't know if I'd accept. The workouts are supposedly unbearable."

Mitchell had all summer to provide Grayson with information about the initiation process, but no, he had to pick right now to ramble on about it. Grayson found a way to excuse himself and headed for Ambrielle's table.

As he approached, he got nervous and decided to go to the bathroom instead. Ambrielle hadn't been lying about her dad—he looked like one mean Lacer. Mr. Stone was twice the size of Dontae from the Ruby I.G. The only average part of his body was his balding head, which was complemented by his wrinkled face, probably from constantly frowning.

Grayson stopped just on the other side of the bathroom door, took a deep breath, and realized he couldn't delay meeting Ambrielle's dad—he had to do it now. Grayson pulled the bathroom door open and walked right into one of the caterers who'd been trying to enter, knocking a tray full of pots to the ground. Luckily there hadn't been any food in the trays, but the clanging noise had still been enough to draw all eyes to them.

Embarrassed, Grayson helped the Lacer pick up the trays. The caterer looked furious. Grayson didn't know if knocking over food trays was a forbidden scenario in the Lacing world, but all the other caters seemed angry too. Grayson didn't care. It wasn't his fault the man had decided to take his work with him to the bathroom. Not daring to speak to Ambrielle's dad after that mess, he went and sat back down by his parents.

Emerson arrived and made his way around the room in his white cloak. Other than the preacher inside the church, Emerson was still the only Lacer Grayson had seen fancy that color. When Emerson reached their table, he and Jeff shook hands. Grayson guessed his dad had forgiven him for behaving in such an "unprofessional manner" during the recruitment process. Jeff got a phone call and stepped away momentarily, leaving Grayson with Emerson.

"Congratulations on the first-round win."

Grayson tried to sound modest by talking up Jasper's training. He didn't need Emerson thinking he had the necklace, too.

"I'm glad the initiation process is going well," said Emerson as he looked around the room, imposing his will.

The way Emerson tried to make his authority known to other Lacers reminded Grayson of how Liam acted when he wanted to impress the I.G.; the only difference was that, as the mayor of Icefall, Emerson had an excuse to act this way. Jeff, who was still on the phone by the front door, waved Emerson over to join him. Grayson continued to snack on his food. He couldn't waste time talking to Emerson anyway. He needed a new game plan to introduce himself to Ambrielle's dad.

With everyone around him engaged in conversation, it would've been a good time to meet Mr. Stone; however, something about his dad and Emerson rooted Grayson to his seat. Grayson racked his brain for possible conversation topics between them. He tried casting a glance in their direction, but Emerson was already staring at him. Jeff had hung up the phone and was now whispering fiercely into Emerson's ear.

Something was going on. Had someone found his necklace? Grayson didn't think his dad would turn him in. Jeff casually moved away from Emerson to the far side of the room. Emerson suddenly became intrigued by a fruit platter next to the table with all the Christmas presents. Grayson was still being watched; it felt like the two of them were trying to sneak up on him.

He considered making a run for it back to his dorm, but it was Jeff who broke into a sprint.

Grayson watched in shock as his dad body-slammed two of the caterers. A fireball from the torch on the ceiling was sent directly at Grayson's chest. He was able to dodge it by falling out of his chair at the last moment, but that didn't stop the table from catching fire.

The guests screamed and ran for the exit. Grayson got to his feet and pulled out his staff. With so many people running and yelling, Grayson had trouble finding his attackers. There he was! The caterer who'd bumped into him by the bathroom was now standing on the balcony, launching fire in his direction.

Grayson saw a Christmas tree to the Lacer's right and was about to send it toward his face when Emerson flew across the house like a hungry eagle and took Grayson airborne. Together the two of them broke through the wall and plummeted into the snow. Grayson couldn't believe Emerson had taken flight. He also couldn't fathom why he'd left the battle.

Grayson scrambled to his feet and tried to run back through the hole they'd just created. Emerson grabbed him by the waist and yanked him down again. Grayson's last view inside Emerald House was of his father and Jasper shielding the caterers from getting through the hole.

"*Get him to the penthouse!*" screamed Jeff as he lost his footing and fell to the ground.

Emerson kicked off hard from the ground. He and Grayson flew away from the house toward Icefall Lane.

"*What are you doing?*" yelled Grayson through the wind, still fighting to get free despite being twenty feet in the air. "We can't leave them!"

Emerson said nothing. Grayson could tell he was exhausted. Surely, he wasn't used to flying with someone else. The two of them crash-landed in an alleyway opposite Marty's Brews.

Grayson had stopped resisting but was now threatening Emerson. "If something happens to my family, I'm going to kill you!" he cried as they stumbled into the first floor of a skyscraper.

"Call E.R.O.L immediately. There's been a breach. We need backup now," ordered Emerson to two frightened women at the front desk of the tower. "And you, get us an elevator to the penthouse."

One of the young girls ran over to the elevator and swiped her key card. The ride to the top was silent. Grayson was overcome with anger. He didn't even know where he was going, probably to some detention cell where he'd be left wondering what the heck was going on for hours.

The elevator slid open, revealing a single door at the end of a short hallway. The receptionist stayed behind while Emerson rushed Grayson forward. Emerson didn't knock; he threw open the unlocked door and said, "We're under attack. I need you to keep Grayson safe while I go back to help."

Grayson wasn't in a detention cell. He was in a dimly lit apartment with thousands of books all around the living room. A hooded figure remained still in an armchair facing away from Grayson and Emerson.

"I told you this would happen, Emerson," grunted the figure as he pulled down his hood and faced them. "Go back now. I'll protect him."

A man with an untidy beard and tangled gray hair rose to his feet. It was Walter Frost.

CHAPTER 15

Chain Link

"You need to go with him and help!" urged Grayson as Emerson charged for the exit. "You have a black diamond necklace. I know you do."

"And so do you," muttered Frost under his breath as he limped toward the window.

Grayson froze. Was it possible that Frost knew the truth, or did he just have his suspicions like everyone else?

"I don't have a darn thing," spat Grayson. "And if you think for one second—"

"Save it, kid. You think I'm just another one of those morons down on the street?" growled Frost, pressing his finger hard into the glass, right down at the never-ending party on Icefall Lane. "Maybe you think I'm just another one of your instructors who doesn't have an ounce of knowledge about how our world works? Your grandfather and I were not raised in such naive times."

Grayson wanted, even needed, to stay focused on what was going on at Emerald House, but Frost's insults about the Lacers of Icefall struck Grayson's interest. All the questions he had about the process of becoming a Lacer could be answered by Walter Frost. Perhaps Grayson's best course of action was to extract as much information as he could while he was stuck in the apartment anyway.

"Your family and friends are going to be fine," said Frost, after a moment's silence. "How many attackers were there? Seven? Maybe eight?"

"No more than ten," said Grayson, thinking back to how many caterers had been carrying in food.

"Has it crossed your mind yet, why a group of Lacers that small felt perfectly comfortable planning an attack at a party where they were outnumbered six to one? I didn't think so," said Frost, still gazing out the window. "It's okay. Your instructors probably won't think about it either. Let me answer the question for you."

Grayson's eyes were locked on Frost. He wanted the man's knowledge.

"It's because the attackers knew darn well ninety percent of them would run. They did scream and run, didn't they?" Frost asked.

"Most of 'em."

"Don't you find it odd that only a select few, fully trained Lacers, felt the need to protect themselves? Hell, I bet your Initiation Group's fighting back more right now than the parents are."

"My dad was fighting back," said Grayson proudly.

"Ha!" choked out Frost. "You think your grandpa would let a man marry your mom without getting his head on straight? Oscar Day would have warned him about the dangers of our world. He would have told him about our purpose here."

"Whose purpose?" asked Grayson, joining Frost by the window where he could see smoke coming from the direction of Emerald House.

"You and me. Lacers. Why did Lacers suddenly start appearing out of the blue? Because we have a purpose."

Grayson thought back to his first day of training. Ridley said the I.G. needed to learn to control themselves so they wouldn't retaliate when humans treated them wrong. Was that the purpose Frost was referring to?

"That's what they want you to believe," said Frost, answering the question Grayson hadn't asked out loud. "But that doesn't seem like much of a purpose to me. What do you think?"

Frost reading his mind hadn't surprised Grayson; he'd been sure Frost had that ability since their first encounter. It was the way Frost so clearly saw things about Lacers that scared Grayson. Why had he trusted this strange group that took him in? Or maybe Frost was the one who couldn't be trusted... He'd been a friend of Oscar's—a man Grayson hadn't even known. What was that worth?

"Then what is a Lacer's *actual* purpose?" Grayson asked.

"There's no use for you to know," said Frost, reseating himself in his recliner. "Even if I told you, and somehow the twisted Lacer Initiation Process didn't make you forget all about it, there'd still be nothing you could do to fulfill it."

It was no use to try and argue with a grumpy old man who could read his mind, so Grayson tried a different approach.

"My grandpa would've told me why I was here. He would've helped me understand what was going on. He would've told me how to handle the black diamond, and he definitely wouldn't have given up on his purpose like you, just because you think it's *no use*," said Grayson, using air quotes.

"You never met your grandpa, kid. Remember? You thought about that when you were deciding whether or not to trust me… Anyway, your mom's coming up to get you," said Frost, picking up a picture from his end table. "If you really want answers to all your questions, there's only one Lacer who can help you, and that's you. But not a you whose mind is stressed and confused. You need to find a place to relax and think."

"That's easier said than done."

"There is one place. Here in the city," said Frost, opening his apartment door for Grayson to leave. "The Stream of Serenity."

"*The Stream of Serenity*," repeated Grayson. "Where is it? There's a bunch of different streams in this city."

"I can't tell you where it is or how to enter it. That's on you."

Grayson shook his head in frustration. There was no reason Frost couldn't tell him the stream's location. As for entering the stream, he didn't need instructions on how to get into the water. Grayson was walking for the exit when Frost set the photograph he'd been holding down on a bookshelf. Grayson paused to look at it. He'd seen it before. The black and white picture showed a curly-haired woman, maybe in her late twenties. Grayson was about to ask Frost who she was when Frost questioned him first.

"Did you have the necklace on when you saw her?" he asked softly.

"Yeah," replied Grayson, thinking back to his final moments of consciousness during the Necklace Raid. "Why exactly did I see her?"

"It's called a chain link. Black diamond holders can see into each other's minds during periods of great despair, exhaustion, or shock. It's supposed to be our one weakness. In my opinion, it's a strength for us right now," said Frost, shutting the door on Grayson as the elevator reached the top floor.

***

After a lot of sobbing from Cristina in the hallway, Grayson calmed his mom down by the time they made it to Icefall Lane. Grayson saw the partying Lacers through a new lens. He maneuvered between the crowd with his arm around his mother. He was sure to keep a lookout for any more of the caterers.

"They've all been arrested," said Cristina. "Dad, Emerson, and a couple of your instructors were able to overpower them. Yes, your dad's going to be okay. He's a little banged up but has no serious injuries. He's back at work now trying to sort this whole thing out."

Grayson insisted on leaving Icefall to check on him; however, his mom assured him there was no need to go. Besides, he would be kicked out of the program if he exited the city under any circumstance. On their way back to Emerald House, Cristina informed Grayson that Ridley had been injured in the attack and was rushed out of Icefall to the nearest hospital.

"Icefall doesn't have a hospital?" asked Grayson.

"No, sweetie. Life-threatening injuries aren't a common issue here."

Emerald House was in ruins. The fire had been extinguished, but the thick gray smoke continued to rise, creating a storm cloud above the scene. Grayson's I.G. and their families were talking in groups outside the house. Everyone's eyes went to Grayson as he walked through the crowd. Emerson stood just inside the hole he'd created while trying to get Grayson out of the attack.

"How's Master Ridley?" asked Grayson, wishing deep down the jerk would be absent from training for a while.

Jasper jogged over to join the conversation. "Ah, he'll be all right. A couple of broken ribs, a broken arm, and uh… there's one more thing. Oh yeah, a dislocated shoulder. Part of the balcony fell on him," he finished cheerfully, pointing to the missing space on the second floor.

"Jasper, where was your brother during the attack? Jeff Day said he didn't see him in the fight," said Emerson.

"I think he was in the bathroom, Mr. Master Mayor," replied Jasper, playfully punching Emerson in the shoulder blade. "I always used to get mad at him for taking so long back when we were kids, but ya know, I guess a man can only go so fast."

Emerson turned away from Jasper and proceeded to explain to Grayson the current situation. "We're going to keep a guard with you until the orchestrator of this attack is apprehended. We have reason to believe you and your grandpa's old necklace were their targets."

"How did they get inside the city?" asked Cristina.

Emerson explained that all eight of the caterers had full-day access passes that they'd stolen from each member of the actual catering team. Apparently, one of the caterers was found dead in his house, which led to Jeff getting a heads-up call from his work. Grayson was glad to hear nobody other than Ridley had been hurt in the attack; after all, he and the necklace had been what those attackers were after.

Emerson positioned himself in the middle of the crowd to make a statement while all the families were still present. He apologized for the lack of security, assured the parents that their kids were going to be safe, and informed them that the Christmas Day activities had come to an end.

Many of the parents were skeptical about leaving their children. After listening to Harlie's parents talk to Emerson, it was clear where she'd gotten her harmless personality. Mr. and Mrs. Laurence were the type of Lacers Grayson could tell were quiet just by looking at them. They both stood a foot shorter than Emerson and held each other close while they whispered questions about the I.G.'s safety going forward.

Grayson walked his mom all the way to the front entry building. Cristina cried the whole way there, saying how she couldn't believe they'd gotten so close to her baby. She was also upset that the coffee maker she'd brought for Grayson had been burned during the attack. At least his dad's "Real Man's Package" full of cologne, shaving cream, razors, and deodorant had survived the fire.

"And all for nothing," she sobbed. "I wish everyone knew you didn't have that stupid necklace."

Grayson felt terrible. If he had just turned it in when he found it, this attack never would have happened. For a moment, he considered telling his mom the truth—but he was too deep into the lie at this point.

"Happy birthday, sweetheart. I love and miss you already! Be safe!"

Cristina gave him one last bear hug and walked away, only checking to see if Grayson was still there five or six times before she reached the car and drove off.

***

"He's the one in the gray jacket," said Grayson, pointing outside his dorm window at a Lacer standing on the dirt path.

"I can't believe they assigned you a bodyguard. If they knew you had the black diamond, they'd realize you didn't need one. Besides, aren't they supposed to be our guards?" asked Ethan, pointing to Spades and Ace, fast asleep on the couch.

"Where's Ambrielle?"

"She's not coming. She's in a bad mood," said Harlie.

With Ambrielle locked in her dorm, Grayson debated against Ethan and Harlie alone.

"Today's actually a great day," said Ethan. "Ridley's going to be gone for a while, and the only evil group of Lacers just got arrested!"

"We don't know if those are the same Lacers who attacked the Black House and killed my grandpa," said Grayson.

"Master Emerson told my parents they were," offered Harlie. "I don't think you have anything else to worry about."

"He doesn't know for sure. Otherwise, he wouldn't have assigned me a bodyguard."

"Why are you determined to believe so many Lacers are bad?" asked Ethan.

"Well, other than the fact that some of them just tried to kill me, other than our stupid instructors, and other than Dontae and Hardy being jerks, I would have to say because Walter Frost thinks so."

Grayson explained that, according to Frost, Lacers were failing to serve a higher purpose, and the Lacer Initiation Process was twisted. "That reminds me. Does either of you know where the Stream of Serenity is? Frost told me it would help me understand all this."

Harlie scratched her forehead. "Selaphiel's Stream is right by the pond, and there's another stream on the far side of the city. I saw it when I was walking with Ambrielle. I don't know its name, but maybe that's it."

"What's a stream going to help you understand? It's a stream of water," said Ethan. "The Lacers on Icefall Lane look like they're doing fine without serving a higher purpose. Why are you even listening to Walter Frost? Over the summer, you told me he was just a grumpy old man who knew your grandpa. Just because he has a black diamond doesn't make him smart."

"He was smart enough to figure out I have a black diamond," Grayson pointed out.

"He what?" gasped Harlie. "Why didn't you tell him you don't have it?"

"I tried... But he read my mind," said Grayson. "I don't think he's going to tell anyone."

"Let me get this straight," said Ethan. "Some random old dude knows you have a black diamond, and yet you're convinced the happy citizens of Icefall are the problem."

"I'm not saying they're a problem… I don't know what they are. I wish Ambrielle was here. She'd agree with me."

***

New Year's Eve was quite an experience at Icefall—not for Grayson, but for pretty much everyone else. The city was louder than it had been all year. From his window, Grayson could see Icefall Lane overflowing. Lacers flew through the sky, probably just using the launch pads for entertainment. Ethan took Harlie over to the campfire by the church so they'd be able to listen to the final seconds of the year ticking away.

Grayson elected not to go. He wasn't in the mood to have fun when Ambrielle remained cooped up in her room. He stayed in all night, thinking about what her dad could have said to her to make her this upset. His only New Year's resolution was to be with Ambrielle during the final chime a year from now…

Training resumed a few days later, with Jasper heading up the sessions in Ridley's absence. Jasper had to be constantly reminded by the other instructors what it was the I.G. was supposed to be doing. He'd always been somewhat of a clown, but with his brother gone, Jasper was completely free to do as he pleased.

"Liam, run in a circle around Spencer," he instructed. "Why? Because it's funny."

The workouts were a joke. Time periods previously occupied with ice baths and push-ups were now filled with playground activities like duck-duck-goose. Grayson started to look forward to training sessions. The I.G. did have to fix the damages to the house, but that was only because Ms. Myles had demanded some productivity while Jasper left to get a soda.

Grayson tried to talk to Ambrielle during training since it was pretty much just free time at this point; however, Ambrielle kept her distance. She spent most of her time mingling with Isabella Parks and Faith Davis from her element group. Grayson suspected she was only doing this to avoid him. He wanted to ask her about the Stream of Serenity and the chain link Frost had mentioned; she just wouldn't give him a chance.

The chain link gave Grayson another reason to be thankful for Jasper's easy workouts. He was much more self-conscious now. He did not want Frost to see his thoughts. Grayson tried not to wear himself down, show his emotions toward Ambrielle, or wear the black diamond; he didn't know if Frost had to be in the same room as him to read his mind or not. Grayson decided that the girl from the picture in Frost's apartment must have been someone he was upset about; otherwise, Grayson never would've had a vision of her. He didn't want Frost to see Ambrielle.

* * *

Whether there were still evil Lacers after Grayson or not, anytime he left training, the residence hall, or just went for a walk, there was his annoying bodyguard. The Lacer always wore the same gray sweatshirt, and one time Grayson caught him looking into the dorm with binoculars. Grayson tried telling the bodyguard that he was perfectly safe without his supervision, but the Lacer would walk away every time Grayson got close to him.

With Ridley gone, Grayson and the I.G. assumed his rules were, too. They ate all their meals at Icefall Lane, no longer bothering to touch the food provided for them during mealtime. Icefall had become fun again; however, Grayson took this with a grain of salt.

"All they do is party."

"They're just enjoying life," said Ethan. "Free food. Free drinks. They're a whole lot better off than our friends' parents back home. Who cares what that old dude says? He's crazy if you ask me. The whole reason we're training is to become like them!"

After a rich dinner, Grayson pulled a reluctant Ethan across Icefall Lane to the far side of the city. The east side of Icefall wasn't a part Grayson was familiar with. They passed Frost's apartment building. The skyscrapers ended shortly after, and another forest presented itself, a forest with thinner trees and a visible sky.

"It's over there!" said Grayson, taking off toward the rapidly flowing water in the distance.

"Do you feel anything? Did you figure out the whole world yet?" asked Ethan as Grayson stuck his arm into the freezing stream.

Grayson didn't answer. The water was cold, but there was nothing special about it.

"Maybe I have to get all the way in."

"Bro… Give it a rest. This stream isn't going to tell you anything. Besides, the sign over there says Muriel's Stream… Nothing about serenity."

Grayson wanted to hit Ethan. He didn't understand how Ethan wasn't even a little curious about a magical stream of water. Grayson read the words *Muriel's Stream* and kicked the snow. A squirrel darted out of its hole at the sign of Grayson's threatening movement.

The animals… Grayson could ask the animals about the Stream of Serenity.

"If you don't want to look for the stream with me, that's fine," Grayson told Ethan. "But I'm going to need your help with one thing."

"What's that?"

"Getting *him* away from me so I can look with Spades," said Grayson, nodding to his gray-hooded bodyguard, who was watching them intently.

During the weeks he and Ethan were developing a diversion plan, Grayson went on walks with Spades around Icefall. He figured this was his best excuse to be wandering around the city. With his bodyguard only a few yards behind him and watchtowers posted on all four corners of Icefall, Grayson had to make it look like he wasn't doing anything unusual. If the bodyguard made a single step in the wrong direction, Spades would fire his snake-like tail to the sky in protest.

After two weeks of aimlessly walking around and dipping his hand in every water source on the mountain, it was time to pull out the black diamond again. On his way up to Ambrielle and Harlie's fourth-floor dorm, Grayson found it painfully funny that he was on the same floor with basically every girl in his I.G. besides the one he liked. Harlie answered the door, barely cracking it open. Grayson told her he needed the necklace from Ambrielle, hoping that would get her out of bed. Harlie grabbed an old shoe and handed it to him.

"Quite the hiding spot," said Grayson, feeling defeated.

"I figured it would be the last place people would expect it to be," said Harlie. "And please don't do anything stupid with it."

Grayson promised he wouldn't, which was true in his mind because finding the stream was something that had to be done.

***

At the end of another easy Friday morning session, Jasper removed the sarcasm from his voice, gathered the I.G. around the lava pit in the fire training station, and announced that Master Emerson would be joining them shortly.

Elliott Emerson paced into the house wearing his white cloak. The I.G. sat up straight and quieted down immediately.

"This won't take long," he said, flipping through a notepad. "I wanted to inform you all that Master Ridley is doing much better and will be returning tomorrow."

Grayson and the others let out a groan, which Emerson ignored.

"We have tightened our security here at Icefall, and I'm glad to see you have been able to continue your day-to-day activities despite the damages to the house."

Jasper started to clap but stopped quickly when nobody else joined him. Grayson raised his hand.

"Yes, Mr. Day?" Emerson prodded.

"Who were the attackers?"

Emerson's face went pink. "The criminals are still under investigation," he said professionally. "We are still trying to determine whether they were acting alone or if they were only a part of something larger."

The entire room went silent. Grayson gave Ethan and Harlie an "I-told-you-so" look—even the instructors widened their eyes.

Mr. Boxer stepped forward. "Is there evidence that suggests the latter?" he asked, nervously rubbing his bald head.

"No hard evidence," Emerson answered, "just the fact that they had information about the original catering team. That information could've only come from someone who has access to your schedule. Like I said, it's still under investigation."

The room remained silent long after Emerson was gone. If Emerson was right, that meant someone inside Icefall, maybe even inside Emerald House, had leaked information to those caterers. Someone inside this very room might want him dead, or at the very least, know he had the necklace.

Grayson left the morning training session with one more thing to worry about. He needed to understand the situation he was in and decided that after the evening session, he was going to try and locate this stream with the black diamond on. Grayson spent all afternoon at Marty's Brews with Ethan, planning a diversion from the bodyguard, who was currently sitting at the restaurant's bar. The plan they decided on was risky, but they both agreed it was the best way to draw the guard's attention off Grayson.

The evening session ended an hour early. Jasper said they were all going to need a good night's sleep for when Ridley came back in the morning. For the first time, Grayson wished training was longer—not because he wanted to delay his search but because he was scared for Ethan. The two boys were the last to leave the house.

"You're gonna owe me after this one," Ethan said as Grayson started off first toward the dorms. "You better find this stupid stream."

Grayson continued down the path, his bodyguard the only Lacer in sight. He slowed his pace and waited for his signal to run. The signal came in the form of a fireball, identical to the ones that the caterers launched at him, flying right past his head.

"*The black diamond is mine, Day!*" bellowed Ethan from the shadows in his deepest voice.

Grayson ran toward the dorms, his bodyguard in the other direction toward Grayson's *attacker*. Grayson jumped through his first-floor window, grabbed the necklace off his desk, and hopped back outside.

"Come on, Spades!"

Spades followed Grayson outside. He clipped the necklace around his neck and ran for the surrounding snow walls of Icefall, his senses stronger than they had been a moment ago. Grayson's original plan was to visit the garden he'd seen his very first night in the city. Serenity was a peaceful word, and that was the most peaceful place he could think of. There would also be lots of animals there to talk to. As he and Spades traveled along the perimeter of Icefall, he heard something strange. He heard running water. There was no water in sight.

Grayson grazed both hands across the frozen snow walls, feeling for anything abnormal; however, it wasn't until after he slowed his deep breathing that he noticed the soothing flow of water was coming from *inside* the snow barrier. There was water inside—he was sure of it. Grayson jogged along the wall, looking for some sort of an entrance. He'd made his way halfway around Icefall and still hadn't found a way in — then he remembered the Necklace Raid.

How did I get through that wall? What did I do? Grayson thought. Well, he hadn't done anything; he'd been pushed through it. But he had to try something. Just as he was about to dive through the snow, he was blinded by a spotlight. Grayson fell to the ground and covered his eyes. Spades quivered in fear.

"We found him!" echoed an overhead voice from one of the watchtowers. "He's okay!"

Grayson knew he was done for. What if Ethan had been caught? That would make it obvious Grayson had set up the attack to get away from his bodyguard. Their fate depended on whether Ethan got caught or not. Grayson couldn't let his best friend be kicked out of Icefall. If Ethan had been caught, he'd just have to tell Emerson Grayson told him to do it.

He heard Lacers running down the steps of the watchtower. Grayson still had the necklace on. With the spotlight on him, he slowly unclipped the black diamond and let it fall through his shirt to the ground. Grayson debated on throwing it into the trees; however, at the very same moment, the necklace went flying across the snow and into a man's hand. Walter Frost gripped the golden chain and disappeared into the darkness, Ethan by his side.

CHAPTER 16

The Stream of Serenity

Losing control of his thoughts wasn't something Grayson would typically be proud of; however, on the night he'd tried to sneak off to find the Stream of Serenity, his mental lapse was probably the only reason he and Ethan were still at Icefall. The chain link between Grayson and Frost had turned out to be a strength rather than a weakness, just like Frost had said.

Grayson and Spades spent the night in Emerald House with a security team on high alert for the attacker, who was still at large inside Icefall. Sleeping on an air mattress inside the dining room wasn't ideal, but Grayson did prefer it to getting kicked out of the initiation process and being considered a Gaven for the rest of his life.

After Icefall had been thoroughly searched by the security team from E.R.O.L, Grayson was sent back to his dorm, where he found Ethan fast asleep and his necklace placed neatly in his desk drawer.

"Frost is one grumpy old man, but I gotta hand it to him; he saved our butts," said Ethan once he'd rolled out of bed.

"What did he say to you?"

"He didn't say anything. He wouldn't talk to me at all. He just kept grunting and muttering stuff. He didn't seem happy," said Ethan before telling Grayson the full story. "Your bodyguard had me cornered. I was about to give up, but then Frost popped out of an alley and sent the dude flying fifteen feet in the air. That's when we came and found you."

"I told you he's a genius. Now, do you believe everything about the Lacers and all their partying?"

Ethan said he trusted Frost more now that he'd met him but wasn't too worried about whether or not Lacers were fulfilling a higher purpose when he was currently Icefall's most wanted criminal.

Before their first training session with Ridley back, Ambrielle and Harlie stopped by to make sure Grayson was okay after hearing about the previous night's attack. Once Ethan admitted it was he who had attacked Grayson, Ambrielle slapped him, and Harlie walked out shaking her head.

"Hey, is Ambrielle still upset about her dad?" Grayson whispered to Harlie.

"Not as much this morning. She said she wanted to talk to you, though."

***

The opening moments of the morning session made Grayson realize how easy his days with Jasper running things had been. Although he had his right arm in a sling, an ace wrap across his rib cage, and a bandage on his forehead, Ridley's demanding personality hadn't been damaged at all. The brief cheerfulness he had shown toward the I.G. for winning the first round of the tournament had evaporated and was instead replaced by a new level of anger. There were many things Ridley had a right to be angry about: Jasper's unorthodox training style, his broken bones, and a balcony falling on his head. But the fact that Ridley took all of this out on the I.G. made it hard for Grayson to sympathize.

Ridley decided to eliminate individual element training altogether to make both four-hour training sessions purely workouts. Grayson wasn't in the same cardiovascular shape he'd been in a month ago; he'd also gotten much weaker. Thirty push-ups made him feel like he was about to have a heart attack. Grayson had been hoping to talk to Ambrielle, but any rest time he had during the session was spent keeling over, gasping for air.

The transition back to healthy food also wasn't easy. Grayson felt like a vegetarian with all the leaves he was forced to eat. Icefall Lane was back off-limits unless, of course, the P.L.s were ordered to run an errand for the instructors, which meant no more eating at fancy restaurants.

"That was fun, huh?" said Grayson, catching up to Ambrielle after the evening session, his black workout shirt dripping with sweat.

The two of them chit-chatted back up to the dorms. Grayson waited eagerly for Ambrielle to bring up whatever it was she needed to talk to him about. He walked her all the way up to the fourth floor until she finally pulled him aside by her door.

"I know I've been distant ever since the Christmas party, but I just didn't know how to tell you." She paused and blinked fast to stop tears from running down her face. "Nothing is going to happen with us anytime soon—we can stay friends, but that's all."

Grayson stood there feeling like his soul had left his body. He didn't move. He didn't speak. That was what he'd been waiting all day for? He hoped Ambrielle would keep talking and say something like "Never mind, I love you," or "Just kidding," but she never did. She squealed out an apology and hurried into her room, wiping her eyes. The door shut behind her, leaving Grayson alone in the hallway.

The pain in his arms from eight hours of push-ups was nothing compared to the hole in his chest. Grayson walked back to his room, where he would spend the next few hours trying not to cry in front of Ethan, whom he couldn't bring himself to tell what had just happened.

Grayson eventually drifted off into an uneasy sleep, where he would be woken up by multiple late-night messages from his joyous instructors. Jasper hadn't sent for him to run any errands, so he was able to go back to bed each time—Ethan wasn't so lucky.

When he arose at five in the morning, Grayson woke up on a different side of the bed than he'd gone to sleep on. He no longer felt like crying; he was angry. His night of disrupted sleep had helped him see the real problem: Ambrielle's father. Ambrielle hadn't meant anything she'd said the night before—that had been her dad talking for her.

Grayson and Ethan were both late for the morning session. It wasn't like it mattered. Ridley had the whole day scheduled for a workout anyway. After a fun hour-long bath in the freezing ice water, Ridley had everyone line up around the pool and stand there. The chilling wind from the mountain swooped down through the open roof. Just as Grayson was starting to dry off, Ridley shoved him back in the water—just him, nobody else. This wasn't the first time since Ridley's return that Grayson had noticed a sense of anger flashing specifically in his direction.

Before the workout started, Ridley had given a speech and said the I.G.'s Necklace Raid victory had been pure luck. He stood directly in front of Grayson for the duration of this speech. Grayson was worried that during Ridley's time away from the I.G., he had discovered the truth. Grayson climbed out of the water, feeling like he was back at Pine Ridge, where the teachers would single him out. He had been late to training, but just like he'd felt while at school, there seemed to be a factor other than his behavior motivating Ridley's actions.

"How bad do you want to be a Lacer?" yelled Mr. Boxer with a snow hat forming on his bald head. "You guys are free to go home whenever you please."

Ridley's presence had resurrected the other instructors' annoying energy. Mr. Boxer, Mr. Hill, Mrs. Foster, and, of course, Ms. Myles would frequently shout motivation such as this during workouts, threatening as many P.L.s as they could to drop out of the initiation process and become Gavens.

Before his talk with Frost, Grayson always thought of all the parties he'd be able to attend on Icefall Lane once he was officially a Lacer. Now Grayson needed something else to drive him to stay in the process. There was always the *"he'd have to return to school and work a desk job his whole life"* motivation, but his new and preferred choice of thought was training to fight Ambrielle's dad. Deep down, he knew it would be a couple of years before he could take down a man that big, but the thought of it would have to do for now.

Grayson took all of Ridley's workouts and punishments head-on. Sometimes he'd even provoke Ridley to keep the other P.L.s safe. It was a good thing Grayson was training hard because the final round of the Necklace Raid was right around the corner, and this time he wouldn't have his black diamond to rely on.

After a few weeks of pure torture, individual element training was put back into the routine, giving Grayson time away from Ridley. He was rusty, to say the least. He hadn't practiced controlling earth without his necklace for nearly two months — element control was much more difficult without that luxury.

"You cannot and will not blow the lead you have. Both houses will be coming for us this time. I will be checking our defenses before the match to ensure jungle animals do, in fact, remain in the jungle," said Ridley, banging his staff at Grayson's feet.

Grayson spent a lot of time reflecting on the previous match, and he hadn't quite figured out why Ruby House hadn't attacked anyone. Not attacking meant they couldn't win.

Jasper laughed when Grayson asked him about this. "Exactly. You see, the other two houses have an unspoken deal. The Ruby team expects the Amethyst team to get our necklace every time, and they don't believe in themselves enough to take anything from the Amethyst group, so they just accept second place every year. They don't care to win as long as we lose. But, hell, now their whole plan is messed up. I wouldn't be surprised if every member from both houses comes for us."

This gave Grayson something to think about. Even if Jasper had been over exaggerating when he said *every member*, he still didn't know how his I.G. would be able to defend their house from that many attackers. Without the animals' help, Harlie's electric moat would be a necessity again this time.

When the I.G. got around to booby-trapping the house for round two, Grayson couldn't even tell what month it was, much less what day. The morning and evening sessions blended, and while he still tried to train hard, lack of sleep was catching up with him. Every bit of his body ached, and his eyesight was blurred.

Since this rigorous training began, Grayson hadn't even considered trying to get through Icefall's snow walls, which he was sure the Stream of Serenity was hiding behind. He had thought about it on off days, yet sleep always sounded more appealing. And aside from the few days he'd taken off to recover from Frost's beating, the gray-hooded bodyguard constantly lingered in Grayson's shadow, making it impossible to explore the sound of running water any further.

Grayson really wanted to talk to his parents about Ridley, about his necklace, and the higher purpose Frost had referred to. After he made it through this first year, he decided that he would tell his parents the truth about the black diamond. He could just wait until summer to get answers to his questions. There was no need to risk getting in trouble. Nothing new had happened since the attack on Christmas.

Grayson's cautiousness did not last long.

On one chilly Sunday morning, he decided to take Spades for a walk. He'd recently felt bad for his guardian because of the switch from Icefall's all-you-can-eat meals to the dining hall's carrots and broccoli. Grayson ran his fingers through the snow on the walls. He couldn't hear the flowing water without his black diamond on, but he was sure it was still there. On the night he had attempted to get inside, he'd wasted all his time trying to find a door. Now Grayson knew what he had to do—he just didn't know how to do it.

With the rest of the day off, Grayson decided to skip his usual Sunday nap to practice moving through walls. He clipped the black diamond around his neck—Spades and Ace watched him curiously as he tried to push himself through the bathroom door. Grayson tried to imagine his body taking on a gas form as he leaned sideways, waiting to fall through. He never quite succeeded, but he did manage to slip and hit his hand on the door handle, waking up Ethan, who actually had been taking his usual Sunday nap.

Grayson had never told Ethan what really happened inside Ruby House; he'd wanted to keep his secret ability a secret. He decided to explain, hoping that Ethan would be able to offer some advice on passing through solid objects.

"That's awesome! I figured you just used the underground roots to get inside… Maybe if I pushed you," he said, standing up from his bed. "That's what you said happened during the match."

Ethan shoved Grayson hard into the bathroom door, giving him a bruise on his shoulder. He remained on the same side. Grayson was rubbing his arm, ready to give up for the day, when Ethan unexpectedly shoved him from behind, sending Grayson directly through the center of the couch. Grayson didn't have to ask what Ethan had been thinking; he already knew.

"You're pretty smart, you know that?"

"Yeah. Yeah. Let's see ya do it without my help this time," said Ethan, pointing back in the direction of the bathroom door.

Grayson knew he needed a running start. He tried to forget he had the necklace on and reminded himself how painful the collision was about to be. Grayson ran right at the door with his eyes closed, jumped face-first at the wood, and then almost smacked his head on the toilet. He'd done it! Instilling fear in himself activated the power.

"I wonder if it works the other way, too," said Ethan, opening the door and helping him off the ground. "You know, like if someone was to punchyouinthestomach."

Ethan swung at Grayson's midsection, knocking the wind right out of him.

"Wh... What th... the heck," gasped Grayson, with his hands on his knees.

"Sorry. Sorry," said Ethan carefully. "I just thought if you could go through solid things, then maybe solid things could go through you."

"You're lucky I still owe you for fake attacking me," said Grayson, steadying his breathing.

***

On top of his daily training, Grayson now practiced jumping through walls. He messed up a lot, so he wanted to take all the time he needed to perfect his new ability. Moving through solid objects would also make escaping from his bodyguard much easier. Once he felt prepared, he would sneak out of Emerald Residence Hall by going through the back wall by the stairs, avoiding his bodyguard at the main entrance.

The day before Grayson felt ready to put his plan into action, he and Liam were paired up with Ambrielle and the other water controllers to craft a new defense tactic for the house: a tree with branches that could shoot out water like a spray bottle. The project was not as difficult as it sounded. Grayson had already grown a couple of trees by the reconstructed moat, and the only thing left to do was bend the branches back into the water. Getting the branches to stay bent wasn't easy. Grayson had to dive into the moat, hold his breath, and shove the branches into the soil, where Liam could then constrict the dirt to hold them steady. It didn't look pretty, but when it was done, the dozens of branches were able to shoot out enough water to blind anyone who came near them.

Grayson and Ambrielle only talked when they needed to. She would suggest an idea, or he would point out a flaw in their defense. Their conversations were strictly business, and there was a lot of awkward tension between them. Grayson was extremely bothered by this, yet he tried to talk to the other girls in Ambrielle's group more than he did to her. He made jokes, played pranks on them, and did pretty much anything he could to make them laugh. Grayson thought he was doing a good job making her jealous until she went to talk to Liam. That whole plan had backfired.

Grayson didn't leave his dorm at all on Sunday. He left his blinds open so his bodyguard could see he was still inside. He faked getting ready for bed and then shut them once the last ounce of light left the sky. Grayson wasted no time getting ready for his escape. He didn't know how long he would be gone, but the I.G. had training at five the following morning, so he couldn't be out too late.

"I'm leaving. Wish me luck," said Grayson, shaking Ethan awake.

"You aren't in danger. This is pointless," he yawned. "If you get caught again this time, I will deny any knowledge of your actions."

"Yeah. Yeah. If I get caught again, I'm going to tell them this necklace is yours."

Grayson wished Ethan could've come, but he had a feeling learning to take people through walls with him was going to be a lot more challenging, if at all possible. He crept silently into the hallway and softly shut the door behind him, tiptoeing his way to the staircase, where he jumped into the brick wall. Grayson didn't stop once he was outside. He kept his same momentum and sprinted through the gently falling powder until he reached the towering snow walls of Icefall. Grayson closed his eyes and leaped forward like he'd practiced hundreds of times.

He stood inside a narrow cave. There were no lights, but the ice around him had a light blue glow, giving the cave a sense of warmth. There was music. It was calm music, nothing like the music played on Icefall Lane. This tune had no words, only the flicker of strings on a guitar. Directly below the rock where Grayson stood, a stream of water, about five feet deep, flowed like a lazy river Grayson had once been to with his friends back home. He stripped down and dipped his toe into the water—it was freezing. The countless ice baths he had taken during training this year had prepared him for this.

As Grayson lowered himself to the water, he felt nothing out of the ordinary. He thought maybe Frost had been messing with him, or perhaps this wasn't the Stream of Serenity he was supposed to find, then he realized he was already being carried downstream. Grayson floated on his back and let the water take him to his destination. He wanted to get out—he was shivering—but the guitar and sparkling ice told him he was in the midst of something magical.

The stream twisted and turned inside the cave, making Grayson feel like he was on a water slide. Suddenly, he heard the sound of steam, like the cold water was leading to a pit of lava. Grayson looked around for a way out, but the walls were too high. He could see a drop ahead. Everything went dark, and Grayson fell like a waterfall.

When he opened his eyes, Grayson thought he was on fire. His body was sizzling, and he felt like needles were stabbing every inch of him. Instead of being in a lava pit, he found himself in an enormous, circular hot tub. The glowing ice and the guitar rhythm remained the same, yet the place felt more alive. The light from the moon shone from a hole in the snow. Grayson maneuvered around a spiraling whirlpool in the middle of the tub and took a seat on an ice bench under the warm water, letting his arms relax in the outside snow. His body had the perfect balance of warm and cold.

Grayson realized this chamber was a place to think freely, without outside influence, without interruptions. He closed his eyes and let his mind wander. He was still aware of his surroundings, but he'd fallen into some sort of trance.

For the next several hours, he couldn't tell if he was awake or asleep. The guitar continued to play without words. Grayson's mind seemed to write the missing lyrics.

You will find your true self as you soak in this stream.
Some will scream, and others will beam,
As they realize things they already know.

This can only help the knowledge glow.

Serenity, you will find,

With an empty and clear mind.

Affect your thoughts,

The outside world shall not.

While you sit and ponder,

Allow negative thoughts to continue to wander.

Peace prevails,

Negativity sails.

Belief is the mind's greatest power,

Use it to heal the physical frame,

Only then can one reach the top of life's tower.

Where all aim,

But beneath is where most cower,

Away from things they could achieve and their true name.

The Stream of Serenity. Grayson's thoughts mirrored themselves from his brain onto the water like a projector. He saw the people he trusted: Ethan, Ambrielle, Harlie, and his parents. He trusted them, but they didn't see the red flags that he saw in other Lacers. He saw the Lacers he didn't understand: Emerson, Frost, and all the Lacers of Icefall. In a dark cloud, he saw his instructors— Ridley, in front of them all. Ridley had changed since his return; his actions told Grayson he had learned the truth. During this breakdown, Grayson remembered something that had slipped his mind.

Ridley hadn't helped Jasper and the other instructors fight the caterers on Christmas.

As his mind naturally drifted to the black diamond, he saw his grandpa, whom he'd never talked to a day in his life, placing one of the most powerful objects on Earth on the backseat of a school bus. Grayson felt like he knew Oscar, like they had spoken that day at the bus stop. He imagined his grandpa riding the bus with him, the two of them talking, and Oscar explaining why he had trusted Grayson with the black diamond rather than giving it to Frost for him to keep safe. As the school bus slowly skated down Icefall Lane and they continued talking, Oscar answered, "Because Frost has already given up."

Grayson had the necklace for a reason. He had a job to do; he just had to understand a Lacer's higher purpose to do it.

From inside the bus, Grayson watched the Lacers on Icefall Lane and asked himself if these partiers were really any better than the people he'd grown up around. The Lacers here on the mountain were much nicer and happier than the people from the world Grayson was used to but were all Lacers this way? Were there more evil Lacers out there?

The more he thought about it, the more Grayson failed to understand why he was training so hard to become a Lacer when they did nothing but drink and party. They had powers—they could do anything they wanted, and this was how they chose to spend their lives?

The bus came to a stop, and as Grayson said goodbye to Oscar, he realized he didn't have to join the Lacers on Icefall Lane if he didn't want to. He could drop out of the Lacer Initiation Process—he already had a necklace.

Maybe Grayson could serve the world more than the partiers. Maybe he was different.

CHAPTER 17

Invasion of Amethyst House

"Were you at the stream all night?"

"Yep."

"You didn't sleep at all?"

"Nope."

"Bro, you're gonna be exhausted this week."

"My head feels clearer right now than it has all year. I'm not sore anymore either."

"Well, that's kinda cool, I guess... Did you discover *a Lacer's higher purpose*?" asked Ethan, suppressing his laughter.

"No, but I—"

"Clark! Day! Drop and give me twenty for not paying attention!" screamed Mr. Hill.

The entire I.G. dropped to the turf.

It had got to the point in the year where Grayson, had he not been able to recall the peacefulness of the stream, felt like he might explode. His instructors had become so ruthless that he considered punching them at least twenty times a session; he knew that was what they wanted. Anytime this urge surfaced, he took a deep breath, closed his eyes, and tried to return to his state of meditation.

Ms. Myles frequently stated that an entire I.G. never made it a year without at least one P.L. dropping out of the initiation process. Her goal was to make somebody drop. She and the other instructors had graduated from simply pushing the P.L.s into the pool to sweeping their legs out or kicking them in.

"Better get used to the pain. The other two houses are gonna bring it to you this time," said Mr. Boxer.

"You can leave! Icefall doesn't need you—you need us!" Ms. Myles would taunt.

While statements like these might have motivated everyone else to stay, they made Grayson uneasy. He no longer wanted to party all the time like the Lacers at Icefall, so why didn't he just drop out? There were a couple of times when Grayson almost went up to Ridley to quit, but Ethan would have killed him. Besides, what was he going to do if he left? Become an accountant? He didn't know what higher purpose he needed to achieve, so reluctantly, Grayson remained in the Lacer Initiation Process, feeling anxious about the direction of his life and the Lacers around him.

Ridley was as cruel as ever. Grayson wished his injuries would heal up; perhaps then he'd be in a better mood. It was now the end of March, several months after the attack that crippled him, yet he continued to limp around wearing the same rib and head bandages. On one snowy evening, Ridley gathered the I.G. around the pool and told them he had good news. Grayson had been gullible enough to believe him.

"You now have less than a month left in your first year of training," said Ridley. "And since all of you seem so keen to stay in the program, we instructors have decided to put together a final, element-related test. Anyone who fails to pass won't move onto year two."

Ethan lost his cool at this news. "That's so unfair!" he yelled. "All the work we put in this year, and then you can just drop us because of one test."

Ridley shoved him in the pool and made the whole I.G. do planks.

Grayson didn't have to worry about the final test as much as the other kids. While they were in their separate training groups, Jasper would make fun of the test, like he did everything else.

"I was thinking maybe I'd let my two trainees design their test this year," he told Liam and Grayson.

"Can we throw a tree across the house?" Liam asked.

"Sure, why not?" said Jasper, shrugging. "But whoever throws it the shortest has to go get me a sandwich."

Jasper said he wanted to spend this last month focusing on deceptive element control—a concept both Liam and Grayson had struggled with the last time.

"Deceptive control can be a lot more than changing the size of your surroundings," Jasper explained. "We're standing in this small little garden right now, but if you can vividly imagine another landscape coming into this one, you can really confuse your opponents."

Jasper aimed his staff up in the sky and then brought it down to the dirt. Grayson now stood in a much bigger garden with many more flowers. It was the one he'd seen his first night at Icefall. Jasper moved his staff, and everything returned to normal.

"It takes a lot out of ya," said Jasper, his face pale, "but it's a great distraction."

Grayson and Liam practiced changing their surroundings. Grayson tried to make the bushes around Liam appear bigger than they were. He pictured every leaf on the bush slowly doubling in size before thickening the stem to sustain the weight change. By the week of the second round of the Necklace Raid, Grayson had managed to fully double a bush size five times while Liam only did it once.

Individual element training for the final test took away a lot of preparation time for the Necklace Raid. Emerald House already had booby traps around every square inch of the yard—that wasn't the problem. The problem was grouping. How would the I.G. split up during the match? Some P.L.s suggested all twenty of them stay and guard the house. If nobody got inside, they'd win.

Grayson figured about thirty-four of the other two teams' forty players would be attacking the house. So even if they all stayed, they would still be outnumbered. He didn't like those odds at all. Grayson had a new plan, a plan he hadn't shared with anyone yet because it was insane.

Since the other teams were going to get inside their house anyway, why not just let them in? If most of the Amethyst team were attacking, that meant *their* house would be susceptible to an attack. His plan was to let both teams get into Emerald House while his team snuck off for Amethyst House. The Ruby team would surely get their necklace back to its home; however, the Amethyst team would have difficulty getting any necklace back to their statue, considering the Emerald I.G. would already be there. That was his plan, defending Amethyst House from its own team.

It was crazy. His I.G. would have to use another team's defenses. In his opinion, this was a better option than waiting to get bull-rushed by both teams. If the plan played out like he thought it would, everything would come down to how many points each team got from entering the opposing houses.

Right now, the score was 9-0-0 in favor of the Emerald team. Grayson had got into Ruby House; that was one point. He'd taken their necklace off its statue, which was another three points, and returning it to his own team's statue had been another five points. Nine points total. If his whole team could get inside Amethyst House, it would at least be enough for second place. As much as Grayson wanted first place, he'd still settle for messing up the other two houses' traditions.

Two days before the match, Grayson pulled the I.G. together during one of their strategizing periods. He'd been preparing himself all week for them to shoot down the idea, yet a lot of his peers nodded in agreement.

"Your plan worked last time," mumbled Ambrielle.

Grayson suppressed a smile when she supported his idea.

"As long as your plan doesn't involve me electrocuting everyone this time, I'm on board," said Harlie.

"Don't act like you didn't enjoy it." Ambrielle smirked.

The I.G. took a vote. This time all twenty hands went into the air. Again, if they lost, the blame would be on Grayson. All of Icefall was hoping for the Emerald team to pull off this upset. The only difference was that Grayson wouldn't be wearing the black diamond this time.

"Nobody stays to guard the house?" asked Xander. "Because Liam and I worked our tails off last time to keep everyone out."

"Well," said Grayson. "I talked to Jasper about this, and he told me at least one of the three selected players has to stay inside at all times. So, Xander, if you're one of three, then I'm guessing you volunteer to stay?"

Xander didn't say anything in return. Grayson didn't blame him; he figured this might be an issue. Ever since he'd mentioned that one person would have to stay back alone, the I.G. had gone silent. Madison Silver moved her way to the front of the crowd.

"That's like a suicide mission," she squeaked. "They're just going to beat up whoever stays."

"No, they aren't," said Grayson. "We just need a good hiding spot."

Since it was his plan, Grayson volunteered to make the hiding spot. The day before the match, he and Liam dug a hole under the tree in the garden. The entrance was away from the statue in the center, so the other teams wouldn't easily notice it once they got inside. They were almost finished when Mr. Boxer interrupted them with an announcement.

"Everyone, get in line! Last workout before the match!" he yelled. "Start running laps. Let's see who's ready for tomorrow."

The I.G. climbed to the balcony.

"Unfortunately, I won't be able to watch this one," said Jasper. "I promised an old friend I'd help him decorate his new apartment.

We might need some help… Grayson, would you mind skipping the workout to help us?"

Grayson jumped off the ladder. Liam glared at Jasper for not getting him out of the workout as well.

"You're so lucky," muttered Ethan.

"Have fun," said Grayson.

Ridley blocked the exit to Emerald House with a look of pure rage written across his narrow face.

"Watch out there, big bro," said Jasper.

Ridley limped out of the doorway. Grayson didn't meet his eyes.

"Master Ridley really doesn't want me to miss a workout," said Grayson as he and Jasper walked through the forest, followed by Grayson's bodyguard. "Who are we helping decorate?"

"You're already in good shape. He'll get over it," said Jasper, flipping his hair. "We aren't helping anyone decorate. I just didn't want our best player to wear himself out before the match. Let's go practice some element control at the lake. What d'ya say?"

During his individual session, Grayson experimented with different staff movements, which Jasper claimed played the most significant role in effective earth control. Jasper also tried to teach him how to tie knots with branches from two different trees. Grayson struggled to lace them together, yet he was sure it would've been an easy assignment if he had the black diamond.

"I prefer to slowly rotate my staff rod in my hands. If I rotate it too fast, the branches tangle and break. Hey, you! You control earth, don't you? Come on over and show Grayson how to tie a knot. I don't think my method works for him."

Grayson's bodyguard, who had been watching from a distance, removed the gray hoodie from his head. He had a thick neck, broad shoulders, and a brown beard. He didn't look happy about being called over.

"Tying a knot isn't going to do a thing," he said in a deep voice.

"You can't tie a knot?" asked Jasper. "What if Lacers are chasing Grayson through the woods, and you need to trip them by tying two branches together?"

"I'd do something else."

"I don't need protection, by the way," said Grayson. "I've been trying to tell you for the past few months, but you don't talk to me."

"Protecting you is my job," the bodyguard rumbled. "Talking to you isn't. They still haven't caught the Lacer who tried to light you on fire, so I'll be around until they do."

Since he couldn't tell the guard that Ethan was the "evil Lacer on the run," Grayson had no way to convince him that the threat had diminished. Even if Lacers were still after Grayson, he didn't feel all that safe with someone who couldn't tie a knot protecting him.

***

He returned to Emerald House as the rest of the I.G. was finishing up their workout. Ethan, Ambrielle, and Harlie walked outside, where Grayson stood waiting.

Ambrielle didn't look happy. "Wow, you look exhausted. Decorating the apartment must've been awful."

"The four of us should go to dinner like we did before the first match," said Ethan, dripping with sweat. "I mean, we're never allowed to go to Icefall Lane, and the year's almost over."

Since Ambrielle had told Grayson things weren't going to work out between them, Ethan had dedicated what little free time he had to making them hang out. Although, deep down, Grayson always wanted to say yes to seeing Ambrielle, he never let himself. On the few occasions when Ethan had invited the girls to their place, she always backed out at the last moment. This time there was no excuse for any of them.

Grayson took his warm, post-training shower, which always felt like heaven in liquid form, put on his fanciest button-down, and one too many sprays of the cologne his dad had given him for Christmas. When the girls knocked on the door, Grayson stood up straight and tried to look as confident as possible. He just wanted to get through dinner without giving it away that he still liked Ambrielle. She turned out to be wearing sweatpants and a jacket, making him feel like he'd tried way too hard.

On the way to Marty's Brews, Ethan and Harlie did a good job carrying on conversations, avoiding the awkward silence Grayson had expected. The restaurant was crowded. Grayson and a tall Lacer with long, curly black hair collided while maneuvering through tables. The first sign of trouble appeared when the four of them reached the table, and Ethan immediately sat next to Harlie, leaving Grayson to be paired with Ambrielle.

The four of them agreed not to talk about the upcoming match at all; they were already nervous enough. They did talk about what a crazy year it had been and how fast it had gone by. They talked about how in a couple of days, they would only have two more years of training until they were officially Lacers, considering they passed their final tests.

"Anybody have summer plans?" Ethan asked the table. "Grayson and I plan on sleeping for most of the summer."

"Ambrielle will be staying with me for some of it, I think," said Harlie.

Ambrielle quickly looked up at Harlie like this wasn't something she'd planned on discussing. "Well, ya know, the more time away from home, the better," she said gloomily while twiddling with her fork.

She was obviously upset—like always, she did everything she could not to show it. Grayson wanted to comfort her, put his arm around her, but she'd probably slap him, so his sweaty palms remained in his lap. He hated to think it, but if things weren't going great between Ambrielle and her dad, then maybe she'd break his no-boyfriend rule. His daydream was cut short when the restaurant door opened and the entire Ruby I.G. walked in.

"Yo, Dontae, he's over here," announced Hardy.

Grayson kicked Ethan under the table. The two boys looked at each other, knowing they were in a hopeless situation.

Dontae approached the booth, his team behind him. "You cheated last time. This time we're taking back what's ours. You can wear the necklace—it's not gonna matter. We're gonna break you and your I.G."

Ambrielle squeezed Grayson's arm under the table as if to tell him not to try anything stupid. Grayson was thankful that Dontae and his group didn't hang around waiting for him to respond because, honestly, he didn't want to fight twenty older P.L.s in a restaurant. Ambrielle immediately released his arm after Dontae left.

Grayson realized why Ambrielle wouldn't date him. She was scared her dad might hurt him. That had to be the reason. It wasn't because she had any problem disobeying her father's wishes. No, it was because she wanted to keep him safe.

Grayson went through the rest of the night with his spirits high. When he got back to his dorm that night, he locked himself in for the tournament. He knew winning, and most importantly, performing well, would not only shut up the Ruby team but it might also make Ambrielle believe he was tough enough to face her dad.

***

"The green cloaks are coming! The green cloaks are coming!"

Just like last time, Grayson woke up from his pre-match nap to find the I.G. in the hallway outside his door. Unlike last time, the energy and excitement seemed to be lacking. Grayson and Ethan went through the crowd, patting people on the back, telling them to keep their heads up, that everything would be fine. But until the three names were called to protect the house and someone volunteered to stay alone, everyone would remain on edge. Liam wasn't shoving the other P.L.s around this time; he looked as though he might puke.

"Come on, Liam, man up," said Xander. "Remember what your dad told us? You don't want God to think you're weak."

Grayson curiously looked in Liam's direction. He would've guessed Xander was too cocky to be religious; either way, he didn't think God judged people for being nervous about a tournament.

Although he should've been just as scared as everyone else, Grayson was too focused on proving himself to Ambrielle, who happened to be walking right behind him as the I.G. made their way into Emerald House.

"You know they're all going to come for you, right?" Ambrielle asked quietly.

"Yeah, I know," murmured Grayson. "And just like last time, I'm going to beat them."

Grayson believed what he had just said. He didn't have the black diamond this time, but he believed in his strategy. After dinner the previous night, he'd made a couple of tweaks to the game plan. It was nothing he had to talk to his I.G. about, just a little bit of time management that could make all the difference.

"Head down. Eyes closed. Toes over the pool," instructed Ridley. It was sometimes hard to take him seriously with his head bandage. "Jasper will be picking the three guards for the house. Jasper, if you will."

"Guard *numero uno*, Ethan Clark."

Grayson's heart dropped. Ethan was one of the few P.L.s brave enough to stay back, but Grayson needed him out on the battlefield.

"Next up, Timothy Addison. And let's see… Liam Dixon."

The I.G. took their time changing into their stealth suits. Once all nineteen of his peers were dressed in their black compression outfits, Grayson called them over to have the dreaded discussion. He hoped Timothy would offer to stay back, but Grayson knew Ethan would volunteer.

"Timothy, Liam, Ethan…" Grayson started. "As you know, one of you needs to stay back and hide. Anyone up for the challenge?"

Ethan tried, "I can—"

"I'm doing it," said Liam firmly, his face bright green like the globe on his staff. "I guarded the house last time. I can do it again."

"That's very brave, Liam," Grayson encouraged. "And I speak for all of us when I say we appreciate it, but remember, you don't need to guard the house. You just need to hide under the tree and stay inside."

Liam nodded. The instructors climbed to the second floor, and the I.G. threw their globes on the ground. The match was about to begin.

"When the horn sounds, everyone stays close to me. Do exactly as I say," said Grayson, trying to sound confident. "And Liam, get the heck under that tree."

OWWOHHHHHH. OWWOHHHHHH.

Grayson and the other eighteen P.L.s slipped out the front door and silently crept down the far-right boundary of the playing field toward Amethyst House. Once they were about halfway, Grayson stopped his team to watch the other group's movements.

It was just like he'd expected. Although he couldn't count how many, he saw a huge mass of Amethyst players running in the middle of the battlefield toward Emerald House. Moments later, Grayson heard a couple of screams. He guessed the Ruby team was already there, and someone had gotten sprayed by one of the trees.

Once the Amethyst team passed Grayson's group, he hurried everyone out to the center of the playing field.

"What the heck are you doing?" asked Spencer Erving. "We could keep going along the edges. We have a clear path. They're gonna see us!"

"That's the point," said Grayson. "We can't let all of them step foot in our house; that's too many points. We need some of them to chase us. Ethan, get their attention. Get ready to run!"

On Grayson's signal, Ethan made a fireball from one of the campfires and threw it next to the I.G. so they'd be bright and shiny for the other team to see.

Grayson waited to make sure some of the Amethyst players saw them, then he screamed, "Run for their house! Don't stop until you get inside!"

Grayson's adrenaline was pumping. His team had a big head start, but they had to get inside and then get back out quickly to defend Amethyst House from its own team.

"Get the ropes out," said Ethan as the I.G. approached the house.

There were no defenders outside the house, nor were there any defenses set up. Grayson threw his rope to the top of the wall, and it latched around one of the spikes. Using the rope, his sticker gloves, and the wall for support, Grayson made it to the top and hopped down onto the Amethyst balcony.

He glanced down to the first floor, and just like when he'd first seen Ruby House, Amethyst House was nothing like what he'd expected. The entire bottom floor, walls and all, were padded with white cushions. There was also a gym and several glass boxes, each large enough to fit a grown person inside. At the center of the padded floor was the statue. Grayson helped pull a couple of his teammates over the wall, hopped down to the first floor, and climbed the statue limb by limb until he grabbed the purple stone around its neck.

"Back outside!" yelled Grayson after counting to make sure everyone on his team stepped foot in the house. "We can't let the Amethyst team return our necklace to their statue."

Once everyone was back outside, the first wave of Amethyst P.L.s arrived. They were not happy. Since the Amethyst team clearly hadn't expected anyone to invade their house, there were no defenses, no campfires, no water sources, no power sources, and no fans. There were a few trees and a light breeze, so maybe Xander and some of the other wind controllers could be effective.

The fight started off like Grayson and Ethan's old school duels — staff on staff combat. As more and more opposing team P.L.s arrived, Grayson was forced to join in. He kept the Amethyst necklace clipped to his waist. It was a good thing he had experience with staff fighting because, just like Dontae and Hardy from the Ruby team, these Amethyst dudes were big. Grayson sent branches in the direction of the other players; he threw dirt up in their faces, temporarily blinding them. He even unsuccessfully attempted to use the underground roots. There was a lot of time left, but so far, his team was holding their ground.

The next batch of opponents changed things for the worse. An Amethyst P.L. grabbed Grayson from behind and put him in a neck-breaking headlock. He thought he was done for, but at the last moment, Grayson was able to gather enough focus to summon a tree trunk and knock him out. When he rolled the guy over, Grayson saw a ruby necklace around his neck. Grayson tried to pull it off—it was stuck. It wasn't the ruby necklace from the tournament; it was the P.L.'s personal necklace. Did these Amethyst players all have their own necklaces?

Grayson made his way through the battlefield, and to his dismay, he saw chains around every opposing P.L.'s neck. Not all of them were using special powers, though—if they were, it wasn't noticeable. One Amethyst girl jumped out of a bad position, took flight momentarily, and landed by her teammate. Yet, it was because of little things like these that the Emerald team was now starting to retreat. Grayson was about to rejoin the fight when all twenty members of the Ruby team approached the scene.

The Ruby and Amethyst teams together absolutely pummeled the Emerald team. Whichever P.L. had the emerald necklace would break through and get inside at any moment. Grayson was forced to do the one thing he had told himself he wasn't going to: Try to return the Amethyst necklace to Emerald House.

"Hey, Dontae, Hardy, Amethyst team, see ya!" yelled Grayson, waving the necklace in the air, taking off in a sprint.

He made it halfway across the field before his legs slowed. Thirty P.L.s were chasing him; if they caught him, he was done for.

The flying Amethyst girl tackled Grayson from behind just as he reached the Emerald front lawn. He scrambled to his feet, picked up his staff, and sent three bushes in her direction, forcing her to dive sideways. He made a run for the front door, but everyone else had caught up to him. Grayson was surrounded, outnumbered thirty to one. He desperately used all his strength to knock over the two biggest trees on the lawn, scattering most of them. He got his hand on the front door.

Then Dontae's fist landed a knockout punch. "I told you we'd break you."

They ripped the necklace off his waist. With no black diamond to evade the attacks, Grayson braced himself for more of Dontae's fatal blows.

OWWOHHHHHH. OWWOHHHHHH.

"No!" screamed Dontae.

Jasper and the other instructors rushed through the front door to stop the fight. Dontae took one more cheap shot, immediately making Grayson's left eye swell shut.

"Get the heck outta here! All ya! The match is over," bellowed Jasper. "Especially you, Dontae."

Grayson struggled to his feet, praying that his team had held off at Amethyst House. Ambrielle, Ethan, Harlie, and the rest of the I.G. all came running to Grayson.

"We did it!" yelled Harlie. "Oh my, your eye."

"I'm all good," said Grayson, giving Ambrielle a confident nod.

"So, did we win?" asked Ethan.

"I'm going to meet with the other head instructors to tally the score," said Jasper. "Normally, Ridley would do it, but he's busy tending to Liam."

Liam! The I.G. ran inside the house, where they found Liam moaning in pain, lying against the side of the tree in the garden. Ridley and Mr. Boxer were kneeling next to him. Mr. Boxer used a first-aid kit to tend to Liam's wounds. Only his cries of pain broke the silence of the night.

"YOU WON! YOU WON!" yelled Jasper as he bounced into the house like a little kid. "Final score: 31-26-20. Let's go!"

Grayson didn't know whether it was okay to celebrate or not with Liam in this condition. With the help of the tree, Liam got to his feet, his eyes swollen, his face bloody. Liam took off running— Grayson thought he was celebrating the win, then Liam shoulder-checked Jasper, knocking him to the ground.

"You idiot!" cried Liam. " If you had just trained me better, I wouldn't have gotten beat up!"

Mr. Boxer and Ms. Myles pulled Liam off Jasper. Nobody could believe their eyes.

"It looks like we have our first Gaven," said Ridley. "Upstairs. To my office. Now, Liam! The rest of you, return to the residence hall and celebrate. We'll see each other on Sunday for your final test. Some of you may, in fact, be joining Mr. Dixon in leaving the initiation process."

When they got back to the residence hall, there was no celebration. Grayson punched the wall of the shower. It was all his fault Liam had been kicked out. It was his plan to have one P.L. stay back. Liam had made it all year, just to be kicked out with two days remaining. A couple of months back, Grayson wouldn't have cared what happened to Liam, but now, with everything the I.G. had gone through together, Grayson felt terrible for him.

***

Grayson looked at his black eye in the mirror. He considered trying to use some of his mom's makeup to hide it before Ambrielle and Harlie came over. He decided against it. The battle scar gave him a tough-guy look.

"I'm glad they didn't beat you up as bad as Liam," said Ambrielle, grabbing a slice of pizza and sitting next to Grayson on the couch.

"Oh, it was just a lucky punch. I was about to take him out when the horn saved him."

"Yeah, right," snorted Ethan, choking on a pepperoni.

Ambrielle just smiled.

"I wish there was something we could do to keep Liam from being dropped," said Harlie. "I really thought our whole group was going to make it through the year."

***

Grayson couldn't sleep that night. He had to help Liam, or at least try to. With Ethan sound asleep, Grayson got dressed and snuck out of Emerald Residence Hall. He needed to tell Ridley it was all his fault. If anyone should get in trouble, it should be him for designing such a dangerous plan.

The front door of Emerald House was wide open, and music rained down from the second floor where the instructors lived. Grayson passed the tree with the bunker on his way to the ladder. He had almost forgotten that Liam was supposed to have been hidden. Had the other I.G.s found him, or had he tried to be a hero and fight them all off? It didn't really matter anymore.

Mr. Hill, Mr. Boxer, Mrs. Foster, and Ms. Myles were inside Jasper's apartment. They sang along to the blaring music as Jasper danced on his desk with a large drink in hand. Through the window, Grayson even saw Ms. Myles smile for the first time.

Grayson continued toward Ridley's quarters. He was about to knock on the door when, through a crack in the blinds, he saw Ridley walking around his apartment, completely bandage- and sling-free. Ridley had been faking all along...

He'd never been injured in the attack. He'd been the one who'd leaked information to the attackers on Christmas. He must've figured out Grayson had the black diamond and ordered the attack himself. Grayson checked to make sure the other instructors hadn't seen him—then he ran.

CHAPTER 18

Deceptive Tradition

"Open the door!" yelled Grayson, pounding his fist against the wood.

"Whatsssyourrrproblem?" yawned Harlie.

Grayson ignored her question, grabbed both her and Ambrielle's hands, and ran them down to the first floor.

"Get up, Ethan!"

Grayson pulled his bed into the middle of the dorm, and everyone followed him into Oscar's underground office. They anxiously paced around the room of mirrors as he explained what he'd seen at Emerald House.

"No injuries at all?" asked Ethan. "You're sure?"

"Not even the arm sling?" wondered Harlie, trying to untangle her hair.

"I'm telling you, he's perfectly healthy," said Grayson. "It's official... He's the one who leaked our party information to the Lacers who attacked the Christmas party. He's the one who wants my necklace."

"Well, it makes sense. During the attack, he was in the bathroom, so nobody saw him get hurt. He obviously hates all of us, anyway," said Ambrielle, running her hand across the glass water tank that encompassed the middle of the wall. "Can we finish this conversation in the morning?"

"Finish it in the morning? We have to do something. We have to tell someone." Grayson had considered going straight to Emerson, but he didn't know how to find him.

"This room is too quiet—it always makes me wanna fall asleep," said Ambrielle. "Ridley's not gonna come after you tonight. We'll find Emerson in the morning."

With all noise of the world above blocked out and the sound of peaceful water flowing around them, Grayson did find himself relatively calm for someone who had just found out his head instructor wanted him dead. The four friends agreed to meet up early the next morning and find Emerson. Wandering around Icefall City at night would've only put Grayson in more danger.

After Ambrielle and Harlie returned to their dorm and Ethan was snoring loudly in his bed, Grayson shut himself in the underground room and sat down at Oscar's desk with his hands in his hair. *I could run away tonight if I wanted*, he said to himself, followed by a lengthy yawn. He could sneak out the back of the residence hall without his bodyguard seeing. *Then... then, I could run through the forest. And then I'd get to Icefall Lane, and then there would be a bus waiting for me. I could get on the bus and leave... And then...*

"*And then you'd be an outcast,*" said Oscar, "*which isn't necessarily a bad thing, but it's a big decision.*"

"*I'm starting to remember,*" said Grayson. "*The stream helped. But why? Why would soaking in the water help me remember these conversations?*"

"The Stream of Serenity is a place to meditate. And only in a state of meditation can one tap into their subconscious mind. I'm about to explain," said Oscar, putting his hand in the air to silence Grayson. "There is nothing special about the water in the stream, only the fact that you believe there is something special about it. When the water takes away the pain in your muscles from training or the pain in your head from lack of sleep, your mind is able to forget about the problems in the physical world and focus purely on the spiritual world, which is what truly matters."

"There is no question concerning the physical world that the spiritual world cannot answer," said Mr. Bruce. "Yet the physical world can answer nothing about the spiritual because everything is set in stone on Earth."

"You have already begun to see the positive effects meditation has on life. The more often you can tap into this spiritual realm, the greater your advantage will be over those who don't. Meditation will allow your ego to evaporate. Therefore, your decision-making will be less selfish and more calculated."

"That makes sense," said Grayson. "I'll slowly start to use this spiritual world to help me make the right choices in the real world."

"There are many real worlds," said Mr. Bruce, with one eye on the road and the other on the chain around his neck. "I am merely bridging the gap between the world Oscar has left us for and the one we are currently living on."

"Grandpa, what world are you in?"

"For now, let's just say I Left yours… However, through their creativity, Lacers do have a way of connecting things that ought to be laced together…"

Grayson smiled. *"Do you remember these conversions, Mr. Bruce?"*

"Oh, not exactly. But I would say I have a great enough understanding of both worlds to know they must be united if we are to have a chance in the war that is to come."

"Could I stop the war by having Emerson arrest Ridley?"

"Who's to say?" replied Oscar. "Just remember, as you decide whether or not to leave the Lacer Initiation Process, as you continue to pursue a Lacer's higher purpose throughout your life, remember, everything happens for a reason. If you carry this mindset, you cannot truly make wrong choices even when you do make wrong choices."

***

Grayson awoke surrounded by his own reflection. He was neither anxious nor scared as he began his day. This Saturday marked the first day of Grayson's last weekend at Icefall. With the I.G.'s final element tests on Sunday, Grayson had two things on his agenda for the day: practicing and making sure Ridley was arrested.

"I think I should talk to Frost and Emerson alone," said Grayson as he, Ethan, Ambrielle, and Harlie set off for the campfire behind the church. "There's no reason for any of you to get involved. If Ridley finds out you're plotting against him, he might target you guys, too."

"I don't care what Ridley does. We all need to stick together until he's in prison," said Ambrielle, setting down the bucket of water she'd brought to practice with.

"Yeah," said Harlie, "our plan was to train for our test and then find Emerson and Frost after. Don't change the plan."

"My test is going to be a joke," Grayson told them. "You all need to practice, so you don't get kicked out of the initiation process—I just need to get this over with."

Grayson continued past the campfire toward the store where he'd gotten Spades and traveled deeper into the city. He hadn't been to this area since he took Ethan to look for the Stream of Serenity. All the buildings were tall; most of them appeared to be offices. Eventually, he spotted the first-floor lobby of Frost's apartment building.

"Mr. Frost doesn't enjoy unscheduled visitors," said the woman at the front desk, "but I'd be happy to give him a call and check."

"Tell him Grayson needs to talk to him about Christmas."

The receptionist wasn't on the phone long after she mentioned Grayson's name. She scanned her keycard, opening the elevator, and Grayson rose to the penthouse.

"What is it this time?" grunted Frost as he washed a plate. "Another one of your friends needs saving?"

"No, but thanks for that," said Grayson, sitting down in Frost's armchair. "I found out who leaked the information to the Lacers who attacked the Christmas party, and I need to find Master Emerson."

Even though the old man continued to do the dishes, Grayson knew he had Frost's attention.

"Yeah? Who did it then?"

Grayson hesitated to tell Frost what he knew. For some reason, he felt like Emerson was the only person he needed to tell.

"Listen, I do appreciate you saving Ethan and me, but I just need to talk to Master Emerson. Can you get me to him?"

Frost made his way over to the couch with a strange expression on his face. "You're not going to tell me who you think it is?"

"Who I know it is," corrected Grayson. "And I don't see why you would care. You never seem too interested in our discussions."

"If you want to find Emerson, then say the name."

Grayson didn't have a real reason not to tell Frost, and he didn't want to waste any more time in his apartment, so he said, "It's Ridley Crimson. He's been faking all those injuries from the attack. I saw him walking around his apartment without his sling or head wrap."

Frost sat down across from Grayson and folded his hands together, lost in deep thought. "Why don't you let me tell Elliott?"

"No, I'd like to," said Grayson with authority. "I'd like to hear him receive the information."

"I'll tell him," said Frost with an unfriendly smile. "And after saving your butt, you better trust me, kid."

"I have a hard time trusting anyone at Icefall after our last conversation," said Grayson. "You can either take me to Master Emerson, or I can start asking random Lacers on the street where I can find him."

***

Emerson didn't live in a penthouse like Frost, but rather an actual house like the one Grayson grew up in. As they got deeper into the city, the skyscrapers disappeared behind them, and a street with ten modern houses and an outdoor stadium came into view. They passed two cement structures, both similar to Emerald House, and a sign that said *Extensive Education*. This must have been the program Ethan's brother Mitchell was enrolled in.

"Be right there," called Emerson, approaching the door in his shimmering white cloak. "Walter. Mr. Day. What can I do for you?"

"Grayson said he needed to talk to you, so I'll let you two get to it," said Frost, heading back down the street.

The white walls and furniture of Emerson's house made Grayson feel like he was in a model home. The two of them headed for the kitchen table, passing stainless steel kitchen appliances and automatic glass doors as they went.

"What's bothering you, Grayson?" asked Emerson.

Grayson got right to the point. "Master Ridley is the one who leaked our party information to the Lacers on Christmas. He's faking all his injuries. I saw him walking around looking perfectly healthy last night."

Emerson was silent for a while, just like Frost had been. "Grayson, I want you to listen to me very carefully. You need to trust that I'll take care of this. In the meantime, you don't speak a word of this. You haven't told anyone in your I.G., correct?"

"No, I haven't," lied Grayson.

"Good. You need to continue to act as if everything is normal when you're around Master Ridley."

"Why don't you just arrest him?"

"We will," assured Emerson, crossing his legs. "We just have to get proof first, that's all. A first-year P.L. accusing their head instructor of something isn't exactly concrete evidence, but don't worry. I'll handle it."

Grayson left Emerson's house feeling more worried than he had been the previous night. Neither Frost nor Emerson had seemed all that surprised by Grayson's news. Were they in league with Ridley? Frost already knew Grayson had the black diamond. What was stopping him from telling Emerson or Ridley?

Grayson purposely took the long way back to the campfire; he wanted to get a second look at the Extensive Education Houses. One had *Sapphire* written in ocean blue across the front, and the other had *Diamond* mapped out in white. Sand pathways and platforms intertwined the Sapphire and Diamond Houses, keeping them above the surrounding lake water. As he got closer, he heard cheers and music coming from inside the homes—these beach houses were probably just another couple of places for Lacers to party.

Grayson got lost a few times on his way back to the campfire from Yahoel's Lake, but he found his destination just as his friends were packing up to leave.

"How did it go? Are they arresting Ridley?" asked Ethan.

Grayson told them how Frost and Emerson had reacted. "I think they're in on it."

"Oh, give it a rest!" said Ethan. "Elliott Emerson is not an evil Lacer. I'm not saying I know Frost, but why would he have saved us if he wanted you or your necklace? He had the darn necklace in his hand."

"I'm sure Emerson will find the evidence he needs quickly. He said he'd get it done. In the meantime, we'll all just stay together," said Harlie, giving Grayson an encouraging smile.

"I don't trust any of these Lacers," muttered Ambrielle. "Just because we don't understand their motives doesn't mean they aren't bad."

Before leaving the campfire, Grayson found the largest tree in the forest and knocked it down by constricting the bottom of the trunk. He swung his staff as hard as he could, sending the tree through the air.

"Twenty-five feet. Not too shabby," said Ethan once he finished measuring.

"Looks like I'm gonna pass my final test."

* * *

Saturday night was Grayson's last night to hang out with his friends. The instructors had messaged the I.G. and informed them that their parents would be picking them up on Monday morning. They'd also said a few P.L.s would be staying at Icefall for the summer.

"I'm going to be stuck here for a month all by myself until Kimberly finishes middle school," said Harlie.

"Maybe I'll ask Emerson if I can stay here with you," said Ethan. "I'd rather be here than at home."

"I don't think that's how it works."

"At least you're only here for a month. Jeremiah can't tell his brother he's a Lacer for three years," said Grayson.

"Don't you mean a *Potential* Lacer?" asked Ambrielle sarcastically.

Grayson most certainly had his own problems, but at least he didn't have to stress about getting dropped after the final test like his three friends; this did not mean he didn't have to listen to them talk about it. Ambrielle seemed like she didn't care. She just laughed whenever Harlie or Ethan brought it up.

Grayson wasn't worried about Ethan getting dropped. He might not have known a lot about fire control, but from afar, there appeared to be a talent difference between Ethan and most of the kids in his element group. Harlie, on the other hand, struggled at times. Grayson figured she would still be okay, but it worried him. He didn't know what he'd do if one of his friends got dropped. Seeing Liam get kicked out had been bad enough.

Grayson saw Liam in the hallway for the first time since he'd tackled Jasper. His face was swollen, he was walking with a limp, and his front tooth was chipped.

"Hey, man—I'm sorry. I should never have put you in that position. Are you feeling any better?" asked Grayson, gently patting Liam on the back.

"It's not your fault," said Liam. "I shouldn't have lost my cool like that. But it turns out I still have a chance to stay in the I.G. Jasper persuaded Ridley to have a meeting with my parents and talk it over. I'll see you tomorrow for the final test—it shouldn't be too bad."

Grayson was relieved but didn't understand how Liam could possibly stay in the process after assaulting an instructor. They'd almost kicked Ambrielle out several times just for talking back to them.

"Yeah, but I know they're never actually going to do it," Ambrielle told him when he shared his encounter with Liam. "They just threaten us. In reality, they do need us to stay in the initiation process. Tackling an instructor is a little risky, but I'm not surprised they're giving him a second chance."

Saturday came to an end, and there was still no word about whether Ridley had been arrested or not. Grayson figured he hadn't been because there was no sign of Icefall Lane celebrating. They would undoubtedly party to the arrest of an evil Lacer. Although it was unlikely, he hoped to wake up in the morning to good news.

At 5 a.m. on Sunday morning, a roar louder than the one on New Year's Eve erupted from Icefall Lane. Grayson and Ethan ran to Emerald House to see if the Lacers' celebration did, in fact, stem from the arrest of Master Ridley.

"Remember, if he's still here, we're gonna be right by you the whole time," said Ethan as they hurried down the path, running late as usual. "And your bodyguard's gonna be inside the house, too."

Ridley was there. And he was back in his sling and headwrap.

"Fire in the hole!" yelled Mr. Hill as he and Mr. Boxer pelted the I.G. with a parade of colorful eggs from the balcony. "Happy Easter!"

It was Easter. That was why Icefall Lane was celebrating.

"And there they are," said Ridley with a fake smile. "A minute later, and you two would have managed to get the entire I.G. dropped."

"We would have managed to do what?" asked Ethan as egg yolk exploded down Grayson's head and onto his black workout outfit.

"Oh, I was just telling the rest of the group about the new rule I've put into place. If one of you fails your final element test, every single one of you will get dropped. Don't give me that look, Mr. Day. You're lucky your earth instructor is giving Liam a second chance; otherwise, one of you would already be gone. However, now it's all of you or none of you. Our city is already too crowded, in my opinion."

"Don't worry, ladies and gents," exclaimed Jasper as Grayson and Ethan filed into empty spaces around the pool. "If you guys all become Gavens, we're always in need of trash collectors. Icefall will be filthy after the other I.G.s are done partying."

The instructors shoved Grayson in the freezing pool at least twenty times on the last day, which happened to be just about the average for everyone else. He kept an eye on Ridley at all times, but nothing ever happened. Ridley remained in his armchair reading a magazine while Ms. Myles and Mr. Boxer had one last go at the I.G.

If it hadn't been for the fear of Ridley killing him at any possible moment, Grayson might have enjoyed his last workout. They'd just had a nice weekend off, so he wasn't tired. Ambrielle kept talking back to Ms. Myles anytime she threatened to drop someone. And it was their last workout regardless of their final test results. Grayson decided not to think about wasting a whole year of his life training only to get kicked out at the end.

After a couple of hours, the workout concluded, and it was time for everyone's examinations. Grayson and Liam went first. Jasper uprooted the tree from the garden and split it in half. Grayson's half was much smaller than the tree he'd practiced with.

"Get the tree across the line, and you pass," said Jasper, drawing a line in the turf with his staff, about ten feet away from the spot where Liam and Grayson stood.

"That's quite the test, Jasper," sneered Ridley.

"Ah, I can't take credit for it. Liam here was the one who came up with the idea."

Liam's face went pink. Ridley now had another reason to want him out of the I.G.

"Ready. Set. Throw!"

Grayson lifted the tree off the ground with his staff and swung it with all his strength. The tree cleared Jasper's line by fifty feet and hit the front door on the other side of the house. When Grayson looked back, Liam still had his levitating a few inches off the ground. He hadn't thrown it yet. When Liam let go, he winced and grabbed his injured rib cage. The tree never made it more than a foot off the ground. The I.G. held their breath and erupted in applause as they watched Liam's tree slide past Jasper's line. Liam fell to his knees in pain.

"My group's done! My group's done!" cheered Jasper, giving Grayson and Liam high fives.

The stress from Liam's tree turned out to be nothing compared to what the other groups' tasks would bring. Ethan and his fellow fire controllers were up next; they had a group test.

"Play catch with this fireball for one minute straight," said Mrs. Foster, addressing her group. "If one person lets it hit the ground or reduces its size, you all fail."

Ethan started off with the ball of fire. He passed it left to Brenda Lewis, who tossed it to Dylan, who passed it to Brooke Lee. Once the ball made its way to the other boys in the group, things took a turn for the worse. Spencer Erving dove to save the ball because of Kevin Workman's terrible throw. Grayson sighed in relief when the fireball returned to Ethan for the last time.

With two groups down, Harlie and her electricity partners were up next. Thankfully, Mr. Boxer had come up with an easy test for Jeremiah, Jessica Baker, and Harlie. They had to turn the AC unit on without hitting the switch and then turn it back off. This test reminded Grayson of his elementary-school days when he wanted to magically turn on the TV because he was too lazy to get up and find the remote. All three of them finished quickly. The I.G. jumped around, cheering.

The wind group was up next. Grayson obviously hoped they didn't mess up, but if a particular group was going to, he would rather it was them than anyone else. Grayson had always gotten along with Timothy Addison, Danielle Green, and Brandi Stark, but Xander Reed remained Grayson's least favorite person in the I.G.

Mr. Hill's test was the same as Mrs. Foster's, but with an actual tennis ball. It was already a windy day, so the four wind controllers had little trouble throwing and levitating the ball back and forth. After the minute concluded, the I.G. went crazy. There was only one group left to go—Ambrielle's.

"Water group, you're up," announced Ms. Myles. "Around the pool, staffs out."

Of course, Ms. Myles had planned the hardest test.

"I'm going to push each of you in the pool, and when you come out, you better not be wet, or everyone fails," she smirked.

"How about giving us a test on something you actually taught us? But I understand that may be hard since you didn't really teach us a whole lot this year," growled Ambrielle.

This was it. How could they possibly come out of the pool dry if they hadn't been taught how to do that?

"You first, Miss Stone," said Ms. Myles, shoving Ambrielle as hard as she could into the water.

Ambrielle aimed her staff at the pool and parted the water away from the spot she was going to land. Once she hit the bottom, Ambrielle circled her staff around herself, keeping the water at bay, and climbed out perfectly dry.

"I'm not even going to brag," said Ambrielle, bowing to her ecstatic audience.

Grayson couldn't believe Ambrielle had managed to pass a test that her instructor clearly meant for her to fail. She'd learned something without being taught it. Grayson thought about the underground roots he could summon, but that was only when he had his black diamond on.

The I.G. wasn't out of the woods yet. Ambrielle frantically yelled tips at Nathan Bowen as Ms. Myles approached him. "Just try to imagine the water flowing away from you as you get closer to it!"

Nathan flew forward. He shifted the water away from himself momentarily, but the second he hit the bottom, he dropped his staff, and the water collapsed on him.

The energy from the I.G. completely evaporated. Grayson felt all his dreams of doing something fun with his life slip away as Nathan came out dripping water. Ambrielle helped Nathan out of the pool as Ms. Myles successfully soaked Isabella Parks and Faith Davis. Madison Silver didn't even attempt to shield herself from the water.

Ridley gathered everyone around him. Grayson hoped he would say Ms. Myles's test was completely unfair, and they all passed. No such words left Ridley's mouth.

"Well, it's been an interesting year. Unfortunately, it's come to an end. Your parents will be picking you up in the morning—yes, even those of you with younger siblings will be picked up tomorrow. There's no law against a Gaven returning home."

"We didn't give in to your stupid process," said Ethan, unable to control his anger.

"Watch your tone, Mr. Clark," warned Ridley. "I'm sure you're thinking this is the last time you'll see me, but unfortunately, you will all need to be back here at 8 p.m. so Master Emerson can officially drop you from our program. Now get going and pack your stuff."

Nobody said a word on the way back to Emerald Residence Hall. Grayson trudged forward, followed by his bodyguard, trying to think of a way to stay in the Lacer Initiation Process. As much as he hated it at times, he always figured that he'd be an Official Lacer one day, not just a Gaven who did chores around the city or went back to the regular world for good.

Grayson went up to his dorm to pack. He really wanted to talk to Ambrielle about her plans now that they'd all been dropped, but she'd run off after Harlie, who'd started crying. Grayson began cleaning up the trash in his dorm; he might as well practice for his future job. When he got to the backpack under his bed, he stopped.

The black diamond. Grayson realized he didn't need to stay in the Lacer Initiation Process. He already had a necklace, the best necklace, the necklace nobody knew he had. He could just share it with his friends if they ever needed to use it, and it would be like they'd never been kicked out. His thoughts were cut short when a Lacer stopped by the dorm to make sure he and Ethan were packing.

"Yes! We're packing! *And tell Ridley he's an idiot if you see him!*" said Ethan as the Lacer hurried down the hall.

Grayson told Ethan that he would share his black diamond with him—this calmed Ethan down a little.

"You better make sure you hide that thing well," said Ethan. "Today is Ridley's last chance to steal it, and who knows if he'll even be there tonight. He said Emerson was going to be the one dropping us."

As he continued to clean the dorm, Grayson debated hiding the necklace in his grandpa's underground room or possibly taking it with him. Something was telling him not to leave it unattended tonight. If he brought it, Ridley wouldn't be able to steal it, and he'd also be able to defend himself if Ridley, or even Emerson, went after him. He would just be sure not to touch anyone while wearing it.

Grayson's wristwatch beeped. *Wear green cloaks tonight. Remember, 8 p.m. sharp.*

"Green cloaks?" asked Ethan.

"I guess they want us to look good for Emerson right before he drops us," grumbled Grayson. "Ridley has the city attacked, and I'm the one Emerson will make leave first. You don't think there's anything wrong with that?"

"Yes, I think something is wrong with that. I just don't think that means Emerson wants you dead."

When eight o'clock rolled around, Grayson and Ethan had only packed half of their belongings; not because they hadn't had time to, they'd just been busy coming up with a way to keep people away from Grayson.

"I can't believe you're risking this again," said Ambrielle as she, Ethan, and Harlie formed a protective circle around him.

Grayson clipped the black diamond around his neck, and his senses enhanced. He felt secure with his second set of eyes, yet a feeling of danger wrenched through his body. Together, the four of them made their way down to Emerald House for the last time in their matching cloaks. There was no sign of Emerson inside the house. Ridley and the other instructors were all present with mocking smirks across their faces. Grayson's bodyguard spectated from the corner—the long gray sleeves of his sweatshirt crossed in front of his chest.

Ridley had the I.G. line up around the pool. Grayson was terrified that one of the instructors would push him in and notice the energy from his necklace. If they did, he would run away from Icefall and never come back. He was about to be kicked out anyway.

"Turn your cloaks backward," instructed Ridley. "Good—now turn and face the person to your left, grab onto their shoulders, and cover your face with the hood on your cloaks."

"Get ready to walk!" yelled Jasper. "Mr. Hill is going to lead the way to Master Emerson's house."

Grayson grabbed Ethan's shoulders from behind, and Harlie grabbed his. With their cloak hoods blinding them, they made their way out of Emerald House.

"I guess they really don't want us to know where Emerson lives," whispered Ethan as he cautiously made his way through the front lawn. "It better be close because I feel like I'm gonna fall."

"It's on the other side of the darn city," whispered Grayson.

Grayson was lucky he decided to bring his black diamond because even though he couldn't see anything, he felt like he still knew what was going on around him. He spent half of his energy trying not to fall and the other half trying to locate Ridley. His senses were thrown off when the line reached Icefall Lane. The Lacers cheered as the I.G. crossed the street, passed Frost's apartment building, and traveled toward the Extensive Education Houses.

"Emerson's house is right down the street," said Grayson, who was starting to realize everything was about to come to an end. He could either stay at Icefall and be a garbage man, having no fun at all, or go work some regular job back in his hometown. What were his parents going to think of him after this?

The line made a sharp left turn, making Grayson stumble as he almost fell down a flight of stairs. This wasn't the direction of Emerson's house—there hadn't been any stairs a day ago. The floor leveled out, and the line came to a halt.

"Turn your cloaks back the right way," said Mr. Hill.

Grayson shielded his eyes from the bright lights above him and flipped his cloak around. He stood in the middle of an outdoor stadium, surrounded by stone benches where the Amethyst and Ruby I.G.s sat watching. Emerson made his way through the audience and up onto the platform with Grayson's I.G. There was no sign of Ridley or Grayson's bodyguard.

"Great. They're going to drop us in front of Dontae and Hardy," whispered Ethan.

"Get ready to take my necklace," said Grayson.

"What? Why?"

"I just have a bad feeling."

Grayson reached up to his neck as casually as possible and unclipped the black diamond. He slid it down his side, clenched it tightly in his hand, and prepared to give it to Ethan.

Emerson stated, "I'm troubled to announce our first Emerald I.G. in sixty years to win the Necklace Raid won't be moving onto their second year of training in the Lacer Initiation Process."

His news was met with cheers and laughter from the other I.G.s.

Grayson didn't care. He didn't care about the other I.G.s. He didn't care about Ridley or even Emerson. He had his grandpa's necklace, and he would do greater things than all of them. He just had to make it through the night without getting caught. He no longer cared what being a Lacer meant. They weren't anything special.

"Now, in all seriousness," continued Emerson. "All of you in the crowd undoubtedly remember this feeling whether it was a year ago or two years ago for you… It's time to congratulate these hard-working P.L.s on a successful first year of training and welcome them into the second year of our three-year program. If they choose to continue, of course."

The Emerald I.G. covered their mouths in shock. Ethan ferociously shook Grayson's shoulders, and Ambrielle, who seemed to have already known this twist was coming, looked like a girl who'd just walked into a surprise birthday party she'd heard about weeks ago.

Grayson didn't know what to think. He'd been so angry with Emerson and his instructors a second ago. Was he just supposed to forget everything since it was a trick?

"Step forward, Ethan Clark," said Emerson.

Ethan skipped his way to the front of the stage.

"Do you choose to continue to the second year of the Lacer Initiation Process?"

"Yes, of course, I do!" Ethan beamed.

"Congratulations," said Emerson, shaking Ethan's hand.

Mrs. Foster was also on stage to shake Ethan's hand. She looked happy to see him finish, despite being a complete pain in the backside all year long.

One by one, each P.L. was called to the front to shake hands with Emerson and their element instructor. Liam, who was still beaten up, chose to continue immediately and received a bear hug from Jasper, who clearly didn't care that they'd been in a fight three days ago.

Harlie chose to continue so quietly that Emerson had to ask her twice. Ambrielle also decided to continue to the second year but didn't even bother shaking Ms. Myles's hand. Ms. Myles didn't seem to mind Ambrielle's rudeness; she clapped loudly and looked sincerely excited to see Ambrielle continue.

Grayson knew his name was about to be called at any moment, and he didn't have an answer yet. He didn't need to continue. He had his staff and his necklace. He could train himself and not have to deal with another two years of punishment. He could get away from Icefall and do anything he wanted with his powers. He knew he was different, and this was his chance to leave.

"Grayson Day," said Emerson, followed by the loudest cheer yet.

Dontae and Hardy stood up from their seats to clap. Grayson stepped forward, Jasper to his left, Emerson to his right.

"Mr. Day. Do you choose to continue to the second year of the Lacer Initiation Process?"

Both answers could turn out well. Both answers could turn out bad. Grayson glanced back at Ambrielle, who had her eyes locked on him, her long black hair waving in the wind.

He couldn't leave his friends.

"Yes, I do," said Grayson, shaking Emerson's hand.

As their hands met, Grayson realized he still had the black diamond in his opposite palm. He had forgotten to hand it to Ethan. Emerson was going to feel the energy. If Emerson hadn't already known Grayson possessed the necklace, he knew now.

CHAPTER 19

Shaders

G rayson tried to yank his arm away, but the damage was done. He walked back into line with his I.G., completely ignoring Jasper's outstretched hand. He saw Jasper shake his own hand as they passed each other. Emerson's eyes stayed with Grayson long after he returned to the line. Grayson put the necklace behind his back and handed it to Ethan, who took it immediately.

"I thought the necklace was supposed to make you smarter," whispered Ethan. "That might honestly be the dumbest thing someone has ever done in the history of doing things."

Emerson remained in his same spot at the front of the stage, showing no sign that he would tell anyone else. Maybe he'd already known—maybe Frost had told him. As Emerson once again addressed the crowd, Grayson started to shake. Everything about the situation felt out of place.

He looked around for Ridley, who was still not in attendance. He found it very odd that the lead instructor was the only Lacer absent. Maybe Emerson had found evidence of Ridley's involvement in the attack on Christmas and arrested him while the I.G. was walking to the stadium. Perhaps Grayson's bodyguard, who was also missing in action, was the one who arrested him.

"Now that each I.G. has completed their ceremony, it's time for the main event," said Emerson, pulling out his staff and moving the stage to the side of the arena. "Instructors, if you could please lead the Emerald I.G. to their seats, we'll get the tournament underway."

With Harlie stationed behind him, Grayson took a seat in the second row in between Ethan and Ambrielle. He was unaware of what tournament Emerson was referring to, but Grayson was happy to sit and watch for once.

"Please give a warm welcome to our first two contenders of the night: Sarah Smith and Mitchell Clark," announced Emerson. "The first round of the Extensive Education Tournament will begin momentarily."

As the Emerald I.G. and other nearby Lacers hurried over to question Ethan about his brother's skills, Grayson smoothly reclaimed his necklace and started making predictions about the upcoming match with Harlie.

"Is it just like the Necklace Raid?" Grayson asked.

"No, the fourth- and fifth-year students duel each other," said Ambrielle.

"I bet your dad told you all about it already," said Grayson. "Just like I'm sure he told you about the instructors pretending to drop us from the program on the last day."

"It's not my fault you believed them. I honestly would have told you, but Ridley had a talk with me at the beginning of the year and said if I spoiled the initiation process for anyone, I'd actually get kicked out."

Emerson informed the audience that there would be eight first-round battles, each lasting a maximum of five minutes. Both

Mitchell and his opponent's stealth suits were lined with a row of silver canisters strapped around the waist.

The two of them were facing each other in the center of the arena, the match about to begin, when a wave of Lacers from Icefall Lane approached the scene. They quickly filled the remaining seats; however, there weren't enough for all of them, so many had to stand and watch from above. Grayson didn't feel comfortable with so many Lacers around him; someone was bound to come up to him, not to mention it made it more difficult to keep an eye out for Ridley.

Mitchell and his opponent extended their staffs to full length as Emerson sounded the commencement horn. There weren't any elements for the two fighters to use. Was this fight going to consist only of the powers they'd gained from their necklaces?

Mitchell answered Grayson's question when he took one of the canisters off his waist, and it exploded with fire. Mitchell sent the fire at the girl's ankles, which she blocked with a gust of wind that came out of her canister. The crowd cheered as Mitchell and Sarah exchanged offensive attacks.

Since it was nearly impossible to get seriously hurt in a stealth suit, Ethan obviously wasn't worried about Mitchell's safety. Yet Ambrielle's jokes about his brother possibly losing in the first round had him nervously tapping his leg. About three minutes into the duel, Mitchell found a weak spot in the girl's defense by forming a rope out of his fire and swinging one of her legs out from under her. He put his staff to her chest, forcing Emerson to call the match.

"That's my brother! That's my brother!" exclaimed Ethan.

Mitchell waved in Ethan's direction before sitting with the other participants.

The night was quite enjoyable. Lacers walked up and down the aisles, handing out drinks and snacks—they were free, of course. Grayson sipped on a coke and shared a pretzel with Ambrielle. Emerson was refereeing the tournament, so he couldn't currently get Grayson in trouble for wearing the necklace even if he wanted to. Grayson's parents were picking him up in the morning; he'd just have to hide the necklace in Oscar's office until then. Since Emerson never saw the necklace, he didn't have any real proof.

When the second match began, Grayson and his friends scooted over on the bench to make room for two newly arriving Lacers— one of them Ridley. Grayson's heart skipped a beat. Master Ridley was only a couple of seats away from him, and the black diamond was in Grayson's pocket.

He elbowed Ethan and kicked Ambrielle to get their attention off the tournament and onto the nearby problem. They both gathered around him tight while Harlie extended her legs into the aisle behind him, making it difficult for people to walk through. With his friends covering him, Grayson strapped the black diamond back around his neck.

"What on earth are you doing?" hissed Ambrielle.

"Protecting myself," said Grayson. "My bodyguard isn't here. Ridley probably took him out."

Grayson kept a more thorough watch on Ridley and his companion with the necklace back on. He blocked out the excess noise and focused on understanding Ridley's conversation. The Lacer next to Ridley fancied an amethyst cloak, and his long black ponytail was tucked neatly into the hood. The two Lacers were deep in conversation, paying Grayson no attention.

"Maybe we should just go," suggested Harlie. "If we go back to the dorms, we won't have to worry about any of this."

"I'm not making you guys miss the tournament for me, especially since Mitchell is still in," said Grayson. "Besides, if we left now, it would look suspicious."

"Yeah, because the three of us practically covering you like a blanket doesn't look suspicious," said Ambrielle.

As the tournament continued, Grayson tried to study the older Lacers' techniques in case Ridley decided to make a move. A girl who stood at a towering height of six-foot-eight didn't use any of her powers and won by tackling her opponent. A boy half Grayson's size won by sending a girl's electricity attack back at her. A Lacer named Luke claimed the latest and perhaps most impressive victory. Luke had glided over the top of his opponent, dropped a wind canister at her feet, and sent her flying out of the arena and into the stands.

During an intermission, Liam hobbled over into the row behind Grayson. Grayson blushed as Ambrielle put her arm around his back to shield him. "Your brother looked good out there," Liam said, making his way toward Ridley and the unidentified Lacer.

As Liam bent down and gave the Lacer next to Ridley a hug, joined in on their conversation, and sat next to them, Grayson remembered what Liam had said about Jasper convincing Ridley to meet with his parents so he could stay in the program. The other Lacer had to be Liam's dad. Grayson guessed that Ridley had missed the completion ceremony because of this meeting. Evidently, it had gone well; the three of them seemed to be joking around.

Grayson wanted to take Ridley's sling and headwrap off and force him to walk around fine without them in front of everyone. Ridley would probably be friendly with all the P.L.s now that training was over, just like the other instructors. Jasper had been the only one who hadn't tried to make life miserable for the I.G., and Grayson hadn't even shaken his hand at the end of the ceremony.

"Yo, Ethan, come on down!" yelled Mitchell once the first round concluded.

"Let's go," said Ethan. "We'll get food after we say hi."

"I'm not getting up," Grayson said. "I don't want Ridley to see me."

"I'll stay with you," assured Ambrielle.

"Okay, well, do you two want anything to eat?" asked Harlie, getting up to join Ethan.

"I'll get something later," Grayson replied.

After Ethan and Harlie left to talk to Mitchell, Ridley stood up from the bench and looked down on Grayson. Despite his body's internal shivers, Grayson did not back down from Ridley's gaze. He had his secret weapon around his neck. The stare-down ended with Ridley doing a quick scan of the stadium, swiftly jumping over the bench, and taking off at a speed walk in the direction of Emerald Residence Hall, his limp non-existent.

"He's going for the necklace," Grayson realized. "I have to stop him!"

"The necklace is around your neck! Let him look for it," said Ambrielle.

"I'm not letting him into my dorm. He'll find Oscar's underground room or hurt Ace and Spades!" said Grayson, getting up to follow Ridley. "You stay here! Go get Emerson. Tell him what's happening."

Instead of following Grayson's instructions, Ambrielle stumbled through the stands, clinging onto Grayson's cloak from behind. Once out of the stadium, they broke into a run across an eerily silent Icefall Lane.

"Go back! You have to tell Emerson!"

"I'm not leaving you to fight Ridley alone!" said Ambrielle as they entered the dark forest.

Grayson stopped arguing. He grabbed Ambrielle's hand and led her over the electric blue bridge covering Adriel's Pond, past the roaring animals deep inside the woods, and onto the path in front of Emerald Residence Hall, where Ridley could be seen pacing through the hallway.

"We've gotta draw him outside so I can use the underground roots," Grayson said.

Grayson and Ambrielle made a break for the sliding glass door, but Jasper popped out from the jungle and tackled them.

"Shhh! Be quiet!" he whispered, helping them to their feet. "Are you insane, going after my brother alone?"

"Yeah, probably," said Grayson. "But you're here now. Let's get him."

"All three of us can't beat him," said Jasper. "If we attack, Emerson and Walter Frost will be here in a second to help him."

"Frost and Emerson are in on this, too?" asked Ambrielle. "Were they the ones who had Emerald House attacked at Christmas?"

"Yes," said Jasper, his usual joking tone non-existent. "You two have no idea what you're in the middle of. My hands have been tied all year long. We need to get out of here, now. We'll come back for the black diamond later. I'm guessing you have it well-hidden."

"I don't have the black diamond," Grayson denied.

"Grayson, every instructor has known you've had the black diamond since the first round of the Necklace Raid. If you have a good hiding spot for it, let's get out of here!"

Grayson took a moment to process what Jasper had said. If Jasper knew he had it, there was no reason not to tell him its current location.

"I don't want to leave," said Grayson, untucking the necklace from his cloak. "I want to get Ridley outside and end him."

Jasper's mouth dropped. "If Frost and Emerson weren't a factor, I'd say let's go for it. Trust me. We've gotta get out of here."

Reluctantly, Grayson followed Jasper through the forest, away from the residence hall, his hand grasping Ambrielle's tightly.

"How are we sneaking out of here?" asked Grayson.

"The southside watchtower," said Jasper.

"We can't leave without Ethan and Harlie," said Grayson as they came to a stop in the same place the spotlight had flashed on him while searching for the Stream of Serenity.

"There's no time," Jasper interjected. "You're the only one they want. Ambrielle, you can stay back. You'll be safe."

"Not a chance," said Ambrielle.

Footsteps echoed down the watchtower staircase, and Liam's father emerged from the darkness. "Norman Dixon," he said in a low, barely audible voice, nodding to Grayson and Ambrielle. "The guard's dead, Jasper. We're free to go."

Jasper nodded. "All right, kids, up we go!"

Grayson grabbed Ambrielle's arm and pulled her back. He thought back to a comment Jasper had made the day they met: *"No decent Lacer would ever kill an animal, so animals don't randomly hunt and kill Lacers."*

Norman had killed another Lacer. He had committed a crime.

"It's okay to kill other Lacers, but not animals?" wondered Grayson.

Jasper swallowed nervously. "You don't understand how bad we need to leave this city," he said sternly.

"Why do we need to leave?" Grayson challenged.

"You're leaving with us one way or another," said Norman, stationing himself behind Grayson and Ambrielle, trapping them against the city wall.

"You're the one who wants my necklace. You *and* your brother are evil Lacers," said Grayson, pointing at Jasper.

"I'm no Lacer. I am a Shader," Jasper said, bowing to the earth. "And the only reason Ridley came to Emerald Residence Hall tonight was to stop me from finding your necklace. I already killed your bodyguard. I guess my brother wanted to protect your dorm in his absence."

"I know Ridley is faking his injuries from Christmas. Do you expect me to believe anything you tell me? You've lied to me all year," said Grayson, slowly walking sideways with Ambrielle.

"Ridley is faking his injuries to help the government build a better case against my friends from the Christmas party," said Jasper. "E.R.O.L's laws are delusional, and my brother is a puppet for playing along."

Grayson took a second to think about what Jasper was saying—if Ridley was faking his injuries to help E.R.O.L, that would explain why Frost and Emerson hadn't been surprised when Grayson told them.

"I know it looks bad. However, we had valid reasons for every crime we've committed," Jasper told him. "I killed your grandpa to balance the world."

Grayson didn't want to hear anymore. The only instructor he had trusted was the reason his grandpa was dead, the reason his mom had spent the summer crying, and was clearly the reason the Black House had been attacked. He had to get away. Grayson pulled Ambrielle up against the snow wall of the city—he faintly heard the familiar sound of flowing water.

"We didn't want to kill you. We still don't want to kill you," said Jasper, inching closer to Grayson. "Come with me. Leave this joke of a city behind, and you'll be trained in a way to fully maximize your potential. Think about how much time you wasted getting your physical body into shape this year. If you leave with me now, I can show you how to condition your mind in a way the initiation process never could."

Intrigued as he might have been, Grayson had already made a series of bad decisions during his first year away from home; listening to Jasper would only add to that list. At this very moment, Grayson learned the true power of belief. Escape wasn't a choice — it had to be done.

Grayson grabbed Ambrielle's shoulder, and together they ducked down and rolled through the frozen wall into the Stream of Serenity.

Jasper and Norman let out furious screams from the other side of the wall — then the mountain shook. Jasper plowed a massive tree trunk through the snow wall, making a hole big enough for him and Norman to climb through. Still in their emerald cloaks, Grayson and Ambrielle dove into the chilly water and let it take them downstream.

"You go right. I'll go left," called Jasper. "Be careful. He's wearing the black diamond."

The stream was too bright to blend into the darkness. It was only a matter of time before Jasper or Norman spotted them.

"We're gonna be okay," Grayson reassured Ambrielle. "We need to reach the heart of the stream, where the walls are lower, then we can get out and go back to the city for help."

He could hear steam coming from the place where the ice water met the circular hot tub. Jasper's footsteps inched closer. The instant Grayson's body submerged into the relaxing bath, his stress alleviated, and his muscles relaxed.

Grayson pulled Ambrielle out of the soothing water, and they made a break for the nearest wall to re-enter Icefall. Jasper rounded the corner and swung his staff at Ambrielle's face, knocking her to the ground. Seeing Ambrielle get hurt unlocked a level of rage Grayson didn't know he had inside himself.

"You foolish, arrogant kid," snarled Jasper as student and mentor exchanged blows. "You're a fool for wearing that necklace tonight."

Grayson's brief moment in the heart of the stream had healed his muscles and was the only reason he stood a chance against his instructor. He screamed, clawed, and eventually shoved Jasper off him, creating distance. Grayson thought this was a good thing since neither of them had any elements to fight with. But then Jasper kicked off hard from the ground and took flight just as Emerson had on Christmas. He knocked Grayson backward into the flowing stream.

Norman Dixon appeared from the opposite end of the cave. He fashioned liquid ropes out of the water, restraining Grayson, and raised him up to surface level. Grayson tried to slip through them using his black diamond; they only got tighter each time he tried. He was stuck.

"Get the girl," said Jasper, spitting blood out of his mouth. "She's seen too much."

Jasper picked up Grayson's staff, and Norman walked toward Ambrielle, who was still lying unconscious on the ground. He was only inches away from her when she rolled sideways off the rocks and back into the spinning hot tub.

The whirlpool picked up speed, violently splashing water around the cave, and a black pit began to slowly open at the center. Grayson saw Ambrielle and a white school bus rotating inside the water. Ambrielle grabbed the bus, and the pit swallowed them whole. The water returned to its calm state. Grayson screamed for help, which resulted in Norman suppressing his mouth with a water rope.

"Forget her! Time to leave!" said Jasper, heading in the direction of the watchtower.

"I thought we'd just be kidnapping the boy tonight, and we'd have to come back for the necklace," said Norman as he pulled Grayson through the hole in the wall and levitated him up the watchtower staircase.

"Yes, I did as well," Jasper said, trailing behind them. "Thanks, Grayson, for making our job even easier. Our lord will be most pleased."

Grayson figured Jasper and Norman weren't operating alone, but hearing Jasper refer to someone as a *lord* made his body chill. There was some sort of revolution going on, and Grayson and his necklace were smack-dab in the middle of it all.

The towering glass buildings and all the ponds and streams of Icefall could be seen from the top of the watchtower. Fighting the force of the water ropes, Grayson cranked his head over the metal fencing, hoping to find Ambrielle below. He had no idea what he'd seen inside the Stream of Serenity; he had no idea how she disappeared. Ambrielle could control water better than anyone Grayson knew—he told himself she would be okay and focused on saving himself. The watchtower guard was sprawled out face-first on the steel platform. And on the other side of Icefall's snow wall, a steep slope led down to the ski resort's highest trail.

"Get the cable on him," said Jasper, tying a strand of metal around the railing of the watchtower. "You lower yourself down first, Norman. Grayson next, and I'll disconnect the cable."

Norman propelled Grayson's restrained body onto the edge of the tower, his focus on his water ropes the only thing stopping Grayson from falling down the slope.

"Let's get the hell out of here," said Jasper, climbing onto the other side of the railing.

Suddenly, on what had previously been a still air type of night, a forceful gust of wind propelled not just Grayson but Jasper and Norman as well off the watchtower. The water ropes around Grayson evaporated as the three of them tumbled down the snow wall onto one of the trails from the ski resort.

Grayson was sure he'd broken a couple of bones. His head was spinning too fast to find Jasper and Norman, but he desperately crawled forward for his staff, which was half-buried in the snow. Grayson looked back up at the watchtower fifty yards above, and there, perched at the top, was Walter Frost. He held a staff so white and shiny, its globe reminded Grayson of the White Earth from his dreams.

CHAPTER 20

Return of Wind and Evil

Frost didn't fly down to the ski trail—he gently glided through the air with as much grace as an angel on Christmas. He landed next to Grayson, and when Grayson looked into his eyes, he saw they were no longer filled with unhappiness or hopelessness; they were burning with determination.

"Get up, kid," said Frost, pulling him to his feet.

Grayson's head ached, and his knees threatened to buckle from his own weight, but he didn't have much time to regroup.

"Where's Ambrielle?" he asked.

"We'll find her after we deal with this. Now get behind that tree," ordered Frost.

Jasper and Norman, who had tumbled farther down the slope, made their way into the clearing.

"Come on out, Grayson," Jasper taunted. "The old man's gonna need your help."

Jasper used his staff to collapse the tree Grayson was hiding behind. Grayson jumped sideways to avoid it, wincing as his rib cage throbbed. He limped back into the middle of the trail next to Frost.

"It was nice of you to leave your apartment for the first time in a decade just for us," said Jasper as he and Norman came to a halt twenty feet away from Grayson and Frost.

"Are you going to keep talking, or do you want to make a move?" grunted Frost. "Oscar's grandson and I are perfectly content right here."

"Oscar Day seemed to have lost most of his abilities in his last days as well. I would know. I killed him."

Grayson waited for Frost to put Jasper in his place. But Frost remained patient.

"Oscar hadn't lost his abilities. He knew when the time was right to pass the torch," said Frost, placing his hand on Grayson's shoulder. "That's the thing about us black diamond holders. We have a better understanding of the world than you brainwashed psychopaths."

"Maybe you've mistaken our intentions," said Jasper, indicating to Norman and himself. "We aren't just two more of Icefall's drunk partiers who suddenly decided we wanted the power of a black diamond. No, we have a purpose here on Earth, and we're here to fulfill it."

Grayson almost forgot he was in danger. Could this be the higher purpose he'd been searching for all year?

"You two don't have a purpose," said Frost, waving his hand in disgust. "You're power-hungry killers."

"We are much more than that," Jasper countered. "We're Shaders, and we're here to balance the world."

"There aren't any Shaders left," Frost growled. "We ended them and their ideals long ago. Just because you discovered their name and want an excuse to do wrong doesn't make you a Shader."

"What if you forgot one? Maybe there's one you didn't lock away or kill during the war," said Jasper, shrugging. "And maybe that one has been gathering followers for years right under your nose and teaching us the ways of *evil*. Only two things are absolute in our universe—good and evil, and you can never fully dispose of either."

"We didn't forget one," said Frost, angrily digging his foot into the snow. "We burned every last book of their teachings. We burned their whole temple down. Whoever you're getting your information from can't teach you true evil."

Jasper laughed. "We learn from the descendant of Bryon Shade himself... You know just as well as I do that he knows the ways of evil."

"Fletcher Shade is dead," spat Frost. "I watched Oscar Day kill him myself."

"My grandpa killed someone?" asked Grayson, taking his eyes off Jasper and Norman to look at Frost. Frost continued to stare at the Shaders.

"Your grandpa never killed anybody," said Jasper. "Shade is very much alive. He can never die."

"He's dead," said Frost, and to Grayson's surprise, he steered him away from Jasper and Norman, back toward the city.

"If he and his teaching are both deceased," Jasper challenged, "then how could I possibly know that Shaders are promised an underground kingdom in hell for doing the God of Evil's work here on Earth, just as the God of Good promises you Lacers eternal life in heaven for doing his?"

Frost stopped dead in his tracks. He looked back at the Shaders.

"I told you…" Jasper said with a smile.

"They do know evil," muttered Frost in astonishment. "I have to fight them. Run up to the city and get Emerson. Tell him everything."

"No," said Grayson. "I'm staying."

"I wasn't asking," snapped Frost. "Now, leave!"

Frost confidently marched down the ski trail. Grayson reluctantly limped up the hill for Icefall's front entrance building.

"I guess we can settle for taking your black diamond instead," said Norman.

"You demons won't be taking anything from me tonight!" yelled Frost as a blast of wind erupted from his gleaming white staff, sending Norman thirty feet down the trail.

Grayson didn't understand how Frost had done it. There was no wind in the air—the gust had come from the staff itself. Grayson couldn't miss this battle. Instead of going back to the city, he crept along the side of the trail and hid in the trees.

Then the tree next to him shook. Its branches transformed into arms, and its trunk split into legs. At Jasper's command, the wooden giant tore from the ground and pounced on Frost. A protective force field crumbled the tree to pieces, but two more sprang into battle. Their roots smacked Grayson in the head, causing him to cry out in pain.

"The boy's in the trees!" bellowed Norman as he returned to Jasper's side.

Jasper aimed his staff at the snow beneath Grayson's feet, and the ski trail disappeared. Grayson was in the garden at Emerald House. There were rows of flowers and bushes but no battle.

By the time Grayson realized Jasper was using deceptive element control, Norman had already had him bound again in water ropes. Grayson's motionless body fell to the snow. The trees and the Shaders simultaneously converged on Frost. The old man closed his eyes and disintegrated into thin air. Grayson screamed.

"You demons don't understand the power of a black diamond when it's used for the right reasons," said Frost, reappearing behind the Shaders and propelling them to the ground with another gust of wind.

Grayson couldn't believe his eyes. Frost effortlessly manipulated the air to camouflage himself as he relocated from spot to spot on the trail, trash-talking Jasper as he teleported. "The ghost of Fletcher Shade hasn't taught you enough," Frost said, dismantling one tree after another and using the branches as his own weapons.

"He's no ghost," said Jasper, struggling to his feet.

Frost had the Shaders on their heels. Norman unfroze a pool of water and attempted to submerge him, but once again, Frost used the attack to his advantage. Norman got leveled by his own wave, causing him to lose focus on his water ropes. Even though Frost was doing perfectly fine on his own against the Shaders, Grayson hobbled onto the trail to end them once and for all.

"Stay on his right side!" yelled Jasper as he and Norman tried to surround Frost before launching their attacks. "Now!"

Jasper raised his silver staff to the sky but had it snatched from his grip by a tree root.

With his eyes closed and mind focused, Grayson sent an angry mob of underground roots at his instructor. Without his staff, Jasper was helpless. Grayson bundled his entire body until his head was red from the constriction. Norman didn't stand a chance on his own. He tried to run down the slope, but Frost pulled him back by his ponytail and used invisible restraints to rest him next to Jasper.

"You're lucky you weren't killed, kid," said Frost, putting his hands on his head to regulate his breathing.

"Walter! Grayson! Are you okay?" yelled Emerson as he ran down the trail. "Miss Stone told me you were in trouble and that Jasper was the one who... Oh my god." Emerson dropped to his knees by Jasper's side. "How could you? After everything... After all your brother's done to put those Lacers away for life... And you've been one of them all along."

"Is Ambrielle okay? Where is she?" Grayson demanded.

Tears welled up in Emerson's eyes. He no longer looked like a powerful Lacer Master; he looked like a broken man who'd just lost a close friend. "She's safe," he said.

"Evil is rising once again," hissed Jasper, looking Emerson in the eyes. "It's been dormant for far too long. Thankfully, you Lacers have been stuck in your cities, partying your lives away, failing to promote any kind of positive change to society in its absence."

Emerson curiously tilted his head to the side. "We haven't promoted a positive change because we're still trying to get humans to trust us after evil Lacers like you attempted to force change upon them," he said, getting to his feet.

"That's a lie," Jasper denied.

"We've been working with human governments all around the world to slowly implement positive change into society ever since Frost and the rest of our war heroes won Karma's War sixty years ago."

"There's no such thing as an evil Lacer," said Jasper. "There are Shaders, and there are Lacers. Shaders never tried to force positive change on society; we tried to destroy the world. That was just a heartwarming lie Frost and the rest of your *war heroes* told everyone, so becoming a Shader was no longer an option."

Emerson looked just as confused as Grayson.

Jasper laughed at their ignorance and continued, "Look what you've done, Walter. You, Oscar, and the rest of you old Lacers really thought you could eliminate the God of Evil's teachings forever. Now we've risen again, and only a handful of Lacers even know what Shaders are. By failing to educate Lacers on the evil half of karma, the initiation process has doomed you all for the war that is to come."

"Tell me what a Shader is," demanded Emerson, slamming his staff into the snow. "No more avoiding my questions, Walter."

"A demon from the pits of hell," grunted Frost. "They're here to wreak havoc, just like we're here to bring peace."

"There is no such thing as good in a world without evil." Jasper smiled. "In some weird way, we are the ones responsible for happiness, and Lacers are the cause of hopelessness and despair. A mix of good and evil keeps the Earth spinning, and we're both just doing our part."

The air around the ski trail and nearby trees became silent. There was a balance—a long-awaited balance.

"You're evil just to be evil?" Grayson asked.

"Yes, but if you really think about what I said, Shaders are also the reason for all things good. Our God promises us a kingdom just like yours."

Frost shifted his gaze from the Shaders at his feet into the eerie stillness of the night sky. "I'm going to bring these two to the Black House," he said. "E.R.O.L needs to see firsthand that evil has returned. Emerson, you need to bring Grayson to the residence hall and secure the city."

"We're going to talk when you get back," said Emerson, putting his arm around Grayson. "And you're going to tell me everything."

Frost nodded and used his staff to lift Jasper and Norman's restrained bodies off the ground.

"Make sure you treat Liam like a hero," said Jasper with one last wicked smile. "Without him, our plan never would have worked."

"The boy helped you take Grayson?" asked Emerson.

"Oh yes, definitely. Not knowingly, of course," said Jasper. "If I hadn't made him stay in the house alone during the Necklace Raid and then told him to attack me after, we never would have gotten Norman into the city. I told him that we pick one P.L. to start a fight with an instructor every year just to mix things up."

Emerson snatched Grayson off the ground and flew him away from the Shaders, over the ski trail, and up to the watchtower.

"Can I tell my friends what happened?" asked Grayson, hurrying down the spiral staircase.

"That's your decision," said Emerson, once again picking up Grayson and flying him to Emerald Residence Hall. "I personally don't even understand what's going on, but if you want to try and explain it to them, go ahead. Lacers should not keep secrets from each other."

"Are my friends here?"

"I believe so. You need to stay in your dorm no matter what. I'm going to lock down the city. I'll make sure the residence hall is well protected."

Grayson thanked Emerson and ran through the hallway to his room as fast as his broken body would allow. Ethan, Ambrielle, and Harlie were anxiously waiting inside.

Ambrielle sprung off the couch to hug Grayson. Her forehead was severely bruised from Jasper's strike. Ethan quickly shoved her out of the way to embrace his best friend.

"Your head!" yelled Grayson, reaching for an ice pack in his refrigerator.

"I'm not the one who needs ice," said Ambrielle. "Look at yourself!"

Grayson stared at his disastrous reflection. The skin on his right forearm had been scraped off, and a steady flow of blood dripped from his neck onto his torn emerald cloak.

"Hello? Tell us what happened!" shouted Ethan, flipping his hands in the air. "Did they catch Jasper? Harlie and I thought you two left to get food!"

Grayson dabbed his neck with a towel Harlie had grabbed for him and leaned back in his desk chair, letting his muscles go limp. "They caught him."

Grayson went through the night step by step, filling in his friends on the events succeeding Ambrielle's blow to the head. He made an executive decision to leave certain details out. He told them all about Frost's heroics in battle. He told them how he had been the one to disarm Jasper. And he told them Emerson was currently securing the city. Grayson did not tell them about Shaders; in fact, he didn't tell them anything about the balance of good and evil or about how both Lacers and Shaders were on Earth to enforce their respective changes on society. Grayson wanted a better understanding of the situation himself before informing his friends.

"So that's it?" said Ethan. "Now that we caught Jasper and Norman, there are no more evil Lacers? They were the ones who killed Oscar and attacked the Black House."

"Emerson is securing the city for a reason," said Grayson, not wanting to leave his friends completely in the dark. "Jasper hinted that there could be more of them."

"Oh, well, there better be!" said Ethan, clenching his fists. "I can't believe I missed out on this fight. I'm definitely not missing the next one. We tried to come tonight, but Emerson had one of his assistants bring us here after Ambrielle told him what happened."

Grayson turned to Ambrielle. "How did *you* tell Emerson what happened? Where the heck did you even go?"

Ambrielle smiled. "You're not gonna believe me. C'mon, I'll show you." She moved Grayson's bed into the middle of the room and opened the trapdoor. "I don't know how I noticed it. I was lying on the ground after Jasper hit me and I realized the calm sensation from the stream was the same feeling this room gave me. I jumped into the whirlpool, and it took me here," she said, pointing to the tank of water that wrapped around the office wall. "And then I ran back to the tournament and told Emerson everything."

Grayson smiled. He couldn't help but feel like his grandpa had somehow played a role in Ambrielle's escape. "How did you get through the glass?" he asked.

"I don't know. It just opened for me when I floated down. Water poured out everywhere, but Ethan started a fire and dried it all up."

Ethan gave Grayson a big grin and a thumbs-up. "By the way, Mitchell came in second place. He lost to that tall girl who didn't use any of her elements—she just tackled him."

Just as everything seemed like it would be okay, Harlie spoke for the first time. "That's too bad about Jasper. He was always so nice. At least now E.R.O.L will be prepared if any more evil Lacers start trouble."

Once again, Grayson couldn't bring himself to make the night any worse for his friends. According to everything Jasper had said about Frost and Oscar lying to the rest of the Lacer community about the origins of Karma's War and a powerful Lacer Master like Emerson not knowing what a Shader was, Grayson didn't see how Lacers could possibly be prepared for another war.

He kept his mouth shut and gave Harlie an encouraging nod. After another couple of bear hugs threatening to break Grayson's ribs further and promising to get up early the next morning to say goodbye before their parents arrived, Ambrielle and Harlie left to go back to their room for the night.

✳ ✳ ✳

On the last day of his first year at Icefall, Grayson woke up early as usual. Tired or not, his body was accustomed to it. He took a warm shower to subside the pain from his injuries, clipped the black diamond around his neck, and left the dorm quietly.

Grayson didn't have any real destination as he set out on foot across the city that had given him a whole new life. He strolled inside the open front door of Emerald House. It was completely vacant. The inside looked no different than it had on the first morning of the initiation process. Four element training stations were set up neatly around the pool, and the emerald necklace on the statue in the middle of the water shone brightly in the morning sun. Grayson made his way to the Necklace Raid rule sheet pinned on the wall; there was nothing about one player being forced to stay back. Jasper had made it up to get Liam's dad inside Icefall.

Emerson trudged into Emerald House. "I figured you would still be sleeping. I was just on my way over to your residence hall."

"Did you already know I had the necklace? You know, before I shook your hand with it on?" Grayson immediately asked.

"Actually, I did. However, I was still surprised you decided to wear it during your completion ceremony."

"Did Mr. Frost tell you?"

"He didn't have to. I watched your performance in the first round of the Necklace Raid," said Emerson with a chuckle. "As a matter of fact, all your instructors were sure you had it, yet they decided against ratting you out. Of course, Jasper Crimson did much worse than that in the end."

"They did a good job pretending not to like me," Grayson said as he continued to glare at the Necklace Raid rule sheet. "I figured they would've told E.R.O.L in a heartbeat if they'd known."

"Their job is to make you angry, so when you face controversy in the outside world, you're able to control your emotions and walk away when you're mistreated. Lacers are kindhearted beings. We're polite and know nothing but love, as I'm sure you've seen when you visit Icefall Lane. I guess it makes sense for those of us who do evil to be classified as something else."

"So, my grandpa and Mr. Frost won a war against the Shaders and then thought they could just stop Lacers from turning evil by pretending evil didn't exist?"

Emerson nodded. "I talked with Walter this morning, and that seems to be my understanding of the situation as well. Their plan worked for sixty years—no crimes, no killings. Last night was my first time hearing of Shaders, and the initiation process certainly never taught me anything about a God of Evil. Walter said there had been signs of evil returning for quite a while. He just doesn't understand how it's happening after all this time."

"Is that why you tried so hard to get Ethan and me to Icefall at my welcome party? Because Frost wanted to keep an eye on me?"

"Yes, he told me to get you here by any means necessary," said Emerson with a yawn. "He wouldn't tell me why. He wouldn't share his thoughts on Oscar's death or the Black House attack, either. I'll admit that without the proper information on what we were fighting against, it was hard for me to keep control of Icefall this year."

Grayson plopped himself down underneath the tree in the garden. His legs hurt from standing, and his mind was depleted from trying to process the current situation. "What's gonna happen to the black diamond now that everyone knows I have it?" asked Grayson, spinning the gem in his hand. "E.R.O.L knows I have it, right?"

"Yes, they know. Walter gave them a full report when he turned in Jasper and Norman. This is the first time an underage P.L. has had a necklace, so this is unknown territory. If I had to guess, I'd say it would come down to a vote on whether or not you should be allowed to keep it. Don't worry about it now. They agreed not to press the issue with all you've been through recently."

"I just have one more question."

"You can ask as many as you'd like, but I can't promise I'll know all the answers."

"Did you know Jasper? Like, personally know him? You looked upset when you first saw him on the ski trail."

"Since we were kids," said Emerson, sinking to the dirt next to Grayson. "He was like a brother to me. We haven't talked as much in recent years—there was a tragedy in his family, and he changed after that. I guess the comedian role he's been playing was just a way to mask what he'd actually become. Killing your grandpa and your bodyguard—a murderer is not something I saw him becoming."

Before Grayson could ask Emerson what tragedy he was talking about, Emerson patted him on the shoulder and told him to go pack. Grayson took one last look inside Emerald House and departed. The city's mayor remained in the garden, too exhausted to get up.

Grayson considered getting something to eat on Icefall Lane, but his parents would surely want to get breakfast when they picked him up in an hour. He walked through the glowing blue forest to the residence hall, where Walter Frost sat outside waiting on a bench. Grayson was sure Frost and Emerson were keeping a lookout on him. He approached the bench and sat next to Frost, whose eyes had the same look of determination they'd had the night before.

Frost exhaled. "Longest night I've had in quite a few years."

"Thank you for saving me, again."

"No, kid, you're the one who saved me," said Frost. "I had given up on trying to fix the problems in this world a long time ago. I was convinced I had already done my part. When you came to me on Christmas and asked those questions, I figured I would let the stream help you form your own opinions. I didn't care anymore. But seeing the flash of my best friend's grandson getting kidnapped made me realize I have plenty left to do before I call it quits."

Grayson gently brushed his shoes back and forth against the mushy snow beneath the bench. "You told me on Christmas that the Lacer Initiation Process was twisted. How can you think that when you're the one who wanted to hide evil in the first place?"

Frost shook his head. "Hiding the ways of evil gave us sixty years of peace; that's not why the initiation process is messed up. Instead of teaching our Potential Lacers to fulfill our purpose of inflicting positive change on the world, we teach them how to control their anger, and then they graduate to a lifetime of partying on this mountain. E.R.O.L's plan is to slowly make people understand that

Lacers are not the harmful creatures the Shaders have made them think we are. In the meantime, we just hide in our cities doing nothing to make the world a better place like the God of Good wants us to."

"How do we know there's really a God of Good and a God of Evil?"

Frost took a thoughtful gaze into the jungle, picking his next words carefully. "About a hundred years ago, each God put one being on Earth to carry out their plans for humanity. Bryon Shade and Tobin Lace were their names. Both gathered followers and trained them. After Shade and Lace died, Karma's War happened. Oscar defeated Bryon's son, Fletcher, and we won, but the human government saw the battle and grouped Lacers and Shaders together as dangerous creatures."

"It's going to be a lot harder for Lacers to promote a positive change now that Fletcher Shade is back from the dead," Grayson replied, looking down at his feet.

"He's not back from the dead. Jasper, Norman, and the rest of the Shaders from Christmas are just believers in his cause. We have to be careful, though—I'm not saying there aren't more of them out there. I still don't know who's teaching this new era of Shaders."

"Well, whoever it is, they really want my necklace."

"Priority number one for next year is making sure you keep that black diamond of yours," said Frost, gently brushing the gem around Grayson's neck with his fingers. "We can't let that fall into the wrong hands... Now go pack; your parents are almost here. And don't sit around all summer—teach yourself how to use your necklace."

"Don't worry about me being lazy," said Grayson, rising to his feet. "I have some neighbors who haven't been ding-dong-ditched in way too long."

***

"There you are!" said Ambrielle. She had finished packing and had already brought her luggage down to the first floor. She helped Grayson stuff his clothes into their carriers while Harlie calmly assisted Ethan.

Grayson noticed his GemPhone resting on his desk. The battery was dead, but the moment he picked it up, the creative energy from the black diamond ignited the screen. The countless messages from his friends made him smile at the thought of going home. He put the phone in his pocket, grabbed Oscar's book from the hidden room, and sealed the trapdoor for good. The book felt like a token of his first year at Icefall.

He had the sudden urge to open it—like it had one last thing to give him—but then all the parents arrived at once, forcing Grayson to stuff it away in his suitcase along with his black diamond.

Rob and Susan Clark shook hands with Ambrielle's dad. Mr. Stone was twice their size and seemed eager to get away from the two cheerful Lacers. They didn't talk long—Susan saw Ethan and immediately ran over to ask about the Necklace Raid and Ethan's performance, at which he proudly told her he'd played a major role in their upset victory. Mitchell appeared moments later and informed them of his second-place achievement in the Extensive Education tournament. Susan whipped out her phone to take pictures of her two "champions."

Grayson's parents were the last inside.

"Grayson!" called Cristina, embracing him in a hug that once again crushed his ribs. "Oh my god, are you hurt? Are you okay? Why do you have bruises everywhere? Are they from the tournament? I have medicine in the car!"

"It's a long story, Mom. I'll tell you later," said Grayson, dreading Cristina's reaction to his near-kidnapping.

"Hello, son. And hello, beautiful young ladies. Grayson, these your girlfriends? Only a joke… just joking," stammered Jeff as he met Ambrielle's father's eyes.

The three families, accompanied by their guardians, plowed through the snowy paths, past the front office, and emerged into the parking lot. Harlie trailed behind—she wouldn't be going home until her sister finished school later that month.

As they loaded up their vehicles for summer, Grayson went around saying goodbye to his I.G.; he was sad to part ways with a group he had grown so close to over the past six months. The only P.L. Grayson didn't get a chance to say goodbye to was Liam. Liam's mom had shoved him in the car and sped off.

Aside from Jasper, all the instructors were present. Grayson could hear many of them apologizing to their element groups for being so harsh.

"We were just doing our job," explained Mr. Boxer. "Every Emerald I.G. has to deal with it. Next year will be different."

It seemed like most of the I.G. had already forgiven their instructors. Grayson leaned up against the side of his car, thinking of his own teacher, who was hopefully rotting away in prison right about now. And there was Jasper's brother standing inside the front office window, his eyes glued to Grayson. It was understandable if Ridley wasn't in the mood to socialize after all that had happened. Ridley himself had spent the past few months faking injuries to get his own brother's colleagues from the Christmas party into more trouble.

Although the glass was slightly tinted, there was no mistaking Ridley's look of fury. Grayson pondered that perhaps *he* was the one Ridley was angry with. Grayson getting Jasper caught surely put a damper on Ridley's reputation. As the I.G. slowly cleared out of the parking lot, Ridley remained inside, not bothering to say goodbye like the rest of the instructors. He might have faked his injuries, but that didn't necessarily mean he had faked his hostile personality— maybe that hadn't been for show.

Grayson, Ethan, Ambrielle, and Harlie huddled up to say their final goodbyes. Dylan came over to show them the bags of food he had taken from Icefall Lane, and Jeremiah waved goodbye from the entrance building before going back into the city.

After Dylan left, Xander came over and rooted his wide body right under Grayson's chin. "If Liam doesn't come back next year, you're going to be sorry," he growled.

Grayson and Ethan both clenched their fists, ready to swing, but Harlie beat them to it. She kicked Xander on the kneecap and sent him hobbling back to his car.

"Do you guys think he's an evil Lacer?" asked Harlie.

The other three were too shocked to say anything. Harlie had just roundhouse kicked the strongest P.L. in their Initiation Group without a second thought.

"We did it, Ethan," said Ambrielle, raising her hand for a high five. "We finally turned her violent."

Ethan couldn't have looked happier. He and Harlie gave each other an awkward side hug, which caused Rob to yell out, "Make sure you get her number, son!"

Ethan's face turned red. Harlie hurried back inside Icefall, clearly embarrassed as well. This left Grayson and Ambrielle in the middle of the parking lot while Ethan screamed at his dad.

"So... um... see you next year, I guess," said Grayson, not wanting to recreate the same uncomfortable scene Ethan and Harlie had been through.

Ambrielle smirked. "Shut up." She leaned in and kissed him on the lips, not just in front of Grayson's parents but her father, too.

Grayson felt like he was dreaming long after Ambrielle pulled away. He wasn't sure if he had closed his eyes or not, but he didn't care.

Ambrielle walked to her car, and her dad immediately started yelling.

Grayson's parents were too busy celebrating to hear him. Cristina had tears in her eyes. "My little boy's all grown up," she muttered as Jeff did a fist pump.

"I told you I don't want you with some little boy who can't take care of himself, much less a woman like you!" bellowed Mr. Stone while Ambrielle put her head down.

Grayson couldn't stand to see Ambrielle upset. He unzipped his backpack and pulled out the black diamond necklace his parents didn't know he had. He clipped it around his neck, not bothering to tuck it into his shirt.

"I can take care of myself *and* Ambrielle," said Grayson, playing with his necklace, speaking directly to Ambrielle's dad. "It was nice meeting you, Mr. Stone. Have a great summer, Ambrielle. I'll see you next year!"

Grayson didn't see Mr. Stone grab Ambrielle, throw her in the car, and drive away. He didn't see his mom stumble against the car door to stop herself from fainting, nor did he see his dad drop the car keys and reach for his glasses to get a better look at the necklace.

Walter Frost stormed across the parking lot, latched onto the collar of Grayson's shirt, and pulled him to the metal railing overlooking the ski resort.

"Jeff. Cristina. I'm going to borrow Grayson for a moment."

"Okay… maybe I shouldn't have shown off to Mr. Stone," said Grayson, tucking the necklace away, "but he was being mean to Ambrielle."

"No," said Frost. "It's fine. But if you insist on making your power known to others, you need to know exactly what you are."

The surrounding noises silenced themselves as Grayson looked Frost in the eyes.

"We are *Life Angels*," said Frost. "And God knows *Creativity* is the only thing that *Effects Reform* in our world."

"We're angels?" asked Grayson, rubbing the flesh on his arms. The power of a being greater than him jolted his body and pumped through his veins.

"Yes, we are angels," said Frost. "Angels are not bound to stay angels forever. We can give in to the temptations that come along with living on Earth. Many of us, like Jasper, have chosen the easy God to follow rather than the merciful God of Good. We must not lose our moral compass of right and wrong—of good and evil. Chances are, neither of us will live to see the positive changes the God of Good wants to bring about in society. All we can do is be decent in our short time here by stopping what's left of the Shaders from tearing people apart."

"Positive change is going to happen in my lifetime. I know it," said Grayson confidently.

"You do, huh?"

"Yes, God just told me."

"The God of Good does not directly communicate with Lacers," grunted Frost, although he sensed Grayson's seriousness and wondered if an exception had been made.

Grayson gazed off into the distant gray clouds. "He didn't tell me himself," he replied, trying to decide if the outline of the fog looked more like Jasper or Oscar—definitely a mixture. "But my dad told me Lacers can accomplish anything they put their mind to. And according to *The Laws of Nature*, that means if I believe positive change is going to happen in my lifetime, it's destined to."

"Do you believe it?"

"I do."

www.ingramcontent.com/pod-product-compliance
Lightning Source LLC
Chambersburg PA
CBHW030154200626
46812CB00017B/1916